DANE:
THE LORDS OF SATYR

Also by Elizabeth Amber:

DOMINIC: The Lords of Satyr

LYON: The Lords of Satyr

RAINE: The Lords of Satyr

NICHOLAS: The Lords of Satyr

Coming soon:

BASTIAN: The Lords of Satyr

DANE:
THE LORDS OF SATYR

ELIZABETH AMBER

APHRODISIA

KENSINGTON PUBLISHING CORP.
http://www.kensingtonbooks.com

APHRODISIA BOOKS are published by

Kensington Publishing Corp.
119 West 40th Street
New York, NY 10018

ISBN-13: 978-0-7582-4128-3
ISBN-10: 0-7582-4128-3

First Trade Paperback Printing: June 2010

10 9 8 7 6 5 4 3 2 1

Printed in the United States of America

For Heather Brewer, Mippy Carlson, J.A.M. Jansing, Debbie Tsikuris, Pam Mann, Katy Marcille, Kimmy Lane, Roberta Espinoza, Julie Kiesow, Tracy Brainard, and all the wonderful readers in my e-newsletter group at http://groups.yahoo.com/group/ElizabethAmber.

—Elizabeth Amber

PROLOGUE

In centuries past, the Satyr lords secretly dwelled throughout Europe, working the ancient vineyards of the wine god, Bacchus. By 1820, their numbers had dwindled until few remained to protect the sacred gate between Earth and ElseWorld, a parallel realm populated with satyr, pixies, nereids, faeries, and other creatures of myth. Thirty years later, a treaty allowed more such creatures to come through the gate, and the satyr flourished in Italy. Other species were less fortunate. A Great Sickness arose, affecting females born of blood other than human, and in great numbers they died or were rendered infertile.

It is now 1880. Interworld travel is largely restricted, except for business or diplomatic purposes specifically sanctioned by the ElseWorld Council. Within a corridor of lands that extends from Tuscany southward to Rome, all is so thoroughly bespelled that ElseWorld immigrants go unnoticed.

Still, the magic that cloaks this territory is fragile, and discovery by humans is a constant threat to a small clan of Satyr lords in Rome. These brothers of ancient royal blood have been entrusted to safeguard artifacts, relics, and antiquities created by their ancestors, which are now under excavation by archeologists.

Upon the coming of each new month, their blood beckons them to heed the full moon's call to mate. To deny this carnal call is to perish. To heed it, bliss.

1

Rome, Italy
EarthWorld, 1880

"*Dieux!* Where the devil is it?"

The sound of the woman's voice drifted to him through a grove thick with olive trees. The early October breeze rattled silvery green leaves on gnarled branches, alternately revealing and concealing the meddling female from view. As she moved past in a direction parallel to him, he angled his jaw so his eyes could follow her.

Perfect. Now he wouldn't have to go hunting tonight.

But he was still in transition, not yet fully in control, and so for now only filed the information of her arrival away to be considered later. Breathing deep of the cool twilight, Dante continued to slowly ease his way into a mind that belonged to another—Dane, his reluctant host.

It's for your own good, Dante soothed. *For your protection. I'll be gone again come morning. Relax now. Sleep.*

But Dane ignored this and fought on with an inner strength

that was as admirable as it was futile. Subjugation could not be pleasant for one so strong willed. This changeover was always a strange time and an uncomfortable one, dredging up memories they would both prefer to forget. So Dante treaded carefully, confident he would ultimately prevail. Just as he had on the night of the full moon last month, and during all the Moonfuls that had come before over the latter half of Dane's life.

In a matter of moments, he'd assumed full possession. He was Dante now. Not a person in his own right, but rather an alternate personality that lay dormant inside Dane and came forth only when required. On occasions such as this one.

Slowly, he uncoiled from his crouch on the forest floor. He shrugged broad shoulders, adjusting himself to the fit of this familiar set of bones and flesh he'd donned. The mind and, therefore, the body were his for the present. He would be master of them only until dawn.

The tailored linen shirt he wore hung unbuttoned and open in front, gleaming white against the shadowed flesh of his sculpted chest. He flexed his hands and found them sore. He noted the ax on the ground a yard away and the felled limbs, the piles of encroaching vines, which had been freshly cut away from twisted trunks nearby.

Ah, yes, he remembered now. When he'd first come into consciousness, they'd been working.

He and Dane.

Two facets of the same mind. Possessors of a single body.

And it was a body women admired, sought, swooned over. Six and a half feet of solid brawn, wide of shoulder, narrow of hip. A strong column of throat, topped by a square-jawed masculine face with a prominent blade of a nose, and crowned with tousled sable hair. A face bearing a distinct resemblance to those of his brothers. It would have been too handsome save for one feature. From below straight brows, eyes of icy silver reflected the world, making him appear otherworldly and strange. Which he was.

Through the fabric of his trousers, he found the feature that perhaps rendered him most aberrant. One he reveled in on these nights. Fondly, he stroked its considerable length with the pad of his thumb as if sharpening a precisely made weapon meant only to give and take pleasure. Already it stood thick and lofty and barely confined within his trousers.

This cock of theirs symbolized the entirety of Dante's role in things. He was the fornicator—only one aspect of the whole that was Lord Dane Satyr. Brought forth whenever this body's lecherous need arose. He relished his role. And Dane envied him for it. Craved it for himself.

A thrashing sound reached his ears. The woman. He'd known she was there all along, of course, had been tracking her with a small corner of his mind. Now his eyes found her again.

She moved heedlessly through the grove, thinking herself alone. Now and then, she paused to tug at a branch, plucking an unripe olive or two from it. Holding these small bits of plunder to her nose, she then pocketed them as if gathering samples. The olives would not be ready for picking for another month, so he briefly wondered at her actions. But curiosity was not a failing of his. Dane, however, suffered from a wealth of it. And look where that had gotten them.

Beyond her, the sun had just met the horizon, a huge ball of juicy orange jailed by black cypress spears that marched along the hilltop opposite this one. It turned her pale skin to gold, the shadows of her face to lovely bruises, her dark hair to coal. She was dressed fashionably and well in a prim gray dress that blended with the trees here. Perhaps twenty years of age or a little older. And shapely.

He smiled. They'd only been here a few weeks, but already he liked this new world. A Sickness had killed many of the female species in ElseWorld that usually served as mates for his kind and rendered others unable to bear satyr offspring. Only the members of the Council had the luxury of keeping their own women. Yet here, women delivered themselves right to one's doorstep.

His prey disappeared into a clearing and he moved after her, keeping her in view. Her head was bent to study something she held. A small book. A page flipped under her lace-gloved hand, a frown creasing the creamy smooth skin between her dark brows as she strained to make out its text in the failing light. Whatever she read on its pages caused her to sigh in frustration.

"Honestly, *Maman!* What am I to do with these scribbles? Couldn't you have done any better than this on so important a matter?" Glancing around, she fanned the gilt-edged book back and forth in one hand with obvious impatience.

Gifted with a natural stealth enhanced by a decade of training and field experience as an ElseWorld Tracker, Dante soundlessly moved in her direction, intent on cutting off her exit to the road. Though she had no way of knowing, she'd come at a most opportune time. Night was falling. A very special night to those of Dane's kind. Once the moon rose, all would begin.

He made a cursory, visual survey of the grove. It was protected. Dane had bespelled its perimeter himself that very morning. If any humans wandered too close, they would find themselves repelled by forces they didn't understand. Since she'd managed to trespass, he could only assume she must be of ElseWorld blood.

His eyes swept her again. She was slender but pleasingly curved. Fey perhaps. On this special night, her blood would be stirring as well, though not as high as that of the satyr. Not as high as his own. When one lived only ten hours a month, one was understandably eager.

A light breeze gusted at his back, whooshing past him to ripple over mistletoe, betony, chicory, fennel, rosemary, and saffron that grew low on the forest floor. He watched it make its way toward the woman, carrying with it his scent.

When it ruffled her skirt and pulled at tendrils of her hair, she stilled—a woodland creature made suddenly and acutely aware of danger. Her eyes shifted in his direction, twin flashes of emerald. His own eyes narrowed and he smiled, pleased at what he'd read in her glance. Recognition. Only an ElseWorld creature could detect the scent of another. His blood pumped a little faster at this confirmation of his initial assumption. A female from his own world would make for a far more interesting engagement than a human one might have.

"This is private land." He stepped free of the forest's shadows into the small clearing in which she stood. She whirled to face him then, her skirts sending the leaves eddying around her. His nostrils flared, waiting for her scent to ride the air in his direction. He'd know what sort of creature she was soon enough.

When her fragrance reached him, its delicate, delicious impact enfolded him like a physical caress. His senses analyzed and sorted through its nuances, and a new prickle of awareness swept his skin. His body reached a stunning conclusion regarding her origins a split second before his mind did. He could actually feel his eyes dilate, his heart gasp, his blood halt in his veins.

"Gods, who . . . *what* are you?" he demanded.

Frozen in place, they simply stared at one another with only a dozen yards of sylvan forest and shocked silence between them. Even the air around them seemed to hold its breath.

Then she pivoted on one dainty, booted foot and hared off. She was getting away!

As abruptly as it had stopped, the pump of his blood resumed, burning through him with its ecstatic gush. His hunting instincts in full force, he loped toward her at an angle, slicing through the forest of Dane's ancestors with ease. The tangled underbrush aided him, snatching at her skirts and slowing her.

His hand lashed out and caught the front of her waist, low between her ribs, pulling her back against him and stealing her breath. She was slight compared to him; her spine easily molded to the cavern of his broad chest. Her hips were lush against his hard thighs. Her hair a silken sweep at his throat.

All of nature seemed to still within the forest as he gathered her to him. He bent his head to bury his face in the tangle of her hair, inhaling deeply. The rightness—the perfect fit of her—rocked him to his very core.

"Who are you?" he asked again.

"No one. I'm no one."

Long moments passed and they were alone in the universe, locked together in an intimate cocoon. The birds fell silent, but his blood sang. The gentle music of a nearby stream ceased, but their heartbeats thundered. His massive frame shuddered under a flood of lust. His balls clenched, his cock hardened, his every sense attuned to her.

He felt Dane stirring somewhere inside him, like someone turning over in his sleep. Her pull was so strong that it was affecting even him. *Who is she?* Dane whispered, but his question, too, went unanswered.

Dante carefully shoved him deeper into their mutual subconscious, where he must remain until this night was done. He'd been protecting him for the past thirteen years and saw no reason to stop now. Not while the danger to them still existed in this world.

Under his palm, he felt the firm stays beneath her gray silk gown. He considered the swiftest way to convince her to allow him to remove them. "Don't fear us. We're like you."

"Us?" She shook her head and tugged at his hands on her waist, resisting the pull he was exerting on her person and her senses. "What are you talking about, monsieur? I only wandered here by mistake, looking for flowers for my table tonight. I didn't know the house was occupied. If you'll let me go—my conveyance is just over there." She gestured toward the road, then as she drew her arm back down again, slammed the point of her elbow into his rib, struggling.

He frowned, startled, unable to comprehend that she might not want him. "Why do you fight?" he murmured into her hair, his voice hot and dark. "Night comes, and with it the Calling."

She gasped, whipping her head around. Her eyes were wary, but in their depths awareness flickered.

The backs of his fingers traced her pale cheek. "You know of what we speak," he accused softly. "Of the Change that will come over us when the sun dies." Each word was bespelled, an enticement meant to lull her senses.

"No." She shook her head as if to shake off his touch, his enchantments, and his intentions toward her. He felt her magic dueling his for supremacy, and it sent a prurient thrill through him. But within seconds, his magic had crept into her consciousness, visibly affecting her. Her body remained half turned away, but she'd relaxed, no longer poised to flee. Her expression softened and a flush of pink stole across her cheeks. Her fingers rose to lightly brush her lips; then they dropped to the neckline of her bodice, restlessly tracing its lace.

"Gods," he whispered. "Everyone believed creatures such as you to be only a myth." He tucked a curl of her hair behind her ear, studying every nuance of her upturned face, wondering about her. Who she was. Why she'd come here.

"I'm fey," she protested weakly.

He chuckled. "Little liar."

Dane with his insatiable need to know would have questions for her when they met with the coming of morning. Let him find answers then. Tonight was for pleasure. His palm warmed on her cheek, casting a Calm over her.

"Stay," he murmured. "Stay with us tonight."

Her will to fight him—to fight her own nature—faltered. Her shoulders softened and her arms went lax. Something hit the toe of his boot. Her little book. Her head lay back on his shoulder and he felt her go boneless against him. When her lips turned into his throat, he knew he'd won her. But it wasn't enough that his magic wiles should woo her anymore. He wanted her with him, desiring him with her body and spirit, and would not be satisfied until she begged him to fill her. He brought her fingers up to the fastenings of her bodice and helped her to work the first of them free.

A strange and sudden numbness came over him then, and his own fingers fumbled, becoming uncoordinated and uncertain. His hold on her slackened. Not because she'd renewed her puny efforts to shake him off but because of . . . something else. Something was wrong.

Dante felt himself waver, felt his consciousness ripple like the waves on a pond that had been disturbed. His hands dropped away from her as the shadow of another presence crowded around the edges of his mind. Dane? No, it couldn't be. Yet it was.

But Dane had never resurfaced during a carnal encounter. It wasn't safe. What if *they* came again and took him back to that awful place? It had driven him into an asylum before. Next time, it might kill him. Dante couldn't let that happen! Protecting Dane was what he lived for.

Don't you remember how things were . . . before? Dante warned. *Don't you value your sanity? You must hide. Sleep,* he crooned.

Get out of my head, damn you! Dane bit out. *I don't need you!*

Stunned, Dante could only stand there, arms useless at his sides as he faded further still, inexorably losing his grip on . . .

Dane sucked in a sharp intake of breath, inhaling his own soul back into his flesh. His mind, his very essence, poured back into his body like wine into a goblet. He was himself again. Alone in his own skin.

He opened his eyes, blinking at the world, seeing it at first as if he were under water. Drowning. He was disoriented, his vision blurred, almost losing his balance for a moment before managing to right himself. His hands found an anchor. A woman.

Her back was against him; her body a warm, pliant, delicious weight in his arms. His palms shaped her ribs, stroking the turn of her waist and hips. Somehow he knew he must hold on to her, as if she were his conduit to consciousness. To salvation.

Things swam back into focus as disconnected flashes. He was in the grove, just as he last remembered himself. He'd been working here on his newly acquired property earlier, hacking away vines to keep them from suffocating the trees.

Then that whoreson phantom Dante had come. Had taken control of him, of his mind, his body. Intending to use it to fuck the night away in his stead. Claiming it was all done for Dane's own good—same as every Moonful. But Dane had interrupted the bastard this time!

How he'd done so was a matter of question. It had something to do with her, this woman who inexplicably stood here with him in the gathering gloom, her head upon his chest, her exquisite body unresisting under his intimate exploration.

Her pale gray bodice was partially unbuttoned, revealing the curves of full, white, perfect breasts. He'd long had a particular affection for this portion of a woman's anatomy. As if in a dream, he watched his hand slip between fabric and flesh, catching on the fine gold chains she wore. Her breast was cool under his fingers, and firm. He found and teased a rosy nipple, dragging the cold metal links over and over it until it drew up tight.

She moaned and touched his wrist, her thighs shifting restlessly against his. His cock surged and he gasped, almost brought to his knees by the sensation. He found its prodigious length with his hand, gripping it through lightweight black wool that could scarcely contain it.

He was hard. He. Not Dante. Was. Hard.

Never in his life had he experienced the hot thrill of his own arousal. Urgently, he turned her toward him, half fearing that she might be a specter herself and fade away. She was comely, with raven lashes and hair, and gently flushed cheeks. His prick was fat and hungry between them, twitching for a taste of her. This was a gift, a miracle wrought by this beguiling stranger.

His arm slanted across her back and his hand met her nape, holding her for his descending mouth. Her fingers threaded his hair, and her kiss met his. She tasted of magic.

He inhaled her scent and found it redolent of ElseWorld. His senses keened, sorting through the soft rainbow of flavors within it. They were unusually complex—a sprinkling of citrus and spice, a dusting of fey glamour, and a heady confusion of other fragrances. But he was a Tracker and would soon have their measure.

Seconds later, his head jerked back. His hands gripped her shoulders and he stared down at her, stunned.

"You're . . . No, it's impossible. . . ." Yet her scent was unmistakable. She was satyr, like him. Never in all of history had a female been born among his species!

"What are you?" he demanded, giving her a little shake. He needed to hear her admit it.

Eyes that were slumberous, the color of spring clover, tangled with his. "I'm emptiness. Want." Rising on tiptoe, she rubbed her lips over his. "Fill me," she whispered.

His hunger shot higher, past all restraint. Urgently, he pressed her back against the trunk of a centuries-old olive tree planted by the ancients and covered her body with his larger one. His hands swept over her waist, ribs, and breasts, learning her shape.

"Yes, we will do as our kind must for tonight," Dane rasped against her lips, his voice rough with need. "But you will answer my questions come dawn."

"*Oui, monsieur,*" she breathed, her eyes dark with passion yet oddly evasive.

She wanted him, whether due to an innate desire or to Dante's magic, he didn't know—was past caring. He led her hand low between their bodies to the monumental erection that threatened to burst from his trousers, then turned his own fingers to rip at fastenings. His cock surged from its woolen prison, finding the warm cup of her palm.

A predatory growl rumbled from his throat when she encircled his root with fingers that didn't quite meet around its girth. Through lowered lashes, his silvered eyes glinted with arousal, watching her face as he drew back his hips, moving himself within her hand in a long, voluptuous drag. Then a push, and yet another withdrawal, this one sending her clasp upward along a length roped with hot, blue veins, until finally she held his crown.

His entire body gave a violent shudder at the seductive stimulation. Never prior to this moment had he felt the throb of his cock under an erotic feminine touch or felt the pleasurable burn of viscous precum welling higher to pool in the tiny slit at its crest. Things other men of virility took for granted. She found his pearly seed and smeared it with the pad of a thumb. Her eyes widened, as if this were new to her, too. With a wicked daring quite at odds with her innocent expression, she lifted the thumb to her lips, tasting him.

As if she'd lit the wick on a keg of blasting powder, his ardor exploded. He crossed her wrists under one hand and pinned them above her head upon smooth, silver bark. Her breasts rose, splitting the gap in her bodice and tantalizing him with her every inhalation.

A stockinged thigh slid upward between his to gently nudge his balls. "*S'il vous plaît,*" she whispered.

"Gods, yes," he gritted. His mouth fell upon hers, parting

soft lips. His tongue pressed inside in much the way his prick would soon breach another pair of lips and mate another feminine mouth. With his free hand, he tossed her skirts higher.

At any other time, he would not have acted so rashly. But it was Moonful, and the urge to cleave himself to her drummed in him, stronger than the beat of his heart or the workings of his curious mind. Though his body had engaged in copulation under every full moon that had passed since his eighteenth year, he recalled none of it. But tonight, he'd conquered Dante. This time, he would remember what he did.

He guided his straining rod past her delicate underthings, and when he insinuated himself between her legs, she shifted slightly, opening for him. Flesh met flesh. Her breathing hitched and a smothered feminine cry of desire perfumed the air. A lecherous rush of answering masculine need sent his fat knob plowing her slick furrow. Unerringly, he found her hot, yearning heart and nestled there, anointing himself with her precious weeping passion. Their eyes caught and clung . . .

High above them, the forest's umbrella rustled in the gentle breeze, parting for the gaze of an unblinking moon, which chose that tender moment to observe them. Its luminescence caressed their entwined figures, calling to them.

"Sweet hells!" Dane's lungs drew up on a harsh, strangled breath as this new divine mistress took him, commanding that he worship her in the way of his ancestors. Demanding that he change; that he engage in the rituals required of all the satyr on this night. His face lifted to her light and he groaned—a dark, carnal sound that threaded the exotic, velvet night.

"Please," came a desperate whisper. The flesh and blood woman in his arms.

But he was caught in the moon's snare now, and could only wait as light and sensation washed over him, from his face down the column of his throat, his broad chest, ribs, and finally belly. Under the fabric of his trousers, a soft downy fur sprouted on his thighs and calves, so fine it was scarcely visible. Yet it was the beginning of the Change that would render him freakish, at least to those in this world, if they but knew.

Dane had never experienced the Change for himself and hungered for it now like a starving man. Need coiled higher in him, and higher. In a moment, when the moon's thrall released him, he would turn the woman he held in his embrace and lift the back of her skirts. Would seat himself at both of her openings. For he would require another sort of mating with her once the moon had its way with him—a dual one.

A moan fluttered from lips that were rosy and moist from his mouth. As if she'd read his mind.

His belly twisted in a sudden brutal cramp, catching him off guard. He gripped his midsection. His other hand released her wrists and balled into a fist on the tree bark. Long moments passed as he was racked by a pleasure so piercing that it was colored with pain.

Freed now, her arms slowly wilted to her sides. In her sweet, clear eyes, he saw fear bloom. Of him or of herself? He frowned. Had Dante in fact bespelled her in some way? Was that why she'd seemed so willing?

"Move. Let me go." Her voice trembled.

His torso held hers fast to the enormous trunk of the ancient tree. "Haven't you ever seen the Change come over a male of your species?" he ground out.

She pressed trembling hands flat on his chest. "No! I don't know what you're talking about. I—"

"It's beginning in me now, here," he interrupted, slicing through her lies. He took her hand and forced it low on his abdomen so she could not help but feel the hard, knotted muscles there. So that she could not deny the truth of what she knew him to be. A male of her kind.

She hesitated and he fought a desperate craving to pick up where he'd left off; to ram himself inside her, welcome or not.

"You won't change in the same way I will tonight, but you must be feeling something. When you turned eighteen, didn't you—"

"No!" She yanked her hand away and struggled against him, denying what she'd guessed he'd been about to say. "I'm not like you!" she shrieked.

Before he could call her on this untruth, his fingers went suddenly clumsy and uncoordinated. He flexed them, trying to shake off the numbness. "No . . . Gods, not yet. Not now."

Dante had returned. And he wanted this woman for himself.

It is how things must be, the voice in his head whispered.

Dane locked his jaw in a grimace, fighting the takeover with every fiber of his being. Knowing it was useless. He studied the woman before him intently, memorizing her every feature. The knowledge that he would not be able to conclude what he'd begun with her was a bitter pill. But he would find her again later, he vowed to himself. One day he would rid himself of Dante and he would have her. Meanwhile, she must be protected. Somehow.

"What's wrong with you?" Dane saw her lips move, forming the words, but she sounded distant, as if she were floating away from him. She was staring at him with round, frightened eyes. Well, not at him exactly. She seemed to be gazing all around him—to his left, his right, above his head—but not directly at him.

"Stay. You'll need me soon, between your thighs," he murmured.

"No! I can't."

But she wanted to. He could read it in her face. "Stay," he rasped again. "If nothing else, you will need my protection. Because of what you are. There are those who would harm you—"

She backed away, shaking her head. Denying him, herself, and what she was.

A lightning bolt of pain shot through his skull. He staggered, catching his weight against the trunk of the nearest tree.

What's your name? he demanded desperately, but his words were soundless now. He was losing her. Losing himself.

He pressed his knuckles to his forehead, trying to force the usurper back. But it was no use. He felt himself subsiding, his mind sliding away from him like the tide washing out. He was succumbing . . . being overtaken by . . .

Dante found himself in control again. He swayed, then shuddered, quickly regaining his equilibrium. He was in pain. His hand went to his belly and felt the hard clench of muscles there. The air in the grove had turned cooler with the night. And the moon had come, bathing him in its glorious light, swamping him in carnal need.

Where was the woman? He glanced up and found her. She'd shaken free of him and his spells, and moved away. Far enough that she might be able to elude him, in his current debilitated state, as the Change overtook him.

As if hypnotized, she watched his fingers in fascination as they smoothed over his belly. In the gathering darkness, the gap he'd opened in the front of his trousers was shadowed, leaving her to guess at what was happening within. Her conflicting emotions were easily read on her face. She was frightened of lingering here with him but could not bring herself to leave.

He stroked himself. "Come here," he beckoned softly. He was between her and the road, and hoped it was enough to deter her from attempting departure while he was in the grip of the Change.

She stepped back, shaking her head. "How dare you cast your spells on me."

He lifted one brow, his gaze on her steady, his voice quiet. "You are wet for us, and not because of any magic. And for all your protestations, you've stayed for more."

But he didn't hear her reply, for a sudden, fierce agony seared him and he doubled over, his hands gripping his thighs to keep from falling. A muscle jumped in his jaw and a raw groan left him as a series of cramps rippled over his pelvis. Long moments passed as he waited for the pain to subside.

He sensed her creeping closer, closer still. Coming to him! He opened his eyes and saw her crouched before him, at his feet. Her pale fingers reached out. He felt her rip something from underneath his boot.

He managed to grab her wrist, staying her. Their eyes locked and he frowned. "Why aren't you affected?"

"Because I'm not what you think," she whispered. She yanked loose. He was weak now, too weak to hold her.

And then she was scrabbling away from him, dusting up leaves in her haste to leave him. She was clutching something. The book. She'd dropped it earlier. It had been under his boot and she'd only come closer to retrieve it.

Wordlessly, she backed away, eyeing him as if he were a dangerous viper. Her little book was pressed high to her breast as if she were trying to keep her heart from jumping out of her chest. She looked uncertain and wary of lingering here with him, but utterly fascinated at the spectacle of his Changing. So much so that she was unable to bring herself to leave.

He leveled his gaze on her. "Don't go. Denying your nature won't change it. You'll need us soon, between your thighs," he said. An echo of what Dane had told her.

Then the moonlight's drench intensified, leaching all color from his skin and strengthening his lecherous desire almost beyond endurance. His back arched on the primal roar of pleasure–pain that erupted from his throat, shaking the very leaves on the trees as the last physical change of the Calling night occurred in him. Standing in a pool of silver, he felt his arms stretch wide, his hands clench tight. His face lifted to pay homage to the luminous orb in the blackened sky.

Moments later, all was ready. He was changed, poised to begin the night. His palm slipped around the thick shaft rooted in his dark thatch. His other fist found the twin column of newly awakened flesh that was rooted only an inch or so above. Moonful had gifted him with this second shaft of bone and sinew—this second cock ripped from his own belly. It extended high and hard from his pelvis, and jerked with hunger. He stroked upward along all ten or so inches of both pricks until his thumbs found and smeared the droplet of moisture that pooled in the crease at each tip.

In the distance, he heard the woman crashing through the brush. Then he heard the clop of her pony cart moving down the hill. She was escaping. Running from him. And from her own need. Deaf to anything he might wish to say to her. He would wipe any memory of her from Dane's mind before he departed from it at dawn. Just as he'd wiped the memory of other, far crueler lovers from his mind twelve years ago.

Instinctively, he moved toward the temple situated on Dane's land, saw it gleaming just ahead. Far below in the valley, he could see the glow of archeologists' lights as they toiled far into the night. The excavations in the Forum went round the clock, week after week. They were uncovering relics and artifacts that had been hidden for centuries.

And secrets, too.

Secrets that must be kept from Dane.

2

Heart pounding, Mademoiselle Evangeline Delacorte struggled to fit the slender blade of the bronze key into the lock in the ornate ironwork gate. A difficult task when her lace-gloved hands were shaking so badly.

Her face was flushed, fevered with an unfortunate illness that came to her with regularity and ever-increasing force. Human females of her acquaintance might complain about their monthly flow to confidantes over tea in the privacy of their salons. Yet for her own safety and that of those she protected, she must remain silent on the subject of her own more unique monthly discomforts.

"Odette? Pinot?" she called, rattling the key in the lock with growing desperation. Why wouldn't it catch? In contrast with her frenzied struggle, the lazy Italian moon eyed her just above the horizon. How long did she have? Fifteen minutes? Ten? She'd never cut her time so close. Just beyond the gate lay a small garden; then beyond that the door to her townhouse. In moments, she was going to fall apart.

Sudden illuminations splintered the sky above her, bursting

like fiery snowballs. She started violently, and the key clanked to the cobblestone lane at her feet.

She cursed under her breath. "Must every night bring another celebration to this ridiculous city?" Bending, she swept her skirt aside and searched the ground on all sides of her.

Footsteps sounded and she glanced up, alarmed. Had the man from the grove followed her? But it was only a group of human revelers scurrying past, on their way to a Roman *festa* of some sort. Decades of excavations in the Forum along Via Sacra had caused a rampant fascination for all things mythological. They were dressed in costume. How ironic that they chose to disguise themselves as the very species that she and other ElseWorld transplants took such pains to hide.

The lone Bacchus among the group wore a garland of olive sprigs and held the arm of a delicate sprite. Accompanying them were several maenads, a fairy with wings that glittered in the dwindling light, and the Roman goddess of love, Venus. A faux satyr was costumed in a dark demi-mask and a cloak. A large, multicolored phallus meant to draw the eye bobbed at an upward angle from the codpiece he wore.

You'll need me then, between your thighs. She shivered, recalling the words of the man in the grove. Gods! How had he guessed when no one else had before in all of her twenty-two years?

Beside her foot, her hand touched metal. The key. When she stood again, a dour face stared back at her through the curls of iron in the grillwork of the gate. She flinched and lay a hand over her heart. "Odette! You nearly scared the life out of me."

The mulatto woman's eyes, startling blue against her coffee skin, narrowed on her. She'd had the uncanny knack of ferreting out Eva's secrets ever since she'd been a girl. Would she guess what had just occurred in that small olive grove on Aventine Hill?

But Odette only darted a meaningful look at the moon.

Clucking, she lapsed into the colloquial mix of her native Else-World and an obscure Italian hill-country dialect as her hands worked the stubborn lock from inside. Then, "You late, mademoiselle! I sent Pinot out looking for you," she said, referring to the diminutive pixie who served them as a combination coachman, majordomo, and bringer of gossip. "I worry you could be out there dead like the others, floating in the Tiber River."

"Obviously I'm not. I'm careful." Eva wrung her hands. "Hurry, will you?"

Finally, the gate budged. It swung open with a protesting shriek—one they did not oil away for it offered advance warning of visitors. At last she was admitted into the garden. As Eva darted inside, Odette peered both ways down the street, eying those who idled there as she shut the gate again. She hadn't yet gotten used to the fact that they no longer dwelled in the dubious district they'd inhabited in ElseWorld, rather than their current, more respectable address on Capitoline, the smallest of the Seven Hills of Rome.

Odette swung the gate shut with a bang and followed behind her, her step ungainly. "Where you been?" she demanded suspiciously.

"I followed the map in *Maman*'s book to the grove." Eva paused long enough to stuff the handful of olives from her pocket into Odette's hands.

"This all you could get? It won't see you through the month."

"I'm lucky to have gotten that much. The land has been occupied," Eva threw behind her as she scurried through the garden's small courtyard and toward the house.

"By whom?"

"Not now." Eva shook her head, nodding toward the two wide-eyed girls who stood barefoot in the doorway. Clad in white linen nighties, they almost appeared to be apparitions. They weren't, of course. But they weren't entirely human either.

"Mademoiselle! You've come!" said five-year-old Mimi. She bounced on her toes in childish excitement. Next to her, eight-year-old Lena was nervously stroking the end of her braid over her lips, looking as if she were nibbling a paintbrush.

"*Vite, bebes!* Come inside—all of you," Eva scolded softly. Bending to give them slapdash hugs, she gently tugged the braid from Lena's mouth, offering her a reassuring smile. Then she skirted the pair and ducked inside.

Lifting her skirts high on either side of her, she raced up the stairs in an unladylike manner. On any other night, Odette would have scolded her.

But tonight, she only called to her from the bottom of the staircase, "All is as you like!" Behind her, the girls peeked from either side of her aproned skirt, fascinated as always by any hints of what was to happen to Eva during this mysterious monthly event.

"Off with you!" Odette shooed the girls toward their room on the opposite side of the house.

"Do as she bids you," Eva called. At the top of the staircase, she rushed down the corridor and flung herself into her bed-chamber.

Shoving the door closed with an elbow, she half fell against it, the weight of her body slamming it shut behind her. Her head fell back and she wrenched open the neck of her bodice. Her corset had become a device of torture. Breath was strangled in her chest, struggling to escape. She ran her fingers down hooked fastenings, popping the uppermost of them open. Released from their decorous silken prison, her breasts swelled within the deep vee. Ah, sweet freedom!

But tonight, these four walls would serve as another sort of prison. One that kept the world out and rendered her safe within. The doors and walls here were thick and the windowpanes doubled. Whatever happened here would be buffered from the outside world and from the two girls who'd become her family.

When she'd come here three months ago, a neighbor had told her that a madwoman had been kept here in this chamber a century ago. And would she not turn mad herself soon? She supposed she was fortunate that her lunacy would only be of a ten-hour duration. From dusk to dawn.

Her eyes opened, darting to the tall cabinet along the far wall. The small door inset at eye level was normally kept locked, but it now stood open to reveal an assortment of crystal jars, vials, cylinders, and other curious items. Pushing off from the door, she crossed toward it, kicking off her boots onto carpeting that had been woven on ElseWorld looms. Eva paused before the cabinet, which had been constructed by fey woodworkers. In fact, the very house itself was under the covert ownership of the ElseWorld Council.

Sitting prominently on a low shelf within the cabinet was a slender glass bottle that to the untrained eye appeared to contain ordinary red wine. It was an ElseWorld relic, found somewhere by Odette, who knew how to locate such things. Beside it was a goblet, which had already been poured, awaiting her. Odette had obviously been here recently, preparing things.

She put the goblet to her lips and took a long draught from it, feeling the sanguine elixir burn its way down her throat. She followed that quickly with yet another gulp. Gasping, she wiped her lips with the back of one wrist. This was ancient drink, a necessary component in initiating tonight's ritual. A ritual that took place only once a month under the fullness of the moon.

One of the powders she'd taken that morning was meant to soften the effects of this Calling, delay its onset. When she'd first begun taking the powder four years ago, it had allowed her to pass nights such as this one with relative calm. But with each successive full moon, the powders' effectiveness decreased. Darkness had only just fallen and already she was near to leaping out of her skin.

Fortunately, the wine would calm her and set her on the inevitable path she must follow tonight. She took a third swallow from her goblet. The entire bottle would be empty by night's end. Would somehow become full again a month from now without anyone having replenished it.

Seconds later, she heard the smooth glide of metal upon metal. Tumblers groaned, falling into place. Her door was being locked from the outside. For a moment, there was waiting silence beyond it. Odette was listening from the hallway.

"I'm all right," Eva called softly. After a slight pause, she heard her servant's familiar uneven step fade down the hallway.

In truth, she was beginning to feel far better than just all right. The elixir was doing its work. Already the pace of her blood was slowing, and her jittery mood was altering to one of arousal, anticipation. In just a few moments more . . .

Eva stared into the goblet, tilting it toward the window in order to see the moon's light upon the wine's wavering surface. Dipping a finger into the drink, she stabbed the reflected orb, watching it turn bloody with the juice of Sangiovese grapes. When she lifted her finger again, several drops fell from its tip upon the breasts that swelled from her gaping bodice. The crimson droplets trickled lower between her curves. She caught them on the pads of two fingers and painted their slick moisture in a light circle over her nipple.

Where *he* had touched her. A prurient thrill prickled over her skin, and her nipple became a hard bead. *Umm.*

Her head lolled lazily to one side and her gaze fell to the bedside table. A basin and linen toweling had been placed upon it. For later—toward morning, when all this would end.

Through lowered lashes, she noted other preparations. Two lengths of silk-twisted rope securely tied to the head of the bed, one anchored at each bedpost. Her eyes skittered across these cords, a little shamed by them. By her need for them. The coverlet had been removed and folded on the dais, leaving only pillows and batiste sheets atop its mattress.

She took another long drink. Then the base of her goblet hit the low shelf with a *thunk*. And without knowing quite how she got there, she found herself standing at the foot of the bed. Her *maman* had found it for her at an auction of antiquities in Else-World, and it had been dismantled and brought here when Eva and Odette had crossed through the gate three months ago. Just after *Maman* had died. Its origins were uncertain, but it had almost certainly been wrought by satyr craftsmen. Her mother had said the owner didn't understand its secrets, but that Eva would.

It was beautiful and stately, made of lacquered olivewood. The head and footboards were done in an elaborate design of stylized grapevines and mythological figures. These disguised a number of intriguing features Eva had discovered on her own over the years. She skirted the tall leather trunk that stood at the foot of the bed rising to the same level as the mattress.

Tracing along the foot rail with her fingers, she found the indentation she sought underneath and pressed. There was a soft *click* and the rail began to rotate. A smooth cylinder about six inches in length and an inch or so in diameter slipped from its moorings within a sculpted design of vines, tendrils, leaves, shoots, and grape clusters in the footboard. Once the rail had twisted half a rotation around, it locked into place with another click. Now the cylinder stood upright, still rooted in the railing. From there it curved upward, angling slightly away from the nearest bedpost. A highly polished phallus of flawless olivewood, it had been purposely placed here for precisely the use she would make of it tonight.

You'll need me then, between your thighs.

A small, anguished moan escaped her. A carnal engagement with the flesh and blood man in the grove had posed too great a risk. But she'd wanted him. And she could still have him. Here. Tonight. In a manner of speaking.

Gazing intently at a vacant space just beyond the bed, she

began to whisper her summoner's spell. The one her *maman* had taught her to help ease her suffering on these nights. Although her mother had imparted the spell, only Eva was gifted with the ability to utilize it. Her mother had been fey, but little of her blood had passed to her offspring. No, Eva's other parent had had far more influence in defining what she was.

As her words were diffused into the room, the air in front of her started to vibrate. Strands of translucent mist slowly began to appear there, where before there had been nothingness. Concentrating, she called up her memory of the man from the grove. The memory of how he'd made her feel, the details of his appearance. He'd been dangerous and forbidden, exciting, handsome.

Stay. Stay with me tonight.

She clenched both fists to her chest to still the wanting that leaped inside her for something she could not have. For the truth was she had longed to linger there with him. Even though it would have been beyond foolish. Even though he'd terrified her with his strangeness and his suspicions about her origins.

But in truth, she was far more strange than he.

On both sides of the gate, it was nothing for satyr males to scatter their fertile seed far and wide among females of human, fey, or any of the dozens of ElseWorld species. And when a satyr son was born of any such alliance, it was deemed unremarkable. The birth of a daughter elicited no special comment either, as long as she bore only the blood of her mother. But what if another sort of daughter were to issue from such a union? A daughter with only the blood of her satyr father, but no hint of her mother's blood?

That eventuality was quite simply unheard of. In all of Else-World history, not a single full-blood female satyr had ever existed in either world.

Until her.

The man had been right in his suspicions. She *was* like him.

Despite the fact that a female of his species was deemed an impossibility.

Of course there were hints of such things in the ancient petroglyphs in the caverns. And the rumors. But ElseWorld scientists and philosophers had long proclaimed the feasibility of a satyr girl-child to be preposterous. A myth. Some even said, an abomination. Yet, here she stood—in danger from both worlds. Simply because of her blood.

Just beyond the bedpost, the mist began to whirl and spin in a blurred confusion of magic. Swaying gently side to side, she continued her mantra in *sotto voce*. With all her skill, she tried to summon a particular likeness from within it. In the past, she'd occasionally conjured a single amalgam of the features of various men she'd met in passing. But never had her desire been so specific to one man that she sought to bring forth a precise replica of him.

Within the swirling mist, a form began to take shape and solidify. Then, born from the ether itself, in the middle of her bedchamber, there stood a man. One that was tall and virile, with silver eyes under straight jutting brows and hair the color of fire-blackened wood. His cheekbones were flushed with vigor, his strong jawbone brushed with a hint of an evening beard. This was a copy of the man from the grove, or as near as she could remember.

But this was no human man. Nor was he satyr. Nor true flesh and blood. He was an insentient being. One of the ranks of those who'd serviced the satyr since ancient times. A Shimmerskin. His singular purpose here tonight was to obey. To serve her. At dawn, he would disappear.

She circled her creation, enjoying the sight of smooth sloping valleys, hills, and plateaus of muscle and bone. His skin was resilient and glimmered preternaturally in the light. He was a head taller than she, with broad shoulders and strong arms and narrow hips. And he was naked.

"I don't have time for this, you know," she murmured to him, knowing he wouldn't be able to comprehend what she spoke. "I have other important business here in EarthWorld, in Rome." Sharing her confidences with an insentient being was foolish, but it gave her solace. "I'm searching for my father. The one who made me what I am."

Her eyes fell to his genitals. Even in repose, they appeared pleasing. If she'd remained in that olive grove on Aventine a few moments longer, she might not have been forced to guess at their dimensions. Regardless, she'd based her creature's phallus on an extraordinary model. Just prior to her eighteenth birthday, her tutor had taken her to view one of the ancient Else-World Wonders—the famous series of marble statues of the wine god Bacchus that lined the mirrored Hall of Vitis Vinifera.

Throughout her inspection of this effigy she'd fashioned, he only stood there, gazing docilely at her. She sighed. This was the difficulty with these beings. They required instruction.

"Come," she bade him softly.

Obediently, he came nearer to tower over her. His stride and movements were strange in their otherworldly fluidity.

Dark lashes amplified the piercing silver of the eyes that stared down at her. Eyes that were vacant.

She lay a hand on his arm. He was warm and smooth. "Bend me to your Will."

He hesitated, unsure. Of course, since he had no Will, he didn't understand. He required more specific commands.

"Remove my clothing," she instructed, and his fingers came to her gray silk bodice, unfastening. He made quick work of it and her corset, skirt, and petticoats as well. Long, blunt-tipped fingers pulled at strings, untying her pantalets, then unrolling her stockings. Soon, only her chemise remained. He reached for it as well.

Suddenly, a ray of moonlight found its way through the window, burnishing her pale skin to gold. And with its coming, a great longing came over her. She shivered and pushed his hands away. "No," she whispered. "Leave it."

Hurrying unsteadily to the bed, she climbed up and swung one leg over the footrail, straddling it. With one knee on the mattress and the other atop the tall leather trunk on the opposite side of the rail, she kneeled there, open. Poised inches above the protruding, olivewood phallus.

High between her legs, her flesh was flushed, warm and plump with her desire—the effect of the full moon. Her fingers found and threaded through the soft triangle of down, parting her folds and slipping between them. She was damp, creamy. A sound that was half moan, half sigh welled from her as her need turned unbearably urgent.

She glanced at her companion. Remembered how the original version of him had wanted her, there beneath the murmuring olive trees. "Come close. Behind me."

"Yes." He moved toward her like a beautiful automaton, dutifully preparing to fulfill the role for which she'd designed him. She grasped the bedpost before her as he straddled the rail on his knees, coming close to warm her spine.

She turned to look at him over her shoulder, catching his eyes. "Take me," she whispered.

As if she'd flipped a switch, his pupils dilated on cue and his expression filled with lust. She felt his prick harden at the small of her back and her breath quickened. With soft words, she told him what she needed from him.

Hands came, big and firm on her hips, positioning her and then guiding her downward. Olivewood kissed her feminine nether lips, parted them. Impaled them. Her eyes fell shut and her chin lifted on an excited murmur.

Hands tilted her hips back and another phallus, this one just as smooth, planted another kiss on the pruney ring tucked within the crevice of her bottom. And then he was pushing, and she was sinking and spreading and gasping at the exquisite, hot bite of him. The fat greedy plum of his crest slipped inside her, a move synchronized with that of another entrance of polished olivewood. She felt them push on, deeper. Deeper still. The long, hard glides seemed never ending.

"Oh!" Her jaw tightened against the need to call for a respite from the tug of hands and gravity, and the push of thick, tandem cocks. He would stop if she asked. And she didn't want him to stop. She wanted this, needed it. Craved it.

And then at last she was crying out, as unforgiving olivewood and hard male filled her completely. His dark thatch cushioned her bottom, and his chin was tucked at the hollow of her shoulder. His chest was an unyielding furnace at her back, his thighs a powerful embrace on either side of hers. And she was full, so, so full.

You'll need me then, between your thighs.

She moaned, remembering. Yearning.

"Make me come," she breathed. Strong, obedient hands lifted her higher, pulled her lower in an undulating motion, and thus began her erotic ride. Murmuring encouragement and instructions to him all the while, she let passion build, fucking herself, letting him fuck her. Urging him on and on and on.

Air quivered from her throat in wild, quick snatches, and his own came at her nape in hot gasps in time with his plunge and withdrawal. Her thighs burned. Her lungs were near to bursting. The bedpost was cool between her swollen breasts, her fingers white-knuckled where they gripped it. And deep, deep inside she was wet, humming, on the brink of something wonderful.

Oh, Gods! Her nipples clenched painfully tight, and she reached for his hands, needing them on her there, showing them how to massage her. The slap of their flesh was an aphrodisiac as he went deep in her, hot in her, long in her. The sweet, steady building of sensation rose in her, higher and higher, until finally, finally . . . *finally* . . . she felt the first delicate contraction. The seizing of her inner tissues that presaged her ultimate finish. Another contraction came, stronger this time, and then another, again and again, and then closer together, and harder, tumbling upon one another. Her exhalations came in rasps and gulps and moans. Her clit twisted and jerked, and her nether tissues fisted on the lengths they stroked. Her entire body tightened, ready, so ready . . .

And then she was coming, convulsing in long, harsh, beautiful waves of sensation that burst stars behind her eyelids and seemed to go on forever and ever, and yet not long enough. All too soon, they subsided to dull echoes of their former strength. She slumped forward, her forehead on the bedpost. Her inner tissues pulsed more gently now, their pace slowing sooner than her heartbeat. Her lashes lifted.

Beyond the window, the moon was a tangerine, pale and huge above paper cutouts of black cypress and oak trees and spires and rooftops. Illuminations from the *festa* under way in the Forum ruins burst and sparkled around the moon, making it almost appear to be weeping for joy.

And then there was empty silence. The dull aftermath of empty gratification. A tear coursed down her cheek and she rested her forehead on the bedpost in front of her, just above her clenched hands. How she longed for something else. Something more.

"You're lucky, do you know that?" she murmured. "Apparently there are legions of men who would pay large sums of money to have me in this way. Yet you don't care. Can't care. And that's what makes you special, and so perfect for this night. In a world that would be all too interested in exploiting me if they knew of my existence, you are singular. Safe. Unlike the pattern I used to make you."

He didn't reply, of course, and was motionless as she pushed herself upward, relinquishing rods of flesh and wood. She needed this dual penetration only once. It was a crucial, necessary beginning to the night. But now it was over, and she would not require it again. She lay back on the mattress, her head on the pillow, and lifted her arms above her toward the headboard.

"Tie my wrists loosely with the ribbons," she told him without meeting his eyes. He obeyed of course, and when he'd completed that task, she sent him to the cabinet to collect several elongated cylinders of varying thicknesses and designs. And a small pot of salve.

Lying there naked, tethered, and waiting for him excited her. Watching him carry these objects to her for the express purpose of giving her pleasure with them excited her as well. Fostered a momentary illusion that he was in control, not she. It was the sort of situation she craved but could never have. Not with a Shimmerskin—they were incapable of exerting command. And it was unwise to seek another sort of partner who was capable of it. Like the man in the grove.

"Beloved," he whispered as his arms went under her thighs, splaying them for his mouth. But only because she'd willed him to do so. Until dawn, everything he would do and say would be programmed to incite her passion. She had but to imagine an action and he would perform it, no matter how debauched. Yet her experience and creativity in these matters were limited, and the ongoing necessity of controlling him would always deflate her pleasure.

The brush of his stubbled cheek as he kissed the inside of her thigh was a tender abrasion that thrilled. She gasped, tugging at her bonds as his tongue lapped at her clit, parted her slit, entered her. She turned her face toward the window, gazing at the bittersweet moon.

He felt wonderful. He would make her come. Again and again.

But it would not be enough.

How she longed to feel the hot spill of a man's semen. Just once. Shimmerskins were devoid of it, incapable of producing or imparting it. She longed for the whisper of love words, sex words that she didn't have to specifically request her mate to utter. She wanted to feel out of control. Bent to a man's Will. To know she'd driven her mate wild to have her under him.

Her eyes went to the array of titillation devices her lover had neatly aligned along the surface of the bedside table, like fine cutlery at a dinner place setting. He would use them on her throughout the night as she wished, and fuck her time and time again through the hours as she directed. Though her flesh would be well satisfied by the time dawn came, it would not be enough.

She could not continue on in this way. Yet, it was widely known that if the satyr did not heed the full moon's Calling in this manner, they perished.

Death or this. It seemed she had little alternative.

The certainty that her needs would go unappeased, that she would always live this way, and that she could not change her situation, was so terrible at these moments that she sometimes feared she might truly go insane.

3

I'm not insane.

I . . . am . . . not . . . insane.

Lord Dane Satyr repeated the words in his mind, trying to banish the cold terror that ripped down his spine. Pain speared through his brain like tiny branches of lightning. His heart beat a harsh, ragged drumbeat in his ears. Behind his eyelids, a blood-red haze singed his vision. Dormant, half-formed memories had him yanking sharply at his arms and legs, and rotating his wrists against unseen restraints.

Mouths, caresses, fists, cocks, slaps, bites, fingers, tongues, pinches, breasts . . . torturous devices. And the hands. Those wanting, needing hands he couldn't escape. They took from him, used him without his consent. Why did he let them? Why couldn't he find the will to fight? He was disoriented, out of control. Helpless. He, the most feared and vaunted Tracker in ElseWorld history.

But back then, he'd only been a boy of twelve.

Come now, be a good boy.

No! No!

And then he'd been free. Running.

Gods! Where was Lucien? He had to get to him. Free him as well.

But the voice in his mind—Dante—urged him on toward escape. *If you go back for him, you'll be recaptured,* it had whispered. *You must flee . . . You must live . . . It's the only way to save him. . . .*

The first fingers of dawn came, stroking night from the sky. The suffocating memories that clutched at Dane's soul like cruel claws were wrenched away. His senses returned to him in a sharp rush of panic. His eyes flew open, and he threw his head back to draw a deep draught of air into starving lungs. He felt confined, choked, and the small muscles of his large frame twitched and quivered with exertion. A fine sheen of sweat chilled his skin in the crisp morning air.

He was naked. On an altar between the thighs of an unknown female. Her eyes were closed in ecstasy, her breasts arched high and shuddering with each rapid breath. They'd been copulating, and not for the first time. He'd just pulled out of her and spilled his seed on her belly. He felt it, slick between them.

Fuck. He'd lost time again.

How much?

Only last night? Or would he look in a mirror to find that years had passed and that he'd grown old and gray? No, his skin was still smooth and his arms as firmly muscled as before. And they weren't tethered.

With the realization that he wasn't trapped, his pulse began to calm. The sensation of restraint had only been due to the fact that his arms were wound through those of his companion, his hands gripping hers fast to the altar. He released her and rested his weight on his forearms.

Somewhere behind him, olive leaves rustled in the early October breeze. He was on his own land. In the small temple on the slope of Aventine Hill. Under the shelter of a wide, covered portico upon a multileveled floor of patterned marble strung with tall columns. An elaborate continuous mosaic decorated its walls, filled with scenes of worship and sacrifice that had been performed here in times past.

His ancient ancestors had likely taken hundreds of females here on this very altar. However, this was the first time he'd had the opportunity to follow in the family tradition. It had only been the night before last that he'd won this temple and its adjacent house and olive grove from the Patrizzi scion in a game of cards.

Another bolt of dread crawled up his spine, catching him off guard. Gasping, he bowed forward. But it was only the scratch of the woman's fingers as they lightly feathered up his back. She locked her legs higher around his hips, rubbing herself against his prick, basting its length in the warm pool of his own spent seed.

"Dante." It was a feminine purr, the sound of a satisfied woman. The name froze his blood.

"Don't," he bit out. "Don't call me that." It wasn't *his* name. It was that of his illicit occupier, the self-appointed fornicator who took clandestine control of his mind, body, and spirit during every encounter of a carnal nature. Dante, who had been with him for half his life now and who stubbornly withheld answers to plaguing riddles. For the past twelve years, Dane had bided his time. Existed in a sort of purgatory on the other side of the gate, performing the duties of a Tracker in ElseWorld's Special Operative Forces. He'd waited in vain all that time for Dante to reveal his secrets. Two weeks ago, he'd finally managed to escape into this world. And now he would ferret out those secrets himself . . . or die trying.

"I'm sorry," his companion murmured in a conciliatory tone. Instead of lust, curiosity now colored her expression. Damn his loose tongue. He couldn't afford to fuel any rumors that the third Satyr brother, who'd seemingly appeared from nowhere two weeks ago, was, in fact, mad.

"That name. It's one I reserve for nocturnal pastimes," he explained coolly.

"Of course. I understand," the woman replied. But she didn't.

The excuse had sounded unconvincing, even to him. What sort of man wished to be called by one name out of bed and another in it? Not a sane one. She was wondering what was wrong with him. Most of ElseWorld already thought him a lunatic, and he'd soon have half of Rome thinking the same if he didn't take care.

Disentangling himself, he sat up from her. His feet hit the cold granite floor, braced wide, and he rested his forearms on his thighs. The floor was remarkably pristine. It struck him then how well-tended the entire temple was compared with the house and grove he now owned. Locating his discarded shirt, he dragged it across his lap, blotting his belly and genitals, wiping away evidence of a pleasurable pastime in which he'd participated, but of which he had no recollection.

A soft sigh issued from several yards away and he turned his head toward the sound. Another female reclined there, her face slack with sleep, her hair draping the floor in a sweep of red silk. He'd known she was there, of course, having scented her the moment he'd awakened. She was pale, her skin almost a blue-white hue and faintly iridescent. Nereid, he guessed. A species that relished violence in their lovemaking. Which explained the scratches he felt on his back. She wore only a slip, creased and twisted high on her hips. Her thighs were sprawled, and though her thatch was moist with his male leavings, it didn't surprise him that he had no memory of mating her.

One of her wrists was cuffed to the scrolled arm of the marble bench upon which she lay. He'd . . . no . . . It had been Dante who'd tethered her there sometime during the night. Not he.

His gaze clung to her briefly, but he couldn't allow it to linger. He found too much pleasure in the sight of a female willingly bound and waiting. Yet upon himself he abhorred chains of any sort, be they constructed of iron, rope, silk, or flesh.

Arms slid around him. His golden-haired lover had come to reclaim him.

"Just because the dawn has broken, there's no reason for you to go tearing off," she said softly. Pushing away his crumpled shirt, she slipped onto his lap, straddling him. And he let her, his locked arms bracing his weight on the altar behind him. Doughy breasts compressed against his chest, and her torso slinked along his like a cat's. Fingers stroked his nape, and soft lips brushed the overnight beard on his jaw.

"Will you have me again?" Her slick gusset rocked over his prick, trying to coax him into entering her. His hands went to her thighs, helping her ride him. He felt the faint etching of scales under his palms. Like the other female, she was nereid. Cupping her ass, he lifted her higher over him and found his cock with one fist.

Then he flinched, feeling a familiar, stealthy presence rise to lurk within him. Like a tendril of smoke curling from a latent fire, Dante was stirring. Readying. Waiting to see if the inferno of lust was to be rekindled. If Dane continued along this path, Dante would surely return. Would take control and revel in the ensuing fornication until all pleasure was finished and all lust extinguished.

It was pointless to continue. Any ecstasy would not be his own.

Still, it was tempting. In the instant before his consciousness was stolen from him, he would enjoy a single delicious spark of carnal satisfaction, like flint striking match before the fire of mating was ignited. Was it worth it? With both hands, he squeezed her ass, moving her hard against him, staring at her quivering, ruddy-tipped breasts, wanting her. Wanting to *feel*, if only for that instant. Yet not wanting to give up control to Dante. She moaned, her fingernails digging into his shoulders.

Delicate gold flashed between her breasts in the fallen tangle of her blond hair, catching his eye. She wore a necklace. His hands slowed on her and he frowned, suddenly recalling another woman with hair as black as a raven's. Recalling another necklace whose pendant had been lost in the shadows of the shapely cleavage hidden within a prim gray bodice. A woman with pale pink nipples, not ruddy ones. A woman with eyes the color of new spring clover, but whose face he could not recall. Last night.

His mind worked frantically, trying to hold on to a runaway memory. There had been a woman in the grove last night! She'd run from him. No. Not from him. From . . .

"Dante?" The woman on his lap drew back to look at him. She appeared to have been trying to get his attention for some seconds. "What's wrong?"

Dane snatched her away, holding her by the wrists, his eyes intense and glittering as they searched hers. "Who are you? How did you get here?"

For a moment, she looked taken aback. Then she sighed deeply, looking disappointed. "Oh. Business already, is it?"

"*Che cosa il diavolo!* What the devil does that mean?" Taking her weight with him, he stood and set her on her feet.

Nearby, the other female had awakened, worked her way loose from bondage, and now stood as well. The golden-haired woman nodded in her direction, including her when she spoke. "We're Council messengers, my lord, arrived only last night. When we came upon you then, in the throes of the moon's Calling, you bade us serve you."

"And we did so. Gladly," the other woman assured him. The two messengers exchanged knowing glances full of memories he didn't share.

Fuck! He'd been discovered. He hadn't expected this so

soon. Ignoring them, he moved away, finding and jerking on his trousers.

"We come from the other side of the gate," they jointly informed him. "We've traveled through watery corridors formed by the rivers and tributaries between Tuscany and Rome."

"What for?" he bit out.

"To find you," the red-haired one said, offering him a teasing smile.

"Nonsense," the other chimed in. "We didn't know he'd be here."

"But you do now, don't you?" He eyed them with silky menace. "How unfortunate for us all."

"Our only intention was to bring a missive," the golden one assured him.

Her companion nodded and withdrew a metal cylinder about eight inches long from her scant belongings. Nereids traveled by waterway and wore little to impede them. What little they had worn now lay damp and strewn on the marble floor tiles, no doubt where Dante had divested them of it last night. Coming to where he stood under the wide portico that ringed the temple's entire circumference, she made to give the cylinder to him. But the golden-haired one, who seemed to be her superior, preempted her and usurped it.

Removing the cylinder's cap with her thumb, she tapped its barrel with one hand, causing a parchment scroll to slide out from it. Her former flirtatiousness returning, she dragged one end of the scroll down the center of his naked chest and lower, staring up at him through her lashes. "I assure you we enjoyed this delivery more than most, my lord."

He snatched it from her before it reached his crotch and saw that it bore the ElseWorld Council's wax seal. Damn! Under his fingertips, the parchment twitched with magic.

His fist tightened around the scroll, crumpling it, wanting to destroy it. These interlopers had come here uninvited, fucked him without his knowledge. Did they think to take him back with them through the gate as well? His blood pounded on a burst of anger. He felt suddenly out of control, violent. "Take this and go back where you came from. Tell the Council they can go f—"

"Dane." The familiar, deep voice calmed him. Grounded him. It was Bastian, his eldest brother. He'd come from somewhere inside the central area of the temple and now stood framed in one of its several arched doorways. He wore a loosely belted exotic dressing gown of Persian design, which he'd no doubt acquired on his extensive travels to various archeological sites throughout this world. Beyond him in the inner temple, Dane glimpsed pillows and furs spread about in a lush, haphazard manner. Several goblets lay here and there winking dully in the dimness, empty and forgotten. Dane scented the woman his brother seemed to have forgotten there as well.

An inch taller than Dane and five years his senior, Bastian had the same silver-gray eyes and muscular stature, but he wore his dark hair closely cropped instead of wild and tousled. And unlike Dane's raw, rugged nature, there was an air of refined intelligence about him.

"Shouldn't you be down in the Forum brushing dust away from some newly discovered bit of pottery right about now?" Dane snapped.

"The digs can wait," Bastian said, eyeing the coil of parchment Dane held.

"Fuck it." Dane ripped open the scroll and unfurled it. Then he frowned, tilting it so the others would see that on its surface there were but a few words and numbers. "This is what you came all this way to bring? An address?"

"The entirety of the message entrusted to us may be shared only when all concerned are present," he was told.

Bastian angled his head over one shoulder and shouted, "Sevin! Get out here."

Within seconds, their middle brother appeared from the far side of the portico, fastening rumpled trousers he'd obviously just donned. "What's so important?" he growled. "It's fricking dawn and I was in the middle of something."

"Two Shimmerskins?" Bastian hazarded.

Sevin shrugged, but a telling grin curved one side of his lips. This was the Sevin that Dane remembered from their youth, sweeping in with his usual humming energy, his dimples in evidence. With the looks of an angel, he'd been gifted from a young age with the luck of the devil. Gentlemen lost their money to him at every sort of game of chance. Their wives offered him their best biscotti and cannoli, and pressed fond kisses on his cheeks. And their daughters offered him far more than just kisses.

Dane had been thirteen when he'd left his brothers for Else-World. Sevin had been fifteen then, and Bastian seventeen. Though they'd been apart for twelve years, the three of them had quickly fallen back into their boyhood roles in the two weeks they'd been reunited.

Sevin flicked a glance toward the messengers and his face turned teasing. "Nereids, Dane? Didn't know you had it in you."

Dane favored him with a long-suffering glance and a rude hand gesture, both of which only served to widen his brother's grin. When he tossed the scroll onto the altar, Sevin nodded toward it, a question on his face.

"It's an address as usual," Bastian told him, shrugging one shoulder. Sevin rolled his eyes. Dane's brows rose, finding his brothers' reactions inexplicable. But before he could query them, the messengers sought everyone's attention.

"We bring a communication from the Council of ElseWorld," they announced in tandem. Steepling their fingers under their chins, both bowed their heads in the traditional salute afforded to ElseWorld sovereigns, having apparently been informed that all the brothers bore more than a hint of royal blood in their veins.

"Go on, then, if you must," Dane grumbled, for it seemed as if they awaited an invitation.

Standing shoulder to shoulder, they began reciting their message from memory:

> *A good Moonful Dawn to you Lords of Satyr,*
> *We write today to express our concern over the recent unexplained deaths in Rome—nine Else bodies found in the Tiber in the past year alone. Add to that a host of minor indiscretions in the use of magic by some of our kind in our Italian colonies, and eventual discovery of our presence there seems inevitable. In that event, our access to the grapevines and olives will be in jeopardy. As will your ownership of land, your wealth, and your citizenship. It is imperative that you maintain a foothold there. And we have a suggestion in that regard.*

"I'll bet," Bastian muttered. The messengers frowned at him, then continued on.

> *All of ElseWorld has a vested interest in ensuring the continuation of your royal bloodline, as it is one of the ancients. Since it is nigh onto impossible for you to breed in our world now due to the Sickness that affected most of our women, our best hope in securing the future of your line lies in the wombs of human females. We compel you to wed with expediency. To acquire human wives who, by the grace of our Gods, will bear you many satyr sons and human daughters.*
> *Gods be praised,*
> *The Worshipful Council of ElseWorld*

"Ah, there's nothing like a good ElseWorld directive in the morning," Sevin noted with a mighty stretch of his well-muscled arms and back, and a total lack of concern at what he'd heard.

"Does it require a reply?" Dane asked. As a defector with far more reason to be wary of the Council than his brother, he carefully sifted their words in his mind.

The messengers looked a bit surprised, but only shook their heads. "It's assumed that you will do your duty."

"Then gather your belongings, ladies," Sevin told them affably. "I'll see you both back to the Tiber to ensure that you aren't intercepted." The messengers would travel through the network of magic that stretched from Rome to Tuscany, where they would return home through the ancient interworld gate. Hybrids of olive tree and grapevine brought over from Else-World had been planted throughout this network and now emitted a constant scent that bespelled every human within. This had the fortunate benefit of allowing Else creatures to go about their business in the guise of humans and made paranormal events seem normal to this world's inhabitants. Still, the magic that cloaked this territory was fragile. The Council was right that exposure seemed inevitable.

After Sevin and the messengers struck out for the river, Dane located one of his boots, sat, and tugged it on. "You were here all night?" he asked Bastian. "And Sevin as well?"

His sibling nodded. "Didn't you feel us here?"

Dane's head snapped up, and each brother somberly searched the other's face. During the Calling, the satyr were inexorably drawn to congregate for the rituals of Moonful. Ancient blood ties linked them, causing them to share emotions and sensations. The rut of one fueled that of the others, increasing the pleasure of all. But last night, Dane had been cheated of all physical gratification by the phantom presence that lurked within him. He remembered nothing.

And he could see in his brother's eyes that he had sensed something peculiar about him during the night. Of course he would have, and Sevin as well. Damn. Dane had hoped to hide this from them a while longer. But the rigors of Moonful had exposed him.

"I wasn't exactly myself last night," he admitted.

"What does that mean *exactly?*" Bastian asked carefully.

Dane speared the fingers of one hand through his hair. "Gods, I hate this." The rest of the world was welcome to think as they liked, but his brothers and he had been close, before. He couldn't bear it if Bastian thought him mad once he learned the truth. Still, he would lay the facts out without apology, and his brothers could take him as he was or disown him. Their choice. He'd been alone half of his life. He would survive.

"I mean I don't fornicate," Dane said baldly. "Another does it for me, in my place. A separate part of my personality takes hold of me—mind and body—during any carnal experience. He forces me out at Moonful dusk, and I am left with no memory of the Calling time when I awaken again at dawn."

"He?" Bastian's set face gave away nothing of his thoughts.

Dane went on, determined to speak the raw truth. "Dante. Because of him, I only mate during Moonful when our bodies demand we succumb. Otherwise, I'm celibate."

"Gods, Dane. One night a month? That sort of denial would kill some men of our kind," said Bastian, with new respect in his voice.

Dane shrugged. There had been times he'd wished he were dead over the years. But the thought of Luc had kept him going.

"Did your physicians in ElseWorld shed any light on this?" Bastian asked. "The Council swore to us you'd be cared for. We wouldn't have let you go otherwise."

"I went into the asylums."

"Fuck." Bastian's clipped curse was a tangle of frustration and fury. Dane's crazed behavior—convulsions, sleepwalking, incessant nightmares—after his abduction had worried his brothers to the extent that they'd agreed to have him deported to ElseWorld for treatment when he was but thirteen.

"You couldn't have known," said Dane. "And the doctors there did have some experience with my disorder."

"Disorder?"

"Dissociation, they called it, caused by a psychological trauma. Something happened to me that resulted in a fragmenting of my personality. It is as if I am divided into two distinct men. One that goes about life, another that fornicates."

"This trauma—it was something that happened during the year of your disappearance?" hazarded Bastian.

"Yes, but the doctors never moved much beyond that initial diagnosis. Treatment was forestalled when Special Ops recruited me. After that, it was easy to go without women. We're trained not to give in to our carnal natures."

"Except during Moonful."

Dane sent him a rueful half smile. "There's no avoiding the ritual then, for anyone. Every species of our world must heed it to some degree, and the Ops didn't want their entire army dead at dawn following Moonful. They brought us ample numbers of females, and I was told Dante enjoyed some fine orgies."

The growing horror in Bastian's eyes told him he was just beginning to fathom how all this had shaped Dane's life.

Dane stiffened. He didn't want anyone's pity. Beyond uncomfortable by now, he'd rarely been so grateful to anyone as he was to the woman who joined them just then from the depths of the temple. Swathed in an overlarge dressing gown similar in design to Bastian's, she carried a neatly folded stack of what he assumed to be his brother's clothing. After she set them on the altar, she went to hug Bastian's waist.

Michaela. Dane found the name from somewhere, realizing he'd met her once before. She was fey and a courtesan—an expensive one who dwelled in the surreptitious business establishment Sevin owned on Capitoline Hill.

Absently, Bastian roped an arm around her, stroking her side. He'd always been a tactile sort, but a woman's curves and a nicely turned piece of pottery seemed to fascinate him equally. Michaela curled into his touch.

Dane angled his chin toward the discarded scroll. "What do you make of that?" he asked his brother.

Tacitly agreeing to the change in subject, Bastian flicked his hand in a gesture of dismissal. "Nothing. We receive these lectures and missives with monotonous regularity. It's most likely the address of a Marital Broker."

Dane laughed, then quickly sobered when he realized that his brother wasn't joking. "You can't be serious. A matchmaker?" He picked up the scroll, studying the address.

"I'm quite serious. They proliferate up north in Tuscany these days, each vying to catch the bigger prize and cast them into matrimonial hell. And now one has come here to Rome. Follow up on it if you feel the urge to find yourself a bride. I, however, don't."

The woman in his arms stiffened at his words. It would have been an imperceptible tightening of muscles to most observers, but Dane had been trained to notice such things. The least little detail was often the very one that led a Tracker to make a capture.

Michaela was infatuated with his eldest brother. However, Bastian's affections had long been reserved for females carved from marble, limestone, and granite. Even twelve years ago, when Bastian was seventeen, flesh and blood women had found their way into his bed on occasion. But with his heart, they'd stood little chance. It seemed nothing had changed in that regard.

"I'll go bathe and dress," Michaela murmured, slipping away from him. "Find me when you're ready to depart." Then, shooting a shy smile toward Dane, she scurried off down the path toward the house.

"She's breeding," Dane announced into the silence that fell after her departure.

Bastian straightened. "How did—?" He expelled a breath. "Sometimes I forget the sort of work you've been doing in ElseWorld all these years."

Dane eyed him. "Is it yours?"

Bastian shook his head. "She was raped a week before we met. She refuses to name the villain, but once I wring his name from her, he will meet with a swift and fatal accident. The child won't reach term."

"Due to another accident?" Tucking the scroll in his pocket, Dane stood.

"I have no quarrel with the child, only its father," Bastian assured him. "However, Michaela was stricken with the Sickness and is unable to bear children. She caught it when she came through the gate. The—"

The rest of what he'd been about to say was interrupted by the sound of footsteps crashing toward them through the grove. It was Sevin, looking as if he'd run the entire way back to them after seeing the nereids off.

"There's been another killing," he announced. "We found a body down by the Tiber as the messengers were departing."

4

Fear boiled in Dane, hot and caustic. "It's not—"

Sevin shook his head. "No. Gods, no. It's not Luc. It's a girl. Fey. Come see what you make of it. Before she's found and her body disturbed."

Bastian threw on his clothes, and within minutes the three brothers were at the foot of the hill, and Dane was standing over the twisted body of what looked to be an eighteen-year-old girl.

Set between Aventine Hill and the Tiber River, this was the Monte Testaccio area, built on pottery shards. The Vinarium—a market dedicated to the commerce of wine—had stood here in ancient times. Traders had carried their vintages here in amphorae from faraway vineyards. Once these clay vessels were emptied, they had been tossed into the Tiber. Eventually, the broken shards had built up so high they'd threatened to block the river itself. They'd been fished out and tossed onshore here. Like this girl.

"She looks to have washed up here, likely having been dumped from farther upriver." Dane kneeled down and pushed her damp shift aside, stoically inspecting her. In Special Ops, he'd dealt with more than one bloated, lifeless body over the past twelve years.

"There are needle marks on her arms," he noted. "And a red ring around each of her breasts."

"What from?" asked Bastian.

"I don't—" As Dane bent to examine her more closely, a pungent odor struck him full in the face. Onions. His insides twisted and heaved. Turning away, he staggered and fell along the shore, fighting the urge to retch.

"What is it? What's wrong?" Bastian demanded from behind him.

"Onions. Fuck, can't stand the smell of them."

"I don't smell them," said Sevin, his tone bewildered.

"Nor I," said Bastian. "But don't forget—in ElseWorld Dane had training that gifted him with an ability to detect the minutiae of scents."

"Do you suppose this is a clue of some sort?" Sevin speculated. "Could she have been murdered in an onion field?"

Their voices seemed distant as Dane grappled with the awful stir of memories that gnawed at him like a shark's teeth. And the guilt. Always the terrible, seething guilt over the fact that he'd come back alive while their fourth and youngest brother, Lucien, had remained missing. He could still see Luc's trusting, terrified face all those years ago. Just as if it were before him now.

It had been a Moonful night when all had gone so awry. Their parents had gone out to the grove—the very one Dane now owned—leaving their four boys in the care of servants. Dane had recently become curious to learn something of these mysterious rites in which the satyr engaged under a full moon. And he had sneaked out, hoping to spy. Unknown to him, Luc had followed.

They'd been boys, not yet men. Luc only five to Dane's

twelve. Both had been years away from fully understanding what it meant to be Satyr, for they would not be physically ready to participate in the carnal rituals until their eighteenth years, when their bodies would finally alter for the first time with the coming of the full moon.

The night should have been safe for them. The grove's perimeter had been bespelled by their parents and the rest of the Satyr clan—there had been far more of them in Rome then—who'd gathered there for the rituals. No human should have been able to pierce the veil of magic surrounding it, and all Else species would have been engaged in the Moonful observances.

Yet somehow, there had already been other spies there in the grove that night, waiting. And when Dane and Luc had accidently stumbled upon them, both brothers had been captured and hauled away. His last memory of Luc was as they'd been blindfolded. When Luc had looked to Dane to save him.

But he hadn't, and for that he couldn't forgive himself. Instead, both boys had gone missing, and only Dane had turned up again a year later. Alone and without any recollection of who'd abducted them or any of the events during the time that had elapsed since then. With no recollection of what had happened to Luc.

If he was still alive these twelve years later, Luc would now be a month shy of his eighteenth year. In four weeks, another Moonful would come, and his young body would alter for the first time in his life. It would put him in danger of exposing what he was to his captors.

Luc. Gods, where are you? If you're alive, please hold on a little longer. I'll find you.

A shout came from nearby, yanking Dane back to the present.

"Fishermen," Bastian murmured. "They've spotted us."

"Summon the *polizia!*" Sevin called, going to meet them. "We've found a body."

Managing to get to his feet, Dane glanced downriver, dragging fresh air into his lungs. In the distance, he saw a faint flash of iridescence—the two nereids heading westward to the Tyrrhenian Sea, where they would then turn north toward Tuscany. After wending their way through a labyrinth of sea, river, tributary, and stream, they would journey overland again for a short distance and then pass through the gate to ElseWorld.

No doubt they would swim swiftly, anxious to deliver their juicy morsel of gossip. The whereabouts of a defector—him. He had two maybe three weeks at most until the Council sent Trackers after him. He would not hide from them. But he wouldn't allow them to take him either. Yet he could think of only one thing that would stop them. This solution had come to him earlier, back at the temple. And now the scroll he'd crumpled and stashed in his pocket weighed heavily on his mind.

The fishermen had arrived and were exclaiming over the body, crossing themselves and muttering as they awaited the arrival of the local authorities.

"They're handling it," said Bastian from behind him. "Let's go breakfast and bathe. You'll be more yourself."

Dane nodded and the three of them headed homeward. "I'll need a lift to Capitoline later when you go," he said matter-of-factly.

"What's on Capitoline?" asked Sevin.

"A wife," Dane replied.

At the first blush of dawn, Eva's Shimmerskin lover departed her bed, returning without complaint to the ether that had spawned him. As her world swam back into focus, she lay there naked amid tangled covers, her skin still flushed from his attentions. Except for her quickened breath, all was deathly quiet. She was alone. Melancholy. She shifted and felt a pleasant, residual tenderness in her private places.

Last night under the full moon, her body and spirit had been driven by a primal instinct to mate. She had been satisfied dozens of times, both by her own ministrations and by those of her conjured lover. With no true Will of his own, he had obeyed her every command. He'd warmed her body with his, but he hadn't warmed her soul as she imagined a flesh and blood lover might have. Whenever she'd lost herself to the pleasure for even a moment, her instruction to him had waned. At such times, he had a tiresome habit of slacking off in his attentions. It was a difficulty that plagued the ritual every month, and one for which she knew no cure.

She'd dominated him and he had submitted to her Will. It was the opposite of what she wanted from a lover. She would have much preferred one who would command her and take charge of matters. One who would lead her with his strength and spirit, into a deeper pleasure of the mind and heart, as well as flesh. For when all were equally involved, would not the pleasure be exponentially increased? This was something she longed to discover for herself.

It was a luxury to wallow in these yearnings for these few moments. She only permitted herself to do so in the immediate aftermath of this monthly event, in the privacy of this room at the coming of dawn. In the full light of day, she'd leave such foolishness behind and go about the business of living a respectable life.

Until next month, when the fullness of the moon came again, reminding her of what she could and could not have.

The lock clicked, admitting Odette. Bearing a silver tray set with a teacup, a teapot, a small basket covered with a linen cloth, and a mortar and pestle, she came to stand beside the bed, staring down at Eva. Just beyond her, the sky was striated with fingers of pink and orange fast giving way to the blue of daylight.

Eva smiled, inhaling blissfully. "Mmm. I smell beignets."

"You always like them since you were *une bebe*." Odette

sent her a fond glance as she set the tray down on the bedside table. Eva stretched her tired muscles, making no attempt to cover herself, uncaring that Odette saw her in this state. For this was the woman who'd helped raise her for the past twenty-two years, and Eva had no secrets from her. Except one.

Her green eyes flitted guiltily to her maidservant, then away. If she told her what had happened in the grove last night, Odette would hound her even more about her safety and would try to curtail her freedoms. After so many years in the family, the woman was more an aunt than a maid or governess, and she would have no qualms about making free with her advice. It was too early to have the incident dissected and criticized. Something about it was too private.

Odette set the basket of pastries on the bed next to her. Then, turning her attention to the mortar, she tossed in a few pinches of herbs and an oval, button-sized seed, and began grinding them together.

Eva pulled a warm, flaky beignet from the basket beside her. Nibbling, she left Odette to her task and rolled onto her stomach toward the opposite side of the bed, the covers tangling around her bare legs. Pulling the table's small drawer open, she found her mother's diary and flipped to the page she wanted. Resting on her elbows, she studied the spidery feminine scrawl.

"Why you read Fantine's prattle?" Odette asked, gesturing to indicate the book. "You got it committed to memory by now, eh?"

Eva shrugged, tracing a finger over the loop of a "y." She'd only found the book after her mother had died four months ago, and she'd read it a dozen times since. "It still smells of her perfume. And I like to see her handwriting. It makes me feel closer to her."

Her eyes slid down the list of names, all male. Fantine's *innamorati*. By now, she had narrowed her suspects to three candidates among the wealthy society here in Rome, based on the dates her fey mother had been with them. One of them had to be her father.

But here was the puzzle. None on the list bore the surname of Satyr. And there had been no satyr in Rome at the time of her conception. She'd concluded that her father must have used a pseudonym. If so, he might prove reluctant to reveal himself to her as satyr, even if she found him.

She tugged at the thin length of gold chain that draped her neck and sawed it between her lips. "What sort of man abandons a beautiful woman full with his child, leaving her to fend for herself?" she mused.

Odette sent her an inscrutable look, continuing her grinding. "A bad one. One you better off not knowing."

"I don't want to know him. I only want to make him admit himself to be my father and to explain his desertion of us."

"So you say," scoffed Odette. "Finding him isn't gonna make things right. Don't expect his heart will open to let you in. You were a love child, but he won't love you."

Leave it to Odette to find her weakest point and probe it. "Believe what you will, but it won't stop me from looking for him."

Thanks to her bedding of this mysterious man, her mother had become with child. Eva's conception had occurred on a night of the full moon, for this was the only time a satyr male could impregnate a female. Yet, even on such a night, the satyr could control his seed. It therefore followed that her father had either been unforgivably careless, or that he'd given Fantine his child on purpose. But it was what happened next that truly confounded her. And had confounded Fantine as well. Eva ran a fingertip along her mother's words, penned twenty-two years ago:

September 1, 1858
I am enceinte! *Such joy!* Mon Ange *says he hopes for a*
daughter. One who looks like me. He sends me to wait for

him in Florence, where we will marry and live as man and wife. Odette is angry at his negligence in getting me with child and has tried to guess his identity. But he is my secret. I won't tell her his name, though she will learn it soon enough when he comes for me. I know I am a disappointment to her, for I was meant to marry well among human society. But my beloved is surely fine enough even to suit the likes of her.

September 14, 1858
Why does my darling leave us here in Florence so long without word? When will he come? It has been two weeks now and I grow worried. And huge.

I now know the truth of what I carry in my womb and wish to share the news with him. Odette has discovered it, of course. She is in a foul temper, muttering and cursing the head of my beloved. For it seems his seed has dominated mine. This child born of our joyful union will not be fey as I am, but will be satyr instead. As he is.

Will he be pleased? He'd so wanted a daughter. But I hope he will be happy with a son, for if it is to be more satyr than fey, then it can only be a son.

September 23, 1858
If there had been any doubt that my offspring is to be satyr, none exists now. The birth is imminent, and just four weeks have elapsed since Mon Ange and I lay together. Only a child of his species requires so little time to gestate. I confess I am glad this discomfort is to be of so short a duration. But Odette nags at me to flee through the gate. And now the ElseWorld Council has sent an escort. It seems that without a husband, I must go into exile. I have sent a letter to Mon Ange, the third I have posted to him

*and gotten no reply. I am fat, penniless, and joyless. All
looks bleak.*

October 3, 1858
*I have a daughter! I am in shock. Odette is as well. We
don't know what to make of it. I bowed to the pressure, so
we are all back in ElseWorld now. No one here knows the
circumstances of my sweet baby Evangeline's blood, and
we shall endeavor to keep it that way. I will keep her safe
and hope my dearest darling comes to us. Evangeline will
need him to protect her. I fear for her if anyone discovers
what she is.*

But Fantine's "dearest darling" had never come for them,
and they'd had no word from him either. Instead, they'd lived
in exile on the other side of the gate, unable to get permission to
return or to communicate with this world. The treaty of 1850
negotiated by the satyr of Tuscany had established immigration
quotas for interworld passage. Then the Great Sickness had
changed things. Traversing the gate from ElseWorld to Earth-
World had become all but impossible, except for diplomatic or
business purposes sanctioned by the Council.

Over the following two decades, Fantine's hope had slowly
dwindled and been replaced by bitterness. She had dedicated
the remainder of her life to keeping the truth of Eva's blood
secret and to schooling her on one goal. When Eva grew up,
she was to somehow make her way back to Rome and wed a
wealthy human as her mother had not managed to.

And Eva had learned this lesson well. When her mother died
four months ago, she had immediately applied for a visa to
come here. In view of the growing need for her particular skill,
and her professing herself to be fey and passing the test of this,
thanks to Odette's powders, a visa had been quickly granted.

"Why wouldn't she say who my father was?" Eva wondered

aloud. "And how could *you* not have known? You were her greatest confidante."

Odette shook her head, tsking. "She a Marital Broker like you, always around men. Too many of them come and go from her bed for me to keep track. I tell her if she gonna act like a *Grande Horizontale*, then at least get paid like one. But, no, she was in love with love, your mother. Happy to have her clients between her legs, while she found wives for them among the humans."

Odette scooped a heap of finely ground powder from the mortar into the teacup. Then she tilted the teapot and filled the cup with steaming water. Fantine and she had worked together to discover the ingredients for this brew through trial and error, and Eva had drunk many a strange concoction during her youth in order to help them determine exactly the right balance.

Odette absently stirred it now with a small silver spoon, waiting for it to dissolve. "My poor sweet Fantine. The years go by and she tired of every single one of them gentlemen—human or Else—long before they tire of her. Was always happy to bid them farewell the minute she got them married off. Never listened to their pleas to keep them as lovers after they wed, so I didn't worry. How was I to know one among them would break her heart and leave her with a *bambina* one day? A good lesson for you."

Eva grimaced. "I know, I know."

"That's good, then." Odette plumped the pillows. "Sit up now, mademoiselle."

Setting the journal aside, Eva pushed herself upright, hugging her knees. By the time the cup was handed to her, its contents had cooled, and she swallowed them quickly and without argument. Having taken this brew nearly every morning all of her life, she was accustomed to its bitter taste and to its more fortunate effect of disguising the fact that she was satyr. Not only that, it rendered her scent so close to that of a fey's as to be indistinguishable, even to the Trackers. They'd detected nothing when she'd been sent to them for species verification. They had declared her to be predominantly fey—the offspring of a fey mother and a human father as she'd claimed. And so she and her maid and servant, Pinot, had been granted passage into this world.

This brew had allowed her to come here. Allowed her to remain here undetected. Its essential ingredient was the small pit of an olive found only in particular trees—those in the ancient groves planted by the satyr. Which meant they could only be found in a single location here in Rome. On land that evidently had been acquired by the flesh and blood male she'd met last night—the sole person who had not been fooled by her ruse. How had he guessed? And why only him?

Eva set the empty cup on the tray. "Was that from the olives I brought last night?"

"*Non,*" said Odette, going to throw open the window. "It's from what we brought with us from ElseWorld's trees. You'll need to go again to the grove on Aventine and gather more."

Go back? And risk encountering *him*? "Why?" Eva asked in alarm. "What was wrong with what I gathered last night? Were they too unripe?"

Odette's coarse, tightly pinned hair didn't sway when she shook her head. "Ripeness don't matter. It's just that the trees you pick from were the wrong ones."

"How do you know?"

"Just do. You follow Fantine's map next time."

Eva spread her hands in exasperation. "I did follow it. It's confusing. Why don't you come with me to help next time if you think it's so easy?"

Odette quickly drew a sign on her chest with a forefinger to ward off evil spirits. "Satyr lands give me shivers, like the dead walking past."

"Yet you'd bid me go there, in spite of your superstitions."

"That grove won't hurt you—you one of *them*. Those old trees sense it's best not to do you harm. You go back there in the next week or so. Don't have to go today."

Apparently considering the matter settled, Odette began straightening up the room, intent on removing all trace of what Eva had gotten up to last night. The bottle of wine that would replenish its own contents within the month was capped, and it and the goblet returned to the cabinet.

Eva slid lower in her bed, feeling suddenly tired. She took the brew every morning, but it only made her sleepy the morning following Moonful. She opened her eyes again when Odette came closer and reached for one of the ropes tied to the headboard.

"Leave them. I'll do that," Eva protested halfheartedly. "I don't like to trouble you." She tried to get up but sank back, a trifle dizzy.

"You rest."

"I should get up. I have things to do. I need to return to the grove for more olives." She yawned. "And I promised to take the girls to tour the ruins."

"You take those little heathens out later. Rest now." Odette tucked her in, as she had when Eva was a child.

"Don't call them that. They're orphans, who lost their mothers to the Sickness. Abandoned by their fathers as I was. They need and deserve our kindness."

Mmm-hmm. Odette untied the ropes from the headboard and looped them around her hand without comment. They, too, would be stowed in the cabinet and Eva wouldn't see them again until next Moonful.

"Really, I'll do all that," Eva insisted again. Her lashes fluttered as she battled sleep.

"No shame in this, *cara*. It's your nature," Odette soothed.

Eyes drifting closed, Eva shook her head on the pillow. She knew better. Fantine and Odette had loved her, but they'd considered her a freak. Their refusal to discuss her "nature," and the strict secrecy they insisted upon with regard to it, had taught her that there *was* shame in this, at least for a woman. Satyr males were revered in ElseWorld, but she—the lone satyr female—was quite simply defective.

Yet they had always arranged for her comfort during the ritual she performed each Moonful. And Odette continued to aid and abet it in every way after Fantine's death, in spite of the fact that she scorned the satyr species in general. By the time Eva woke again, the cylinders on the bedside table would be cleansed and returned to the cabinet. The phallus at the foot of the bed would be polished and rotated back to its former position among fanciful vines and clusters of grapes carved from olive-wood.

"I don't know what I would do without you, Detty," Eva murmured dreamily, hardly noticing she'd used her childhood nickname for the serving woman. Upon the first Moonful after Eva had turned eighteen, Fantine had been confronted at last with undeniable proof that her daughter was truly satyr. A faraway, longing look had come into her eyes. One that said she was remembering Eva's father. But all she'd said was, "Well, we must make do." But it was Odette who had done the practical things that had helped Eva to survive undetected.

"*Dear Maman.*" Eva sighed, her eyes drifting closed. "I miss her."

A gentle hand adjusted the coverlet over her. "Sleep now. Dream of that rich husband you gonna get soon."

Eva nodded into her pillow. She'd marry well into the ranks of this human society, and somewhere in heaven her *maman* would know and be proud of her success. But for herself, Eva wished for only one thing. To find her father. In heaven, she hoped her *maman* would understand it was something she needed to do.

A smile touched her lips. One like that of the beautiful Fantine, who'd felled half the men in Rome and then gone on to do the same in ElseWorld's French Enclave.

"Pretty smile like that. You'll have your choice of men. But you'll marry human, not a satyr like ruined your poor *maman*," Odette said, satisfaction coloring her voice. "You show these Roman curs who the Delacortes are. You make them pay."

It was a maxim Eva had been weaned on. From childhood, she had been groomed to avenge the wrongs this world had done her mother.

"Rest, *bebe*. Odette's gonna keep you nice and safe." She lapsed into *voces mysticae* then, the chants and protection spells that she'd whispered over Eva for as long as she could remember. It comforted Eva to hear her familiar words, and she drifted off into a drug-induced sleep.

"That's it." Bending closer, Odette gently pulled back the coverlet, then stared down at her for a long moment. She curved a palm along Eva's cheek almost reverently, then slowly ran her hand downward, over her throat, a breast, ribs, until finally her hand came to rest on her belly. "That's my good girl. Dream of babies. And revenge."

5

"Good Gods, I believe you *are* insane after all," said Sevin, as their carriage drew to a halt.

"You're not the first to think so," Dane replied.

Capitoline Hill was thick with monuments, museums, and Medieval and Renaissance palazzi. But tucked among them, the three brothers had found the address written on the nereids' scroll. Dane had insisted. Staring from the windows of Bastian's carriage, he and Sevin studied the three-story brick and stone townhouse. Squeezed between taller and more stately edifices that shadowed it, it had a charm of yesteryear, and it reeked of ElseWorld magic.

"It's owned by the Council," said Dane. "I can scent it."

Sevin grimaced. "It seems fitting somehow that it's located here, near Tarpeian Rock, where men have historically been thrown to their deaths."

Dane heard a snort of laughter from Bastian, who sat behind him on the leather seat.

"Really, brother, what are we doing here?" Sevin persisted,

only half teasing. "I strongly suggest that you run while you still can."

"You heard the Council's missive," said Dane. "We're obligated to wed where our seed will find purchase and thrive. That necessitates a human wife."

"We've received at least a dozen such letters. It's not our obligation to populate this world with our kind," said Bastian. "If you're concerned the nereids will report your whereabouts—"

"I'm a deserter. Of course they will," said Danc, cutting him off. "In a few weeks, Trackers will come for me. But if they find me already wed to a human and breeding her—and if the whole matter was arranged by the Council's choice of matchmaker—what can they do? I'll have accomplished what their letter asked of us. They won't uproot me." He shifted, reaching for the door.

"It's too great a sacrifice," Sevin protested. "Why not go into hiding until they give up searching for you?"

"Because Luc turns eighteen soon," Dane gritted. "My search for him can't wait."

"Do you think we haven't searched for him all these years?" Bastian asked, his steel-edged words slicing the thick tension that suddenly stretched between them.

Dane opened the carriage door, his emotions roiling. Didn't they understand that he alone was responsible for Luc's disappearance? He'd led his five-year-old brother to his doom. Therefore, he must be the one to make things right. "I know you have. But *I'm* the one who lost him. I must be the one to find him." With that, he swung down and headed for the townhouse.

Beyond its ironwork gate, two small girls played in the garden. The younger one noticed their carriage and approached the gate, a question in her eyes.

"Don't wait for me," he called back to his brothers. "I'll find my own way home."

"Come away, Mimi," the older girl cautioned as he approached, shooting him a suspicious glance. His nose told him both were blends of fey and human.

The one called Mimi stubbornly wrapped her chubby fingers around the gate's grill and stared up at him. The question that had been in her wide doe-brown eyes now fell to her lips. "Are you here for a bride?"

Eva heard the merry stomp of children on the stairs as she climbed from her bath. She took the robe Odette held out and slipped it on, tying its belt. Only two hours had elapsed since she'd taken the olive powder, but though her body still ached from the exercise of last night, she had awakened from sleep refreshed.

"There's a man in the garden!" Mimi shouted, dashing into the bedroom. "He came in a beautiful carriage like Cinderella's fairy godmother made!"

"You let him in?" Eva said, alarmed.

"Only because he had this," said Lena. She handed over a crumpled scroll of parchment and its magic tickled Eva's fingers.

Odette came closer to help scrutinize it. "It bears the Else-World Council's seal," she noted.

"And our address," said Eva.

Waiting for their verdict, Lena tugged a strand of her long silky hair between her lips and began chewing it. When Eva had first found the girls on the streets of Rome, they'd been abandoned and begging for water and food during the heat of summer. Lena's hair had been nibbled away to different lengths, as short as she could reach with her sharp fairy teeth. Eva had rescued them, and they were now firmly entrenched in her home and her heart. And in typical fey fashion, Lena's hair had already grown halfway down her back in just the few months since they'd come.

"Whoever he may be, he's definitely a client," Odette pronounced at last.

"Then it was all right to let him in?" Lena asked hopefully.

Leaning down, Eva gently pulled the damp strand of hair from her mouth and smoothed it over one thin shoulder. With her thumb, she soothed away the frown between Lena's brows. "It's all right, *cherie*. But from now on, alert Pinot or one of us when clients arrive, *oui*?"

"But we *are* alerting you!" Mimi declared. Then she sneezed. One of her favorite occupations was investigating the items on Eva's dressing table and she'd been sniffing a box of perfumed powder.

"I meant *before* you let anyone in," added Eva.

"Good for nothing Pinot! He should have been on guard outside," Odette grumbled, making for the door. "When I find him, I'll smack his backside."

"Have our visitor wait in my office." Eva grabbed the woman's arm in a warning squeeze. "And none of your tricks."

"I don't make the tricks. *You* make the tricks." Odette winked, pulling away. Harmful magic had been outlawed in the Twelve Tables in the fifth century B.C.E., but Odette paid that no heed. Eva had grown up at her knee, weaned on her chants, tablets, and the strange little dolls she made.

The minute she left the room, Mimi climbed up to begin jumping on the bed. Her nose was dusted white with powder.

Eva clapped her hands. "Stop that for a moment and turn around, little ones. Has Odette been taking care of you?"

Both girls presented their backs for inspection and she smoothed the flat of her fingers over their shoulder blades, feeling for the bump of feathers through the fabric of their dresses. It saddened her that they must all hide their natures; but in this world, it kept them safe and was for the best.

"Excellent," she said. "You're smooth as humans."

"But I want to grow my wings!" shouted Mimi.

"You can't," scolded Lena, shaking a finger at her in imitation of Odette. "Wings are bad. We must clip them so humans won't guess what we are."

"Wing-y ding dings!" Mimi insisted in the high-pitched voice that only a young girl of five could achieve. "I want my fairy wings so I can fly!" She spread her arms on either side of her and jumped in circles around the bed.

Lena rolled her eyes, hugging the bedpost, but a tiny smile tugged at one side of her mouth.

Eva put her hands on her hips. "How do I look, girls? Shall I meet our new client like this, in my robe?" She made as if to leave the chamber.

"No!" The girls giggled over the scandalous notion, laughter changing even Lena back into a child for the moment.

"Well, then, you must choose a dress for me while I fix my hair. Go to my armoire and select something proper for a matchmaker to wear, will you? *Vite!*"

As if she'd been charged with a duty upon which the fate of the world rested, Lena dragged a stool to the armoire and began rifling through the gowns that hung within it. Mimi hopped from the bed to the floor in a move that undoubtedly rattled the chandelier on the ceiling below stairs, and joined her.

While the girls argued over the merits of each gown, Eva slipped on her underthings behind a screen and then sat at her dressing table. Quickly, she arranged her dark hair in a twist and stabbed it with an abalone comb to hold all in place.

Although she'd come to ElseWorld with her own agenda, she must also satisfy that of the ElseWorld Council, which meant these appointments with clients they sent her from time to time. This would be her fourth such client in three months. Thus far, all had been male—one fey, one Elemental, and one a centaur, who walked on two legs except when affected by a full moon. She'd managed to match them all with suitable human females, who remained blithely unaware of their new husbands' peculiarities thanks to carefully applied magic.

She didn't mind utilizing her skill in this way. It was the reason she'd been allowed to come here after all. And it was the sole source of their income. If she balked at an assignment, the Council might summon her back through the gate. Odette and Pinot as well, which would leave Mimi and Lena here to fend for themselves. They all depended on her for their livelihood, and she must not fail them.

"I'm ready," she announced, turning to the girls. "Now, let's see—what have you chosen for me?"

When Lena and Mimi displayed their selection, their faces were so full of a need to please that Eva didn't have the heart to tell them how unsuitable it was. Hiding her dismay, she proclaimed it perfect for the occasion and stepped into it. Dressing on her own was far easier since the bustle had gone out of fashion two years earlier, though Parisian fashion plates in the ladies' journals hinted at its imminent resurrection. For now, the popular styles remained slim and tight-fitting with a train.

After she'd hooked the gown's fastenings, she drew on long white gloves to disguise wrists that were chafed from the ropes of last night. "Go! Both of you. Find Odette and Pinot. Ask them to tell our guest that I'll be down in just another moment."

"Wait!" begged Mimi. "No gloves. Wear your *maman's* jewels. Pleeese!"

"I'll go," said the ever-obedient Lena, leaving the room to search for Odette.

Opening the enameled box on Eva's dressing table, which had fascinated her from the moment she'd seen it, Mimi selected an assortment of rings, necklaces, and bracelets. Eva tugged off the gloves and waved her closer. "Hurry, then. Bring them."

After she'd been more than sufficiently weighted with sparkles and gems, Eva declared, "All right. It's enough." She gazed at her reflection in the mirror, smiling ruefully. The emerald taffeta ball gown with its long train and abundant jewels was a ridiculous choice for morning. But the sense of pride she'd given the girls by wearing this ensemble made it the perfect choice. What did it matter if her client thought her eccentric? Those in her profession usually were.

Quickly, she and Mimi made their way downstairs and stepped into the small, stately salon that served as her office. Her newest client stood inside examining a mosaic puzzle box that had been her mother's and now sat on a shelf behind her desk among curios, children's fairy-tale books, periodicals, thick tomes, and other clutter.

His back was to her. It was broad, his shoulders wide. His hair was dark, and he was at least a head taller than she. And familiar. Her nape tingled with a strange, sudden awareness. Instinctively, she took a single step backward, contemplating flight.

Seeming to notice her arrival, he turned her way and paused, his silver gaze sweeping her.

Oh, Gods! It was *him!* The man from the olive grove.

Mimi skipped inside, but Eva only stood there frozen in the doorway waiting for recognition to fill his expression. Instead, there was only faint surprise. And humor. He was amused by her clothing.

But he didn't recognize her!

Dane sat across from the occupant of the desk, genuinely intrigued by her as he hadn't been by a woman for as long as he could remember. He hadn't given any thought to what he'd expected a matchmaker and her premises would be like, but he was certain that if he had, he could not have imagined this. For there was nothing at all expected about this room and its bizarre occupants.

In the garden, he'd been briefly interrogated before being

invited inside by the diminutive, stocky man who appeared to have more than a few drops of pixie blood in him. In true pixie fashion, the fellow was fixated on matters of finance and had discussed the matchmaker's exorbitant fee even as he led him to this salon. A mulatto serving woman had arrived next, her face dour and suspicious. Her blood was so mixed that it was impossible to discern her ancestry even with his gifted nose. Likely over a dozen ElseWorld species had gone into the witch's brew that had spawned her.

Then had come the return of the two little girls who'd admitted him to the garden to begin with. They sat together on the carpet now, the older one sketching, and the younger one playing with a toy steam locomotive and making soft chugging noises.

And finally he'd been confronted with this mysterious woman—Mademoiselle Evangeline Delacorte, she called herself. The matchmaker. Seated opposite her with a desk between them, he studied every detail of her person without appearing to. A trick he'd learned in Special Ops.

She resembled an ancient Egyptian scryer, with kohl around her eyes, rings on every finger, and bangles thick at both wrists. What sort of female wore a provocative ball gown to conduct business, other than a courtesan? A tangle of necklaces draped her opulent bosom, an aspect of a woman that he was particularly drawn to. He shifted in his chair, causing its leather to creak, and looked away. Were he to become too enchanted with her charms, it would be tantamount to an outright invitation to Dante to join him in his skin.

The moment she'd come into the room, the matchmaker had ducked her head and quickly located a gauzy veil, which she'd draped over her head and shoulders. While it was transparent and did almost nothing to obscure her features, some form of magic had been woven into it, for he found that when he looked away, he couldn't recall her face. But stranger still was the fact that her scent was so elusive that he couldn't quite make out her species. This above all piqued his curiosity. In ElseWorld, his ability to distinguish one scent from another was legendary. However, something within him—Dante, perhaps—was purposely impeding his ability to read hers. Why? She and her entourage presented a puzzle. Something he'd never been able to resist.

"You've come to me seeking a bride?" It was the second time the woman had asked him the same question. It was rhetorical. The scroll the Council had sent to his brothers lay on the desk before her, bristling with ElseWorld magic and her address upon it plain to see. Her fingers stroked its edges restlessly. She was nervous. Which usually meant someone was hiding something.

Dane crossed one booted ankle over his opposite knee and crossed his arms. "No, I come to you seeking a foreman for my grove."

The older girl glanced up from her drawing. "But Mademoiselle doesn't locate foremen," she informed him with a seriousness that sat strangely on one so young. "She finds brides."

Mimi, who'd driven her train beneath the matchmaker's desk, peered out at him and nodded. The serving woman squirmed on the corner chair where she sat with her mending. The girls' precocious behavior irritated her, and it was clear to him that she had no great affection for them.

"Then I suppose I'll have to settle for a bride instead." He looked directly at the object of his interest then, determined to learn more of her. "Tell me," he asked the mademoiselle, "what sort of credentials does one require to become a matchmaker?"

"Marital Broker," she corrected. "As was my mother and her mother before her, I'm a fey-human blend. Certified as predominantly fey. Mine is an inherited talent, and the Council wouldn't have sent you to me if I weren't good at my job." Her tone held a note of challenge as if she assumed he'd refute some or all of her statement. Curiouser and curiouser.

The pixie, who sat perched on a high stool before a *scrivania,* paused in his scribbling. "She's the best."

Mademoiselle Delacorte reached over and patted the diminutive man's arm, bestowing a fond smile on him. "Why thank you, Pinot."

The older girl had moved to sit in the window seat and continue her drawing where the light was better. The younger one still played under the matchmaker's desk, peeking out at him when the mood struck her. Now and then the matchmaker would absently stroke the child's hair, and she would preen under the attention. The old woman silently glowered, and the pixie hunched over the notes he was taking of their meeting, his eyes studying Dane like a hawk's.

To most, it would have been an unnerving scene. Yet Dane found something compelling and comfortable about it. Though they were an odd assortment, he sensed they were a family. The other four people in the room revolved around this veiled woman as if planets basking in the warmth of a feminine sun that held them all together with its gravitational pull. He felt an odd sort of yearning to join in their orbit of her. To have those soft fingers caress him as well. Shrugging off the foolish notion, he asked, "How do we progress? Do you have a catalog of female prospects I might peruse, or—?"

A giggle came from below the desk and Mimi's eyes popped up over the edge, laughing at him. The matchmaker shook her head. "It doesn't proceed in that way," she said. She seemed to be gazing past him—above his head, then to each side of him. It was a peculiar thing to do, but there was something uncannily familiar about it.

"How, then?" he asked, wanting to hear her voice again. There was something familiar about that as well.

"First, you'll provide information to help me form a profile of the sort of lady who'd suit you as wife. Later, I will select and recommend several eligible candidates. I'll arrange for you to meet them. Together, we'll ascertain which lady among them is most appropriate for you and your situation in life. You'll woo her and then wed her. Does that sound agreeable?"

Dane frowned. "It sounds complicated. How long will all this take?" He had more important things to do with his time—like finding his younger brother.

"It's difficult to say. But the sooner we begin, the sooner 'all this' will be done." Before he could respond, she sat back in her chair with the air of someone who was about to tease him and was feeling pleased about the prospect. "To begin things, my girls have some questions," she informed him. "Lena?"

The older of the two girls paused in her sketching and looked up at him. "Do you prefer rice pudding or chocolate?"

Mimi came to lean against the arm of his chair, staring at him with great concentration. The pixie held a pen over his paper, preparing to record his forthcoming reply as if it were of great import.

They were ridiculous, the lot of them. Yet he found himself answering gravely, "Chocolate, absolutely."

Lena almost smiled, but then seemed to remember herself and simply nodded before returning her attention to her drawing tablet.

"*Merci, cherie.* And now, Mimi?" the matchmaker invited warmly.

The younger girl leaned closer to him, her scent redolent of perfumed powder. Her brown eyes were so clear and sweet that it almost hurt to look at them. Had he ever been that innocent? "Do you prefer thunderstorms or sunshine?" she demanded.

"Some of each. But what has this to do with anything?"

"Do you prefer puzzles or paints?" she persisted.

He glanced at the matchmaker, suspecting ridicule.

"If you like puzzles, you might wish to wed someone complicated and intellectual," Eva explained calmly, as if the child's questions were the most sensible in the world. "If you like paints, you might be more suited to someone with a sedate, creative disposition."

"Puzzles, then."

"Do you prefer kittens, children, horses, or ladybugs?" the little girl enquired.

"For lunch or for breakfast?" he returned with a straight face.

Mimi gasped in horror; then realizing it must be a joke, she burst into giggles, bumping her small fist against his shoulder.

"Mimi!" This sharp scolding issued from the serving woman, her first word in his presence. But the irrepressible girl only shot him another grin and then skipped off to stack various items on the matchmaker's desktop in what appeared to be the beginning of some sort of childish construction project. Meanwhile, Lena drew ever more furiously as if fearing inspiration would depart before she could finish.

"Exactly how do you go about choosing a wife for a man you don't know?" he asked the matchmaker. "I mean, what are the mechanics of it that make you better able to select a suitable mate for me than I might choose on my own?"

Mimi looked over from her building and piped up. "She watches to see which lady jumps at you."

Again, he looked to the matchmaker, a brow raised in question.

"She's describing the nature of my gift," Mademoiselle Delacorte told him. "You may not be aware of it, but every species has a sort of glow around their body, like a large halo or outline." She waved her hands toward him in a vaguely circular fashion to indicate his periphery. "They're called auras, and like my mother before me, I'm one of the rare people who can read them."

"Meaning?"

"Perhaps 'interpret' is a better word for what I do. Your aura is like your signature. No one else's is quite the same. It's constantly changing shape and color as your mood changes."

She used her hands when speaking, and he noticed that whenever her bracelets separated, she kept repositioning them to hide her wrists again. "Your aura will tend to flare outward when a compatible partner draws near, almost as if to embrace her. A female's does the same in reaction to a potential male partner, though it's not as dramatic. Nuances in two auras upon their meeting indicate whether a particular combination will prove harmonious and fruitful."

"Fruitful," he repeated.

Lena looked up. "Whether you'll have babies," she informed him.

The matchmaker shot a speaking glance at the serving woman, who immediately stood and clapped her hands. "That will be all, girls! Out to the garden. Now." The two girls were summarily hustled toward the door.

"I thought we were going to the ruins today," complained Mimi.

"Later, *cara*," she was told.

"For you, signor," the older one said on her way out, handing Dane the drawing she'd been working on. It was a portrait of him, unfinished.

"Thank you," he said in surprise.

"What a lovely gift, Lena," the matchmaker told her. "And how thoughtful."

"Your children?" Dane asked a moment later, nodding toward the door through which they and the serving woman had departed.

"Nieces." The explanation fell easily from her lips. But at the same time she took hold of a snow globe, which had been serving as a paperweight on her desk, and placed it before her as a sort of barrier between them. An unconscious gesture that hinted at a lie. Definitely hiding something. "They're in my charge now that their parents have passed on. Lena's quite a good artist, *n'est-elle pas?*"

"Quite." But he wouldn't let her dissuade him from his questions. Setting the drawing aside, he sat back to offer her the illusion of safety. "You're French I gather. And recently arrived in this world. So how is it that you're already so well entrenched in elite Roman society that you are invited to gatherings where you might locate eligible partners for your clients?"

Her eyes narrowed on him for a long, considering moment. "You're a Tracker," she accused slowly, as if only just realizing it. Her face drained of color.

He quirked a brow. "I was. Is that a problem?"

Her gaze flicked to the pixie and back to him again. "Why would it be?" Her fingers rose to fuss with the low neckline of her bodice, drifting over breasts that were smooth and full and perfectly rounded, with a deep shadow between. His eyes keened on the gesture, remembering it somehow. Suddenly, he wondered if he'd met her before. She noticed the direction of his gaze and dropped her hand to her lap.

Sensing a weakness, he probed it. "Trackers make some people uncomfortable. Particularly those with something to hide."

A flush of alarm filled her face. "I've nothing to hide from you, monsieur."

"Then why the veil?" he demanded softly.

"I always wear it to meet clients."

Another lie. Her hands clasped together on the blotter and she leaned forward, wanting him to believe it. "Now that I know your occupation, I comprehend why your every statement has the quality of an interrogation. And I'll gladly supply you with whatever information is necessary to set your mind at ease, as long as it's reasonable and relevant to our negotiations. So, in the interest of full disclosure—I'm the bastard daughter of a liaison on this side of the gate, but I was brought up in the *Enclave a Paris* in ElseWorld by my *maman*, Odette, and Pinot."

"Which explains her accent," the little man Pinot threw in.

She nodded, continuing, "I received a visa to cross through

the gate into this world a few months ago and have matched numerous Else species to humans since then. I make it my business to infiltrate polite society for the benefit of my clients. Now, if that sufficiently satisfies your curiosity, may we continue?"

With her hands primly folded atop her desk, she'd addressed him in the manner of a governess speaking to a schoolboy. She had a way of cocking her head and gazing at him through her lashes that rendered her every glance an unwitting invitation. It made him want her. Made him want to introduce an alternate scenario between them in which he might play schoolmaster to her schoolgirl, in games more intimate than this one. His trousers suddenly seemed uncomfortably tight. He shifted in his chair again and glanced at the pixie. He was staring in his direction, at his crotch. Good Gods! When he saw that he'd been caught out, the pixie only grinned and went back to his infernal note taking.

"I wonder at something," Dane said, swinging his gaze back to the woman.

"Of course you do," she sighed. "Really, this is going to take all day if you don't allow me to take the lead."

"Just one question more," he assured her. "And that is—if my brothers and I are being pressured by the Council to wed humans and be 'fruitful'—why aren't you?"

"I am. If I wish to stay in this world, I must wed within it." She shrugged a shoulder in an innately French gesture. "But there is no hurry in my case. The Council only cares to rush weddings that will result in offspring."

"You had the Sickness?"

She nodded and went on, explaining something of how she'd become ill. But he was only half listening, concentrating instead on her body language and the rhythms of her speech, knowing he'd learn more in these ways than in the content of her answer.

His eyes narrowed on her face, trying to more thoroughly pierce the mysteries of her veil. Her fingers rose to adjust it as if she were worried he might succeed. With the lifting of her hands came a metallic *clatter* as her wealth of bracelets fell toward her elbows.

There were abrasions encircling her wrists, he realized. Fresh, made by ropes. She'd been bound. Recently. By a lover? Seeing the direction of his gaze, she covered both wrists with her bracelets again. His eyes caught hers, and beneath the veil a slow blush stole over her cheeks.

An imagined scene came to him, appearing in flashes. Of her, restrained on the altar of the temple on his land instead of the nereid. Of him lifting her skirt, her petticoat. Of him spreading her thighs. Ripping her pantalets to get at her . . . moving over her . . . in her.

And suddenly he was falling away, feeling as if the floor had just been pulled out from under his feet. Another's presence was rising in him. Dante. The takeover had never begun so swiftly before. It was disorienting.

Not now, fool! he raged silently. *They'll see and have us sent to an asylum again!*

The matchmaker shoved back her chair and rose, her eyes wide on him. "What's happening to you?"

6

Dane bent forward, his head dropping between his knees, elbows planted on his widespread thighs. His eyes were screwed tight and his mind throbbed with the infusion of another's thoughts into his own as the interloper thrust his way in. He took his head in his hands, thumbs pressed at his temples to still the chaos within him that worsened by the second. He would have given anything for relief. But he would not give himself over to Dante without a fight.

"Fuck you," he grunted.

The matchmaker's voice stiffened. "*Pardon?*"

Damn. Had he spoken aloud?

"Signor!" The serving woman had returned and now stood in the vicinity of the doorway to his left. The pixie's chair scraped the floor as the little man jumped to his feet.

But trapped in a terrible state of confusion, Dane didn't look their way. What the hell was going on? Dante had come, splitting his head open with an unseen ax and forcing himself in where he wasn't wanted. But for some reason, the bastard didn't seem to be forcing Dane out as was his usual practice.

Dane wasn't himself anymore. Yet he wasn't completely Dante either. Unlike other similar incursions in the past, he still remained fully aware.

Why is it different this time? Dane demanded silently.

Because of her. *Her presence is changing us. Blending us.*

Dane's mind ached wretchedly as the intrusion proceeded. His dark lashes fluttered, and his head lowered until his chin brushed his chest. For a moment, swallowing became difficult as his body experienced a strange paralysis. In the background, he heard the other three occupants of the room discussing him. He groaned.

"What is it? Are you ill?" It was the matchmaker's voice, concerned now. Her soft fingers came at his elbow.

Instantly, his numbness passed and an unusual clarity filled him. Always before, he and Dante had taken turns inhabiting this body. But now they shared it, co-existing in a state of awareness for the first time. And the uppermost emotion simmering in that awareness was a fierce desire for the woman who now knelt before them. They wanted her. It was instinct, inexplicable and primitive and hungry.

"Evangeline," Dane murmured, tasting her name. Savoring the fact that she was near.

"Eva," she qualified.

"Eva." He glanced up, needing to see her. She was kneeling on the carpet between his splayed thighs, her worried green eyes searching his. But her eyes weren't just green. They were the color of . . . clover in the early spring.

We know her, Dante whispered, smug. He'd known all along, Dane guessed, and had been keeping it from him. For his own good as usual, no doubt. The bastard.

With dizzying speed, Dane suddenly recalled meeting her in the grove at Moonful, only last night. Recalled wanting her. Recalled the feel of her against him. Warm and sweet. Lust burst in him and spread like a flash fire. If the pixie's eyes were on his crotch now, they were going to bug out of his head. Without looking away from her, he nodded to indicate the servants. "Tell them to go."

"What?" Eva rocked back on her heels, startled. She seemed to be looking beyond him in that way of hers, on all sides of him, rather than directly at him. He could well imagine what his aura was telling her about his mood now.

"S-something's different about you," she murmured.

"Whatever is happening to me has something to do with you," he said.

He needed to keep her with him. Needed *her*. If she left, this wonderful lust that filled him would go with her.

"Stay with me." He reached for one of her wrists, rubbing his thumb over the chafing on its vulnerable inside. Her pulse was rapid and warm. She somehow made him feel more connected to things. Were she to abandon him, he knew Dante would usurp him entirely, and Dane would be lost again to the tangled web that was his mind.

Her maidservant ventured closer, hovering just behind him. "Stop that, signor! Stop him, Eva. Pinot, do something!"

"Why not let her make her own choices for a change?" the pixie replied in support of him. The two servants began to squabble.

Ignoring them, Dane lifted Eva's wrist to his lips, kissing the delicate lacework of blue-white veins. Her scent was suddenly clear and delicious, like none he'd ever experienced. His tongue flicked out, tasting her. He detected a hint of fey. And a hint of human, but that seemed false. What was she?

I don't know, Dante whispered. Was he lying? Impossible to know.

Born with a hyperability to detect scent, Dane had been trained to refine it when he'd become a Tracker. For nearly a month, upon his induction at age thirteen, he'd been exposed repeatedly to an almost infinite variety of scents in order to induce a sensitization to them. He'd been obsessive, honing his olfactory abilities until they were the most acute in the entire force. Which made him extremely valuable to them now—a man they would not let go easily from their ranks.

Silver caught green and Eva shivered. Her pupils darkened with a comprehension of exactly what he wanted of her. Desire flashed across her face and battled there with good sense, as she struggled to decide on her reaction.

"Eva!" Her maid lay a hand on her shoulder, giving it a stern little shake.

"Tell them to go," Dane commanded softly. His voice drifted off on the last syllable, grew more sensual.

We want her.

"I want you," he murmured, low and urgent.

Awe lit her face, and need, and then acquiescence, all in quick succession. "Odette, please fetch some water to revive Monsieur Satyr," she instructed. "Pinot, locate the smelling salts."

Odette's eyes darted between Dane and her, obviously not liking what she read on their faces. "He seems well enough."

"Go," Eva told her.

She wanted him! Through the veil, Dane could see it in the flush of her cheeks, in the rapid pulse at the base of her throat. Could see his own desire reflected in her eyes.

Abruptly, he was on his feet. Moving past her, he grabbed each of her servants by an arm. Firmly ushering them out of the room, he then slammed and bolted the door behind them. Then he turned back toward Eva.

Our Eva.

She'd risen to stand beside her desk. His long legs ate up the floor between them in a half-dozen strides. Looking vaguely alarmed, she backed around her desk to trap herself neatly in the angle formed by a floor-to-ceiling bookshelf and the large window where Lena had sat, which looked out on a pocket lemon orchard.

Without pause, he found her and drew her close, wrapping one arm around her waist and cupping her veiled cheek in his palm. Their bodies aligned and fit like two interlocking puzzle pieces, until they seemed to breathe as one. His mouth brushed hers through transparent gauze and his exhalation impressed the veil between her lips; then hers soughed it back between his.

Never before had he felt the joy of a sexual quickening. But now his cock was hard at her belly, caged within his trousers, full and heavy and wonderful. He'd been a boy of twelve when he'd been abducted, and in all the years since, Dante had wrested control of his body during every carnal experience. Now he was a man with a man's tremendous hunger. And in this room, he was going to knowingly fornicate for the first time in his life. With a woman. This woman. He wanted to see her.

His fingers gathered her veil into a fist, yanked it off, and then thrust it away. Beneath it her skin was soft and smooth, her hair a rich blue-black. Eyes that were lined in heavy kohl regarded him with naked longing.

She's ours.

"Mine."

Dane's lips curved and he smiled into the beautiful face of a miracle.

Lord Dane Satyr sent her a sexy, beguiling smile that Eva would never have guessed him capable of when she'd first found him in her salon. He was a conundrum. Last night in the grove, he'd guessed she was satyr, and yet today he didn't remember and seemed instead to have accepted her claim to fey-human ancestry.

Even stranger was the fact that his aura had altered drastically over the last ten minutes. First, it had been a corona of translucent silver, then a mix of silver and gold, then it had swung to pure gold, and then it had moved back and forth along the same spectrum. Something similar had happened when they'd met under the full moon last night. It was as if he were a mix of two men, and was in continuous transition between them.

But whatever was happening to him—it didn't matter. Not now. She wouldn't let it. For this stolen instant of time, *this* was what mattered. This magical thing that sizzled between them. She wanted more of it. Feared it would be snatched away if she didn't act quickly.

She put her hands to his shoulders and rose on tiptoe, her lips searching his out again. She'd refused him last night in the grove and then longed for him later with a soul-deep desperation. This was a second chance with him, and she would take it. The prospect of making love with one of her own kind was so appealing that it completely overwhelmed any arguments she might make with herself against the idea.

Odette hammered a fist on the door. "Let me in!"

"All is well," Eva called to her over his shoulder. "I merely need a few moments with Monsieur Satyr in private." She smiled up at him, feeling mischievous and excited. He'd crowded her back against shelves thick with the fat spines of her books, his belly pressed to hers. She felt his male member between them, standing long and thick and rigid. Was he truly going to put himself inside her, here in the salon? High between her legs, her private flesh pulsed, wanting.

His lips caressed her cheek, her throat, her shoulder. The beat of her heart tripped as the backs of his long fingers tangled in her necklaces and slipped inside her bodice to stroke the warm curves of her breasts. And then came his mouth.

Odette banged upon the door again. "Evangeline! Are you to be his *zoccola* now? His *puttana*! Open this door! Send that *bastardo* away!"

"Tell me, mademoiselle," Dane murmured, "is your woman right?" His words were a seductive tease at her breast. His tongue swirled over a nipple. His teeth bit gently. "Are you my little slut now?"

Between her legs, the pulse turned into an ache. Her palms went up the hard contours of his ribs and chest, exploring them through fine lightweight linen. "Are you a bastard?" she challenged lightly.

"Sometimes," he replied with an honesty that wooed her trust.

At the continued rapping upon the door, Eva fidgeted. "She'll upset the girls. I'd better . . ." She sent him an apologetic look, beginning to pull away.

With a lift of a hand and a careless flick of his fingers in the direction of the door, he caused the shouts and knocking to fade away. She glanced at him, startled. "What did you do?"

"Only made them forget us for a while and go about their own business." His hot mouth captured a nipple, drawing on it and sending sensation thrumming straight to her clit. Big hands bunched her skirts and lifted them. "Now, I wonder—will you spread your legs for me, pretty *puttana*?" The low, beguiling words were a summons to carnal pleasure.

It was his voice, and yet in an odd way she didn't understand, it was not. Not entirely. But any concerns or curiosity about this were washed away by the rising tide of her lust to have him.

Through fabric, she drew a fingertip up the length of his manhood. "If I do, what will you give me?" she whispered.

Silver glinted and he smiled into her eyes. "What you need." Their eyes clung as he flipped up a froth of petticoat and skirt, and his knee pushed between hers. What he was offering was what she craved. A stolen interlude with one of her own kind. No promises, no regrets. She would make herself vulnerable to him. Would savor every moment of this, every touch, for who knew if such a chance might ever come again?

She yielded to the hard thigh that moved higher between hers. Her restless hands stroked up his back and down again and lower, shaping his rear. He was warm, masculine. Thrilling. Almost the same as the replica she'd created last night, and yet so wonderfully, vibrantly different. So real.

His hand found the opening in her pantalets. Hard knuckles brushed her soft, downy pelt, then turned, palming her. She gasped into his shirt and gripped the bunched muscles of his arms, scarcely daring to breathe as her entire concentration focused on his touch.

The air around them went abnormally still as two fingers pressed the length of her nether lips. They forked, spreading her for the long finger that pushed at her opening and then slipped inside her. She was still tender due to last night's occupation in her boudoir, and this wonderfully amplified the effect of his intrusion.

"What have we here?" he chided gently. His words were dark, his voice graveled with need. "You're wet for me, little slut."

But his words only made her wetter, made her flesh hum with pleasure. Her stockinged calf rose along the back of his thigh, and she opened herself, inviting him to do as he would with her, entrusting herself to his care. Two fingers drove deep, stroking once, twice, again, drawing moisture from her and pulling it upward to paint her clit with her own honey.

"*Chers Dieux! S'il vous plaît,*" she begged.

"Yes, we want to please you."

We? What did he mean? There was only him here with her. Him rubbing and pressing her sensitive nub. Him sawing fingers in her slickness. Him finding just . . . the . . . *right . . . mmm . . .* spot. Gods, were his fingers bespelled? It was certain that no Shimmerskin had ever made her feel like this! Her hands fisted in the fabric of his shirt and she turned her lips to the hollow of his throat, tasting him.

"Yes, I think maybe you like this," he murmured. "Especially on certain nights when the moon is full."

It took her a moment to understand his meaning, but then she blinked up at him in confusion. Even this close, his eyes were like mirrors, revealing little.

"You know," she whispered in shock.

"Yes, Evangeline. I know." He spoke now in that different, even darker voice. And for the moment his aura turned to pure spun gold with nary a hint of silver. "I know what you are, though I've made him forget."

It wasn't exactly an explanation. But his fingers kept working her, gliding back and forth in a heady, erotic rhythm.

"Your blood is our secret for now," he told her. "Our secret . . ." And then his aura shifted again, silver slowly mixing with the gold.

Her mind swam in confusion. "If you've known about my origins since you arrived here today, why did you pretend otherwise?"

"Pretend?" The inflection in his voice suddenly had a different flavor. He sounded as if he had no idea what her question meant or why she'd asked it. It was as if—as if a different man now spoke to her.

Mmm. What were those talented fingers of his doing now? She struggled to focus on their conversation. It was important, wasn't it?

Hot lips nuzzled the sensitive place behind her ear. "Why were you on my land last night, Eva?" He was all silver again, smooth. The interrogator now—autocratic and demanding.

His touch made her want to admit everything, but she bit back the truth, giving him only part of it. "For the olives. I have a map." She was riding his hand now, her breath fluttering from her in soft moans.

"In your little book."

"Mmm. Before her death, my mother drew it. Of the olives on your land. I trespassed only to have some."

"And why not just tell me this when I chanced upon you in my grove?"

"Because you were in a state much like this one and in no mood to listen."

Oh! A new sort of tremor shivered up her channel. If he kept this up, she was going to come under his stroke, during his questions. But he'd felt her reaction and his fingers left her.

Her eyes flew open. "But—"

"There, you see what I can do with just a fingertip?" he murmured. "Imagine what I can make you feel with this." Cupping the back of her hand in his, he helped her to palm the contours of the treasure that lay hidden within the crotch of his trousers. He was arrogant, confident in his masculinity and his attractions, full of himself. It was exactly what she wanted in a lover.

The knowledge that he would not require instruction from her and would not obey her every whim was incredibly exciting. She didn't know what would happen next, or how all would unfold between them. He was in control—her guide in this new sensual wilderness—and it would thrill her to bend to his Will.

"Come inside me," she pleaded, her voice an urgent, hopeful prayer.

Although she couldn't read her own aura even in a mirror, those of others were easily deciphered. His reacted strongly to her plea and enfolded her like great, beautiful wings of silver and gold light. His booted foot slammed flat on the low window seat to one side, and he pulled her thigh so it rode his; then he took her other thigh over his opposite forearm, his hand cupping her rear.

She sucked in her belly on a harsh intake of air as his other hand rammed between them, tearing open the fastenings of his trousers. He took his naked length and plowed its hot, velvet head along her damp furrow. Nestled it at the open, petaled rose of her that blushed and trembled for want of him.

He knew exactly what she wanted and was going to give it to her. She cried out softly as his smooth heat parted her glossy lips. His plum was a smooth purpled fist, pressing her wider, making her gasp for him. She spread for it. Panted for it.

She moaned and arched her back as it slipped inside her. Her nether lips held it dear, hugging its plinth, and then commenced to provide the length of rod that followed it with one long, slick, tight kiss. His gaze burned over her with fierce concentration, watching her face as she took him.

He was thick and never ending, stretching and filling her with unforgiving, wondrous steel. And all the while he pushed into her, he murmured dark encouragements in a mix of Italian and Else languages, promising there would be pleasure, telling her how much her body's hot welcome was pleasing him. How much he wanted to fuck her. How hard. How deep. His words were raw, their brush over her skin erotic. Oh! It was all so perfectly glorious she wanted to weep, wanted to slow everything down, and at the same time to make it happen more quickly.

Her head fell back on a shuddering moan. The scent of lemons reached her. A citrus garden was just below and workers were busy there. Would someone see? Would they watch as he drove onward, deeper and hotter . . . and deeper still?

"Look at me," he demanded, and she did. Their eyes clung as he plumbed the depths of her hot, wet heart. She smiled at him, her eyes misting with a delirious, poignant, carnal joy.

Dane grappled with the soul-altering phenomenon of finding himself buried to the hilt inside a woman for the first time in his life. Inside *this* woman. With all the others—and there had been many—Dante had always done this deed for him.

"Yes," she moaned softly. The sexy contrast of her hot, welcoming cunt and her sweet, prim voice drove him wild. His boot left the window seat and hit the floor, his legs braced between hers. His big hands wrapped around her bottom, holding her so she moved only as he chose to allow. He fucked her intently, in a hard, rolling motion, clenching his ass as he bucked into her.

The dark sex words he whispered to her weren't all his, and his actions weren't all under his control, but for the first time in his life, he was completely and gloriously *aware* during the sexual act. His concentration was all for her, and he noted her every reaction, her every gasp and murmur, the sensation of her moving on him, determined to miss nothing. And Dante was right there with him, an equal partner, reveling in the fucking, in the kaleidoscope of emotions that charged through their shared body.

In and out in long glides, he hunted his pleasure in her with primitive strength. Plunging, grinding her, rubbing her clit against him just to hear her mewling whimpers. To hear her beg him for more. Passionate half-formed words fell from his lips and hers, and mingled on the air. Damp tendrils of raven hair curled at her temples. Bodies rose and fell as one. His hand at her nape. His lips at her white breast, along her throat, on her red mouth. Her sweet mouth, whispering to him, encouraging him.

And through it all, he could *feel*. Could feel her slit give for his crest, feel his repeated invasions dilate her. Feel her tight, sultry embrace along every single nerve ending that corded his length. Could hear her quick intakes of breath. Smell her need. And his own.

The rhythmic slap of their hot flesh was raw and erotic. She was a siren, beckoning him with her slick promise of gratification. He felt powerful, in control. After a lifetime of sublimating his desires, it was a tantalizing thrill greater than any he'd ever known.

Hot sparks of lust pricked him as he and Dante had their way with her. Her flesh yielded to him, her slit licked at him, her breasts shuddered, and she rose to her toes under his every slam. Books jostled on the shelf behind her. Something crashed to the floor and splintered around his boots. It was heaven. He wanted it to go on and on. Wanted to carry her off with him to one of the mating caves in ElseWorld where copulation might go on to the exclusion of all else for weeks at a time. Where law forbade interruption. Where they could remain until he'd gotten his fill. A hundred years from now. A thousand. More.

"Oh, Gods, yes!" she moaned. Her back arched and her hands gripped the edges of the shelf on either side of her hips, her knuckles turning white. Her ankles linked at his back.

His balls drew up into tight fists. His cock trembled with the need to ejaculate. Then he groaned and slammed into her as far and high as it was possible for a man to go. His body pinned hers to the wall. Her wet, feminine heat coddled him deep, so fucking deep. They hung there for a taut instant of time, hovering on a precipice, shivering with the need to finish. Her lips parted and her head fell back. His thighs and body held hers wide. Owned her.

"Going to come," he bit out.

As if in response, her nether throat milked at him, gently, once. A second time, harder. She inhaled sharply and lifted her chin, her eyes shut tight.

Then came an earthquake of sensation rushing through his cock. Ropy, streaming spurts of cum shot from him in hot, violent shudders, marking her forever as his. He felt her orgasm break over him the same instant he went off, and heard her smothered cry.

It was spectacular, a shock to his system. Never had he experienced his own coming. Until now. With her. It was fucking amazing. To think that he'd been denied this prurient joy for so long!

They arched together and bowed as their coming swelled and receded. Her flesh sucked at him, drained him, and he gladly filled her, again and again and again, and he prayed to his Gods that it would never, ever end.

Eventually, eventually, his heart slowed, and hers. He remained between her legs, his cock still buried in her, his cum still pumping desultorily inside her at intervals with the aftershocks of his coming. They were both slippery now with his leavings and her juices, and a light sheen of sweat cooled his spine.

They sagged together, drained, replete. It had gone on forever but had still been too quick for him. He would have her again after this, in just a moment, he promised himself.

She's good. Soft. Ours, Dante whispered from somewhere within him. *Imagine how it will be when we fuck her next Moonful.*

It would kill him, Dane was sure of it, but he would gladly die to have her under the full moon. To join himself to her body in the way of the Calling, with two cocks instead of one, until she was so full of him she would know herself to be truly and irrevocably his.

Dante's presence ebbed then and he was gone. There were only two of them now. Eva and Dane. Woman and man. Lovers.

A breath of satisfaction shuddered from her lips. "I'm not sure we got that quite right," she said.

His head lifted and their eyes caught.

She was smiling at him, shy and sweet. "I think we may have to try again, just to be sure. How long will my family continue to forget us?"

"As long as I Will it."

Her smile deepened and she sighed, a blissful sound. Idly, her hand smoothed his hair, his nape. His eyes went to her bodice and he lowered his head, kissing the curve of her breast.

This time there had been no jarring awakening after lovemaking. He could recall everything that had happened with her. Knew precisely where he was—still joined to her, loath to part. He would remember the miraculous joy of this time with her for the rest of his days. He felt good, happy, in a way he could never recall having felt before.

"What the devil are you wearing anyway?" he teased, his mouth still attentive at her breast. Him, teasing? He'd never teased anyone in his life!

Her smile flashed again, wry now. "The gown? Mimi and Lena selected it. Beautiful, is it not?" They shared a moment of humor as he finally realized why she was dressed in such a manner.

"You're a rare woman. I don't know of another who'd wear such a 'beautiful' outfit just to appease her children." He kissed her smile.

What are you doing?

His head jerked back as the unknown masculine voice shrieked inside him. It was appalled, frightened. Unfamiliar. New.

Eva said something more. But she seemed far away, her words coming from a tunnel. Dane frowned, a feeling of disquiet slipping down his spine. What was happening to him?

I want to go home.

"Who's there?" he demanded. "Dante?"

"What?" Eva asked blankly.

But Dane knew the answer to his question with a terrible certainty. Dante only served a carnal function and had gone now. There was someone else inhabiting him. Someone he'd been unaware of until this moment. Another part of him, hidden all this time, deep within the recesses of his fractured brain.

He stepped back, pulling out of her. His nape prickled with fear, and he glanced around, feeling hunted. The sensation of someone chasing him speared terror down his spine, but there was no threat here. He was remembering something. Something from the time he'd been abducted. This new part of him had knowledge of that time, could help him find Luc.

"Where's Luc?" he demanded. But he got no answer. And then Dane was ebbing away, his sense of self washing out with the tide. Drowning in the murky swamp of his suddenly over-populated mind.

Eva peeked up at Dane as he pulled from her, feeling almost shy with him now. Her pulse was still racing, her knees still quaking. Her lover—how good it felt to think of him in that way—stood there, big and strong and handsome.

He glanced down at himself, seeming bemused to find his trousers around his knees. Yanking them higher, he tucked his manly parts inside and quickly fastened them, staring at her intently all the while.

As if he didn't recognize her.

A strange tension fell between them, and her smile faded. She studied the halo of light around him, as was her habit when she required clues to someone's emotions. Throughout his visit here today, his aura had been dazzling, all molten silvers, strong steels, and flashes of gold. These colors had come and gone, fluctuating, first one dominating and then the other. At times, they'd mingled and sometimes warred as well. But now his aura was changing yet again. This time to an entirely new moody gray. Never had she witnessed so many differing components in one person's aura.

An oddly boyish expression touched his features. He seemed younger. Young. A flush tinged his cheekbones. And then his head was jerking back from her, his eyes wild and shocked as they took in the room.

She straightened, letting her skirts drop, feeling suddenly unsure. It was as if he'd become a stranger. "What's happening to you?" she whispered "Your aura. It's . . . different . . . again."

Without a word, he made for the door, flinging it wide. Lingering at its threshold, he paused to look back at her. Sudden urgency filled his expression. "*Bona Dea*," he said obscurely. The words burst from his lips, running together in an almost unintelligible way and seeming to surprise even him.

She blinked. "What?"

But he'd already quit the room, slamming its door behind him.

Eva stared at the door, feeling completely disoriented. Her very first flesh and blood lover had just rushed off after coitus with her as if fleeing the hounds of hell. What was she to make of that? She ran her fingers through hair disheveled by his passionate hands and lay a palm over a breast still tender from the pull of his mouth.

She shifted her weight and her private flesh gently trembled with an echo of the profound orgasm he'd given her. A tiny dribble of his spill trickled down her inner thigh, and her breath tripped. She stared ahead with unseeing eyes, remembering how wonderful it had felt to hold the length of him so deep inside her. Remembering the hard thrust of him. The warm feel of his body. He'd determined the tempo of his stroke, had held her as he wished, done with her as he pleased. She'd felt the throb of his balls at her bottom, felt the heat of his seed flashing through the long vein in his male member. Then had come his hot, wrenching spurts, the slippery warm flood of his seed. The first a man had ever given her.

It had been perfect, beautiful, just as she'd always dreamed it might be. He'd been so, so much better than an ethereal Shimmerskin.

Another slow trickle followed the first high along the inside of her thigh. And a tear of joy coursed down her face, keeping pace.

She tightened her inner muscles, finding them weary, chafed, well-loved. Hugging his seed and the memory of him close.

Him. His seed. She wanted more.

7

A snaking line of a six men followed Gaetano through the twisting, dimly lit tunnel. All were human and known to him, and each willingly held his bound hands before him as they navigated the uneven ground with a difficulty that, at times, caused them to curse and mutter. Threaded through a ring at each wrist was a long cord that stretched from the first man to the last, preventing hands from reaching upward to remove the blindfolds Gaetano had given them.

Unfettered, he held one end of the cord like the leadstring a mother used to keep her children from roaming too far. They were some of the most powerful men in Rome, but on these special nights, they were like eager children.

Gaetano held the sole lantern, and for some time their path continued on, rough and irregular, but it would smooth out ahead. He'd explored this extensive labyrinth from childhood, and knew it well. Although there was only one true path to their destination, he took them on a number of detours. He chose a varied route every month, so none would learn the way.

One of the men behind him stumbled and sputtered an oath. "Is all this secrecy really necessary?"

"A small price to pay for your evening's entertainments, don't you think?" Gaetano replied.

"*Si*, count your blessings," said another. "We could've been forced to spend an evening in the company of our wives upstairs."

"Wouldn't mind it once," someone muttered from in back. "Like to see what they get up to while we're down here."

"Have you ever dared?" asked another of his charges.

The question was directed at him, Gaetano knew. He shrugged, refusing to say. He'd been glad enough to be quit of his home tonight, though. He had news to share that would bring his family's ire his way and he was in no hurry to incur it.

Another answered in his stead. "He values his life too much, no doubt, like the rest of us. The ladies guard their secrets dearly." There was a general rumble of agreement.

"Ah, here we are at last." Coming into a large circular area tiled with beautiful, timeworn mosaics, Gaetano hung his lantern on its bronze hook. Several torches burned in sconces placed around the underground room. Long ago, it had been vented so none here would suffocate. He'd made a survey above ground in his youth but had been unable to determine where the smoke eventually exited. The ancients had been superb architects, and he had the greatest admiration for them.

"Sergio, the rope," he said, by way of announcing their arrival to the blind attendant. By dint of long practice, the grizzled man groped his way along the line of men and unfettered their hands.

"Welcome, Sons of Faunus. You may remove your blindfolds," Gaetano instructed, although they'd all done so already, upon being freed. But this was the traditional announcement made to begin these nights, and calling them by their group's official moniker was a way of empowering them. Now they were no longer attorneys, businessmen, and politicians. They'd become ordained Sons, free to engage in activities that would never be condoned by society.

Sergio wound the cord around his wrist and on his way back to his perch, he tossed it onto a hook on one wall. Just below it stood a chipped stone table upon which sat a large bowl, bottles of wine, and goblets.

Sybaritic statues of marble and granite graced the circumference of the room, placed at intervals between the nine doors that encircled it. All were closed, save one that opened to a room that was currently occupied only by a narrow bed and a few other furnishings. Beyond the other doors, a similar room extended from the central salon, like spokes from a wheel hub.

A tenth opening had no door and led to a short hallway, and beyond that was a smoking room with periodicals, a selection of erotic devices and literature, more liquor, and cards. A gentleman's room, for later.

Drinks were poured and cigars handed about to those who wished to partake, and there was desultory conversation. Several perched on the chairs that sat here and there around a platform about the size of a breakfast table in the center of the room. What they would do here tonight wasn't important in itself. But it was a time-honored ritual their wives insisted on each month as a companion to their own secret rites upstairs.

"Anything new on offer?" one of the men enquired.

At the question, a new energy permeated the atmosphere. Eager eyes sought the doors.

"Of course," Gaetano answered in his silky, cultured voice. He unlatched and opened one of the doors off the central room and swung it wide.

The young woman seated inside the cell calmly registered his arrival, blinking her brown eyes at them. He gestured her forward. "Come, girl."

Obediently, she stood, a ghost of a smile shaping her lips.

When she came to him, he led her out into the room, assisting her up the steps to the small platform in its center.

Then he left her there to be gawked at and went to pour himself a drink and speak to Sergio, the attendant. "Any trouble today?"

"None. Calm as lambs, the lot of them," he was told.

Gaetano had long since ceased wondering what this grizzled fellow got up to, stuck here day and night. Sergio had kept his mouth shut for nearly two decades of service. That was enough to suit him and the family.

Behind them, the gentlemen prowled around the female like hungry lions. She stood there, docile and unconcerned, wearing a shift of translucent fabric.

Much later, after he guided these men back upstairs, Gaetano would return here to sleep. He'd far rather have his own bed upstairs, but it wasn't his decision. Like a mole, he must come here every night while Sergio slept, keeping watch on things. This situation had earned him a reputation among the house servants, who'd speculated and spread rumors that he spent his nights in the beds of a variety of ladies all over town. He relished his undeserved reputation, and it provided him with a convenient alibi. For if word ever got out as to where he actually spent his nights, the *polizia* would have something to say about it.

The girl on display behind him barely registered it when one of the voyeurs lifted her forearm. His fingers slid across the blue veins at her inner elbow, like he was a playing a stringed instrument. "You've drugged her?" he asked, noting the punctures.

"As always," Gaetano replied.

"What with?" Adie Arturo was one of the most skilled physicians in all of Rome and always asked the same fool questions. As if Gaetano would reveal their methods!

He tried to keep the irritation from his voice when he answered, "It won't affect her performance."

"You know better than to ask," admonished another man. Ridolfi. A high-ranking member of the *Arma dei Carabinieri,* one of the military escorts of the state sovereign.

"What is she?" Arturo persisted, eyeing her skeptically.

A strange question, but all here knew what he meant. Gaetano took a sip of wine before replying, "She's whatever you wish her to be."

For over a century, several generations of these gentlemen's families had shared the secret of this place. Shared the knowledge that their world had been invaded by creatures from another. They took great pains to ensure that no one else discovered this secret, for they viewed ElseWorld beings as subservient only to them and wished to reap the benefits of their servitude without hindrance.

Arturo chomped on his cigar. "You know what I want."

Gaetano shook his head. "They don't exist. Female satyrs are a myth. Besides, I can tell you that if we ever find such a creature, we won't loan her out." He gestured toward the girl on the platform. "Why not try this one instead?"

"She's fey. I thought you had something new for us," Arturo pouted. Such an annoying man.

"She *is* new. Very new." Gaetano paused for effect, then, "An *innocente verginale.*"

A frisson of avidity lit the eyes of the group. Ridolfi rubbed his palms together briskly, his voice keen. "Let's get to it, then."

Going to the table, Gaetano lifted the bowl from it. It was passed around and each man removed an identical ring from the smallest finger of his left hand and dropped it inside.

When six rings had been collected, Gaetano drew one out. He read the initials inscribed inside the ring and handed it to its owner. "Arturo."

Arturo rocked on his heels. "First pick. My lucky night." He lifted the girl from the pedestal with both hands at her hips. "Sorry, friends. You'll have to make do."

The others watched enviously as he took her inside her little cubicle and kicked the door shut behind them.

"Sergio!" At the snap of Gaetano's fingers, the guard stood and then made the rounds of the circular room, unlocking five other doors in turn and pushing them wide. As if they were zombies, the occupants of each room came to loom in their respective doorways at his summons. Some were male, some female, and one was a little of both—a hermaphrodite. Like the girl, their lips bowed upward in vapid smiles, and their eyes were dreamy and drugged.

Another name was chosen, and another man chose a partner and a room. And another and another.

Gaetano wondered if their wives knew what they got up to. When he saw these men outside this place, they would never speak of these goings-on. Instead, they would smile and converse about politics, drink and smoke, and attend the races and galas together with their families, all very respectable. The thought of cards had him running worried fingers through his white-blond hair.

To distract himself from his misery, he peeked into one of the glass peepholes set in the nearest door, which allowed the guard to keep watch on the occupants. Ugh. The huge white ass of Maggio, owner of one of the finest restaurants in Rome, confronted him, jiggling as it pumped into the ass of the woman he'd chosen. She was at least twenty-five and had been here over half her life. She was looking a little shopworn, Gaetano mused idly. About time to find a replacement. But he'd just sent the fey girl to the river, and two unoccupied rooms would annoy them upstairs.

He meandered to the next door where Ridolfi and Luigi were

engaged with "it," as Gaetano had dubbed the hermaphrodite. Ridolfi stood behind their victim, his cock imbedded in its ass or its gusset, hard to tell which. The judge knelt in front, sucking it off. Anyone viewing the scene would assume the hermaphrodite was willing, for its cock was tumescent and its hands were stroking Luigi's head. But it was the drug Gaetano fed the creatures here that kept them calm and willing. Yet, soon there would be no more of the drug to be had, for he'd lost the source of it. With a terrible sinking in the pit of his stomach, he threw himself on one of the couches.

From across the room, he heard the sound of Sergio, jerking himself off. The servant's ear was pressed to a door, listening to the slap of bodies within. Then came the moan of him coming in his own hand. A sigh; then he tucked his prick away and headed for his perch.

Gaetano stared at the water stains on the ancient ceiling painted with glorious exploits of Roman gods, thinking frantically. How could he repair the damage of what he'd done before he was found out? He'd been drunk a few nights ago and been taken advantage of by that fucking Satyr at cards. Dane. Where the devil had he come from so suddenly? His brothers were annoying enough. Half the women in Rome were in love with them. And now this new one would doubtlessly come along and take the other half for himself.

"What's wrong with you, boy?" asked Sergio.

"I lost the grove at cards."

The unseeing eyes in the wizened face grinned, gleeful at the trouble this mistake would cause him. "Boss won't like that. Where you going to get the olives for the drug now?"

Gaetano lay the back of one wrist over his eyes. "I'll fix things. Don't worry. And don't mention this or it'll go ill for you."

"So what's the problem with you, eh?" Sergio asked. "You

can't get your sausage hard or you can't spill your seed? Or you can't make babies with what you do release?"

"None of your damned business."

The guard shook his head. "Does *anything* stir you?"

Gaetano hated the pity in his tone. The nerve of this lowly old scum of a servant to feel sorry for his betters! It made him furious. "Something does, as a matter of fact." Leaping up, he stalked to him and grabbed the man's balls, twisting them hard. "Inflicting pain."

He wrapped his other hand over the man's mouth to still his shrieks as he held him there for a moment. Then he let go, and Sergio crumpled to the floor, whimpering.

Gaetano straightened his shoulders, feeling marginally better. He took a key from its hook, opened one of the doors, and entered a small room. A young man sat on the edge of the bed, wearing only a loincloth. The room's sole occupant, he was ethereally handsome, his body strongly muscled. Gaetano went to stand before him and took his chin in his palm, tugging his face upward. Strangely beautiful eyes flashed silver. So like his brother's.

When this one had first come to them thirteen years ago, he had been five or so. They'd only been able to siphon his tears at first, using the onions to bring them on. But eventually he'd grown old enough to give them his male seed. In a matter of weeks, he would become a man in the way of his species; then they'd put him to even more profitable uses.

He opened the front of his trousers and drew one of the fellow's hands to hold him. Though the touch of them gave him no particular pleasure, he liked seeing those hands on him, doing his bidding. It made him feel powerful. But in such large hands, his poor prick looked small and pathetic and limp. His face twisted with impotent rage.

At the card table that night, he'd wanted to tell that bastard Dane Satyr about this so badly, wanting to hurt him with the secret news. *I know where your precious brother is*, he'd wanted to say. But of course, he hadn't.

So instead of hurting Dane, he would inflict hurt here in this room. He dug a thumb in the hinge of a jaw with one hand and opened his trousers with the other. "Come on now, Lucien. Open up," he said softly. "There's a good boy."

8

"*Un cadeau*! A present!" called Mimi, dashing from her French studies into Eva's salon.

"Give me that package, you little demon child!" shouted Odette from the corridor behind her.

Quickly, Eva tucked away Lena's portrait of Dane, which he'd left behind that morning, into her desk, not wanting to be caught mooning over it. And reluctantly she pulled her thoughts away from her favorite recent occupation—fond remembrances of their lovemaking. Neither her puzzlement over his precipitous departure and fluctuating auras, nor Odette's lectures and grumbles had been able to dampen her glorious mood.

A giddy Mimi screeched to a halt beside Eva's desk. "Your gift—it rattles, mademoiselle!" She gave the box in her hands a shake to demonstrate. "Oh, may I open it? Please!"

"No, you may not!" Odette informed her, entering the room hard on her heels. Snatching it from her small hands, she plunked it on the desk before Eva. "From Lord Satyr, via messenger."

Dane's writing was strong and sure, black slashes on white. At the sight of it, Eva's heart rose in her chest, riding a crest of delight. No man had ever sent her a gift before. Her own *maman* had received many such parcels—perfume, jewelry, silks—from her *"senori and messieurs,"* as she'd called them, and each delivery had created great excitement in the household.

"Found them!" Pinot entered, bringing scissors. She used them to quickly snip the ties and then carefully unwrapped the box, planning to save the paper in the drawer along with his portrait.

Mimi looked on, bouncing on her tiptoes. "I hope it's bonbons!"

"It's not for you, girl, whatever it may be!" said Odette.

Eva knew that look in Odette's eye. She'd felt the smack of her hand more than once growing up when she'd misbehaved. Mimi apparently noted it as well, for she sought refuge on the other side of Eva's chair, as far as she could get from Odette and still witness the grand opening of the gift. Eva frowned at her maidservant. They'd discussed how the girls were to be reared and she wouldn't tolerate harsh punishment. Lena'a and Mimi's lives had been hard enough on the streets. In this house, they were to be treated with kindness.

Sensing the tension, the usually sober Lena leapt into the breach. "Who cares what it is! It's from her handsome beau. Oh la la!" she said in her best imitation of Eva's French accent, then pretended to swoon onto the couch, sending Mimi into a fit a giggles.

Since Lena kept her emotions under tight lock, it warmed Eva's heart to see that she cared enough for Mimi to momentarily break out of her shell.

"We needn't rely on strange ElseWorld men to bring us gifts," said Odette. "Eva's gonna find a rich human husband soon. We'll buy our own gifts then with his money."

"She's right. Still, Lord Satyr *was* handsome, wasn't he?" Eva sent the girls a wink. The package was open at last, and she pulled an envelope from it.

"A letter?" Mimi pouted in disappointment.

Inside was a sheet of paper with a signature at the bottom done in the same strong black slashes. *For your services,* he'd written. Eva paled, before she realized he meant her matchmaking services, not services of a more personal nature. She turned it over, then back again. There was no mention of the fact that he'd enjoyed or even remembered their time together. With a creeping sense of foreboding, she pulled a second sheet of paper from the parcel and examined it.

"Another letter?" Mimi drooped further. Eva shook her head, her own hopes wilting too. "No, it's . . ."

She dropped it on the desktop for them all to see.

Pinot's eyes lit and he gleefully scooped it up. "A bank draft."

"Did he sign it?" Odette asked anxiously.

He nodded. "Payment in full! I'll go make the deposit." With that, he dashed off for his hat and coat.

Tears of disillusionment burned Eva's eyes. After what had happened between them, Dane still expected her to find a human bride for him? An odd, aching sort of grief filled her. She turned away, surreptitiously brushing tears from her cheeks with her handkerchief.

Odette rubbed her back as if she were still a child. "Poor *bebe*," she murmured, low so the girls couldn't hear. "You see? You give your body to him, and you see what he does? Satyr men—all Else men—they're the same. They'll take advantage if you let them. Better to marry a human you can control with your magic."

Odette was right. Stiffening her spine, Eva stuffed her handkerchief and her tears away. She was being ridiculous. Naturally Lord Satyr expected her to keep to their agreement. What else? Had she imagined he would come back this afternoon, declare his love for her, and decide to ignore the Council's command? Naturally he wouldn't. No more than she'd changed her mind about her plans to find a human husband. Nothing had changed. They both needed to protect their families and fortunes, and that meant obeying the Council's wishes.

She'd only been upset because what had happened between them had been so new to her. Because she'd never been with a real flesh and blood man before, that's all it was. And he was Satyr, for Gods' sakes—Satyr males were renowned for their lovemaking skills. Of course it had been an overwhelming experience!

And it *had* been overwhelming. So different from what she'd done every Moonful since her eighteenth birthday. So exactly what she wanted. It had felt like a beginning of something, not an end. But perhaps he had not felt the same way.

"Letters don't rattle," said Lena. "There must be something more." Behind her, Eva heard the girl thrashing around in the parcel. Then, "Aha!" A triumphant Lena held up a small box and gave it a little shake. "It rattles."

Mimi brightened expectantly. "Bonbons?"

"Jewels would be better," said the pragmatic Odette. "We could sell them and buy plenty of treats then, and dresses, and maybe a new carriage."

Taking the box, Eva lifted a small pouch from within, which she then tilted so its contents spilled onto her desk. A single green oval tumbled out and then another. And another.

"Olives!" Lena exclaimed in surprise.

Eva pressed her fingers to her lips to still their trembling and stared, touched by the simple gift. She'd wanted his olives, and he'd gifted her with dozens of them. A thoughtful gesture, swiftly delivered. He must've gone straight from her to the grove and gathered them.

"*Un, deux, trois . . .*" Mimi began tapping each with a fingertip, practicing her counting.

"What kind of gift is this?" Odette said sourly.

"They're the olives we need for the powders," Eva explained. "From the grove described in *maman*'s little book."

"You told him?"

"Only that my mother had picked some there."

Odette's lips tightened with worry. With a word to the children, she banished them back to their lessons. Once they'd gone, she launched into another lecture. "You listen to me. You don't be foolish like Fantine. This satyr man'll give you his semen. His bastards maybe. But he'll give his heirs to a human woman. His wife. He's gonna do what the Council tells him. Mark my words."

"Did I ask for his children? His ring?"

"You know what happens to you on nights when the moon comes full. You'll wind up with his brat in your belly without meaning to. These rich and mighty satyrs. Thought themselves better than your mother. Spilled their seed in her and gave her trinkets in exchange for her heart. Then what? They abandon us all!"

"That was *maman*. Not me!" Eva argued. "Is it so wrong of me to want to hold on to my sanity? Last Moonful night I . . ." her voice faltered with emotion and she clasped a fist to her chest. "I just can't do that anymore, Odette. Not alone. I need him."

"No! You'll get a human husband—"

"Who won't know what to do with me on those nights!" Eva finished for her, trying desperately to make this woman who'd helped raise her understand. "I'll have to bespell him and hide what I am from him. You know what the moon does to me. Can you blame me for wanting a liaison with one of my own kind? Just *one* night a month."

Odette's startled eyes searched Eva's. After a long moment, her expression filled with reluctant acceptance. "You gonna keep on with Lord Satyr, then? No matter what I say, you'll let him in your bed?"

"I don't know. He hasn't asked." Eva uttered a rueful laugh. "But maybe I'll ask him. You said the powders would keep me from conceiving, even when he's at his most potent under the full moon."

"You don't fall in love with him, though, eh?"

"No, I won't fall in love with him." Eva rubbed a hand across her forehead, feeling suddenly weary. She'd been weaned on her mother and Odette's tales of this world and their views on the workings of men's minds. On their notions of how to catch and control a human husband. There'd always been so much pressure to follow their wishes. To find a way to rise in the ranks of human society that had spurned Fantine twenty-two years ago, deeming her too lowborn for them. Sometimes the idea of exacting revenge on a society that had never done any wrong to her seemed so pointless.

"At any rate, I *will* be seeing him again," said Eva. "We've entered into a business transaction. I must do the work he pays me for. And I won't let him think he has hurt me." She angled her chin higher. "He *hasn't* hurt me."

"All right, *bebe*. All right," Odette soothed.

"Now I'm going to help the girls with their lessons."

Still worried, Odette watched her go. Surely Eva wouldn't be foolish enough to fall in love like her mother. She was stronger than Fantine. But nothing was certain until her Eva was safely wed to a human.

The next morning, Dane found his brothers in the Forum ruins surrounded by Rome's seven hills, under the protection of a large white canvas tent. As usual, Bastian was toiling over some precious bits of stone and pottery set on a long table. Dane assumed the bits were more important than they looked, for Bastian was in charge of the digs and put his attention only to the rarest and richest of findings. Sevin slouched on a chair, his boots propped on an overturned crate. Behind him were shelves lined with assorted tools, urns, busts, reference books, and a scrolled copy of Giambattista Nolli's map of Rome. All the sides of the canvas had been rolled up save one that had been left down as a wall to cut the rays of the piercing Italian sun.

Just outside, fashionable ladies strolled gravel pathways in the areas of excavation that hadn't been cordoned off. Admiring eyes lingered on the tent, some hoping in vain that the three handsome men beneath its awning might notice them and pay them heed.

"I'm fucking useless." Dane threw himself into an empty chair, then stood again almost immediately to begin pacing. Bracing his hands high on the reinforcement bar above the tent's entrance, he stared out at the ruins. "I've been over this entire excavation site three times in the two weeks since my return. And nothing. I don't recognize a damn thing. And I don't remember a damn thing either. It's as if I was never here."

Bastian looked up from his examination of a shard of painted terracotta. He was wearing a pair of glasses Dane had never seen on him before. They were thick and greatly magnified his eyes, obviously for doing close work. He let them drop lower on his nose and stared at Dane over the tops of them. "We've been over the entire site as well, many times. Especially the area where you were found wandering upon your return a year after your disappearance."

"But the excavations have been ongoing since you left," Sevin put in. "Things have changed over thirteen years. Digs and rubble have altered the landscape, making it near impossible—"

Dane slammed his fist on the bar under his hands, making the tent shudder. "I'm not giving up, damn you. Luc is not dead!"

"We're not suggesting he is," said Bastian.

Sevin straightened, his boots hitting the floor. "We feel him with us as well. Here." He thumped a fist to his chest. "As preposterous as it might seem to some, we believe he's still alive, too. But this nebulous 'feeling' we get from him supplies us with no direction, no clue, no proof as to his existence or his location. What would you have us do?"

"Hell if I know." Full of restless energy, Dane paced the carpet that had been laid as a temporary floor. He picked up a vessel from Bastian's worktable at random, carelessly tossing it from one hand to another. "I'll have to begin again. I'm overlooking something. I know the clues are right here somewhere under our noses." He paused, examining the urn he held more closely. It depicted an old man beating a young girl with sticks of myrtle while tempting her with wine. "What the devil is this hideous thing?"

"A priceless relic once used in the worship of Bona Dea," Bastian informed him. A sudden shiver slid down Dane's spine as if a cloud had covered the sun for a moment. He seemed to lose himself in the object, floating away on a half-formed memory.

Bastian reached over and took the vessel from him, then set it back in its precise place on his meticulously organized table. Instantly, Dane shook off whatever macabre sensation had momentarily seized him, unable to recall exactly what had just happened.

"We want to find Luc as much as you do," said Bastian. "It's why I was originally drawn to this sort of work, why I felt driven to uncover the Forum's secrets. I still hold out hope they'll lead us to him one day."

"So you see—" Sevin began. But suddenly, Dane held out a hand, halting his brother's speech. Someone was coming. A woman. Eva.

"*Excusez-moi, messieurs?*" she said, stepping inside a moment later, and folding her parasol closed.

At her arrival, his brothers stood in deference. She was as beautiful as he remembered, just as fresh and fine, and dressed in a gray gown similar to the one she'd been wearing in the grove. Its prim lines made him want to take it off of her so he could trace the curves he now knew lay beneath it. He shifted, fastening his coat—his prick had noted her arrival as well.

A knowing smile flitted over Sevin's lips. Dane moved behind Bastian to distance himself from her, needing time to recover. He'd kept his lust on a tight rein all these years, never succumbing to it except during Moonful, when his baser instincts overwhelmed him. Yet the minute she'd arrived, all restraint had departed and he was instantly hard for her. He didn't understand it. Didn't trust it.

Unaware of the nature of his thoughts, Eva glanced at Bastian's collection of bric-a-brac interestedly. "I do hope I'm not interrupting. I brought my nieces to wander the ruins this morning, and I noticed your tent. I've come to see Monsieur Dane on business." Her gaze swept him and her cheeks heated.

What business? Had she come to lambaste him for attacking her yesterday? Or better yet, had she come for more of the same? He didn't remember the latter part of their encounter and that made him uncomfortable. When he'd come to again, he'd been back at the grove, standing in the center of the temple. How he'd left her and returned home was a mystery.

Noting the tension between them, Bastian said, "Since my brother's manners are lacking this morning, I'll introduce myself. Bastian Satyr. And this is Sevin."

"Dane's brothers," Sevin added, his expression brimming with curiosity.

She smiled and nodded politely. "Evangeline Delacorte."

"The matchmaker," said Dane, folding his arms. Bastian's eyes widened as they went to him, sensing intrigue. Sevin raised his brows, smirking at him over her head, and Dane scowled. Like him, his brothers had assumed a matchmaker would be a wizened woman of advanced years.

"I prefer the term Marital Broker," Eva corrected.

"Then Martial Broker it shall be," said Sevin. "Welcome to our humble tent, mademoiselle."

"Mine, actually," Bastian murmured sardonically.

Ignoring him, Sevin took her hand and kissed it in the French way, on the wrist. When he straightened away from her, a slight frown marred his brow. He sent both brothers a speaking glance. He'd wondered at her lack of scent as well.

"Thank you." Eva smiled prettily at them, oblivious to the undercurrents. Then she turned to Dane, not quite meeting his eyes. "I wished to let you know that we have an engagement tonight." She handed him a card bearing an address on Capitoline. "A Pretender Gala."

"You're inviting me to a ball?" Dane said, taking it.

She nodded. "At Palazzo Nuovo. It's how my work on your behalf will proceed. Over the next few weeks, you and I will attend functions and entertainments where there are sufficient numbers of suitable unmarried young ladies of human ancestry. You'll mingle. I'll observe. I'll facilitate introductions as needed. After each event, we will begin to narrow the list of candidates."

She turned to his brothers. "I hope you'll both be coming with him?" she asked, looking between them.

Sevin started to agree, his eyes sparkling with humor at the notion of being there to witness Dane's courtship of a gaggle of strange females.

"My brothers are otherwise engaged," Dane informed her, his eyes daring his brothers to contradict him.

Tenacious, she directed another question to his brothers. "Oh. By any chance, are you both looking for matrimony as well?"

"No," Bastian and Sevin said at the same time. Without moving, each seemed to withdraw from her and her suggestion.

"Pity." Obviously disappointed, she handed each of them her card. "Do let me know if you change your minds."

Eva turned back to Dane then, her gaze more direct than it had been. It was nearly his undoing. He had to find an outlet for the energy that filled him, and quickly, or he wasn't sure he could keep himself from doing something foolish. Something with her. Something extremely gratifying that would likely cause Dante to return.

"Would you care to stroll the ruins with me for a bit?" she asked, as if they were only passing acquaintances, ignoring the fact that he'd been inside her only yesterday. It made him want to drag her off behind one of the tumbled ruins and remind her of exactly how close they'd been. "The weather's fine today and there's another matter I wish to speak to you about."

Glad of the chance to direct his mind to something other than fornication, Dane lifted the flap of the tent for her to precede him. He glanced at his brothers over her head and shifted a shoulder in answer to the curiosity he read in their faces, for he didn't know what she wanted of him. Then he was outside with her and they were walking among the ruins, as if they were humans without a care, both out to enjoy an autumn afternoon together.

"I want to thank you for your gift of the olives," she began once they were alone. "And for your payment." She opened her parasol with a distinct snap.

Dane glanced at her. She sounded oddly miffed regarding the payment, but he smiled to himself, imagining that her pixie financier had been thrilled. "You could have thanked me inside."

"Yes, of course." Her hands gripped the stem of her dainty parasol tighter. "Well, the truth is that there is another reason I wished to speak to you privately. Two reasons, actually."

"And they are?"

"Most importantly, I wish to ask that you keep my species a secret."

"From humans, do you mean?"

"From anyone."

"Why? Are you ashamed of being a fey-human blend?"

She looked at him beseechingly. "Oh, please. Consider what might happen to my girls if . . . fey-human?" She darted a look at the tent behind them. Then her glance bounced off his to study the horizon, an intent frown marring her brow. "Your brothers know I'm . . . a blend?"

What was going on here? Dane glanced over his shoulder toward the tent. Bastian and Sevin were standing shoulder to shoulder unabashedly observing them. Having them nosing about in his business was taking some getting used to. He'd been alone half of his life and had forgotten what it was like to have family meddling about in his affairs.

He took her chin in his hand, but she wouldn't hold his gaze. "First lesson a Tracker learns is that when a suspect avoids your eyes, there's a lie hovering on her lips."

Eva pulled away at that and stared him straight in the eyes. "It's true that my mother gave her fey blood to me. However, she was a courtesan and would never say who my father was. He may not have been human as I've claimed, but I do believe he is here in Rome. It's one of the reasons I came here. I'm searching for him. There, was my gaze direct enough to assure you I don't lie?"

That explained her odd reaction when she'd told him she was human-fey. She had been fudging the truth as he suspected. But that didn't explain why he couldn't scent her. Maybe it had something to do with his attraction to her. Or with Dante's involvement.

"I'll tell you a truth of my own. You're the only person I've ever been unable to scent. It makes me curious."

"Oh?" she said, sounding a trifle alarmed. The pace of her footsteps increased, as if she wished to run away from his words.

He caught her wrist, detaining her. "You said you had another reason for wishing to speak to me in private."

Her other hand tightened on her parasol and she sent him an inscrutable look. "Yes, of course. Well," she tugged away and took a fortifying breath, gazing off into the distance. "After the way you left, I wasn't sure. Umm. That is . . . Was all to your liking yesterday?"

Did she mean—? Yes, her blush told him she did. How could she doubt his enjoyment? He'd gone at her like a ravenous beast. "Yes," he growled. "You were to my liking, Eva. Very much so."

She darted another glance his way and flushed again, beginning to twirl her parasol. "Well, in that case . . . I was going to ask if you might possibly be interested in . . . in entering into an arrangement with me, separate from the brokering of your nuptials. It's completely up to you, of course, and I won't harbor any ill will if you refuse. And we'll just forget I mentioned it if—"

He interrupted what appeared to be a never ending sentence. "What sort of arrangement?"

"A liaison," she blurted.

9

Eva pressed her gloved fingertips to her lips as if hardly able to believe she'd actually uttered the words.

Dane could hardly believe it himself. She was offering him exactly what he wanted. The desire for her that had kindled in him since he'd seen her in the tent leapt higher. He was sorely tempted to take her up on her offer and even found himself eyeing nearby monuments, weighing their suitability as locations for a clandestine rendezvous with her this very minute. But he'd learned past lessons well, and his first instinct was always to mistrust. Any kindness was suspect, any offer potentially nefarious.

She'd wandered off the path and he took her elbow, redirecting her. "Careful there. You're on shaky ground."

"Oh, I'm sorry!" she said, turning contrite eyes on him. "I didn't mean to make you uncomfortable. I simply—"

"You misunderstand," he said, gesturing to a nearby pile of rubble. "Bastian warned me that some of the tuff foundations there are particularly unstable."

"Tuff?" She gazed about them.

"Some sort of porous rock left behind by ancient lava flow. The Romans used it as a building material in the old days because it was easily formed into bricks. But time and the elements have eroded it and rendered it weak. There was a cave-in just yesterday over at the Servian Wall." He paused, smiling in self-deprecation. "As you hear, my eldest brother will soon have me transformed into an encyclopedia of antiquities."

"I was glad to meet your brothers," she told him, latching on to the new conversational direction with a relieved fervor. "For I'm determined to secure them as clients in my business."

"Then I wish you luck and patience."

"Securing them would raise my standing with the Council. And your brothers would certainly curry favor with them as well were they to decide to wed."

"My brothers don't care about marriage or about winning the Council's favor. Eva, about your offer—"

She rushed into further speech, cutting him off. "The arrangement I suggested—I meant only during Moonful. Once a month. Take some time to consider the matter before you answer."

She waved at someone beyond him. "Well, here come Lena and Mimi. I've given you the address of the gala. You'll be there?"

"Yes, but—" He reached out to her, but she sidestepped and gave him a false smile. "Excellent. Then I'll see you there at nine this evening." And without looking his way again, she scurried off.

Damn. Dane stood there, watching her warmly greet her girls. She was a natural mother. Since he must wed, he would gladly take her to wife but for two things—she was not human and she could not bear his children. Not if she'd had the Sickness as she claimed. She was right to seek a human husband, for this would lend her the most security in this world. And the Council would never sanction a marriage between her and an Else male, and most certainly not with a satyr like himself, who was expected to breed. Still, he could continue on as her lover. And would.

Up ahead, Eva greeted a blond woman, who'd apparently been minding the girls. The woman glanced his way and then whispered something to Eva. They were discussing him.

Bastian walked up behind him, handing him the end of a tape. "Here, Sevin's gone off to his salon, so you are left to help me measure this wall." His mind still on Eva, Dane did as Bastian asked and they stretched out the tape along one edge of a crumbling foundation.

"What's going on with her? And you?" Bastian inquired as he jotted a figure in his notebook.

They moved to another side of the foundation and measured again before Dane replied. "Two nights ago in the grove, there was a woman."

Bastian wrote another notation. "A woman?" he echoed, sounding distracted.

"I mean aside from the nereids."

Bastian looked up, his attention caught. "A stranger?"

Dane nodded. "And I felt something with her."

"What do you mean?"

"I mean I *felt* something with a woman. For the first time in my life."

"Go on," Bastian said, sounding intrigued now, as they moved to a third edge of the wall and ran the tape along it.

"It happened shortly after Dante had taken control. I suddenly emerged from stasis and she was just there. With me. Standing calmly in my arms. And I was hard, dying for her. Before I could act on it, Dante returned and I was forced out again. The next thing I knew I awoke in the temple that morning with you and Sevin nearby. And she was nowhere to be seen."

"Why didn't you mention this before?"

"I thought I'd dreamt her." It had seemed likely, for he'd had plenty of imaginings and nightmares after his abduction.

He'd been hysterical and fearful for a while, unable to tell dream from reality. Deemed a security risk, Council authorities had taken him back to ElseWorld and remanded him to the custody of physicians, who'd used their torturous medical devices on him to effect a "cure." He might still be in their dubious care had the Special Ops forces not come calling and determined he was Tracker material. Their training program had been rigorous, but it had given structure to a young life that had been ripped apart. He'd learned to survive.

"Who was this woman, and how did she get on your land? You'd bespelled the perimeter of the grove. I felt it that night. If she intruded, she must've been of ElseWorld blood." They moved to the fourth side, measuring for the last time.

"I *know* who she is." Dane dropped the tape to the far edge and stepped on it with his boot to secure it in place. "Evangeline Delacorte."

"The matchmaker?" Bastian's brows rose and his eyes found her where she and her group were examining the Septimius Arch at the far end of the ruins. While the two women were both daintily picking their way, the children were making a lively game of hopping from one stone to another without touching the ground. "Quite the coincidence."

"Exactly," said Dane. "She said she'd been hunting olives in the grove that night."

"Olives, at night?" Bastian echoed, shaking his head dubiously. "And when you went to her townhouse yesterday? I sensed you were 'with' someone."

Damn, having brothers around again was definitely taking some getting used to. Dane shot him a look. "I had her."

Bastian's gaze whipped to him. "You? Not Dante?" As if to put a point on things, his measuring tape retracted with a snap as he finished his notations.

"Both of us. I was there with Dante all the while, or for most of it. I faded in and out. I was there at the finish; I remember that much for a fact." The corners of his lips curved in a half smile.

"Gods, has that ever hap—"

"Never. And I'm only telling you for the bearing it may have on this whole mystery. Because I think she could be the key to locating Luc. I don't recall where he and I were held captive, but if anyone has that memory aside from our abductors, it must be Dante."

"I had the same thought at the altar after you first mentioned him," Bastian admitted.

"I doubt he'll give anything up just for the asking," said Dane.

"But what if *she* asks?"

The two of them glanced toward Eva and her entourage. She was tending to one of the girls who appeared to have fallen and scraped a knee. "I'm not telling her about him. She'll run screaming," said Dane.

"Maybe she doesn't have to know. Maybe she could be bespelled long enough that she might serve as a sort of medium, allowing us to question him, to unlock whatever secrets he guards."

"She suggested a liaison," Dane admitted.

"Then I strongly suggest that you agree."

"Before I forget, I brought you the cream I promised," Alexa Patrizzi said when Eva left Dane to join her among the ruins.

Eva took the squat jar from her friend, perplexed.

"For your little Lena's scar," said Alexa.

Overhearing, Lena put two fingertips over the small slash near the left corner of her mouth, looking embarrassed that her defect had been noticed.

"It's from an old family recipe," Alexa went on. "And just look at my mother sometime if you want proof that it works.

Nary a freckle, scar, or a wrinkle can be seen on her face. It's sure to help your girl." Alexa didn't notice Lena's discomfiture, for she was too busy glancing over at Dane and his brothers. Any minute now she would ask about them.

"Thank you," Eva said simply, and pocketed the jar away without examining it, so as not to embarrass Lena further. She hadn't asked for the cream, but Alexa was sometimes overly concerned with outward appearances.

"You're free to explore, but not too far," Eva called to the girls, sensing their desire to roam. "Just keep where I can see you and you can see me."

As the children dashed off to play, the two women linked arms to mill through the excavations together. They'd met two months ago at a gathering for young ladies arranged by one of the society matrons, and they'd formed an instant friendship. Back in ElseWorld, her *maman* had required much of her attention, and Odette had guarded her too fiercely at times. As a consequence, Eva hadn't had many friends in her life, and now she was learning how wonderful it was to form such a tie.

She'd justified the friendship to Odette by saying that alliances with humans were a necessary part of the marital brokering profession. The making of inroads into the upper crust of society bought her access to events where her clients could mingle with highborn eligible partners. However, Eva and the girls must still guard their tongues with regard to certain subjects when they were in Alexa's company. There were some secrets that could not be entrusted to humans, even those one counted among one's friends.

"Thank you for watching the girls for me," said Eva.

"Certainly. But do tell me—what were you doing with the infamous Satyr lords?" Alexa glanced behind them to indicate Bastian and Dane, who seemed to be measuring something with a tape.

"Infamous?"

"Handsome, then. Tall, dark, and brawny. Need I continue?"

Eva studied Dane's broad back, which was turned her way, remembering the feel of it under her hands as she'd held him yesterday in her study. Remembering how his crisp hair had felt threading through her fingers. How his kiss had warmed her breast. How strong and capable his body had felt against her smaller one.

When she'd seen him again just now, a sweet yearning had pierced her. Had she just made a fool of herself with him? Did he think she was trying to cling? She sighed inwardly. She cherished the memory of their passionate interlude and could not be sorry for what she'd proposed to him just now.

He was the only ElseWorld male who had guessed the truth of her despite the powders she took. It must mean something. That the liaison she'd suggested would be right between them. Still, there was also the puzzle of why he seemed to have forgotten what he knew of her blood yet again. It was all very perplexing, and she longed to discuss the matter with Alexa and to garner her opinion. But of course, that was impossible.

"Well? Is it a secret?" Alexa prompted. "I've seen the one wearing glasses before, and the other one who left the tent earlier. Bastian and Sevin?"

Eva nodded, unsurprised that Alexa had noticed them before now. Tall, broad shouldered, and exuding masculine confidence, they were difficult to miss. "They're brothers."

"I know that. But who's the new one?"

"A third brother, Dane."

Alexa took another peek at the men working at a distance behind them. "Goodness. They do grow them large in that family."

Eva smiled to herself. Her friend had no idea. The two women fell in step again, wandering through the Arch of Septimius Severus.

"Come on, I saw you speaking with them," Alexa prodded. "What are they like?"

She shrugged. "Intelligent, wealthy, handsome."

Alexa's eyes widened with feminine interest. "How terrible that sounds!" she said, and they shared a grin. "How do you know them?"

"Through friends," Eva hedged. "Dane wishes to wed soon, and I'm helping him with introductions into society."

"He has told you he wants to marry?" Alexa said in surprise. Her gaze swung to him and she eyed him speculatively.

"He's not for you," Eva hastened to add.

"Spoilsport." Alexa sighed. "My mother wouldn't allow it anyway. Unfortunately, I'm already engaged in all but the final asking to Signor Fitzgerald. But I can still look, can't I?"

They shared a smile. "No harm in looking," Eva agreed.

Alexa stole another glance at Bastian and Dane. "Can you imagine a wedding night with one of them? I'd be frightened out of my wits!" She leaned in, whispering, "I've heard they sport a second member in their trousers."

"No!" Eva tried to appear convincingly shocked. And she was—shocked that Alexa knew!

Alexa let out a peal of laughter. "It's true, I tell you. And I've also heard they know well what to do with both of them."

"That's absurd."

"Well, of course it is. But what if there were something to it? Just imagine," said Alexa.

"Where did you come by this oh-so-accurate information?"

"Like everything else, it's a rumor started by the unearthing of artifacts here in the forum. I was told by a reliable source that there's a particular statue of a satyr enjoying a Bacchanalia in one of the temples. It holds a wine goblet, has furred haunches, a tail, and its male"—she leaned close again—"parts are high and at the ready for entertainment." She fanned herself.

Both appalled and amused at once, Eva sputtered with laughter. "Artistic license I imagine. You'll be pleased to know that Dane has promised to attend the Pretender Gala tonight. So you may judge him for yourself. I predict you'll find him quite tame."

Alexa pouted prettily. "I hope not!"

Eva giggled again, enjoying her ribald sense of humor. Most women in Rome seemed to have one, but the wealthy ones usually kept it hidden. When she wed into their ranks eventually, Eva vowed she would not be so stiff. After all, Alexa wasn't, and she was the issue of one of the most affluent, esteemed families in all of Rome!

And she had a very eligible brother. One who was rich, highborn, and human. A gentleman who satisfied all of Eva's *maman*'s requirements. Marriage to him would provide safety for those in her household. It was a bonus that he was the brother of her dearest friend.

She'd been waffling, but there and then, Eva decided that she would set her sights on Alexa's brother. She would woo him and take him as a husband. But she would not bear his children, for if the Council discovered she'd lied about having contracted the Sickness, they would revoke her marriage and her visa. She'd quickly find herself back in ElseWorld, obligated to wed and conceive the children of the next eligible satyr on their list of breeders in line for a wife. And this would without doubt reveal her species.

She glanced covertly back at Dane again and started when she found him staring at her in return. Their eyes locked. From this distance she couldn't read his expression. But something about the set of his shoulders seemed determined.

Turning away from him was one of the hardest things she'd ever done, but she forced herself to do so. To place him firmly in the category of lover, not husband. Both men she was pursuing would be at tonight's gala. She would yearn for one, but she would wed the other.

10

As Dane and Eva entered the Hall of Emperors within Palazzo Nuovo that night, they were greeted with music and the sight of humans dressed as faeries, nereids, and a host of Roman gods, goddesses, and creatures of ancient myth. Dane placed his hand at the curve of Eva's lower back and leaned into her. "You didn't tell me this was to be a masquerade."

Far more aware of his casual touch than she let on, Eva adjusted the shimmering white mask she wore, her only concession to the festivities. They'd met just outside in the foyer and now joined the throng of elite Roman society assembled here in the Renaissance palazzo designed by Michelangelo himself. This hall in which the gala was being held was additionally populated with statues and busts of long-dead Roman emperors. Guests wove around them treading upon a patterned floor of black and white marble.

"I'm quite sure I mentioned that we'd be attending a Pretender Gala," Eva told him.

"And what is that exactly?"

"A ball in which the upper classes make a pretense at bringing mythological beings to life. Your eldest brother's work in the Forum ruins has inspired them. Every time his smallest discovery is made—a bit of mosaic or a new bust—it is an excuse for yet another costume ball to celebrate it. These events are a constant feature of society here in Rome these days." She gestured toward two men they passed, who were both costumed as satyrs. "And since you are the real thing, I saw no need for a costume. Besides I want the ladies to see you displayed as you are to full advantage."

He sighed. "So I'm to be a piece of meat in a butcher's window?"

Amused by his long-suffering tone, Eva made the mistake of glancing up at him. He was searingly handsome tonight in dark eveningwear. The aura of every female that passed responded to him. But she wouldn't share that information with him yet. Men sometimes were made nervous by the fact that women were intensely aware of them. It was as if they expected women to wander about in a cloud, oblivious to anything remotely associated with matters of attraction, leaving men to do any choosing of partners.

Dane's hand at her back was light but directed her confidently among the throng. She reveled in this small measure of his masculine mastery over her, and for the moment it was easy to pretend to herself that she was his and that he was hers. They hadn't mentioned the offer she'd made in the ruins, but it lay between them, a taboo at present.

With the donning of her mask tonight, she had forced herself to take on the persona of a Marital Broker. It was time to send him off to select another woman, one who would be his wife. Casually, she pulled away from him. "I'd like a drink," she said, suddenly needing something to sustain herself for the task.

As Dane lifted two glasses from a passing tray and handed one to her, she took note of the other ElseWorld creatures who mingled here with costumed humans. All were clandestine and taking care not to congregate, but she felt their furtive glances. An awareness passed between them all as if they recognized that they were members of some secret organization.

Pixies that stood to half of Dane's height threaded their way through the crush, bearing trays of drinks and hors d'oeuvres atop their heads. They often found employment as waitstaff in this world and were easily trained for such tasks as this. Now and then they executed complicated whirls and flourishes that had the guests clapping.

As she and Dane paused beneath one of the large centaur statues, an actual centaur clopped past. He winked at them. She smiled secretively and took a sip of her drink.

Dane glanced at her in question. "An acquaintance?"

"A former client. Happily wed due to my efforts on his behalf, I might add," she said pointedly.

Her eyes swept the crowd, and it amazed her that humans were oblivious to things that were so obvious to her and Dane here tonight—the sparkle of skin, wings made of flesh rather than fabric and sequins. A centaur that appeared to walk on two legs rather than his actual four. It was stunning that no one in EarthWorld had yet realized they'd been invaded by species from another world.

"How can so many clues be overlooked?" she murmured, shaking her head.

"They see only what they expect—what we mean for them to see. But one day something will go awry and their eyes will be opened."

"All the more reason we must find a wife for you as soon as possible," she said, giving herself a stern, silent lecture. She would send him off as she must, and she would focus her mind on other business here tonight—searching for her father and wooing Alexa's brother.

"And what about your husband?" Dane asked. "Who have you set your sights on?"

Was he a mind reader? "Your future spouse may be my business, but mine isn't yours," she returned. Setting her drink on a passing tray, she handed him a card from her pocket.

"What's this?" he asked, sounding wary.

"Your engagement card for tonight."

"Five names? You've been busy," he said, tucking it away in a pocket as if he intended to ignore it.

"In a few moments, I'll introduce you to all five ladies I've selected as candidates," she warned. "You may make your own additional choices as you prefer. That part of things is fluid. Once we separate, you are to dance and converse with any number of eligible partners. But if you are distracted too long with one, expect me to interrupt. No more than two dances per lady, none consecutive, and I want to see you circulating."

"Slave driver."

She flashed a teasing grin. "I'm pleased you understand my role in things. Your objective tonight is to meet a wide variety of potential partners. Once you've been sufficiently introduced, I'll set you free to roam as you wish."

"And where will you be?"

"At hand, observing. Your aura will react to the more suitable partners. I'll take mental notes. And if you wish to be extricated from an uncomfortable situation, just signal by running your right hand through your hair." She placed her hand on his arm. "Come, I see the hosts. Let me begin the introductions."

"If we're coupled in their minds, won't that be a deterrent to finding prospective candidates?" he asked as they made their way across the room.

"It's the 1880s, signor," she informed him. "Rules of society aren't as stringent as they once were. Men and women can meet in public as friends now, without incurring undue scrutiny. And if ladies see you accepted in the company of another woman— myself—you'll appear safe. A good choice for a husband."

In the crush, someone knocked into her and he pulled her

back against him. "Safe?" he whispered against her hair. "Is that what a woman truly wants in her husband?"

Eva's heart thundered in her ears and she let herself melt against him for a stolen moment. "It's what I want. But only in my husband, not in my . . ."

"Lover?"

The crowd parted and she pulled away. Smiling politely as they joined the matrons, she began introductions, which took them on a circuit around the room and absorbed them for the next half hour.

"Evangeline!" It was Alexa Patrizzi, all smiles and dressed as a peach-gowned Venus. Alexa hugged her and then glanced coquettishly toward Dane, silently begging an introduction.

Eva sent her a small frown.

"You said I was to judge him for myself," Alexa murmured in an innocent aside.

"Signorina Patrizzi, Signor Satyr," said Eva, bowing to the inevitable. Alexa could be tenacious when she wanted something. However, Eva was pleased to note that, although her friend's aura was excited by Dane's presence, his own remained calm and constant. Eva stood largely silent as they chatted briefly, but when several other of Alexa's friends joined their circle, Eva prepared to fade into the crowd, thinking no one would notice. But as she made to step back, a strong, masculine hand grasped her arm.

Dane bent lower so only she would hear. "Will you be all right on your own?"

"Of course," she said in surprise. None of her other clients had bothered to wonder how she might fair alone at these gatherings.

"No last-minute instructions or advice?" he teased.

"Only that you are to be polite and charming, and that you are to weigh the candidates well. Remember, you're selecting the . . . mother of your children." It was the same advice she gave all her male clients before releasing them, but now for some reason, she stumbled over the words. Embarrassed, she twisted her arm slightly and he released her.

Yet foolishly, as she walked away, she wished he had held on.

A gloved hand snared Eva's wrist as she wove her way through the gathering. "Yet another Venus," said a cultured male voice. "I warned my sister that her choice of costume was destined to encounter much in the way of competition here tonight."

Eva turned to see Alexa's brother, the very handsome, very rich, very blond, and quite unmarried scion of the Patrizzi family. Of impeccable background, his family had been one of the ruling ones in Rome for a century or more. A decade or so older than she, he was distinguished and steady, and an appropriate choice for her. Unlike Dane.

"Signor Patrizzi." Eva dragged her thoughts from Dane and managed a smile and even a small curtsy for the man she'd set her sights on as a husband. "The statue of the Capitoline Venus here in the palazzo inspires many like your sister to don such a costume. However, I am not in costume at all, as I'm sure you are aware. But let me see—" Her gaze swept him consideringly. "You wear the thunderbolt. You're Jupiter, King of the Gods?"

"Exactly. And as ruler of the heavens, I hereby command you to dance with me," he said, offering his arm as the musicians struck up.

He was attracted to her. She'd known that for some time; but because the gossips were always watching, he'd rarely so blatantly singled her out. Though she wanted nothing more at that moment than to leave him and tuck herself away in some secluded corner where she could observe Dane from afar, she instead smiled, took his arm, and let him whirl her into the company of other dancers.

She'd danced with him before and found his gentlemanly touch and bland aura pleasant enough, yet now both irritated her. Why? Nothing had changed, except . . . her eyes found Dane across the room. A pretty auburn-haired woman was flirting with him now. Her bright pink aura reached out for him, as if to wrap him up as her own special gift and tie him with a gay bow. She was attracted to him. Very attracted. But as with all the other women in his orbit, Dane's silver aura failed to stir for her.

Feeling selfishly relieved, Eva sent her own partner a dazzling smile. His fingers tightened on her and he swung her deeper into the dancers, and she lost sight of Dane. "You keep a rather close eye on that gentleman," he remarked.

Surprised, she glanced up at him. He angled his head in Dane's direction to indicate of whom he spoke.

He continued, "Didn't think I'd notice? I'm interested in you, haven't you guessed? Forgive me if I'm a little jealous."

This declaration should have gladdened her, but instead it only made her a little depressed. "You needn't be," she said. "We're only acquaintances. He's new to this society and interested in marriage. I'm helping him settle on a suitable partner."

He laughed, drawing attention their way. "You're matchmaking?"

She shrugged, annoyed at the denigrating way he said it. "It amuses me. I have an intuition for matters of the heart."

"But how fascinating," he said. "I had no idea you truly were a Venus. Tell me how you go about it."

"Simply by making introductions," she said; then she forced the conversation in a more desirable direction. "Tell me, sir, are you hoping to wed?"

He perceived this as a flirtation and launched into light banter meant to amuse her. He was as easy as his sister, and she found she could relax with him, ignoring him for stretches of time and then easily picking up the thread of his conversation in order to offer sensible replies. In truth, she was feeling a little bored in his company. Odd, for they'd met a half-dozen times before, and she hadn't been bored by him then at all.

The musicians had stopped their playing, but his gloved hand squeezed hers. "Another dance?"

She forced a dimple to appear in her cheek. "Wouldn't that be a bit scandalous?" It was tantamount to an announcement of an engagement, surely he knew that.

He stepped closer. "I'll risk it."

But did she want to? She knew she should take him up on it. She should steal him out onto a balcony afterward and hope he mustered the courage to kiss her. It would seal their alliance. What was she waiting for?

She turned to look toward Dane. Three young ladies surrounded him now. And he was running his right hand through his hair—the signal that he needed her!

"Oh dear." She glanced up at her beau. A proposal seemed to be hovering on his lips. Dane was ruining this chance for her. But she wasn't sorry. "You'll have to pardon me, I . . ."

"There you are, *caro*," a perfectly modulated feminine voice said from behind them. They turned to see the matriarch of the Patrizzi clan, Serafina. She'd brought a pretty young lady in tow, one obviously intended for her son. She nodded stiffly to Eva and then said to him, "You remember Signorina Claiborne?"

After a bit of chatting during which Signora Patrizzi managed to largely exclude Eva, her son was soon paired with this new partner, though he didn't look pleased about it.

Meanwhile, across the room, Dane was set to rub his scalp bald with his right hand.

"Please do excuse me." Not waiting for an acknowledgment, Eva left her current company and headed his way.

Eva slipped into the group surrounding Dane, which consisted of three of the names on the card she'd given him, as well as three other ladies. All eligible. All interested in him, if their auras were any indication. She tried not to think of them in his bed, of him kissing their lips, of him pressing his body to theirs, and moving between—

No! She must only think of these women as objects on a shelf. Dane would choose one just as if . . . as if buying a hat. And in that vein, Eva was to function only as the shopkeeper, helping him make a selection. She would not imagine how or where he would wear the hat once he bought it. Or how much he might come to love it over time.

Trying not to attract attention to herself, she glanced at him in silent question. Why had he summoned her?

"Ah, ladies, you must pardon me," he announced. "I've promised this waltz to Mademoiselle Delacorte."

With a bow toward six downcast faces, he took her arm and pulled her into the midst of the dancers. He was warm and smelled of various fragrances, having danced with various women. It irritated her.

"You gave the signal. What's wrong?" she asked in a clipped tone.

He stared down at her for a long moment; then a slight smile touched his lips. "I missed you."

"What?" She jerked to a halt. "This isn't a joke, Dane."

He swept her off again, barely missing a beat. "I wasn't joking." When she opened her lips to scold him again, he added more seriously, "I wanted to warn you about the man you've linked yourself with." He nodded toward Alexa's brother.

So he had noticed them together. "What about him? His sister is my dear friend and he's—"

"A pompous ass."

She gasped. "A case of it takes one to know one?"

"Perhaps," he said unrepentantly.

"He's none of your business, nor is my association with him," Eva said firmly. "As for you, you're proving a rather difficult subject I'm afraid. Have you felt a particular interest in any of the ladies here thus far?"

He shrugged. "They're all the same."

"Maybe on first acquaintance, but Signorina DeLuca is considered a great wit. And Signorina Constazio is quite learned and thoroughly enjoys picture puzzles. You did say you liked puzzles."

"Ah, yes, I recall. That day in your study." His eyes twinkled devilishly. "How well I remember many pleasurable details of that afternoon."

She blushed, as he had intended. Suddenly, the offer she'd made in the ruins spiced the air between them with promise.

He drew her close. "Come home with me where we can be private."

"What?" She gazed into eyes of lambent silver. His aura was steady, certain, reaching out to her as it hadn't with the others.

"Your offer of a liaison. I'm accepting it, Eva. Come home with me. There's no one else here I want."

"You mean now?" Heat prickled over her cheeks and she felt a bit faint. No, they must wait. Mentally, she counted the nights until Moonful, until she could have him. There were far too many.

His hand crept to her nape, warm and sure. "Remember how it was between us?" he coaxed. "We could have that again, just minutes from now, in my carriage. In my bed. Against my wall. Me, inside you. Come." He stopped dancing and took her hand, tugging her toward the nearest exit. She was halfway across the room with him before she remembered herself and pulled away.

"Stop! I didn't mean t-tonight," she stammered, clasping her hands together at her waist.

"Why not tonight?"

Because you might become addictive. Because if I am with you too often, I will want to give you my heart and you might break it. Because I don't want to wind up like my maman. "Because it would be unwise to form such a casual habit. I'm pleased that you are in agreement with my proposal, but—"

"Only pleased?"

"*Very* pleased, then." He was too arrogant. Too confident. Precisely the sort of man she lusted for. But she couldn't let herself want him too much. "As I told you, I mean to reserve our rendezvous to Moonful nights exclusively. To those times when our human spouses simply won't do for us."

"Neither of us is married yet."

She frowned. "I might have become engaged a moment ago if you hadn't cried wolf just now."

"To that idiot you were dancing with?" His outrage only stoked the fire between them.

"Enough," she said, cooling it. "Let us shelve this discussion until later. If you wish to continue as my client, you will reserve your comments to the business at hand tonight. Which is that of finding your new wife."

He shoved his hands in his pockets, looking irritated. "Just choose any one of them for me and be done with it."

"I'll do no such thing," she said, appalled. "This is a woman you'll have to live with for the rest of your life!"

"Hardly. I intend to set her up in a house of her own and visit her bed only long enough to get her with child. As long as she's a decent woman of respectable nature, she'll please me."

"You really want me to choose your wife?"

He nodded. "You'd probably do better than I. And while we're at it, why not let me choose your husband in return?"

Eva expelled an annoyed breath. "In that case, your task would be far easier than mine. For I've already chosen him."

"Patrizzi?" A muscle twitched in Dane's cheek at her curt nod. "A little old for you, isn't he?"

"What? No!"

"Pardon me, I overstep." He gave her an abbreviated mockery of a bow. "I have little doubt he'll fall at your feet."

She heard him mutter something more regarding the other man doing so due to the elderly's requirement for a cane, but she chose to ignore that and only shrugged. "Of course, I look like my *maman*. But I'm smarter than she was. I won't let wayward desires rule me. Now, circulate. When next we meet, I'll expect a full report from you regarding at least two ladies you met tonight whom you admire."

Eva stalked across the room and sequestered herself in a nook. There, she planned to secretly nourish her obsession with him by observing him to her heart's content for the rest of the night. But it was not to be, for a voice spoke at her elbow only a moment later. "He's handsome."

Eva turned to see Signora Patrizzi beside her. She, too, was looking at Dane and had apparently spotted Eva observing him. She was an uncommonly beautiful woman, but Eva peevishly wondered what she would think if she knew that her aura was an unattractive shade of puce.

"Signora." Eva nodded politely to her but ignored her conversational gambit, hoping in vain that she might leave the subject of Dane alone.

However, Serafina only set her fan fluttering to disguise the fact that they were speaking together. "I do hope you haven't set your sights on my son," she said casually. "He's well aware he's meant for better things."

Eva's ire rose. Women just like this one had battered her mother's self-esteem. "If you were so confident of that, you wouldn't be here now warning me off."

Serafina waved politely at an acquaintance across the room. "I didn't mean to upset you. I only wished to save you some wasted effort and inevitable disappointment. Good evening, signorina," she said, and then departed without another word, leaving Eva stewing in her own annoyance.

"Witch," muttered a voice.

Eva looked around. A tray resting a few feet away lifted a

few inches, revealing the grinning pixie under it. She grimaced. "Pinot? What are you doing here?"

His twinkling eyes disappeared as he lowered the tray to rest on his head. "I'm working, what does it look like? I like to earn a little money for the house when I can. I don't need two women to keep me."

"Spying, more like. You don't fool me." Waiters had plenty of privacy beneath the trays, and Eva was well aware that some took advantage. The hands of a pixie were always busy, thieving the occasional purse or gold watch, or sometimes even rifling the guests' pockets just for the fun of it.

"A little of that, too. People forget we're under these trays. Because they don't see us, they think we don't have ears. Makes it easy to learn the news." Pinot rocked back and forth on his booted heels, cocky. "Yes, *lots* of news to be learned."

"Such as?"

"Such as news about a certain gent who's listed in your *maman*'s little book. A Signor Rrrusso," said Pinot, rolling the Rs in an exaggerated way, so as to mock the gentleman's elevated social status. "I have it on good authority that he's right over there, by that statue."

Russo was the first of the names on her short list of candidates for father. Excited, Eva followed Pinot's gaze. "Which statue? There are hundreds here. What does he look like?"

"Hard to miss him. He's the taller of the three Brethren of the Misericordia—the Brothers of Mercy. Over there, all costumed in black like tall, skinny crows. Gives me the willies."

Eva found the trio with her eyes. Their black hoods were thrown back on their shoulders and their long robes dusted the ground. They'd donned black silk masks to partially cover their faces.

The true Brethren were Capuchin monks, who did works of charity. They were a familiar site at funerals and in city streets as they rushed the desperately ill on litters toward hospital. But they were never present at balls.

"Why are they dressed that way? The Capuchins aren't exactly creatures of Roman myth," she observed.

"Who knows? But one of the waiters here works in Russo's household. It's him all right, but he's no monk."

"No, I'd figured out that much myself." She gave him a surreptitious pat on the shoulder and then headed for the black-caped trio. "Thank you, Pinot. I think I'll drift that way."

"Not so fast." Pinot abandoned his tray and trotted after her. "I'm coming. Odette will skewer me if anything happens to you. Besides, I want to eavesdrop a little."

Eva turned to forestall him.

But Pinot pointed ahead of them. "No time to argue. He's getting away!"

"Gaetano!"

Gaetano Patrizzi stood at the large casement window at the front of the Palazzo Nuovo's Great Hall, twisting the gold ring on his smallest finger and watching Eva escape. Two stories below, the equestrian statue of Emperor Marcus Aurelius sat upon a pedestal in the center of the piazza, glinting in the wavering torchlight. Two figures scurried past it along the black and white trapezoidal pavement. Evangeline and her strange little gnome were departing the Pretender Gala on foot.

When he eventually wed her, Gaetano planned to make sure that cretin disappeared from her entourage, forcibly if necessary. And she wouldn't be dancing or consorting with his nemesis—Lord Fucking Dane Satyr—any longer, or his brothers either.

Having spotted her, Gaetano had intended to follow her like a bee after honey, but now it appeared he was to be waylaid by the very last person he felt like conversing with. His mother, Serafina.

"Gaetano, I'm speaking to you," she said in her imperious way.

"Yes, what is it?" Behind them, the musicians played on, and the din of conversation was deafening. But here in this nook, they could be clandestine in their discussion.

"You've been impossible to find recently." Standing with her back to the window he faced, she leaned toward him. "Sergio has complained that our charges are growing restless. He requires fresh serum. Why haven't you gathered more olives to make it?"

Anger surged in him, and suddenly he was glad at the news he was going to deliver. He turned her way, wanting to see her face when he told her. "Because I lost the grove."

"What?" she asked blankly.

He folded his arms and lounged a shoulder against the glass, taking pleasure in turning the knife. "I lost it. In a game of cards." And now the final stab. "To Dane Satyr." Her face mottled, and she could only stare at him. Rendering her speechless for once made him feel powerful.

A sharp pinch came at his ribs and he yelped. "Damn it all, Mother!"

"If we were alone, I'd slap you as well," she told him, unrepentant. "This could ruin us, you worthless cur. Oh, why was I cursed with such a son?"

His hands fisted at his sides. He was the one who'd been cursed. She had much to pay for. One of these days . . .

"I'll speak to our attorneys tomorrow and have them approach Satyr with an offer. We have to maintain control of that grove. Our little business is done for if we lose it."

"What's the matter, Mother? Afraid your looks will fade if you don't have your creams and lotions?"

"Shut up, fool. That's not all that's at stake. If news of our work leaks, our reputations will be in tatters. The family fortune gone in an instant." Her face turned conniving. "But Satyr has even more to lose than we do. His entire world would be exposed if we tell the secrets we know. He and his family would be locked up as fearsome freaks."

Gaetano turned back to the window. Eva was no longer in sight. "If you think he'll sell the land back to us, think again. I offered on it right after I lost it and one other time since. I saw how badly he wanted it. Called it his heritage."

"Just because some distant ancestor of his planted its trees, that doesn't entitle him to them. And I'd like to see him prove his claim without revealing what he is. I'll make an offer to him. If he doesn't see things our way, our lawyers will sue him."

"His brothers might have something to say about that. They've acquired some powerful allies in the government. Especially the eldest, Bastian. His finds in the Forum are earning him friends in high places."

"I'll manage something. We'll have the grove back, don't you doubt it. Women left to clean up a man's mess, as always." She sent him a look of disgust.

"What are you two arguing about?" asked Alexa, coming over to them. "It's a party. Time to enjoy yourselves. Time enough for squabbling tomorrow."

"Which reminds me," Serafina went on, berating him without pause. "I don't approve of you consorting with Alexa's little friend."

"Eva?" asked Alexa.

Gaetano ground his teeth. "She's much preferable to your choice for me. The Claiborne girl has the face of a horse."

"And the bank account of Midas, as well as a fine pedigree," Serafina scolded. "After you tell me you lost the grove, I'm in no mood to humor you regarding that French tart."

"Don't speak that way about Eva," said Alexa. "You hardly know her. And what do you mean he lost the grove?"

"I mean he lost our olive grove on Aventine. In a card game. To Dane Satyr. Now I must hire lawyers to get it back," she said.

"Then go and get on with it, and leave me in peace. As for the French tart, I plan to wed her," said Gaetano. He'd have pursued Eva regardless, but it was a bonus that his mother detested the idea.

"Wife? I hardly think so," Serafina scoffed. "You will stop your pursuit of her. Nothing can come of it and it's an embarrassment. She lives in a rented townhouse, for goodness sake. And she's hardly of our status. No, I don't think so."

Gaetano's stomach roiled with anger. Eva wasn't polished in the stilted way of the women his mother chose for him. But a man didn't care about such things. He wanted Evangeline Delacorte, and by God he was going to have her. Alexa put a comforting hand on his arm, but he shook it off. They'd always gotten along well enough, but Alexa's willingness to pacify their parent was beginning to grate on him.

"Shouldn't you be mingling, Mother?" Honestly, sometimes he wanted to throttle her.

Serafina nodded. "I see our attorney over there. I might as well broach the matter of our little difficulty."

"Or I could wed him," Alexa offered, drawing two pairs of startled eyes her way.

"Who, the attorney?" asked Gaetano. "How would that help?"

Serafina stared at her, intrigued. "You always were a smart one. You'd be willing?"

"You mean to wed Satyr?" Gaetano demanded, fuming as he finally comprehended things. "No, I forbid it!"

"Honestly, Tano, as if you had the power to forbid anything. Come, Alexa, let us discuss this matter without further distraction from your brother," said Serafina. With a diffident swish of her skirts, she took Alexa's arm and made to leave him.

But before they departed, she couldn't resist one last dig. "Remember, I hold the purse strings in this family, and I'm sure your gambling would suffer if you were cut off. Let tonight's dance be the last you enjoy with your little mademoiselle."

After they'd gone, Gaetano turned and banged his forehead to the window glass. "But I *feel* something with her," he whispered. His gaze searched the piazza below. Of course, Eva was long gone by now.

Shifting so his coat would hide what he did, he cupped himself. His cock was flaccid as usual. Had he only imagined it had stirred when he danced with Eva tonight? No, had happened before in her company. It was real, and she was the only woman who'd ever affected him in that way. He was almost afraid to take her under him in bed, fearing that in the end, he might discover that he was as impotent with her as with all the others he'd tried. But the possibility that this was not the case was a lure he could not resist. He would woo her with drink or drug one night soon and try her on. And if he was successful at bedding her, his mother would relent.

Then he could have the delightful Eva whenever he wished. Could wed her. Sleep with her in his own bed on fresh sheets. Upstairs, not down in the dank labyrinth that ran beneath his home.

Just then, he saw Dane on the tile below, moving in the direction Evangeline had just gone. Damn. Did the man think to steal everything from him?

11

"What is this place?" Pinot whispered.

"Shh!" said Eva, batting at him to stay behind her. "I don't know. I've never noticed it before." Hidden at the bottom of a staircase in the shadow of an enormous stone griffin, they stared at the mysterious building at the top of the steps.

"Nor I," said Pinot. "And I often pass this way."

They'd followed the black-caped gentlemen from Palazzo Nuovo for several blocks, until the trio had taken the stairs up to this stately three-story edifice. Along its façade, a series of sash windows alternated with Corinthian pilasters crowned with carven olive branches. Something flickered beyond one of the glass panes. A candelabrum.

"It reeks of magic," said Eva.

She felt Pinot's head nod at her elbow. "A Council building," he whispered. They were still on Capitoline, not far from their own home. From somewhere behind them in the distance came the clink of pickaxes and shovels working around the clock to uncover ancient mysteries in the Forum ruins.

"I'm going in," said Eva, when a group of naiads arrived and took the steps upward toward the building. "Go home."

"Forget that. I'm coming, too," insisted Pinot. "This is far too good a mystery."

"Hurry, then, if you must, and keep up," she said. Together, they ascended the steps. Attaching themselves to the last party up the stairs, they attempted to surreptitiously enter through the arched doorway with them.

"Halt!" A gargantuan one-eyed creature barred the threshold, just before they made it inside. A Cyclops. Not the first Eva had met, but certainly the largest. At his side, a three-headed guard dog sniffed at them for a long, considering moment during which they held their breath. Her mind raced, trying to think of a plausible excuse that might gain them entrance. Difficult when she didn't know what this place was.

But when the dog didn't devour them, the sentry muttered, "Cerberus finds you acceptable."

"Well, good. Then . . ." Eva tried to edge around him.

"However, I don't." The Cyclops blocked her, eyeing the pair of them like some giant, supercilious butler who'd spotted vermin. "Where's your card?"

Card? Eva and Pinot exchanged furtive glances.

"I forgot it?" Eva offered, having no idea what he was talking about.

The big eye narrowed. "You don't sound too certain."

"We're friends of the three Brethren of Misericordia who entered earlier," Pinot piped up.

"Yes! Right. There they are," Eva said, spying Signor Russo beyond the Cyclops. At the far side of the room he and his companions disappeared through a red velvet curtain. Smiling with what she hoped was confidence, she took Pinot's hand and again tried to sidle past the guard.

And yet again, he blocked them. "No card, no admittance.

Not without the boss's approval." Leaving Cerberus to stand watch alone, the Cyclops took her arm in one hand and Pinot's collar in his other, and hustled them both inside and through the velvet curtain.

They quickly found themselves in what appeared to be an elegant sitting room dotted with small tables and couches. Perhaps two dozen people were ensconced there, mingling and chatting. Unfortunately, Signor Russo and his companions were not among them. No one glanced up as they entered, and Eva gathered it would have been considered gauche to take too much notice of anyone in particular. There was something indefinable in the air here that encouraged discretion.

Before they got much farther, a masculine voice stopped them. "Mademoiselle Delacorte?" Dane's brother Sevin was approaching. "What are you doing here?"

"I might ask you the same question," Eva parried. He was dressed more formally than when she'd last seen him, in black silk. She'd been so intent on Dane when they'd met in the ruins that morning that she hadn't really noticed how handsome his brother was. His hair was dark like Dane's, his lips full and sensuous, his eyes a clear sparkling blue, his shoulders broad.

"I'm the proprietor." Sevin waved the guard off, then acknowledged Pinot with a nod and took her elbow, leading them both farther into the room. His touch was firm and masculine and confident, yet it didn't affect her in the same melting way Dane's did. "You've come ahead of schedule, actually," he told them. "Once you'd resided in this world for six months, you would have received an invitation."

"It's the *Salone di Passione*, isn't it?" Pinot guessed suddenly, sounding excited. Trust him to have heard of this place. He sniffed out information like a bloodhound.

A corner of Sevin's mouth curved upward in tacit confirmation.

"What?" Eva asked blankly.

Just then, a young man passed them, gesturing toward Pinot as if to draw him away. He was tall and slender, and attractive in a boyish fresh-faced way. Eva looked down at Pinot and saw him blush.

"He's a friend," Pinot explained, making to leave them. "I'll just be a minute."

Once he left them, Sevin steered her to one side of the room so she could better take it all in.

"A passion salon?" she queried. "What is this place and why haven't I ever noticed it before?"

"The building is bespelled so the uninitiated won't take note of it, or of any comings and goings from it that might bring on an investigation. To nonmembers, it appears to be merely an impenetrable thicket. I can only assume that your association with my brother has had the effect of prematurely rendering us visible to you."

Fascinated, Eva studied her surroundings, noting the risqué frescoes and mosaics on the walls and floors, the brocade couches, and the bubbling fountain at which guests periodically refreshed their drinks. "What goes on here that's so secret? Does the Council know?"

Sevin nodded. "They sanctioned it. I broached the concept to them five years ago, presenting it to them as a way of staving off trouble for our kind on this side of the gate. ElseWorld immigrants needed a safe, private location to congregate for conversation and concupiscent engagements with like-minded partners. Coming here helps limit the potential for inadvertent exposure were such engagements to take place outside these environs."

Sevin believed he'd created a haven for all ElseWorld creatures. Yet without her powders, Eva knew she would be as endangered in this place as she was outside of it. For if she were to reveal herself to him and his brothers as a female satyr, there would be no sanctuary here for her. They would turn her over to ElseWorld authorities if they knew. Wouldn't they?

"What's through there?" she asked, pointing toward a drape that obscured an arched portal. Since Signor Russo hadn't lingered here, she deduced that he must have passed into the next chamber.

"The main salon," Sevin readily explained. "This is merely an anteroom, used to engage in verbal foreplay. Some guests never move beyond it. For them, a little flirtation with members of their species is enough. However, if one is looking for more, there is the main salon through that drape. But first, partners can spend time here in this room negotiating terms if they wish. Then, when they move on, they can arrive with a plan and already in character, so to speak."

"And if one arrives here without a partner?" she asked. She glanced toward Pinot and was jolted by surprise to see him locked in an embrace with his friend. Selfishly, she'd never before thought of him as having a personal life outside of the one her household provided.

"Then this can serve as a setting in which to meet one before entering the main salon. As I've suggested to Dane on numerous occasions."

"He's a member? Oh, of course. He's your brother after all," she mused, not altogether pleased at the thought of Dane here, with other women. "He might have told me."

Sevin sent her a knowing look, a twinkle in his eye. Had he been testing her to gauge her reaction to the mention of his brother?

"It could impact his marriage prospects," she improvised hurriedly. "And mine. Even if the perimeter is bespelled, what of these people?" She gestured toward the room's occupants. "They'll have seen him, and now me. It increases the risk of gossip that might prove detrimental to our hopes to wed within the human community."

Sevin was already shaking his head before she finished. "Although everyone is visible to everyone else here, upon leaving these premises, you'll find yourself unable to recall anyone's precise features or identity. There is one exception, but it requires a specific invitation. It's done in that way." He indicated a couple across the room, who were standing close together. Briefly, each placed their palms over the other's eyes, then removed them as if removing blinders. "Now neither will forget what passes between them here tonight."

Eva looked down to find Pinot at her side again. His friend hovered near the front door, as if preparing to depart, and Pinot was casting him longing glances. "You want to go with him?" guessed Eva.

"No, I'm staying with you." But he looked torn between duty and a desire to enjoy himself.

Sevin offered his hand then, shaking Pinot's. She liked that he treated him as an equal. Some men didn't. "Sevin, Dane's brother," he said, introducing himself. "I'll make sure she gets home safely after her visit."

"Go. I'll be fine," she assured the pixie.

"All right, then." With a bit of a swagger, Pinot sauntered over to his young man. Arm in arm, they departed the salon. How fortuitous that Pinot's protective instincts had been dulled by his infatuation. Now, if she could slip free of Sevin at some point, she had a question or two for Signor Russo.

"You're welcome to take a tour," Sevin suggested, gesturing toward the arched entrance to the main salon. "Unless you're intolerant or easily shocked, in which case I advise against it."

"Though I'm not sure about the latter, I'm innocent of the first. But don't I have to be a member?" she said, already moving toward the curtained opening. Even she, with her lackluster olfactory abilities, could detect hundreds of different scents emanating from beyond it.

"Not if you're with me," he assured her. "However, if you plan to join us again, you'll first have to go through our orientation process. There are standards and policies by which everyone must abide. All prospective members are carefully screened before they receive a subscription card."

Eva considered that, wondering what the screening entailed and whether Odette's powders could withstand the scrutiny. The fantasy of coming here again at some point for a carnal purpose appealed. But shyness blossomed in her at the thought as well. Would she dare?

The two burly guards on duty at the entryway to the main salon stood aside as they approached. Sevin parted the velvet drape with one hand, and then they were inside.

The complex, evocative scent of magic that permeated the room was the first thing that struck her. And the décor was a feast for the senses—lush, predominantly done in reds and golds. The gilded, coffered ceiling reached three stories high, and there were balconied seating boxes encircling the room's vast perimeter, much like those in the *Enclave a Paris Opera House* in ElseWorld. Massive candelabras forged of precious metals unknown to humans were ensconced between the boxes, bathing the floor where she now stood in an incandescent light, while at the same time washing the boxes in half shadow. She saw clandestine movement in some of them and briefly wondered what the occupants did up there in their sequestered quarters.

"Come." Sevin took her arm and they began to walk the perimeter of the room. He was silent, allowing her to absorb the sights at her own pace. Guards in severe, tailored black studiously ignored them as they passed. They were stationed in unobtrusive locations, their sharp eyes making sure all ran smoothly.

The expansive room was mildly chaotic and in its center, a carousel turned with mesmerizing slowness. Wildly painted and lacquered dragons, unicorns, and other fantastic creatures pumped up and down, their backs eerily bare of passengers for the moment.

On short pedestals set here and there around the room, life-size erotic statues stood, some fully nude and others partially so. She assumed they were stone, until they all suddenly moved on cue, switching positions to the strains of the soft music that emanated from an indeterminate location. The partners of some now paired themselves with new partners, while others posed alone. They were alive, she realized, and had only been painted to give the illusion that they were sculpted of marble. Their poses were overtly sensual, meant to titillate. A woman's head was thrown back in ecstasy as her lover's lips pressed themselves to her breast. A man caressed the face of a woman who kneeled at his feet, her hands cupping his genitals, her adoring face upturned to his. Two women embraced, their bellies pressed together and their hands linked at each other's back.

She blushed and felt Sevin's amusement. "As it turns out, you are, in fact, quite shockable, aren't you?" he teased.

"I didn't promise otherwise, if you'll recall," she said, smiling faintly in return. And she *was* shocked, but the salon's air of freedom excited her as well. Here, fantasies could blossom and flower, unfettered by shame. Anything seemed possible, and acceptable.

"Are you certain you want to stay?"

Eva nodded. Not only because of her search for Russo, but because this place fascinated her. ElseWorld species of all kinds milled about, some in translucent veils. Others were in costume or in street clothes, or even half naked. It was hard to be circumspect when she wanted to stare. "Who are all these creatures?" she asked, as they continued on their stroll.

"A broad spectrum culled from the ElseWorld population of Rome and beyond," Sevin readily informed her. "The salon boasts over five hundred members from all over Europe."

Her eyes widened.

He chuckled. "Not all here at once."

Two well-dressed gentlemen sauntered past, eyeing her, and Eva edged closer to her escort, uncertain of what they might want. Sevin put a hand at her back. He and the men exchanged potent glances, seeming to recognize something about her that she didn't yet understand. Her gaze found the floor, and she suddenly noticed that it became glass in places. Below the glass was a continuous, lighted pool in which mermen swam. It seemed she'd tarried too long in one place, for several of them had gathered to stare upward, their vantage point allowing them a clear view of what lay under her skirts. With a little yelp, she moved aside to an opaque piece of flooring.

Sevin laughed, displaying white teeth. Several females looked in their direction, drawn to the sound and to his dark good looks. The mermen winked at her irreverently, and with an iridescent flash of their tails, swam away.

From the corner of her eye, Eva saw an expanse of black and turned to see the trio of hooded gentlemen she and Pinot had trailed here. One held aside yet another curtain that hung in a doorway, and they all went inside.

"Anything attempted without a partner's full consent is forbidden here," Sevin was saying. "Other activities a partner might consent to are off-limits as well. There are some things I haven't the stomach for, and since it's my establishment, I set the rules."

A woman came up to Sevin then, her arms sliding familiarly around his middle. She rose on tiptoe and whispered something in his ear that caused him to glance upward, toward the largest of the opera boxes. It was covered with smoked glass that made it impossible to see inside it.

Taking advantage of his distraction, Eva slipped away, intent on following her quarry.

"I'm not interested in force," Dane stated unequivocally, as he and Bastian observed the scene unfolding below. From the secluded balcony above, they had watched as Eva and Sevin entered the salon a few moments earlier.

Having tracked Eva and her pixie here by means of the pixie's scent, Dane had come upstairs to the balcony knowing it would provide an overview of the salon, making it easy to locate her. The smoked glass surrounding their box was transparent from their side but impenetrable from the floor below. The enclosure also served as Sevin's luxurious office, but Dane had found only one of his brothers here.

"She's already offered you a liaison," Bastian replied firmly.

"With conditions."

As Eva's eyes lingered on one of the living tableaus of statuary, Bastian sent him a significant look. It was a foursome she admired, three men gathered around a single female, all standing frozen in place. Two males were at the female's back, one with his hands covering her eyes, the second with his fingers trailing the crease in her buttocks. A third man faced her, wrapping her hands around his cock. "It's easy to see what draws her interest. Domination. Multiple partners. Give her what she wants. Sevin and I will easily oblige if you require us."

The thought of dominating and controlling Eva appealed, and if he were honest with himself, the notion of sharing her under certain circumstances did as well, but he would not be so easily manipulated. "Your habit of issuing orders grows tiresome. I've managed on my own all these years without your help."

"Giving orders is a big brother's *raison d'être*," Bastian said with an amused quirk of one brow. "And I'm proud of the man you've become. Others might have been crushed by what you've been through."

The two didn't look at one another as he spoke, but Dane was moved by his brother's words. "Well?" Bastian prodded. "You have only to join us here when Dante comes and we'll help you question him if you require us."

Dane angled his head toward the third occupant of the room lounging on the couch behind them, a tacit warning to Bastian to be careful in what he said regarding Dante. "So I'm to use Eva as a tool."

"Use her as you must for the good of our family. For the good of Luc. You'll give her a night of pleasure in return. Everyone wins."

Whatever had happened to Dane during that missing year had left him with an abhorrence of any sort of restraint and of any attempt to control him. Yet it had also engendered in him an appetite for a measure of control over his partners in carnal engagements. The very thought of dominating Eva's soft body with his, of having her willingly entrust herself entirely into his keeping in the name of pleasure, was a balm to his wounded soul.

Dane slanted a glance in his direction. "I'd forgotten how persuasive you could be."

"Cold logic," said Bastian. "It's what I'm good at."

As they watched, Sevin turned away from Eva for a moment when his assistant approached him. In a furtive move, Eva slipped away and then dashed inside one of the semi-private rooms.

"What the fuck?" Dane said in alarm. The words had hardly left his lips and already he was through the door and taking the stairs downward three at a time.

Bastian remained in the office, watching.

"Cold logic is my very favorite thing," teased a feminine voice from the couch behind him. "Perhaps I could warm it for you?"

Though he didn't reply, Michaela rose and came to stand before him, her slightly rounded belly bumping his hard one. "Shall I stay?"

"Your choice."

"Then I choose to stay." Her hand shaped his prick through his trousers.

"Why?" he asked gruffly, covering her hand with his.

"My reasons are my own," she told him with a demure smile. With sure, skilled fingers, she unfastened his trousers. His phallus jutted free from them, vein-roped, ruddy, and almost frightening in its size and power. She took it between her palms, and her eyes slanted upward to meet his. "Not so cold after all," she teased gently.

He grunted, his eyes glued to her face, wondering why he could never read her expressions so well as he could those of others. Wondering why he cared. Her hands stroked downward on his shaft as she sank to her knees in a swish of silk. Her lips parted just enough to reveal the flat of her pink tongue, which then journeyed from his root upward along the underside of his length, tracing the vein that would soon carry his cum from his balls and into her. Too soon, if she kept this up.

"Your lips are magic," he murmured, petting her hair. It was a fact. Only one in five hundred thousand ElseWorld females were gifted with such a mouth. The mere touch of her lips or tongue on the flesh could make a man—or a woman—come in an instant. She'd done it to him the first time they'd met. Before he'd known what she was. But he'd since raised his guard.

When her talent had first revealed itself in her at a young age, she'd been sold by her parents into the *Academie du Grand Horizontales*, where she'd studied the Arts of Companionship. Bastian knew little else of her past, except that somehow she'd wound up here, working in the salon. And that she'd had the misfortune to find herself attracted to him.

She resided here he knew, but he'd already decided he would

take her into his home on Esquiline while she recuperated from her inevitable miscarriage. He did care for her in his own way. His brothers thought him incapable of love, but he only shunned entanglements, for he was interested in his work and disinterested in fidelity. And he wouldn't apologize for that. He had scrupulously informed Michaela and his previous partners of this fact well in advance of entering into relationships with them. His passions burned highest for the mysteries in the Forum, and he wouldn't apologize for that either.

The point of her tongue rubbed at the sensitive groove on the underside of his crown, then swept up to press at his cock-slit. Gritting his teeth against the swift rise of lust, he looked away from her and through the window. Belowstairs, Dane entered the salon, spoke to Sevin, and then passed through the same curtained entrance that had earlier admitted Eva.

Obviously considering the matter well in hand, Sevin went off to take care of some problem his employee had brought to him. His brother relished the success of his salon, but the furious pace of its expansion was fast reaching a crisis point.

Michaela's fists were stroking him now in long, slow, wet sweeps from root to crest, forcing pre-cum to well in his slit with each drag. Every time her fist met his plinth, those lips—those magic lips—met her fist from the opposite direction, and her mouth and tongue suckled the pearls of seed from him. Bastian sucked air between his teeth. Cum roiled in his balls, and hot, pagan lust boiled higher in him. His palms struck the smoked glass, making it shudder as he braced himself against the sudden and intense need to come.

Enough! A flash of anger filled him that she had gotten through his defenses so quickly and he glanced down to issue a cutting comment. She'd been watching him, but her eyes dropped under his. And somehow, he found himself instead murmuring, "You should find someone else. A man who can offer you what you deserve."

Her mouth slowly released him with a wet, lingering kiss that caused his prick to jerk and the long muscles in his thighs to twitch. "You're giving orders again," she whispered, "I distinctly heard your brother try to dissuade you from that."

"It's a habit."

She glanced at his cock pointedly, then caught his eye. "A *hard* one to break apparently."

His eyes darkened and his voice turned suggestive. "Let me show you exactly how hard." Long fingers tangled in her soft hair, holding her as his other hand brought his cock to her mouth. "Open for me." A primitive power surged in him as he watched those full red lips obey him. Take him. Stretch for him. He felt himself glide over her tongue. Felt her swallow his tip into her throat, watched her take all of him as few women could do.

He craved the strange connection he felt with her at times like these almost as much as the sex, but it made him wary, too. Her hands clenched his ass as if to keep him lodged inside her forever. But he contracted the muscles of thigh and hip, rocking himself out of her, then back into her liquid heat. Her lips bowed and pursed as he fucked her mouth. She moaned and he felt her anticipation for him rise. A warm shiver of exhilaration flooded him. "Gods, that's good, Michaela."

He felt his balls draw up tight, his cock swell. Her head went back against the wall and his cock followed. He braced his forearms above her, his head bent between them to watch her take him again and again. He wouldn't last much longer. A few moments more and he'd be issuing orders to her again, this time to swallow his seed. Yet with her mouth thus pleasantly occupied, she would not fault him for it.

When Sevin's attention left her moments earlier, Eva had taken advantage and slipped behind a row of columns, then ducked into the room where Signor Russo had gone earlier. Once inside, she was greeted with the slapping sound of leather.

She froze, waiting for her eyes to adjust to the dimness. Her first impression was that she'd entered an austere cloister. All was done in dark colors with fat, cream-colored candles clustered around the room casting a golden glow. Two dozen visitors sat upon rows of uncomfortable-looking stone benches, aligned in three semicircles facing the small stage. All eyes were riveted to the three Brethren who stood there, and her own followed suit.

Signor Russo had removed his hood but was otherwise still garbed in his long robes. However, his two companions had removed their hoods and cowls, leaving on only the skirts of their garments, and were familiarly kissing a woman, costumed in the habit of a Sister. Eva jerked as the slap of leather sounded again. Russo was holding a flogger! He brought its thongs down across the buttocks of one of the men, who flinched and then resumed his kissing even more fervently. As if he'd enjoyed the fall of the lash! Eva put a hand to her mouth to still her gasp. No, these men were most definitely not true Capuchins!

As she watched in consternation, the female slid lower, going down on all fours. The men sank to their knees. In an instant, the back hem of her habit was hiked up to reveal a white bottom, which jiggled between her black skirts and black stockings. Using her mouth and the availability of her rear entrance, she began to pleasure both men. Russo looked on and raised the lash, striking his own flesh over his shoulder. The leather straps sliced the fabric of his robe and the small audience clapped.

Eva took a step back, thumping into the wall. She'd never watched someone else copulate. And she couldn't just walk up to Russo and tap him on the shoulder with her questions. If he was her father, it was horribly inappropriate for her to see him like this. She fumbled along the wall for the curtain, intending to leave. A hand slipped around her upper arm and another covered her mouth, muffling her shriek as she tried to struggle away.

"Trawling for clients?" The question was a suggestive growl at her ear. Dane.

"Oh, it's you. Thank goodness," she whispered. Relieved, she ceased struggling and turned into him. His hand went low on her back, rubbing lightly. "What are you doing in here?"

"I followed one of those men on the stage from the gala," she said, her head buried in his chest. "A Signor Russo."

"Pursuing yet another octogenarian?" Mild humor laced his voice. "I begin to be truly concerned at your taste in partners."

"He's no more than forty-five," she grumbled. "The perfect age to possibly have sired me."

"Russo?" Above her head, she sensed Dane glance toward the stage. "I don't think so. He prefers men."

"What?" she sputtered. "But what about the . . . the Sister?"

"Also male."

She peeked at the stage, and her eyes widened at the goings-on there. She could see now that the person in the role of the Sister was, in fact, male. "But my mother's journal mentions him. She was a courtesan. A very comely one. Do you think he might have made an exception for her?"

He shrugged. "Anything is possible."

"What is his species? Can you tell?" she asked eagerly, causing his eyes to narrow.

"Your mother's book didn't lend any clues as to your father's identity or species?"

"I have numerous names, that's all. My olfactory abilities are next to nothing, but yours seem to be excellent. Can you—"

His nostrils flared almost imperceptibly. "He's fey."

"Oh," said Eva, her hopes wilting.

"You don't think your father could be fey?"

She was tempted to tell him the truth. He was a Tracker. With his nose, he could probably help her locate her father if she provided him with enough details. What could it hurt? He would never jump to the conclusion that she, a woman, might be satyr.

"Actually, my mother has hinted that he was satyr."

Dane shook his head at that. "I haven't scented any satyr here tonight, other than my brothers."

"You could help me find him, though, couldn't you, if he is somewhere in Rome?"

A potent pause, then, "Is that what you're looking for Eva? A father?"

"I told you I was."

"Why?" He lifted her chin on a finger, searching her eyes in the dim light.

She didn't quite know how to answer him. Why *was* it so important to her? "Everyone has a need to know their parents."

Something shifted in his eyes, in his touch. A new understanding. "Or maybe what you're truly seeking is not a father at all, but rather a strong male presence of another kind in your life." That hand at her back was roving lower now, still rubbing in slow circles, tantalizingly close to her rear. It was making it difficult to think about anything else. "I watched you from the balcony before I came down here," he continued. "I saw what interested you. Domination. Multiple partners."

His words were soft but struck her like staccato bullets, and she stiffened, her eyes darting warily to his.

"You're ashamed," he murmured, gentle surprise coloring his features. "No, don't be. Shame is an emotion that serves no purpose in what's between us. We'll hurt only ourselves if we don't satisfy our passions. Do you wish to play daughter to my role as your strict father? I can do that. Want to play nun to my priest? Naughty schoolgirl to my schoolmaster? I can do those as well. Whatever you like." At last his hand rubbed over her buttock, squeezing and sending a hot thrill through her.

Shocked at herself for being titillated by his suggestions and wandering hands, she pushed him away intending to quit the room. But instead she found herself standing before him uncertainly and studying his face. She felt laid bare, her most secret desires exposed. It felt good and freeing and worrisome all at the same time. She had never allowed herself to so blatantly consider such notions, even in her own imagination.

"Don't be disgusting," she said faintly. Her cheeks flushed under his knowing gaze.

He reached out and tucked a wayward strand of hair behind her ear. "It's play, Eva. For pleasure. Simply fantasies played out between consenting adults. I trained as a Tracker, remember? We're taught how to tease, how to lure our suspects on, to know what will push them to the precipice of pleasure time and time again . . . until that pleasure becomes so acute that it is almost pain, and they willingly surrender what we want of them."

The suggestive scenario he painted opened up a Pandora's box of salacious fantasies in her mind. Fantasies she'd always kept carefully locked away from the light. Her heart ached with a tentative gladness, yet she was almost afraid to let it blossom. To believe that she wasn't alone in these desires that had always seemed too deviant to put into words, much less into action. Yet this man was telling her that her particular fleshly desires were acceptable, and more than that, he was offering to make them reality.

"Only think how empty you will feel if you leave me and this place," he went on. "Think of the pleasures you will miss. There's much more to be seen here, more to do. So stay, Eva. Stay with me."

12

Dane pulled her unresisting body against his, his hold undemanding for the moment, his hands slowly roaming her, gentling her. She couldn't miss the fact that he was hard and twitching to have her. If he didn't soon, he would explode. Yet at the same time, he relished the waiting. Relished the sensations of his rushing blood, his prickling skin, his tumescing cock. The touches between them were a sweet torture, the brush of her skin like an aphrodisiac. It was all still new to him. So wondrous.

Through her skirt, he traced a finger up the divide in her buttocks and back again, slowly, almost to her cunt. She shivered and leaned into him. Their thighs aligned, and his cock grew fatter, longer, hungrier for her. Somewhere deep within him, Dante stirred, restless to take her. But he—Dane—now controlled when it would happen. Tonight, for the first time, their two male presences no longer chafed and repelled one another. Instead, there was a true mingling taking place between them, like tendrils of smoke interlacing steam. Yet the balance in their relationship had irrevocably shifted. Now it was Dane who was in command.

Because of Eva.

Their mutual craving for her had blended them into this great tangled confusion of ferocious need. And Dane would use that need to his advantage tonight. Though Eva didn't know it, she was to be the instrument that would allow him to interrogate his latest subject, Dante.

He would take things slowly, drawing out the pleasure and tempting all those within their unusual ménage—Dante and Eva and himself. He would lure Dante until he grew desperate to have her. And still he would deprive him. Would not give him release until he supplied much-needed answers about Dane's past. About what had happened that long ago night and during that lost year.

And this was all to be done for Luc's sake.

But Dane would take this ride along with Dante with reluctance, for he was already randy to pin Eva to the nearest wall with his prick. But so it must be. He would endure, and he would make it good for Eva. For all three of them in the end.

He glanced over her head and saw that a third of the audience had joined the cast onstage. The orgiastic frenzy now under way was unlikely to please her sensibilities when she noticed. Wrapping an arm around her, he took her outside and steered her in a direction away from the salon door, resuming the tour her precipitous flight had interrupted with Sevin.

"As I've told you, my suggestion of a liaison between us extends only to Moonful," she was saying in that dubious, prim voice that only made him want her even more. "Reserved for nights when our human spouses cannot do for us."

"ElseWorld demands that I marry a human," he argued complacently, secure in the belief he would convince her, because inside, she wanted what he did. "A marriage for the making of children. The keeping of property. The vows I'll take are necessarily false. I'll keep up the pretense, but nothing more."

"That's a difference between us, then," she said in quiet

earnest. "I'll only break my vows to my husband during Moonful out of necessity, when my blood calls me to abandon him for a male of our own world."

She was foolish to think she could compartmentalize her passion in that way, but now wasn't the time to quibble. He turned her toward him, hands on her shoulders. "Yet tonight no impediments stand in our way. No wives. No husbands."

Around them a sensual kaleidoscope whirled, but for the moment, neither noticed. She looked up at him, searching his face, hope lighting her own. "True."

"Tonight there is only us. In this place. A fitting location for an exploration of what our liaison will entail. A haven in which to enjoy a taste of one another before we enjoy the full banquet at Moonful." His hands slipped down her upper arms and linked at her back. Hers rose to his chest.

Then her breasts lifted on a fortifying breath as she seemed to reach a decision. "Very well. How shall we begin?" she asked shyly, and he smiled, more relieved than he cared to admit to himself.

"What would bring you the most pleasure?"

"I'm not sure." She glanced around, appearing to suddenly recollect their surroundings. "I don't have a broad knowledge of carnal matters."

His eyes traced down her sternum, traveled the line of fastenings between those luscious breasts of hers. "You'd been mated before our afternoon together."

She nodded, looking suddenly uncomfortable. "For reasons I cannot tell you, in those prior situations it was necessary that I give direction to my partner and assume all control. It's not what I wanted. I-I longed for the opposite situation. I still do."

His curiosity leapt at this mystery, but his cock leapt as well. His hold tightened on her. Eva was his, but he sensed she wanted to push the boundaries of what was comfortable for her, and that she wanted him to guide her in this. It was what he wanted as well. Over her head, his glance shot to the smoked glass veneer of Sevin's office, sensing that both of his brothers were now behind it, watching. He would take her there later, but not until Dante and he and she were so rabid to have one another that they couldn't wait another moment. He would give her pleasure there, but he would use her to pry secrets from Dante as well.

With a hand at her back, he nudged her and they began to walk again, side by side. He felt the heat of glances around them from some in the salon. There were those here who admired her and envied him, and wished to join them.

Dane was picking up where Sevin had left off, Eva realized, offering her a tour and a chance to consider the exotic possibilities presented on every side. Her glance happened upon a woman escorted by two gentlemen, each with a hand at her waist. She caught Eva's eye and winked as the trio slipped through a door and closed it firmly behind them. Eva frowned after them, strangely anxious to know what they would do so secretively.

Her eyes flicked along the wall and saw it was perforated with more such doors at irregular intervals signifying that smaller and larger rooms lay behind them. And sometimes instead of a door, only a velvet or brocade curtain filled one of the entrances.

"Everyone here chooses whether to be private, semi-private, or on public view," Dane told her, noting her interest. "While a shut door is not to be opened, a curtain is an invitation to enter a chamber and observe in a semi-private environment, such as with Russo and his companions. Still others choose to put themselves on public display." He gestured to encompass the main room. "Their presence here in the central area is an invitation to watch. And if one is specifically invited, to join in."

Eva's gaze followed his hand and she gasped. Only a dozen feet away there was a massive, semicircular liquor bar of polished mahogany and brass, around which stood four females and one male in various stages of undress. None of their faces was visible, for their backsides were toward the room and their torsos bent forward at the waist so they half-reclined facedown on the smooth surface of the bar. Libations were being bought and sold in the expanses of space between these living, breathing decorations, and the patrons largely ignored their presence except for slipping them the occasional fondle. Each of the five seemed to be wearing bracelets. No, they were ropes!

"Are they manacled?" she asked, breathless.

"Willingly," Dane noted. Lending tacit approval to her voyeuristic impulse, he leaned back against a tall, thick column and took her back against him, wrapping his arms around her and letting her linger to watch. The warmth of his chest spread over her back, and his legs braced long and hard on either side of her.

Two of the women at the bar wore only their chemises, gartered stockings, and heeled slippers. The other two had kept their corsets as well, but none was fully dressed. The lone male among them wore only boots and trousers that sagged unbelted at his lean hips. Two burly men of indeterminate species tended the bar, and Eva gained the impression they also kept watch over those secured atop it.

As she observed, two gentlemen—both fully and well dressed—visited the bar to refresh their drinks. One palmed the buttock of a woman restrained there consideringly, as if judging the worth of a melon in a market. The men stood on either side of her for a moment, touching her lightly and discussing her merits. Then the man nodded to some suggestion his companion made and dropped something small into a cup beside her head on the bar. As his friend looked on, he then lifted the back of her chemise and opened the front of his trousers. She wasn't wearing pantalets and he easily thrust himself into her feminine slit. The woman's hands fisted and she jerked, her head rearing up.

Eva gasped and put a hand to her own belly, as the muscles

high between her legs leapt in an empathetic response so strong it was almost as if the man had entered her instead. She blushed, realizing Dane must have noticed her reaction.

But unable to tear her gaze away, she watched on as the man grasped the brass rail on either side of the woman for leverage and began his mating in earnest, slamming in and out of her. He didn't touch her with any other part of himself, keeping their contact purely libidinous. And still his friend looked on, casually sipping at his drink. A few thrusts later, the man pulled out and left her. He hadn't finished. His member was still red and swollen when he lowered her chemise and left her for the female stationed next to her. Another coin went into another cup. Another chemise was lifted.

Still, Eva's gaze remained on the first woman, whose longing for fulfillment was a tangible thing, even from a distance. Her hands flexed on the ropes that held her wrists and Eva's fists clenched in compassion. "It seems an intrusion to watch her," she whispered.

"They're here because they want others to watch," Dane said, and a note in his voice told her he'd been affected by the scene as well. "The second man who only observes is the first woman's partner. He will continue to return to her throughout the night, bringing others. A nominal price has been set for her favors. When she has earned enough coin in her cup, the game is over and they'll find their release together. It will be all the more intensely satisfying for the waiting."

Another man came now, visiting the woman under her partner's watchful eye. A coin went into her cup, but then this customer opened his trousers and slipped on a French letter before penetrating her. Eva sent Dane a questioning glance over her shoulder.

"You're wondering why the letter, since Elses are unable to communicate disease," he said. "Some men simply enjoy withholding something of themselves as part of their play."

"Play?"

"Sex play."

She rolled the phrase in her mind, considering its possible meanings. "It sounds so intriguing, so freeing." She sighed wistfully. "But a lifetime of indoctrination is not easily disposed of in one evening."

"Your first effort need only be a speaking of the truth. Tell me what you want. Break the chains. Release yourself from the shame others would use to tether your desires."

At his words, Eva felt a recklessness surge up in her. Her hands went low on either side of her to rest on the fronts of his thighs. Under her palms, his long muscles turned to rock and she felt his heart pound at her back.

"Yes," she admitted softly. "I do want those things you mentioned before, and more." It was difficult for her to say the words, but her deep yearning forced them from her. "I long to be with a man who will manage carnal matters between us. Who knows what I want without my asking."

"In that last requirement, you'll chance getting a man who takes what *he* wants from you, rather than giving you what you want. No man is omniscient. Let tonight be a beginning between us. We'll explore what you want, what you like. And I'll give you an understanding of what I want in return."

She nodded, her throat tight with excitement. "What I want . . ." Her hands moved higher behind her and between them, coddling his cock. It reared up, forcing itself into her caress. His jaw nuzzled her temple, his voice a warning growl, "Eva . . ." With one palm half atop the other, she stroked him. He was so long, so hard, so hot.

He groaned and reached around to cup the lush weight of her breasts, massaging and finding her tightened nipples through the fabric of her bodice with the rub of his thumbs. Right there in the middle of a room full of strangers.

"You're mine now." It was a rasping, masculine demand against her neck. "Say it."

"I'm yours." For tonight. She lolled against him, enjoying his hands on her and hers on him. His thumbs and fingers pinched her nipples into hard beads, shooting sensation right to her clit.

"Do you see those men?" His lips brushed her ear. "The ones watching you?"

She forced her lashes to lift and looked ahead to see three tall, wide-shouldered, well-dressed gentlemen some distance away. Their eyes were hot and roving her with blatant admiration. Dane's hand flattened on the vulnerable expanse of flesh above her bodice and dipped inside the fabric to claim her breast. Like hungry magnets, three pairs of eyes riveted on that hand.

"They know I have you." Behind her his mouth dusted her nape. "That you are unobtainable. Yet still they can't help themselves and they devour you with their eyes."

Under her dress, her breasts swelled and her nipples became highly sensitized to the scratch of her prim cotton chemise and his masculine touch. The restraint of the garments themselves— sensible items of clothing she'd donned many times without thought—now seemed suddenly and strangely erotic.

"Show yourself to them," Dane ordered calmly.

"What?" Her hands went up to cover his at her bosom.

"Lower the front of your bodice. Slowly, provocatively. Show them what I have. What they desire."

The very idea shocked her to her core. Yet her reaction to it shocked her even more so. A prickle of excitement zipped over her skin. This—this was what she wanted. A partner who was . . . creative . . . daring . . . in control. She felt safe with him, yet his suggestion felt risqué and salacious and wonderfully unsafe.

"Your body is beautiful. And none will remember you once we all leave here tonight. It's only for our mutual pleasure that we whet their appetites and offer them a glimpse."

He drew her fingers to trace along her neckline, rubbing the tips of them over the fastenings of her bodice. Of their own volition, her hands began to work at the hooks. Tension filled the men across the room, and she watched their eyes fix on her fingers at her bodice as she slowly, provocatively revealed the corset beneath.

Dane was an unyielding, rock-solid presence at her back, his support lending her security and strength. His hands swept over her ribs and waist and hips and belly and back again, painting her with desire. His head was bent over her, his cheek on her hair as he intently observed what she gingerly revealed. And he offered gentle encouragements, telling her how beautiful she was. How smooth her skin. How full her breasts. She reveled in his compliments and in the lustful gazes of strangers.

Long moments later, her bodice sagged open to her waist. And those hands of his took swift advantage, moving upward to widen the gap and plump the undersides of her breasts, forcing them high and accentuating her cleavage until her nipples peeked above her corset and chemise, standing rosy and pert. One of the men across the way threw back his drink and another gulped hard, shifting his weight.

"And now the rest," Dane instructed softly. Her obedient hands went more easily now to the top of her corset. With each hook she popped, the tension wound tighter in the men across the way. When she was done, bodice and corset were gaping, just wide enough to do more than hint at her curves.

One of the three men set his drink on the nearest surface with sufficient strength that she heard its slam. She straightened, suddenly unsure as he came toward them to stand only a yard away. Beyond him, his companions had moved together, discussing her *sotto voce*, as if she were a priceless bit of statuary on auction. Her eyes skipped around the room, and though she saw the occasional eye turned her way, for all intents and purposes, she, Dane, and this man were alone in their encounter.

"He won't touch you unless you invite him," Dane murmured at her ear. She looked at him then, over her shoulder, saw the avid light in his eye and knew this excited him as much as it did her. "Your choice. I'll be here," he told her, and linked his hands at her midriff. "You're safe."

Her teeth tugged at her lip and she glanced at the stranger, shy, but intrigued. Her nipples were tight with a sweet pain, and without thinking she soothed them with her fingertips and felt both men react. Her yearning to explore this opportunity they offered was so intense it was like a living thing inside her.

With shaking hands, she reached for the edges of corset chemise, and bodice, and peeled them back, exposing her breasts. Behind her, she sensed Dane watching the other man's interest keen further. "You may touch them," she offered softly.

The man stepped closer, so close she could feel his body's warmth, and she scarcely dared breathe. He smiled into her eyes. He was tall, almost as tall as Dane.

His gentleman's hands were smooth and warm and confident as they covered her breasts and rested there, unmoving. His gaze fell to them and he squeezed her gently, and again more firmly, and then again, flattening her nipples under his palms and dimpling her flesh with his long fingers. It was wonderfully strange, having two men hold her a willing captive between them in this way. It made her feel restless, eager for more.

After a long, ponderous moment, the man looked at Dane over her head. "Do you share?"

Eva trembled, her eyes going wide. She wasn't ready. And somehow Dane knew. She felt him shake his head and was relieved.

The stranger's lips curved regretfully. "You're a lucky man," he said. "Perhaps another time."

"Perhaps," Dane agreed.

Giving her breasts a last, lingering squeeze, the hands reluctantly drew away. The two men nodded civilly to one another; then the stranger rejoined his companions.

Eva swiveled in Dane's arms and his gaze immediately dropped to the rise and fall of her bosom. He swallowed visibly.

"Would you really have allowed him to join us?"

"As he said, perhaps another time. If you want it." His hands came, dark against the white of her breasts, and he held her as the stranger had, as if he enjoyed the memory of other masculine hands having held her thus. "It excited me to watch him desire you. To know you'd promised yourself to me, and that I could limit the favors you'd bestow on him. Or on another partner we chose, on another night." Two fingers dipped in her shadowed cleavage, tracing a curve as if he were fascinated with her shape and texture.

She smiled, glad that he enjoyed her body. Never had she dreamed she might find a man like this, one whose desires aligned so well with her own. Before tonight, she'd thought herself wayward, debauched even, because of the very hungers he so readily accepted and fostered in her.

"How lucky I am to have found you," she said. "A man so exactly what I wanted. So handsome, so passionate. So honest."

Dane froze. *Honest.* Her word bit at him. But he couldn't be completely honest with her. What would she think if he told her he was two men, not one? She'd summon the *polizia* and have him locked up. He almost wouldn't mind as long as they locked her in with him. But where would that leave Luc?

"Come," he muttered. She clutched her bodice together in one hand and let him lead her away.

"Where are we going?" she wanted to know.

"Upstairs to a private room, one exclusive to my brothers." When they came to a door marked PRIVATO, his face hardened briefly and shadows of regret crossed his features like storm clouds. "There's something I should tell you first—something about me you should know," he ground out. But his bleak tone frightened her and she put her hand over his mouth, shaking her head. Then she grabbed his hand and pulled him toward the door he'd sought and opened it herself, glad when he followed her inside.

Together, they hurried up the stairs. On the landing, they paused and he pushed her against the wall, kissing her deeply, as if he couldn't wait to have her. His hand went under her skirts and two fingers plunged inside her.

"Gods, you're so fucking wet," he groaned against her hair.

With a rustle of petticoats, she hooked a knee around him. "Now. Please."

His aura had been silver for most of their time together tonight, with only occasional flecks of gold. But now the gold was flaring higher as if fighting free of some invisible restraint. She could feel his desperation, but he grimly pulled away and rushed onward and upward, dragging her with him. Finally, they reached the haven he sought. He threw open another door with one hand, and together they stepped into the magic beyond.

In the soft glow of muted light, she gained a vague impression of sofas and cushions, exotic spices, erotic frescoes . . . and surreptitious movement! His two brothers were there, she realized, and their presence startled her into stillness. Each of them already embraced a woman. Sevin was lying atop his partner, moving on her, one of his legs between hers and his trousers lowered only enough to expose the dimples on either side of his lower spine. Bastian was nude—what she could see of him—and lying on a dais among velvet cushions like some sort of exalted sultan, his powerful hands roaming the scantily clad woman he held. Both men had glanced up at their entrance. Something significant passed between the three brothers, but then each went back to what they'd been doing.

Eva looked at Dane, finding his gaze fixed on her like a predator's on prey. "This is how things will be for us at Moonful," he told her. "Does it bother you that they're here?"

She shook her head, so eager to have him now that he could have brought hoards of others—an entire audience—into the room and she wouldn't have objected.

He grabbed and kissed her then, deeply and with raw, pent-up passion that drove every thought from her head. And then her back was on pillows and he was forcing her wrists high over her head, his chin nudging her bodice lower, a hand ripping at fabric, and his mouth falling hot on her breast.

Cool air found her legs as he pulled off her skirt and pantalets. A hand shoved under her rear, lifting her. In one long stroke he thrust into her core and she cried out in relief. And then he was slamming into her over and over with a savage hunger he did nothing to disguise. She arched under him and then all too quickly was tumbling into orgasm, tripping and fizzing into splendor, her tissues rhythmically milking at him like slippery fists. Her breaths came in pants as she bowed with each thrilling wave of fierce pleasure. And he rode her all the way, giving her what she needed, plunging into her slick response in a measured rhythm that filled her in just . . . the . . . right . . . *ahh!*

It was perfect. So perfect that her orgasm had nearly subsided before she realized that he had not come with her. She looked up at him, disappointed, for she remembered the heady feel of his spurting seed and wanted it again. His jaw was clenched and she stroked its sandpapery texture.

"What do you need?" she whispered.

His eyes searched hers for a long moment. When his voice came, it was low and dark. "I need you to do something for me."

She felt the sudden arrested attention of his brothers, but she was beyond caring. "Yes, anything," she pledged, his undying slave now, wanting him to find the same release he'd given her.

He stood and lifted her to her feet, his body between her and his brothers. She wove her fingers in his hair and pulled his head away, her gaze questioning.

"I need you to put your mouth on me," he rasped. "To suckle me for however long it takes."

Grasping his meaning, her eyes dipped between them. His cock angled high, its thick stalk corded with veins and its crown flushed sanguine with need. She licked her lips, suddenly thirsting for a taste of this new pleasure. Her knees folded, but he caught her as she began to sink. "Don't stop, no matter what happens," he urged. "Not until I finish."

Her eyes widened, but she nodded. "I won't." It was a whisper, a promise.

And then his hands were on her shoulders, pushing her to her knees. His legs adjusted wider for her and a broad hand threaded her hair, holding her, as his other led his cock to her mouth.

"Take me." His voice was rough and fierce, vibrating with hunger.

She wet her lips again and parted them, let his smooth strength stretch her kiss wide. She tasted herself on him and his own salty tang. Her hands rose to the shallows on either side of his hips, feeling his muscles tense as he guided himself deeper. He leaned into her and the coarser texture of his shaft glided along her tongue.

When his crown nudged the back of her throat, she breathed through her nose and forced her muscles to go lax, allowing him deeper.

Both hands held her, fingers tense and tangled in her hair, his head bent to watch her take him. "That's it. Relax for me," he urged in a tight, velvet voice. "I have more to give."

And then he was in and then quickly pulling back, slick and slippery now. And then filling her again. And suctioning away, working in her mouth, back and forth in long, sleek strokes, in time to the rhythmic flex of his hips.

His pace soon began to quicken, his thrusts coming shorter and faster, his body straining. Anticipation filled her as she imagined him spilling his seed in her mouth in warm, wonderful spurts.

Gods! It was like burying himself in a fistful of warm honey, over and over. Dane had never been so desperate to shoot off. He felt Dante sharing the moment, but it wasn't like before. This time, they weren't vying for control. Rather, it was as if two men held the reins of a runaway carriage. Both enjoying the ride together. He'd forced Dante into the background, but now Dante's hunger was his hunger, and it was pushing past his control.

Do you want to come? Dane demanded silently.

Fuck, yes! What do you think? You want it, too, you bastard, came the reply that only he could hear.

Then tell me what I want to know. What you know about Luc. Where is he? What happened to us thirteen years ago?

I don't know!

Liar.

Grimly, Dane pulled out of her, his cock still fat and hungry, and glistening from her mouth. Leaving her just then seemed the hardest thing he had ever done in his life.

Dante shrieked inside him, calling him every foul name he knew.

Tell me what I want to know and I'll let you have her mouth again, Dane promised, praying Dante would agree and end their mutual misery.

"Dane?" It was Eva. Her voice seemed to come from miles away.

The memories you seek. They aren't mine. They are yours to unlock.

"Is that some sort of riddle?" Dane said, unaware he was speaking aloud now. "Are you saying you don't know what happened to us years ago?"

That's right. I don't keep that secret.

"Then who the hell does?"

"Dane, what's wrong? Who are you speaking to?" It was Eva again. She had stood and pulled on her skirt and was clutching her gaping bodice together in a belated attempt at modesty. The prim schoolmarm had returned. And she was afraid.

With a part of his mind, Dane noted Sevin ushering the other two women out of the room, heard the soft whoosh of the door closing after them. Noted Bastian go to Eva and put a hand at her back, soothing her. She struggled briefly, but he curved his palm at her cheek and bent his head to hers, murmuring, casting a Calm over her.

But by then, Dane's thoughts had turned inward. Caught up in his private nightmare, he left his brother to manage her. "Answer me," he demanded of Dante. "Who knows these things if you don't?"

Daniel. The young one.

"Daniel?" Fingers of terror walked down his spine. There was someone else inside him? "Is he here now, with us?"

He's always here, just asleep. That's all I know.

"Is there anyone else? Anyone besides us and him."

No! Now let me come!

Sevin's hand came at his shoulder, jarring him back to reality. "Are you all right?"

Dane flicked a glance at Eva, who was leaning against Bastian. "Don't let her leave." He turned his back on them all and took himself in hand. In an efficient series of jerks, he spent himself. Dante cursed with relief and then was gone. Wearily, Dane went to the stack of linen toweling neatly folded beside the corner washstand and cleansed himself.

"Well? What did you find out?" Sevin demanded.

"Who the hell is Daniel?" Bastian gritted at the same time.

"Another personality apparently," said Dane. He went to Bastian and took Eva, and holding her against him, felt himself grounded again.

"What happened?" she asked woozily.

"You need to tell her," said Bastian. "Or let her go."

"More orders?" Dane grumbled.

"Tell me what?" Eva asked, pulling away. Averting her eyes, she fluttered a hand in their direction to indicate her discomfort with their nudity now that matters had gone serious. "And would you all please . . . ?" Dane watched her fasten her corset, hiding her breasts away, and it felt like a repudiation of what they'd shared. His eyes narrowed.

Sevin tossed Bastian's trousers to him and then revealed some of the truth. "My brothers and I were orphaned here when our parents died of the Sickness. Dane was lost shortly before then, at age twelve."

"Lost?" she echoed. Dane turned away, running a hand over his face, wishing she didn't have to hear this.

"Abducted and found again a year later," Bastian said, taking up the tale as he slid into his shirt. "We had—have—a fourth brother, Lucien, who was lost with him. He hasn't been seen since. And Dane has no memory of the year he lost. So now you know the part of the story that belongs to all of us, but any more is only his to tell." He nodded in Dane's direction.

Eva was closing her bodice now, almost dressed. And when she was all trussed up and respectable again, she would leave him. Perhaps forever, if he didn't explain. If he didn't at least try to make her understand the incredible truth.

"Dane, earlier, who were you speaking to?" she ventured softly. "Your aura changed then, from silver to gold and back again. It has happened before with you. As though you were two different people in one body."

"I am." His curt admission cracked in the room like quiet thunder, and then words were pouring out of him as if from a lanced wound. "Something happened to me while I went missing that year. Something unspeakable. The memories of it are locked inside the minds of . . . two . . . other personalities buried inside me. At times, they surface and take control of my speech and actions."

Eva came to him, her gaze a soft mix of horror and empathy. "That explains some things."

"I'm sure." He took a deep breath. "I couldn't get any answers from Dante, the one I know best. Until you came."

At that, the truth of her part in tonight seemed to dawn on her and her expression tightened. "You were using me to draw out his secrets." The brothers' stony silence damned them. Quickly, she found her slippers and tugged them on. "Then now that my usefulness has ended, I'll bid you good night."

But Bastian barred the door with a casual shift of his body. "You are more important to all this than you think," he told her. "We believe the secrets his mind holds could lead us to Luc. Dane's sanity could be at risk here, and Luc's very life. This brings urgency to our need to get answers, by any means necessary."

"Shut up, brother," said Dane, pushing past him. The last thing he wanted was for her to think him insane. "Come with me, Eva. I'll see you home."

She let him take her downstairs and outside into the cool night. "It seems like a year has passed since I went inside this place," she said, gazing up at the stars with a melancholy air.

"None of it matters," he said. "You won't remember tomorrow. I didn't invite you to."

"Oh." She sent him a sideways glance. "Does that mean you won't remember either?"

He shook his head. "The satyr are the only species who don't require a formal invitation. I'll remember."

"That's hardly fair." Though she was glad it meant *she* would remember as well. There were many parts of this night she would never, ever want to forget. In future lonelier times, she would reflect on them like cherished sepia photos of her all-too-brief salacious past.

But Dane only shrugged. "Sevin's salon. Sevin's rules." He whistled into the night and they heard the clop of hooves.

"Men," she grumbled. "It annoys me that you can make things happen with so little effort. Were I to whistle, I assure you no carriage would appear."

He smiled at her, masculine charm tilting at the corners of his lips. "Then it seems you must keep me around, if only for convenience sake."

She sighed. "Dane . . ."

"You were not just a tool. Not just a pleasant way to pass a night," he said, shoving his hands in his pockets. "I admit I was afraid to tell you the truth. Afraid you'd think I was a freak. You wouldn't be the first."

"You are not a freak," she said passionately. She had good reason to know how that label could hurt. Yes, she was angry that he'd kept secrets from her, yet wasn't she harboring secrets of her own? If she were brave enough to reveal hers, what would he do? Tell the Council? Or protect her instead, and jeopardize his own future and his family's? She wouldn't risk either consequence, and she wouldn't ask him to make such a painful choice.

The carriage drove up and she turned to him. "There is to be another gala tomorrow night," she offered solemnly. "In *Circo Massimo*, near the Forum. You'll come?"

He made a frustrated sound and stared off into the distance toward the eerie glow of the Forum lights. "My interest in finding a human wife wanes," he said, but then he looked at her again and nodded. "But I'll be there." When she moved to the carriage, he stepped closer. "One thing, Eva, before you go . . ."

And then, gently, he placed his palms over her eyes and spoke as if casting a spell. "I invite you." And then his hands were gone. "To remember."

Her heart melted at this gift, though he had no way of knowing his invitation had not been necessary.

"Thank you," she whispered. And then she planted a quick buss on his lips and stepped into the carriage, sitting back so he wouldn't see her face crumple with emotion. He'd had so much loss, so much pain in his life, so much uncertainty. Yet he had faced her bravely tonight and admitted the terrible truth of his past and present, and now had trusted her to safeguard what she'd learned. She put a hand to her tightened chest, feeling the awful knot of her own secrets lodged there unspoken, for she could not find the courage to be as honest in return.

"Tomorrow night, then." He smacked the side of the carriage and it lurched off.

She peeked at him from the blind, eyes clinging to his figure until he was swallowed by the night. "Yes," she whispered into her lonely carriage. "Tomorrow."

13

———————

"Carmen! Come in from the rain, *cara*. The night is atrocious." Serafina Patrizzi shut the door and clasped her longtime friend's impressive girth in a perfunctory hug. "You've come alone?" she enquired, ignoring the girl who trailed her friend.

"My Alfredo is in Venice on business," Carmen replied.

"It's just as well. Our men departed for the bowels of the earth an hour ago, and he would have been left behind. It's so good to see you. It's been too long."

"It's the cholera that keeps me away. The epidemic is driving all of my relatives from Naples and into my household here in Rome. My mother, my grandmother, my nine cousins, and on and on. Bah!"

"Goodness! How do you deal with so many?"

"It's a trial," said Carmen. "I tell you I scarcely have time to myself. I know I must look a bit haggard."

"Hardly."

The two women smiled at each other, enjoying their little joke. Both were uncommonly youthful for their ages. But they worked at maintaining their looks most diligently.

"And who is this?" Serafina asked, finally deigning to notice the young woman behind Carmen. She took the girl's chin between thumb and forefinger, tugging her face left and right. "Very nice."

The girl pulled away, a trifle suspicious.

"Her name is Nella. I met her only this afternoon when my carriage took a wrong turn and wound up on Esquiline." Carmen paused, shedding her wrap and brushing a few errant raindrops from her skirts. "She has freckles on her cheeks as you see. Except for that she's a darling girl."

"How old are you?" Serafina asked.

"Sixteen, signora."

"A lovely age!" Carmen declared. "But the unfortunate dear is unmarried and recently bore a stillborn babe, can you imagine? She has complained that her bosom is paining her, swollen as it is with a mother's milk, yet no child to take it from her."

Both women glanced at the girl's breasts, then exchanged significant looks. Nella folded her shabby shawl modestly over her bodice.

"Oh, don't be shy. It's just us ladies here," Serafina teased.

"I told her she will have the young men lining up to marry her if she just rids herself of those awful spots. I knew that she could benefit from our cosmetics, so I invited her," said Carmen. "I hope it's not an imposition?"

"No, indeed," said Serafina. Smiling at the girl, she took her work-roughened hand, patting it. "I myself once had a freckle. Right here." She touched a fingertip to her nose. "But within a few days after using our cream, it was gone. Poof!"

"I can't pay," the girl admitted, relaxing under Serafina's easy manner.

"No matter. Come along." Serafina took her arm, leading her into the house. "You'll help us with our work instead."

"Is that Carmen I hear?" called a voice from farther down the corridor they entered.

Turning inside a doorway, the two women joined four others in Serafina's tastefully decorated private salon. It had been done in the Tuscan style in ambers and rusts, with at least two dozen busts and paintings culled from the ruins of the Forum itself. Shelves built into one wall were neatly stacked with smooth jars, vials, and small boxes, all similarly labeled.

"Carmen. At last!"

Carmen opened her arms wide in boisterous greeting. "Anna! Leona! Magda! Cecile!" She kissed each in turn on both cheeks.

"Finally, we can begin," said Leona, as she began to fill six golden goblets from a bottle of wine. And then a seventh silver one filled from a different bottle.

"I can't help if I'm late," said Carmen as she settled herself in a chair. "But you'll forgive me when you see what I've brought. A young lady to help us with our good works. Step forward, Nella, and let everyone see you."

The girl lingered in the doorway, unsure.

"Nella has freckles she wishes to be rid of," Serafina confided to the others. "It is only left to us to determine which of our creams might be most effective for her." She gestured the girl closer. "Come, we won't bite. We need to see you to judge what will suit."

Hesitantly, Nella took a few steps into the room. Seeing the girl was eyeing the refreshments on the tea cart, Serafina urged her to try what she liked. "Here, you must have a cannoli, yes? And, Leona, give our guest a bit of wine."

At the offer, Nella's suspicions gave way to hunger. Looking like she'd died and gone to heaven, she gobbled the sweet and three more, then tossed the offering of wine down her throat as well. Her six hostesses sipped from their golden goblets, watching her.

"Is that the freckle cream?" the girl asked, nodding toward the jars on the shelves.

"Yes, but ladies never begin business with gentlemen watching. They prefer us to be decorative rather than industrious," Serafina instructed.

Nella wrinkled her nose in puzzlement.

Serafina set her drink aside and stood, and her companions followed suit. From a stack on one of the shelves, she handed the girl several pieces of velvet, each the size of a small tablecloth. "Here, you must help us, *cara*."

"Yes, while she still can," Carmen chuckled into her goblet. One of the others gave her an elbow in the rib, shushing her.

"Veil the men with these, there's a good girl," said Serafina. When Nella still looked confused, Serafina gestured toward a row of busts atop pedestals. "The marble heads over there." She demonstrated, draping a painting of Bacchus with another length of cloth. The other ladies each took up dark gauzy veils themselves, each covering several pieces of artwork.

"No, not that one dear. Only the men," Serafina cautioned when Nella went to drape a bust of Diana the Huntress.

"Why?"

"It's tradition," Carmen told her.

"When do I get the cream?" Nella persisted.

"Soon. But we have an order in which things must be done on these occasions," said Serafina, draping a bust of Cicero. "We have a new treatment for lengthening the eyelashes also. The maschera, also known as rimmel. Would you like that, dear? Longer lashes?"

"Do you think I need it, signora?" The girl raised a finger to brush her lashes, as if to test their thickness.

"It couldn't hurt, could it? Gentlemen admire such things."

Once every masculine bust and painting had been shrouded, Serafina announced, "Gather around, ladies."

Nella perched on the small couch then and allowed her skin to be treated.

"There. Just wait a bit and we'll wash it off when it's time," Serafina told her before turning to the other ladies. "Any other complaints?"

Carmen lifted her skirt. "I have a bothersome mole to be treated on my knee."

"That's a wart," Anna declared, peering at it.

"Mind your own business, *strega*." Carmen shoved her skirts lower.

Anna shrugged in the blithe Italian way. "If you don't wish to hear the truth, don't ask."

Conversation continued as an errant wrinkle was treated, a liver spot on the back of a hand, a blemish, Carmen's knee.

The creams were set aside a half hour later, and Serafina said, "There, that's done. On to paperwork and orders."

"I'm pleased to report that business is excellent, particularly in Paris, and income is up," said Magda.

"We'll need to obtain more raw materials. Coal dust, petroleum jelly, vinegar, apples, clay, glycerin, and of course, the olives most importantly," said Leona. The other ladies perked to attention as she turned to Serafina. "About the loss of your grove—"

Serafina stiffened. "What about it?"

"I had the news from my own son who was there at the card table that night," Leona informed her. "He claimed one of those Satyr lords won it from your boy."

"The olives cannot leave the family," Cecile said in distress. "What if we are found out!"

"Shush! Do calm down, Cecile. I'm taking care of it," Serafina said in irritation. "I plan to offer my daughter to Lord Satyr, as wife, in order to bring the land back into our fold."

"Alexa?" asked Leona.

"Do I have another daughter?"

"Does she agree?" asked Carmen.

"It was her suggestion," Serafina told them.

"Before they wed, we'll induct her into our group, of course," said Magda, flipping through her book. "When you have a date, let me know and I'll adjust our meeting calendar to allow for the ceremony."

Serafina nodded. "There is the small matter of my lack of husband to perform the rite with her."

"You really should get married again, *cara*. Isn't your bed cold?" Anna nagged.

"It's as warm as I wish it to be," Serafina replied briskly. She'd loved only once, and the object of her affections had not been her husband, but rather the inconstant Angelo.

"Well, then, who will volunteer their husband to stand in during the ceremony?" asked Carmen, glancing around their circle.

"That won't be necessary," said Serafina. "Alexa has a brother. He'll do as I tell him."

"I thought he was impotent," Cecile pointed out.

Several of her cohorts winced at her plain speaking, Serafina noted, but still listened avidly for her own reply. "Anna is treating him," she said. "We expect a good result in the near future." She hated the pitying looks she received. If only it had been Angelo who'd spawned her son. Then he surely would not have been impotent!

She glanced to the couch, hoping to divert attention from her family's ills. "Oh, look, Carmen's protégé has fallen asleep." Standing, she went to the girl and adjusted her head at a more comfortable angle, then wiped the cream from her face. "Good, the cream has done its work. See how pretty she is. A worthy gift for our goddess."

Then she turned back to the others as they all draped their hair with the ceremonial veils. "Light the flames, ladies. We begin."

14

Eva came awake to the sound of splashing water and conversation. Pinot was filling the coal box and water was running into the porcelain tub in the lavatory off her bedchamber in preparation for her bath. It was morning.

"What kind of woman stays out half the night with a man?" Odette muttered as she worked the pestle in the mortar on the bedside table, preparing Eva's morning powder.

"Humph!" said Pinot, heading for the door with his empty pail. "Any kind. Her man's handsome, old lady! More handsome than most. With a big one in his pants."

Eva smiled into her pillow.

Odette reached out to swat at him, but he was too fast for her and scampered into the hall. "What do you know about that?" she demanded.

"My eyes are just the right level for judging such things. I know what he's got. Our Eva's a lucky one to have caught his attention, that's for certain." Pinot raised and lowered his brows, then burst into laughter as he headed downstairs.

"He's right," said Eva, letting Odette know she was awake.

"It's the nature of the satyr to be carnal. Just as it is yours to be disapproving."

Sitting up in bed, she downed the potion Odette handed her, trying to ignore the woman's glower. She rocked her lower jaw side to side gently. It was sore, a subtle reminder that last night with Dane had not been a dream. She stood, her lips curving in a soft secret smile, remembering the best parts of her time with him. There had been plenty of those.

Odette's lips tightened as she waved her toward the bath. "What you got to smile about? You got no husband. You gonna be a whore now instead, huh? Just like your mother."

Eva stepped into the steaming water, sighing with pleasure as she folded herself obediently into the tub. "Umm, this feels nice," she said, studiously ignoring the woman's foul mood.

"Lie down with dogs, you gonna get fleas," Odette groused. "But we'll wash any fleas off you now, eh, and you forget about that man from last night. Think about securing a proposal from Signor Patrizzi."

Such a proposal was the last thing she wanted to think about, but Eva nodded and leaned forward. Odette began to soap her back, just as she had every morning since Eva was a girl. "I meant what I said before, Odette. I can't do . . . what I did last Moonful any longer."

"You not have a choice, *bebe*. You *maman*'s fault for mating herself to a satyr and getting you in her belly. But don't you worry, that Patrizzi gonna take care of you on such nights once you belong to him. Raise you arms now."

Obediently, Eva raised both arms and the cloth swished under them each in turn, over her breasts, and down her belly. "I am an adult now and must make my own decisions. I'm going to continue to see Dane," Eva announced baldly. It felt good to say it aloud. "Just a few visits with him every month, is that too much to ask?" she rushed on before Odette could object. "If I can't have him, I'll be reduced to visiting the *wall di fori*, hoping for another of my own species to come along at random. Would you prefer that?"

Odette smacked the rim of the tub with the flat of one hand. "You stop that dirty talk! Where you hear about that?"

Eva rolled her eyes. "I'm twenty-two—I hear things!" She wasn't about to mention she'd learned about it from Dane himself.

"You gonna throw all your promises to Fantine away? Forget why we come here?" Odette accused.

Eva sighed. "I haven't forgotten. I'll wed Patrizzi if he asks. If he doesn't, I'll marry another human in order to keep all of us safe. But I'll spend my Moonfuls with Dane, if he'll have me. And maybe a few other nights besides that."

"Foolish! Just like Fantine!" said Odette, fairly scrubbing Eva's skin raw as she launched into a rant.

"A human husband will not comprehend what I need at Moonful, don't you see?" Eva broke in.

Odette pursed her lips, obstinate. "You bespell him then, make him think he has you. This isn't a difficulty. You got other men to take care of you on such nights. Men with skin that shimmers, that you conjure with this," she tapped a finger at Eva's temple. "All right now. Up."

It was impossible to explain the subtleties of what she needed on Moonful nights, so Eva didn't try. She stood and let Odette pat her dry.

"You be careful! If they find out you satyr, they hunt you," Odette went on. "Bad ones out there. Girls go missing. I hear things at the market."

The weight of Odette's expectations and worries grew more oppressive as each day passed. Last night, Eva had tasted freedom with Dane. She wanted more of it. The need to break free from stale promises made in girlhood to two bitter, lonely women tore at her, but she only slipped into the dressing gown Odette held for her and went to the window. "Where are the girls?"

"At music lessons," said Odette.

Nodding, Eva sought an outlet for her frustrations, and when her gaze settle on Fantine's journal, she found one. The question of her origins still plagued her, and she would put her mind to further investigation. She went to her desk, penned a note, and handed it to Odette. "Have Pinot deliver this and tell him to await a reply."

When she saw the name on the letter, Odette grumbled something about a dog with a bone, but she did as Eva asked. And that very afternoon, having received a reply to her note, Eva arrived at the foot of Capitoline Hill at the northwest end of the Forum.

The second man on her mother's list awaited her there in the shade of the massive white marble arch of the ancient emperor, Septimius Severus. The Venetian painter Canaletto had depicted it in oils nearly one and a half centuries earlier when it was still half buried in sediment, before the excavations of the Forum had begun in earnest.

She circled the arch, wanting the light to throw itself across his face, not hers. Odette had accompanied her and now waited within view in a small patch of shade nearby.

"Signor Arturo?" Eva called out softly.

"*Si?*" The dapper, gray-haired gentleman turned her way. His eyes were green, like hers. And was his brow drawn in an arc similar to hers as well? Hope rose in her. Was he satyr? Was he her father? And if he were, would he admit to either?

"I've so wanted to meet you," she told him, her excitement mounting as she climbed closer.

"You're the one who sent the note?" He flicked an ash from his cigar and the gold ring on his smallest finger winked in the sunlight.

She nodded. "As I mentioned, I believe we have an acquaintance in common."

"Oh?"

"Fantine Delacorte." Eva held her breath, waiting, hoping.

His brows rose as recognition filled his face. "Now there is a name I haven't heard for far too long," he said slowly. She stepped into the light then and let his gaze sweep her. When he raised his eyes to her face, they filled with shock. His aura blanched a split second before his face did, the mind slower to catch up to the soul's recognition. He stepped closer. "Who are you?"

"Your daughter. And hers."

He chuckled and took a long drag from his cigar. "I hardly think so."

"What were you to my *maman*?"

"Her financier for a time. Her admirer. Never her lover, not for lack of trying on my part. I doted on her for almost a year and it came to nothing." A faraway look entered his eyes. He flicked another ash. "She had a way with her, your mother. You're beautiful. Like her."

Eva's fingers went to her hair. "She was blond . . ."

"And a notorious flirt. But your face, your shape—they're like hers. So, what is it you're after, signorina? Money? I've got plenty of that, for a pretty girl who's interested."

"Interested in what?" she asked blankly.

An unhealthy attraction flared in him, tingeing his aura with bilious colors. "In earning it on her back, in my bed."

She stiffened, repulsed. "You're old enough to be my father, monsieur!"

His green eyes narrowed against the tendril of smoke that curled from his cigar. "Thought that's what you came for," he mocked. "A father."

Eva gasped in affront. Turning on her heel, she scurried away fuming. His taunting laughter followed her. Well, that was another name she could knock off her list. What an awful man! Thank goodness he *wasn't* her father!

"Well?" asked Odette, when Eva joined her where she waited on the periphery of the ruins along Via Sacra.

Eva shook her head. "It wasn't him. He's odious. How could *Maman* have consorted with him, even in passing?"

Odette shrugged. "Fantine loved men. And they all treat her nice, even if she didn't let them in her bed. Kept us in style. While it lasted. What you gonna do now?"

"There's one final name to consider on my short list before I weigh the entire list again for possibilities I overlooked," said Eva. "Angelo Sontine. But my inquiries about him have netted nothing thus far."

"Best that way," Odette snapped. "No good can come of you looking."

"I disagree, I—" Eva stopped in surprise. Across the Via Sacra a distance away from them, Dane stood at the entrance to the Mamertine. Alexa and her mother were with him.

Odette grabbed her wrist. "You not going over there to him. I'll pitch a fit if you try."

"Of course not," said Eva, tugging away from her. "He's otherwise engaged, and it's time to collect the girls at music instruction. But I *will* see him tonight," she added pointedly. "There's to be another gathering, this one in *Circo Massimo*, if decent weather holds." They strolled on, and Eva wondered what in the world Alexa and her mother could be about, speaking to Dane. In the ancient Roman prison, of all places.

"Signor Satyr?"

Dane clenched the railing on the porch in front of old Mamertine Prison, taking deep draughts of air into his panicked lungs. He'd ventured down into the cells just now, and the tight, moldering quarters had made him drastically claustrophobic. He'd only managed it for a few minutes, but that had been more than enough.

He was in no mood for company, but Gaetano Patrizzi's mother and sister were bearing down on him, taking the stairs up to the porch. Serafina and Alexa. He'd met both the previous night at the gala. Eva had introduced them. What the devil were they doing here?

The prison was on Capitoline Hill adjacent the Forum, near where he'd been found garbed only in a loincloth and wandering that day a year after his abduction. He'd come here today in search of answers.

An isolated prison seemed the perfect location to have held Luc and him at one time, perhaps in some subterranean chamber. Constructed over two and a half centuries ago, the prison was part cistern, with a spring at the lowest level near the cells where prisoners in ancient times had been thrown, and strangled or starved to death. It was connected to the Cloaca Maxima, the first well-developed sewage system in history, according to Bastian. Long ago, government officials had surreptitiously flushed the bodies of dead prisoners through it into the Tiber River. Which he'd thought might explain how the fey were winding up in the river now.

Yet so far, nothing here seemed familiar to him and he'd found no evidence of any prisoners having recently been housed here. Nor had there been any anterooms off the main cells below, which might have held Luc and him all those years ago. Another dead end.

"May we have a private word with you?" asked Signora Patrizzi. Dane shrugged and then gestured them inside the main chamber to sit on a bench along the wall. There was no one else here at this hour, and the room was clammy and uncomfortable. It had a grisly history and was no place for two ladies to visit. But they'd come uninvited and he wasn't going to interrupt his investigation to bother moving with them to a more suitable location.

Serafina whisked dust off the bench with her handkerchief and then sat, motioning her daughter to do the same.

"Do sit," Serafina invited him.

He folded his arms, eschewing the bench opposite them. "What do you want?"

Something about the woman disturbed and choked him as the cells had done, making him long to return outside into the fresh air. Her son affected him in the same way, but not the daughter. Alexa. He remembered her from last night. She'd been livelier then, but her mother's presence today seemed to have a dampening effect on her charms.

Serafina removed her gloves and draped them artfully across her lap. "Very well. I'll go straight to the point, signor. I wish you to return to me the land you stole from my son at cards."

He'd expected as much. "I assume you refer to the grove and house your family stole from mine thirteen years ago?"

She shrugged. "I don't recall any objections from your parents at the time."

Anger flared in him. "Because they were dead." His parents had been brought down by the Sickness while he and Luc had been missing. He'd never seen them again after he'd been abducted. "My brothers and I were young then, without money or power. But I warn you that's no longer the case."

"This is a fruitless tangent," she said mildly. "The fact remains that I want the land. And my attorneys assure me I have good cause to sue for its return. My son was inebriated with liquor you provided that night at the card table. The game took place in an unnamed establishment owned by your brother, which strangely, no one can seem to locate. Coercion, etc., etc." She fluttered a hand.

"It's only five acres, overgrown with vines and weeds. You didn't tend it well over the years you've owned it. I wonder that you now claim it's so dear to you."

Her lips tightened. "Will you return the land or not?"

"Mother," Alexa murmured in soft censure, but they both ignored her.

"Not," he replied.

"A case between us could sit in the courts for a decade. My attorneys could arrange things so you don't have access to the land during that time."

"Why is it so important to you?" he asked again.

Serafina took up her gloves and slapped them into her opposite palm. "Because it belonged to my ancestors decades before your family came here. Your father stole it from mine in much the same way you've taken it from Gaetano."

"And centuries before any of that, *my* ancestors planted the olive trees there. Surely that lends my family the prior claim."

"Prove it," said Serafina, in the haughty tone of one who believed her superior social standing and wealth would assure her of victory in any argument.

Dane ran his fingers through his hair, fearing she was right. "Name your price and I'll pay it. And we'll forget the winning of it in a wager with your son."

Her eyes leapt as if this was an offer she'd hoped for all along. "Excellent, but it's not money I'm after. I happen to have a solution that might solve this to the benefit of everyone. May I put it to you?"

"If it involves divesting my family of the grove, save your breath."

She went on as if she hadn't heard. "I gather from the gossips that you are set on acquiring a wife?" She glanced at him enquiringly.

He kept silent, sensing a trap.

"And of course, you've met my Alexa?" she added pointedly.

Understanding dawned and he straightened, his eyes going to her daughter. She flushed under his notice. "You want these five acres so badly you're willing to sell your daughter for them? To a man you know nothing about?"

Serafina shrugged, her expression mild. "You and your

brothers have shown a decided knack for accumulating wealth and land." Her gaze swept him. "And you look like good breeding stock."

Alexa shot her a horrified look. "Mother, please!"

"For you or your daughter?" he said, goading her.

"You needn't be crass." Serafina stood and began strolling the circumference of the room, idly noting various details. She soon neared him, gazing into the hole in the floor that led to the tullanium, the deep cells where prisoners had once been kept.

"Interesting place, isn't it?" she offered softly for his ears only. "I can gather evidence that could land you in such a place."

Every muscle in Dane's body tensed, but she hadn't finished. "I can have the police visit you and your brothers in your precious grove one night under the full moon. Your behavior there might raise eyebrows," she went on. "It would be a shame to see men so full of vitality incarcerated, left to wither away."

Gods! She'd found them out!

"I wonder that you would wed your offspring to one you consider insane," he mocked, but inside his guts were roiling.

"We both know you're not insane, but I want that land," she persisted. To her daughter, she said, "Dear, please excuse yourself so that I may speak privately to Lord Satyr."

"Why?" Alexa asked, looking thoroughly confounded by the bits she'd overheard. "This involves me. Surely I should be here?"

"Step outside," Serafina insisted. "I'll join you in a moment."

With a sigh, the girl headed for the door, but Dane caught her arm on her way out. He'd smelled the faint scent of her attraction to him last night and again now. But still he asked, "You want this? A marriage to me?"

She looked up at him, her eyes shy but hungry. "I will bow to my mother's wishes." Then with a glimmer of the liveliness he recalled from his dance with her at the gala, she added, "And you are far preferable to her previous candidate for me I assure you."

"That's enough, Alexa," said Serafina. "Wait for me at the bottom of the steps."

"Alexa knows nothing of your world or your kind," she told him once her daughter had gone. "I suggest you keep it from her. She's never excelled at safeguarding secrets. So, do we have an agreement?"

Dane's thoughts whirled. This woman had the power to destroy his family. And to expose ElseWorld! But he despised being manipulated. "I could simply throttle you instead."

"I wouldn't advise it. There are others in my inner circle who know what I know about you," she threatened. "Come now, you want a wife. Why not have Alexa? You can see she's willing."

He knew precisely what was holding him back. The thought of a woman—any woman—in his arms or his bed other than Eva held no appeal. But he had to choose someone or give up any hope of remaining in this world or finding Luc. He heaved a frustrated sigh. "The grove stays in my family," he warned.

She nodded, but he didn't trust her and would have it in writing before any wedding took place. But for now, he only nodded his agreement. "And I'll want children of her."

Excitement lit Serafina's eyes, obviously pleased she'd won. "Will you wish to wed before the next full moon?"

He stepped closer, intimidating her with his size. "Tell me exactly what you know about us. And how you know it."

Her eyes flicked beyond him to ensure that her daughter was out of earshot. "I know enough. I was involved romantically with one of your kind many years ago," she admitted. "A satyr by the name of Angelo Sontine. A tall, strapping gentleman, much like you and your brothers. Do you know him?"

Dane shook his head.

She looked a little disappointed at that, but only slipped on her gloves. "I'll bid you good day, then. And I'll be in touch."

Her gaze was that of a woman in her forties, but her figure and face were those of a woman only a few years older than Eva or her own daughter. He frowned. "How old are you?"

She smiled, moving away. "I'm the mother of two grown children. You can't expect me to own my age, surely?"

Gaetano Patrizzi stood at the entrance to his bedchamber, glowering at the pair of women who approached him from the hallway.

"Gaetano! What a handsome boy you've become. And still not married?" The *strega* took his chin in her fingers. "When you going to make some babies for your mama, eh?" She gave him a hard little pinch as if he were an errant schoolboy.

"Do you think I wanted this situation for myself any more than you?" He pulled from her hold, annoyed.

Unfazed, *Strega* Anna patted his cheek with her smooth palm. Like most of his mother's friends, her skin was remarkably unlined for her age.

"You'll father children yet," Serafina declared as she and her friend barged past him into his room. "Who else to carry on my legacy but my only son? Still, time is passing, and I'm not getting any younger."

"Nor older," the *strega* quipped.

Both women broke into titters at their private jest.

"But now on to our patient." Anna gestured toward Gaetano's trousers. "Take them off, hurry up, and lie down. I have other patients to see."

Seething with resentment, Gaetano divested himself of his trousers and flung himself on his back upon his bed. The *strega* waddled closer and examined his limp phallus, tsking. She pulled out a jar full of a green substance. "Here, we'll try this today."

"Another potion?" Gaetano lay his forearm across his eyes, resigning himself to submitting to yet another humiliation from this woman. She began applying her green paste to his genitals with her fingers. "God, what a stench! What is that foul stuff? It smells like death." He covered his face with a pillow.

"That pillow brings up a matter I would discuss with you both," the *strega* announced, setting her jar aside. "We've been at this for years now. At this point, I'm ready to suggest something more drastic. What do you think about asphyxiation?"

Incredulous, Gaetano threw the pillow off to glare at her. "What?"

"Historically, it's a treatment some in my profession have prescribed for your condition," she went on, perfectly serious. "After all, male victims of public hangings have been observed to develop an erection, sometimes even ejaculating. Some take their death erection to the grave."

"Really?" Serafina asked, sounding fascinated.

"I won't submit to such a thing," Gaetano announced.

"I want grandchildren out of you," said Serafina. "If we exhaust all other measures, you'll do it."

The *strega* tried to reassure him. "It's only a little discomfort. And think of the reward if it works. Isn't there some lady you'd like to poke?"

A vision came to his mind unbidden, of him taking Eva to his bed and plowing her. Of having her honeyed slit yield to his cock, while gazing into those green eyes of hers.

The *strega* gasped. "Saints in heaven! The paste is having some effect!"

Following her gaze, Gaetano glanced down, hardly daring to believe his own eyes. His cock was tumescent. It bobbed, making an effort to stand.

The two women huddled, bending close to study it. "Is it enough?" Serafina asked anxiously. "Could he get it inside a woman like that?"

"It's a beginning," encouraged the *strega*. "Only a little stiffer and he would manage."

"Enough to give her his seed?"

"If not, he could take himself in hand and spill into my syringe. If he can make seed, I can insert it into his wife. And then"—she snapped her fingers—"all the grandbabies you want!"

"I don't have a wife," Gaetano interjected.

Serafina patted his arm, beaming at him. "Well, in view of this development, perhaps we should purchase more of this paste and then go about finding one for you. But we'll have to give the poor lady a clothespin for her nose with this stench." Both women laughed.

"It's not the paste," Gaetano told them, irritated.

They turned to stare at him.

"Of course it is," said the *strega*. "What else?"

"Then what is it?" his mother asked at the same time.

"A woman. A particular woman I was thinking of just then," he insisted. "Evangeline Delacorte."

His mother's face flushed. "You lie. You're attracted to her so you're trying to trick me into giving my approval."

"No!" He gestured to his distended prick. "You see this? It happened last night at the ball when I danced with her, and two times before that when in her company. Just now, when she came into my mind, it happened again. So now do you comprehend the reason for my interest in her?"

Serafina tapped the well-manicured fingernails of one hand on his bedside table, making an audible clicking sound. She glanced at her friend. "What's behind it, do you suppose? Why this French girl? Someone so unremarkable, so unsuitable."

"Does it matter? She's what I want," Gaetano interrupted. He fanned his nose. "Wash this damn stuff off, will you? It's on my hand now, too. God-awful stink."

The *strega* went for a basin. "Men often find a lowborn

woman stimulating," she threw over her shoulder in answer to Serafina.

"I am surprised, though," Serafina mused as the *strega* returned to wash him. "I always assumed it would take an Else-World female to stir him."

"Evangeline is of ElseWorld blood."

The women gaped at him in astonishment.

"She went to the *Salone di Passione* last night," Gaetano informed them. "Didn't leave until this morning."

His mother's eyes sharpened. "You went to her after I warned you not to? How far have things gone between you? Have you—?"

He looked away. "Nothing's happened. But I know she's one of them. And she's not fey. If I didn't know better, I'd say she was satyr herself."

Serafina's interest was truly caught. "Will she accept an offer from you?"

His gaze shot to her. "Of marriage? Last night you told me not to dare dance with her, now you're ready for me to announce nuptials?"

"Of course, what else? If she can get a rise out of you, you can whelp heirs on her. Every doctor we've seen has agreed that your seed isn't problematic, but rather your ability to deliver it between a woman's legs."

"What if she won't have him?" asked Anna.

"She'll have him," Serafina assured her. "Anyone can see what she's after. Her eyes light up at the thought of his social standing and his lira."

"Maybe it's me that puts the light in her eyes instead," said Gaetano.

"Maybe," his mother agreed doubtfully.

"What if she doesn't bear his offspring when all is said and done?" asked the *strega*, beginning to pack her little bag again.

Serafina shrugged. "What's another body in the Tiber? The

fish will make short work of her. Another tragic disappearance to puzzle the *Carabinieri*."

"And then we can always try things my way—" The *strega* made a wringing motion with her hands.

"I'll choke *you* if you try it," Gaetano warned her.

She just smiled, pinched his cheek again, and bussed a parting kiss on Serafina's. "*Ciao*. Let me know if you need me again."

15

The scene of the outdoor gala was brilliantly illuminated as Eva stepped from her carriage that night. Eagerness rose in her at the thought of seeing Dane again. Though they'd known each other less than a week, she felt more connected to him than anyone she'd ever met. She'd dressed in her best for him, in a gown of creamy taffeta. Odette had tucked pearls in her hair and supplied her with a surfeit of unwelcome advice regarding what she was to accomplish tonight. Securing a human fiancé being at the top of the list. However, Eva had decided to ignore her. She felt that she and Dane had come to an understanding at the close of last evening, and a fragile hope now blossomed in her that they might somehow make matters work between them.

Pinot jumped from his seat at the front of the equipage to hand her down and then drove off to an adjoining lot with the other conveyances, where he would spend the evening gossiping with the coachmen.

Tonight's event in *Circo Massimo* was meant to encourage interest in the ongoing digs in the neighboring Forum, and various statues had been temporarily relocated here. Carved of white marble, they lined the well-groomed lawn on either side of the *Circo* like ghostly soldiers.

In the middle of the lawn, gleaming candles bobbed like fairy lights in the hands of the guests. Decorative lanterns had been set out to mark the pathways. Situated in the valley between Aventine and Palatine hills, this oblong track where chariot races had once delighted ancient audiences was now filled with banquet tables and a large wooden platform for dancing.

The pinnacle of society were in evidence here, their purses fat. Guards policed the perimeter above the valley, ensuring that the guests and their jewels were safe from vagabonds who roamed the areas nearby. Torches lit the stairs, which had been built at intervals on the sloped sides of the *Circo* for the occasion. Along these same slopes, marble seats had once risen high for the crowds of ancient Romans who'd come here seeking entertainment.

"A bit of the goddess Luna for you, signorina, to light your way?" A candle was handed to Eva, representing the Roman goddess of the moon. Smiling, she accepted it from the attendant and went to take the arm of the escort who was charged with guiding guests down the steps so no one would take a tumble. A strong arm suddenly usurped the escort's, taking hers. She looked up, but her hopes that it might be Dane were quickly dashed.

"Good evening, Signor Patrizzi," she said, trying to hide her disappointment. Only a week ago, she would have been delighted that he had singled her out.

"Gaetano, please. We're friends now." He covered her hand on his sleeve with his own. "Very good friends, aren't we, Evangeline?" The determined look in his eye was worrisome. Was he in a mood for proposing? She wasn't ready. Not yet.

"Oh, look at the delicacies that have been laid out for us," she enthused when they reached the bottom of the stairs. Pointing toward the tables in unfeigned delight afforded her an excuse to move away from him.

Under a series of striped awnings, tables groaned with crostini, ravioli, cakes, cheeses, and every other sort of foodstuff. In the middle stood an enormous ancient fountain shaped to resemble the Roman god of the grape, Bacchus. Wine bubbled from a half-dozen spigots hidden within it. Much of the fruit on view was delicate and had been grown here in this world from ElseWorld seed. Tomatoes shaped like stars, grapes of unusual flavor. It seemed impossible that humans didn't notice the change in their produce and menu. But the differences had come on gradually, and the magic that draped all of Rome and Tuscany had fortunately lulled them into acceptance.

She sensed Gaetano's impatience but took her time examining the items on display, conversing with the cooks regarding the merits of each and greeting acquaintances as they passed. With furtive glances, she searched the distance for any sign of Dane, hoping he might rescue her from an imminent proposal. A perverse desire on her part, since she'd been wooing this very gentleman for weeks.

"Evangeline, I would speak with you on a particular matter," Gaetano began, in a pompous, rehearsed tone.

"Oh?" She sensed what was coming and her heart thudded with a peculiar desperation to stave it off. Silently, she lectured herself. She must let him propose, for the good of her girls, herself, Odette, and Pinot. She and Dane could still have one another occasionally. It had all been decided. So—

"Eva!"

She turned, vastly relieved to see Alexa waving and hurrying in their direction. "Look, there's your sister!"

"She can wait." Taking her arm in a proprietary manner, Gaetano tried to steer Eva away.

"Oh dear." Eva dropped her candle purposely and it winked out, allowing Alexa to catch up with them.

"Darling!" Alexa kissed her cheeks fondly when she reached her side. "Oh, have you lost your candle? Tano, why don't you go off and get her another? That will allow me time to tell her my news!"

Gaetano tried to protest, but Alexa waved him off. "Do run along, brother. You already know, and I want to tell Eva when it's just us."

With an abbreviated bow and a disgruntled sigh, Gaetano marched off on his mission.

"You'll never guess!" Alexa whispered, drawing her away from the tables.

"Then tell me," said Eva.

Alexa took both of her hands in her own, her eyes alight with bottled excitement. "I'm engaged!" she announced dramatically.

"What?"

"I'm engaged—to be married."

Eva squeezed her hands, completely taken by surprise. "But that's wonderful! How did it happen, and when? And why are we whispering about it?"

"Because Mother wishes to make a formal announcement in the papers before the news is spread widely. And perhaps because I'm afraid to shout it to the world lest I find out it's a dream. You're the first I've told."

"And your fiancé? Who is it?" Eva smiled, wondering which of Alexa's many admirers had finally won her. "Signor Fitzgerald?"

Alexa wrinkled her nose. "No! Not him. Do you think I would be this elated? It's your protégé, Lord Satyr," she announced, her eyes sparkling.

Blood fled Eva's face in a torrential rush, leaving her pale and momentarily speechless. Her vision swam with a prickle of spots, and a cold perspiration dusted her upper lip. Light-headed, she fanned herself in an effort to remain upright. "Dane?" she managed finally.

"Yes!" Alexa bounced to her toes, like Mimi when she was excited. "I must admit to you that my mother had a firm hand in things, but I owe you great thanks as well, as you are the one who introduced us at the gala."

No! She was to lose Dane so soon? And to her dearest friend? Please, no, let this be a mistake. How she wished she could escape instantly in a poof of magic like in one of Mimi's fairy stories. But she couldn't even manage a conventional departure, for her knees were shaking too badly.

Beside her, Alexa rushed on, so preoccupied that she was oblivious to Eva's distress. "You'll wonder where the ceremony is to be. And the details of my dress. I'm—"

"Is it a l-love match?" Eva interrupted weakly.

Alexa nodded. "On my side at least. I was drawn to him immediately. But in all honesty, I can't say that he has any great affection for me. I shall work on him, though. He must be enamored to some degree or he wouldn't have offered, no matter how my mother cajoled him, *si*?"

"But I thought you were so sure that a wedding night with him would frighten you out of your wits," Eva argued, desperate to turn this nightmare around. "What about that statue with the two—?"

"That was just silliness. The ancient Romans had all sorts of strange ideas—faeries and the like. Men can't alter their bodies to grow a second appendage." Alexa shot her a mischievous grin. "Although I wouldn't mind if it *were* true. As to our wedding night, I confess I'm almost looking forward to it."

Gaetano returned then, with a candle. And somehow Eva found herself setting it aside and whirling onto the platform of dancers in his arms without being quite aware of how she had gotten there.

"Finally, I have you to myself," her partner said in a satisfied voice.

"Umm-hmm." Leaving him to keep up the conversation, Eva let her mind race down a path she didn't want to follow. She would have to give Dane up! Her heart thumped with a dull, pounding grief. But she knew she must. For to take him as a lover—even only during Moonful—would be an unforgiveable betrayal to Alexa. The loss of him just when she'd come to care for him threatened to make her physically ill.

"Well, Evangeline? I'm asking you to marry me. To be my wife," said Gaetano.

She stared at him blankly. While she'd been daydreaming, he'd been proposing?

"It's what you want, isn't it?" he added. "I didn't mistake your interest?"

"You do me a great h-honor," she stammered. "But—can you allow me some time to consider your offer? It's so . . . unexpected."

"I'm disappointed," he said, a coolness seeping into his voice. "I'd hoped for a quick assent. But while you consider me, remind yourself of what it is that I offer you. Respectability. A fine family name and deep pockets. A secure future. I know these things must be important to you in view of your parentage."

"What?" She shivered, suddenly fearing that Odette's dire predictions regarding the exposure of her species might be coming to fruition. She tried to pull away, but he continued dancing, carrying her along with him and holding her even tighter. He was stronger than he looked.

"I know that your mother was a courtesan here in Rome, and that you were born in Paris. That you're a bastard." A life in Paris was a fiction she'd woven for Alexa, but he'd learned the rest on his own somehow.

"It doesn't matter to me," he continued with grating magnanimity. "I want you, Evangeline. Marry me."

"Your mother won't agree," she argued, weakening. She just wanted to leave. To go nurse her wounds in private.

"She will. She has." The music paused and they found themselves along the edge of the platform. He tugged her down the three steps to the shadowy lawn.

Why was she hesitating? She couldn't have Dane as her husband, even if she refused this man's offer. Dane belonged to Alexa now. When Eva next met him, having a fiancé of her own in place would serve as a convenient barrier between them.

Gaetano's hand curved at her neck and his fingers slipped under her hair. Her head fell back and she gazed up at him through her lashes, wishing herself anywhere but here. His eyes filled with heat and an arm locked her close. She felt suffocated. Felt hope shrivel. His mouth lowered. He was going to kiss her. Ugh. She closed her eyes.

Suddenly, it came to her that if she wed this man, she would often find herself in the company of his sister and her new husband. No, that would be too awful! She would have to find another suitor. Just as he made to kiss her, she opened her lips to refuse him.

"Patrizzi!" snapped a voice as dark as a thundercloud. Dane.

They jerked apart to see him standing a few feet away, Alexa's arm tucked through his. Eva's eyes locked on those entwined arms, and she felt a sinking in the pit of her stomach. She couldn't bear this. She had to get away before she broke apart in front of everyone. But before she could make her excuses, Gaetano slipped a hand around her waist as if to claim her.

Dane included them both in his black, condemning look. Eva felt a trifle guilty, as if he'd caught her betraying him. Nonsense! She was doing nothing of the sort. He was the one who had gotten himself betrothed!

Alexa clapped her hands in glee. "You've asked her, haven't you, Tano? Oh, Eva, we are to be sisters! I knew he was set to propose, but I couldn't let the news leak beforehand." She reached out to embrace her.

When she stepped closer, Dane did as well. His sleeve brushed Eva's bare arm. An innocent touch, but it sent a lick of fire through her. Her eyes burned with unshed tears.

"Oh, I know how you feel. It was the same when I found out I was to wed Lord Satyr," Alexa said when she drew back, completely misunderstanding the reason for her weepiness. "But stop, you'll make me cry as well and our faces will be spoiled."

"You interrupted us, dear sister," Gaetano chided. "I'd only just asked her."

All eyes went to Eva. "And I've given you my reply for now," she told him gently. She would refuse him, but not in so public a way.

A half hour later, Eva managed to find her way free of Gaetano. She escaped the festivities and was leaving the ruins without farewells. Tears that had simmered close to the surface since she'd first heard Alexa's news now splashed upon her cheeks. Oh, Gods—Dane was to be wed! She lifted her skirts, scurrying faster and keeping her head down so no one would see. She needed to find Pinot. To reach the carriage. To make her way home to sob the night away.

Along the outskirts of the *Circo*, a hand caught her waist and another covered her mouth. The hard strength of a man came at her back, and she struggled. "It's me," said Dane. She stilled cautiously and let him draw her farther away from the confusion and lights. Seconds later, they confronted one another in a secluded bosk beneath the shadows of umbrella trees at the *Circo*'s edge. The atmosphere was brisk with the coming of autumn, and redolent of cypress and their mutual, impossible hunger.

Eva drank in the sight of him. He was so handsome in dark eveningwear, looming tall and strong, his crisp shirt gleaming white in the dim light. Her heart squeezed, knowing he could not be hers again.

"You're not going to wed him," he announced, breaking the silence.

She sent him an affronted glare. "Yet you will marry Alexa?"

He sliced his hand in the air as if to cut that part of his life away from the life he wished to make with her. "She makes no difference to you and me."

"Your auras are incompatible. You should have consulted me before offering for her. Do you love her?" she asked, hardly daring to breathe as she awaited his answer.

He shifted impatiently. "What do you think?"

"I'm asking."

"Her mother knows about our world and has threatened to expose the news," he admitted.

"What?" Eva sputtered. "I can't believe it! Alexa could never keep such a secret to herself."

"I doubt she knows, but her mother claims others do. Don't worry, I'll ferret out their names and it will all be taken care of soon enough."

"But," she said in bewilderment. "Then why marry Alexa?"

"Because I want the grove, and her mother wants to fight me on it. You knew I would wed at some point. What does it matter to whom?"

"But you'll make her miserable."

He flashed a grim smile. "I assure you I will not."

Eva gasped, shrinking away. The image of him with Alexa. In *that* way. She couldn't bear it. She looked across the lawn, wanting to grab his hand and run from their obligations. But wherever they went, they'd be faced with them again. Some things could not be outrun.

"And what of you?" he demanded. "Is that why you agreed to wed her brother? In a fit of pique over my engagement?"

"Fit of pique?" she echoed in outrage.

"Choose someone else. I won't see you marry that ass." Dane folded his arms, insufferably confident in his ability to get his way. "Or better yet, let me find someone for you, as I suggested before."

"So you would dictate my choice of husband, but I—a counselor charged with finding you a wife—will have no say in your choice?"

"Gaetano Patrizzi is old enough to be your father."

"He's no more than thirty."

"He's forty, if he's a day." His expression went pitiless. "But how perfect that will be—the father you've always wanted. And him tied to his mother's apron strings. The three of you will make a fascinating triangle."

Eva made as if to slap him, realizing too late that he'd been goading her and hoping for such a reaction. He pulled her against him, his hands stroking down her back. Oh, Gods, it was heaven to lie against him, the swine.

"There, that's more like it," he murmured into her hair. "I thought I'd lost you."

He hadn't lost her, he'd pushed her away. "Alexa is my dear friend. I won't sleep with her husband."

"I'm not—"

"Or her fiancé," she said pointedly.

Dane stared at her in consternation. She recognized that look by now. Arrogant as always, he assumed that if he found just the right key, he could open her heart and mind to him again. But she would be strong.

"Our original intention to betray our marriage vows seemed far less objectionable when your wife was a nameless, formless specter. Now I can see that such an arrangement would never have suited." She sighed shakily. "It has only been days, but already I care for you too much."

"Then don't give up what we have."

As if it were so black and white! Eva looked him directly in the eye so he would see her determination. "I've had few enough friends in my life and won't throw one away. Let Alexa be the mother of your children. Something I can never be." Though she'd lied about having the Sickness, what she said was still true in a sense. The Council required unwed fertile females to register themselves as such and to breed with a succession of partners they selected. An intolerable prospect, and it also involved more tests and the risk of exposing what she was. "The Council—"

"Fuck the Council. I won't let them stand in our way."

She stepped back, bumping a table of clean linens behind her. No, they were the coats and cloaks of the guests, and had been stored by the servants here out of sight on a long table. Only then did she realize that servants had used this as a temporary staging area, for it was stacked with boxes along one side as well.

"Alexa stands in our way," she insisted. "And an entire country will be between us as soon as I get permission from the Council to relocate to Paris or Tuscany. I won't wed Gaetano, but I still intend to wed a human, one who can provide for my family."

Dane took her shoulders. "No. Eva, no. I'll worry about you if you're so far away. Worry the day will come when your husband will discover you're not human. Things could turn ugly between you. If you remain in Rome, at least I'll be near enough to help—"

"Human men are easily tricked. I'll bespell my husband when the full moon comes. He'll lie in his bed and dream of what we do together and never know any of it happened."

He gave her a small shake as if trying to instill sense in her.

"Even a weak man is physically stronger than a woman." His mouth firmed with new determination. "Why not forego a husband completely? I doubt the Council will pressure an infertile woman into marriage. You could live in lodgings I provide instead of theirs."

"As a whore like my *maman*? And cry into my pillow on the nights you are with Alexa? No, I watched my mother cry over a man on too many bleak nights. I won't be like her. I have obligations. To protect and provide for Mimi and Lena and Odette and Pinot. They all depend on me. I won't let them down."

"Then kiss me farewell," he demanded bitterly. "And remember what you'll be missing when you lie in your human husband's bed." Hard hands pulled her close and hard lips fell on hers.

"Dane." It was a cry for leniency, a breaking of a heart, a woman pushed against a wall with none of her choices agreeable. "Please. We shouldn't."

"You taste of your tears," he murmured, unmerciful.

Eva gripped his shirtfront, greedy for this one last kiss. But one kiss turned into more, each more desperate than the last. A touch, a gasp . . . Hands cupped her bottom and he pulled her over him as he half sat on the table, drawing her thighs up on either side of him. Her knees dimpled the cushion of furs, silks, and satins, and he dragged her against him so his manhood stroked her privates through layers of fabric. Their lips clung, moist. All was surreptitious need and quick gasps and muffled moans, and she would stop it in a minute. Just another minute.

"I'll give her up," Dane gritted against her mouth. "Wed you instead. I don't need my own children. We'll have your nieces. They are enough."

She shook her head. "But not human. Not what the Council wants for you. Wed Alexa. She is what you need. If our world is discovered by this one, a human wife and children will strengthen your hold on your land, your future, all your brothers have worked for. You must—"

"Eva? Oh! Lord Satyr! What?" Alexa's voice diminished to a horrified squeak.

Eva pushed away from Dane in a swish of skirts. Alexa stood a few feet away at the edge of the bosk. Behind her were Gaetano, her mother, and others with shocked faces, avid ones. A group that had been leaving the festivities and come for their wraps.

Alexa's complexion turned a ghastly white as she looked from Eva to Dane and back to Eva. Tears welled in her eyes. "How could you?" she asked miserably.

"Alexa, I—" Eva took a hesitant step toward her, but what excuse was there for this?

"Come, darling," said Serafina, gathering their wraps and tugging at her daughter's arm. And then Eva's dearest, only, wonderful friend was gone.

Gaetano shot Eva an angry glance. Dane stepped closer and put his arm at her waist. She looked up at him and intercepted the obnoxious challenge in the hard stare he sent Gaetano, almost begging for an altercation. She stepped between the two men and put a hand to each of their chests to defuse their antagonism.

"I'm sorry," she told Gaetano, but he only sneered and pushed her hand away, and then left in the wake of others who had already secured their belongings and gone.

"Go after Alexa," Eva told Dane. "You must repair the damage between you. It's the right thing for everyone." She could see that now. But why couldn't her heart?

He shook his head slowly.

"Your family is in danger of being revealed if you do not!" she insisted.

Dane remained obstinate. "I'll visit her, but only to break off our engagement."

"Then do as you must, but don't visit me again," she told him, making to go. "I-I need time to think."

He grabbed her wrist, his face tough and almost brutish in a way she'd never seen it. "You won't disappear to Paris, or through the ElseWorld gate?"

She pressed a hand to her lips and shook her head, afraid that if she spoke, she'd burst into tears.

"Promise me."

She nodded and pulled away, fleeing to her carriage and wondering how all had gone so wrong in so short a time.

16

"I must tell you something," Eva said as Odette helped her dress the following morning. "Last night, Gaetano Patrizzi asked me to wed him, but—"

Delight shone from Odette's eyes. "Glory! Our dreams are coming true, *bebe*!" She made as if to hug her, but Eva forestalled her.

"Wait. Let me finish. I won't be wedding him."

"What? You refused him?"

"No, listen, will you? I never got a chance to reply to his offer before I was caught in an indiscretion with another gentleman."

Odette's face suffused with angry color. "With Satyr? It was *him*, wasn't it? That one that came here for a wife and found you instead." She pointed in the direction of Eva's study, where Dane had first taken her.

Eva nodded, blushing. "Signor Patrizzi saw us together last night. His mother and sister saw us. Others did as well. Our plans must change as a result. Gaetano won't want me any longer, and

I can't just meld into the upper circles of society now to find another like him to wed."

"Let me think. We figure something out." Odette stood on a stool and lowered a pin-striped skirt over Eva's head.

Eva was shaking her head when it appeared again. "There's something else you must know. An even bigger difficulty." She gestured to the mortar in which Odette had prepared her morning draught. "These powders I've been taking. They don't seem to be working as they used to, at least not during Moonful."

Panic filled Odette's expression. "What?"

"Four years ago, when I began taking them, the moon was slow to affect me during the monthly ritual," Eva explained. "Its effects began gradually and peaked only when the moon was highest in the sky, and then eased off well before dawn. My need was far less overwhelming than it is now. When the full moon came a few nights ago, I felt it within the hour. And it was a difficult night to pass alone." She held up a hand before Odette could interject. "Shimmerskins aren't enough anymore. Do you understand?"

"I told you, you just need a husband," said Odette, adjusting the skirt around Eva and then helping her slip into its matching jacket.

"A human husband isn't going to be enough for me. Not ever."

Odette's voice rose. "But Satyr *is*? What you think he'd do if he find out what you are?"

Eva deflated slightly. "I don't know."

"You stay away from him and he won't find out. That's the only way."

"I can't. He owns the grove now," Eva argued. "He won it from Gaetano Patrizzi, gambling. We'll have to ask him for the olives now and then."

Odette began to pace, her uneven gait becoming more pronounced in her agitation. This wouldn't do, she thought. All had been so perfectly arranged in her mind. If she could only come upon a solution, all could be so again. Ownership of the grove must be returned to the Patrizzi scion. Eva would win him as her husband and have access to the grove to hide what she was from him. It was how things were meant to be. How they must be.

"If I'm to wed someone from this world, we'll have to leave Rome. Get permission from the Council to relocate to Paris. It's where they wanted to station us in the first place based on my facility with the language. But we asked to come here, where *Maman* wanted me to find a husband. And where I hoped to find my father. Well, that's not going to happen now."

"Satyr's not gonna let you go. Not easy. I know men like this. If he finds out what you are, there'll be trouble."

"If I'm careful, he won't find out."

Odette raised her eyes to the heavens as if seeking divine guidance. "He's a Tracker! Of course he will. What you think will happen then? He'll turn you in to the Council, that's what. What about Fantine? Your promises to her. And me. You throwing all that away? What about your girls? How you going to protect them if you're exposed? And maybe that Satyr will decide to keep you in his own private harem or sell you to his friends instead of telling the Council. Who knows?"

"That's ridiculous," said Eva, fluttering a hand in the air to dispel her foolish notions. Fully dressed now, she headed for the stairs. "Dane doesn't wish me harm. If I'm determined to go, I'm sure he'll be reasonable and provide us with enough olives every autumn to keep me safe. He was to wed Alexa, but now—"

"The Patrizzi girl?"

Eva nodded, looking fretful. "That's a long tale, and I haven't the heart for it now. Suffice it to say that since she has

seen me with him, I'm not sure there will be any wedding between them." Suddenly heavy with grief, she drew on her gloves
and opened the front door. "I can't talk about this anymore.
I'm going out. Please watch the girls."

Eva moved down the garden path. With a screech, the gate
opened under her hand and then banged shut behind her.

"Wait." Odette followed her and clutched at the gate's grill,
gazing at her through it. "Never told you before. But you need
to know now. This leg," she said, slapping a fist on the damaged
thigh that caused her to limp. "A man gave me this leg in his
anger years ago. A man who say he love me. You be careful,
bebe. I worry for you."

"I know you do," said Eva.

"Where you going?" Odette called after her.

"To mend a friendship I hope," Eva called softly, and then
she was gone.

Odette paced the sidewalk, rubbing the scar on her thigh
where her abusive lover had lamed her years ago. She'd still
loved him even after that. But he'd found another to love. And
so she'd had no choice but to make him sorry for his defection.
Very sorry.

She turned to walk in the opposite direction again, oblivious
to the view of the Forum excavations beyond the railing. Under
her breath, she rehearsed what she would say when the door
across the lane finally opened to spit out the Patrizzi matriarch.

"Can we go down to wander in the ruins?" Mimi asked for
the fiftieth time. She'd brought Mimi and Lena along to stroll
with her, as an excuse for her presence here in this fine neighborhood. A servant walking two well-dressed children along a
vantage point above the Forum ruins wouldn't attract undue
attention. But they'd been here an hour now, and Eva's orphans
had grown bored and begun whining.

"Can we?" Mimi begged again.

"Quiet or I'll sic demons on you," said Odette. Mimi's eyes widened and she stepped closer to Lena.

"We're cold," Lena complained. "Either take us home or let us return there on our own."

"Shush, I tell you! You'll wait here and be quiet about it," she said. She went to give Lena a smack, but stopped, hearing the door open across the way. The one she sought stepped out at last. Gaetano's mother, Serafina Patrizzi.

"I'm going to speak to someone," she told the girls.

"Who?" asked Mimi, trying to see.

"A grand, rich lady, too fine for the likes of you. Stay here until I return, if you know what's good for you."

"When will you be back?" Lena demanded to know.

But Odette was already crossing the street and didn't bother with a reply. "Signora!" she hailed. "I would speak with you regarding . . ."

A driver wearing dignified livery stepped in front of her, preventing her from reaching the carriage. "Away, old woman! What do you think you're doing?"

Odette craned around him, calling out. "If you want Evangeline Delacorte for your son, you'll listen to what I have to say."

Serafina paused, her foot on the carriage step. Though she didn't deign to turn her head and acknowledge her, she asked, "And what would you know about that?"

"I'm her serving woman. Been with her since she was born. And with her mother before that."

"What could you possibly have to say that would interest me?" Serafina asked, sending her a quick glance.

"You're interested, all right. Because I know how he can still have her."

"I'm not accustomed to conversing in the streets. Ride with

me. I'll give you ten minutes. Driver, circle once around the park and then return us here."

Odette swung up, entering the carriage behind the woman, noting the fine leather cushion and the expensive smell. Soon her Eva would ride in a carriage like this one and Odette with her. She stroked a hand over the velvet curtain at the window. She herself would be in charge of Eva's servants. No more menial work. They'd be living like queens, her and Eva.

"Well?" asked Serafina.

"You want my Evangeline for your son?" Odette asked. "Or is it just him that wants her?"

"You're here to give *me* information, not to ask questions. What is it you have to say?"

"First, I want the answer. Gossips say you run things in your family. I don't think your son would have offered for her if you didn't want her for him, too."

"Why should I want her when she has embarrassed all of us with Lord Satyr?"

"But you do?" Odette insisted a little desperately. She didn't know what she'd do if this family didn't want her girl.

"My son wants her. And I want grandchildren from him."

Odette smiled in relief. "Good, then. That's what I want. It's what her mother wanted. My Fantine. She was foolish. But Eva is—"

Serafina gasped. "Fantine? *The* Fantine?"

Odette nodded, a proud smile playing on her lips. "You remember from when she was here before, eh? All the men wanted her back then. But she fell in love with the wrong one." She fisted her hands on her lap. "Won't let that happen to my Eva."

"Judging from her appalling behavior last night in the *Circo*, it seems it already has."

"Satyr?" Odette curled her lip. "Bah! I know how to fix him."

"*Fix* him?"

"You want the grove and my Eva for your son? What you willing to do to get those things? Those my questions to you. Before I give you any answers."

Serafina considered her. "I'd say I'm willing to go to great lengths to have those things."

"But him, your son? She humiliated him. He still wants her?"

"He'll do what I say. But how do you propose to convince her?"

"Satyr is all that stands in our way. If he disappears, Eva will come to her senses and turn back to your son."

Serafina's brows rose. "If he *disappears*? How will you manage that?"

Odette's expression turned crafty. "The *Defixios*."

"Binding spells? Curse tablets? If that rubbish is all your plans amount to, then we have nothing more to say."

"Done it before, twice. The man that gave me this lame leg? Disappeared." She snapped her fingers. "And Eva's father that got my Fantine big with child? Gone. Like that." She snapped again.

Serafina's eyes sharpened. "I remember Fantine had a string of admirers here in Rome. Who exactly fathered her daughter?"

"Won't say. Eva can't know."

"But *you* know, don't you?"

Odette sent her a sly look. "I'm the only one who does, and I'll never tell. The fewer who know, the safer that secret remains."

"You'll tell me or I won't help you. I want babies from my son." Serafina leaned toward her and eyed her significantly. "And I want to know precisely what sort of babies I can expect from his marriage with your Eva."

A chill drifted over Odette. "What you mean by that?"

"You know what I mean." Sitting back, Serafina put a perfumed handkerchief to her nose and opened the window of the carriage to let a breeze in. A strange, spicy odor emanated from the serving woman as if she'd sprung from a crypt of demons that very morning. "I'm asking if the moon affects the girl."

The mulatto's eyes rounded in her dark face. She was offensive, grasping above her station, and a little nervous at being in the midst of such great wealth but trying not to show it. She would be easily manipulated.

"You know about all that? And you still want her for your son?"

"Of course. Her heritage is the very reason I want her. I'll confide something to you in hopes you'll confide in me in return. Mademoiselle Delacorte stirs my son when little else does." She inched closer. "Come, now it's your turn. I must ensure that offspring will ensue from the pair of them. My Tano has difficulties in that area, and I may have to facilitate things. So tell me, can she only get with child during Moonful?"

The serving woman panicked. "No. No, I've got to go," she said, trying the door.

Serafina put a gloved hand on her arm and her voice turned soothing. "Don't be stupid. Answer me. I don't mean any harm. What's your name?"

"Odette."

"Well, Odette. I'm not going to the authorities. Quite the opposite. I'm inviting Eva and you into my family. To share in our home, our societal position, and our wealth. You could both travel like this every day." She gestured around the sumptuous interior of the carriage. "You could dress well, dine well. What do you think of that?"

Odette swallowed the bait. "Yes, it's what I want," she said eagerly.

"Excellent. But for that to happen, you and I must first become allies. So let us speak frankly. Fantine was fey, was she not?" Serafina enquired casually, as if such a question were nothing out of the ordinary.

When Odette nodded, her pulse raced. Gaetano had been right, then. Eva had ElseWorld blood in her veins. "Who was Evangeline's father?"

Odette withdrew slightly, dubious. "You not gonna tell her? Or anyone else?"

"She doesn't know?"

"No, the less she know about that the better."

"I promise, then."

"Well, then, it was Angelo Sontine." With a fingertip, Odette drew an invisible sign of some sort on her own chest and spat from the window. "I curse his name every time I speak it. He gave my Eva his blood, made her the rarest of Else creatures—a female satyr. Ruined any chance Eva had to be normal. And ruined my Fantine for anyone else. But I made sure he paid for all that."

As the woman ranted on, Serafina blanched at the revelations that tumbled from her lips. Eva was of satyr blood? And fathered by Angelo? *Her* own, beloved Angelo? All this time, she'd thought him alive and living a happy life on the opposite side of the gate in that other world of his, with Fantine. But to find out he was dead!

"You remember him?" asked Odette, wondering at her silence.

"What? Yes, but only by name," Serafina lied.

She could see that Odette didn't believe her. After all, Angelo had been as handsome as a dark angel, and charming and rich. But she must convince her. "I was twenty-five, already married and a mother when I met him. We didn't move in the same social circles. Why am I telling you this? We've agreed that we want the same thing, but you seem to have it all figured out, with your *Defixios*. What do you need from me with regard to Lord Satyr if you're so powerful?"

"Before I say, I need to know your son is gonna want her

after I do the deed. She needs a human husband. Your son's babies for me to look after. A fine house."

"She'll have those things if Dane is gone."

"Promise me. Swear on your life."

"I swear."

"All right, then, I'll tell you. It's not just the curse tablets I employ. I'm skilled in the art of poison making. Gave those other ones poison to finish them off and then pushed them in the Tiber myself. There were inquiries from the *polizia* when the bodies were found, but there wasn't enough left of them after the fish enjoyed them to recognize. They didn't have family to keep an investigation going, so nothing came of it. This Satyr, though, he's got brothers looking out for him."

She'd poisoned Angelo! A hot mix of anger and grief boiled in Serafina, making her wish she could kill this woman herself, but all things in good time. "What do you propose?"

"I can get Satyr dead, but I need help getting him from town into the river this time. Older than I used to be. Not as strong."

"We're almost home again," Serafina noted, glancing from the carriage window. "And what's this? I see your Eva and my daughter Alexa up ahead."

Alarmed, Odette peered out at the road opposite the house, looking toward the ruins. Those two little brats were gone! How was she going to explain their loss to Eva?

"Not that way. On this side, standing on the sidewalk," said her companion.

"I know that. I'm hiding. She'll have too many questions if she sees me with you."

Serafina nodded and rapped on the roof of the carriage. As the driver let the steps down, she told him, "Take this . . . lady . . . around once more and then return here and drop her off."

"No, take me home now. To Capitoline."

"Very well. Take her to the address she specifies on Capitoline, and put the carriage away afterward. I won't be attending my luncheon after all." Then to Odette, she asked, "When will you do it?"

Odette flicked the driver a glance. "Soon. Can't be sure yet. Who'll you send to help when it's time?"

"Gaetano. He will know how to handle things." Without another word, Serafina took the driver's hand and alighted from the carriage. How wonderful that this repulsive serving woman had appeared, willing to take the risk in such a murder. Afterward, Gaetano could be depended upon to make sure that both her victim *and* she wound up feeding the fish.

"Alexa!" Eva called, paying no heed to the carriage.

So ill-bred, Serafina tsked silently. Shouting on the sidewalk. She despised women who raised their voices in public. A well-modulated tone was one of the hallmarks of a lady. After the girl wed Gaetano, etiquette lessons were obviously in order. As she stood on the walk running the names of possible tutors through her mind, Eva caught up with Alexa.

"I thought we were to meet at the market on Aventine this morning," she said breathlessly.

Alexa whirled on her, anger coming off her in waves. "Don't pretend all is well."

Eva turned beseeching. "Please, can't you forgive me? We didn't intend to hurt you."

"Yet you did," Alexa replied.

Serafina let them argue, taking the time to examine Eva's face, studying it for similarities to that of her dear Angelo. She had his dark hair. The line of jaw and brow were the same. The cheekbone resembled his, and the way she gestured with her hands so animatedly.

It was all so like him that a shadow of poignant grief passed over her. He'd been the only man she'd ever loved, and she'd lain sobbing in her bed for weeks when she realized he had gone from Rome without a word. It had been a fleshly love, for he knew what he was about in bed, as all satyrs did. But it had been love, at least on her side.

If Evangeline truly bore his satyr blood, she was one in a . . . Well, there had never been such a creature to make comparisons! The possibilities for her were endless. Determination filled her to own this daughter Angelo had created in his cuckolding of her. To make a fortune from her for decades to come. And if Eva suffered for her father's defection in the process, so much the better.

"Please." Eva extended a hand toward Alexa.

Alexa shook her head. "I cannot be friends," she said, sounding overcome. "Not yet. Give me some time. Then we'll talk again."

Eva nodded, accepting the rebuff, but looking more hopeful now.

"Come, Alexa," said Serafina, urging her toward the steps to their home.

Alexa made to go, then paused and glanced back at Eva. "Will you continue on with him?"

"With Dane?" Eva's voice softened with confusion. "I—I don't know."

Alexa sighed, as if she'd expected as much. "At least you won't marry my brother. I couldn't have borne it if you and I had been forced to share the same household."

As Alexa ascended the stairs, Eva looked so bereft that Serafina gave her arm a pat. "Don't worry. She'll forgive you. I already have, and Gaetano as well. We still hope to welcome you into our family." She turned and took the stairs, leaving the girl staring after her openmouthed with shock.

The moment she entered the house, Alexa pounced on her. "I heard what you said to Eva, Mother! How dare you? This is my business."

"You know how I hate raised voices," said Serafina, removing her gloves in quick jerks. "But it's propitious that you should mention business—"

"What's going on?" asked Gaetano, coming downstairs.

"I'm glad you're here, Tano. I've decided it's time your sister learned the truth about the workings of our little family business."

Gaetano's eyes shifted between them. "Why?"

"Because the other Daughters and I have agreed it's time. Shall we go?"

"You're coming down, too?" he asked.

Serafina nodded. His surprise was understandable. She rarely visited the labyrinth—usually confining her visits to the annual ritual when she and the other Daughters descended together without the men. In the interim, whenever they secured new victims for the cells such as little Nella, it fell to her son to escort them into the bowels of the earth.

"Down where?" Alexa asked blankly. "What business?"

"Our cosmetics, of course. Haven't you ever wondered how they were made, and where?" Serafina asked.

"Well, yes, I've asked you many times, but you said young ladies were not to concern themselves with matters of finance and manufacture."

"Ah, but you're grown up now, and one day you and Tano must carry on for the family when I'm gone. It's time you learned your heritage." Serafina led her two children into her elegant salon, the one where she held her ladies' gatherings. Along a far wall, she pulled a lever that turned the bookcase filled with jars and vials, and Alexa gasped. An opening had appeared behind it, leading to a tall, crude tunnel hewn from rock. Serafina stepped inside and lit a decorative lantern with a matchstick.

"Why didn't I know about this?" said Alexa, moving to peer inside. "It's rather gothic. Frightening, actually."

"You haven't seen anything yet," murmured Gaetano.

"Come along." Serafina nodded to Gaetano, who lit another lantern and gestured for Alexa to precede him through the labyrinth. "The first thing you must understand," Serafina went on as she led the way along the serpentine corridor, "is that there is a world beyond ours, accessed through a gate in Tuscany. Your friend Eva is from that world, as is Lord Satyr."

Alexa stopped short, and Gaetano bumped into her. "What?" she asked faintly.

"Why does she have to know?" Gaetano demanded in frustration.

"But how adorable," cooed Serafina in surprise. "You, playing the protective older brother. That will work nicely into my plans, for your sister is to be inducted into womanhood soon. And you have been chosen by the Daughters to stand in for your father with her."

Gaetano shook his head, stunned anew by his mother's brand of casual cruelty.

"What are you talking about?" asked Alexa.

"She wants me to act as Faunus with you," Gaetano gritted angrily. "A man who sought incest with his own daughter Bona Dea—as in our own Bona Dea Cosmetics. I'm to get you drunk, then bed you. They'll likely drug you as well so you won't remember afterward."

"No! Stop it!" Her face blanching, Alexa put her hands over her ears, then turned to run back the way they'd come.

But Serafina grabbed her wrist, drawing their faces close. "I know it seems strange now, but you'll grow used to it. It's a tradition in our family." She smoothed back a stray lock of hair that had fallen across Alexa's brow. "My father bedded me when I was your age. But your father is dead, so Tano is my choice for you. Better he than one of the bloated husbands of the other Daughters."

Alexa shook her head, her eyes terrified. "This is all too heinous. You can't mean it! Either of you!"

"We're descended from Gods, Alexa!" Serafina exclaimed. "Bona Dea and Faunus dictated long ago that a mating has to occur among family before you can wed. It's a divine rite of passage. Be proud."

"Proud? I've never been more ashamed!" Alexa began backing away. "Wherever you're leading me, I don't want to go. I can only hope I'll awaken tomorrow and find this was all a nightmare of some kind."

Serafina sent a speaking glance toward Gaetano. "Stop her!"

But he didn't budge, allowing Alexa to escape in the direction of the house. "I'm not going to let you hurt her. She's my sister, for pity's sake. I don't mind all the rest." He gestured toward the tunnel farther ahead. "But I'd rather go on as we were before. She doesn't have to know everything."

"Oh, stop your hysterics. It's time she grew up and shouldered her share of the work. Aren't you tired of doing it all? After all, you're to be a husband soon, with more responsibilities."

"And who exactly am I to marry?"

"Evangeline Delacorte, of course. Nothing has changed there."

"As easy as that?" he scoffed. "You wish it and it will happen? She'll leave her lover and return to me?"

"Have no worries on that score," she said smugly. "Dane Satyr will soon meet an untimely end."

His brows rose. "How?"

"Not by my hand. Her maidservant visited me this afternoon. She is conveniently determined that Eva wed you and has agreed to poison Satyr. I only tell you this because your assistance may be required in disposing of him afterward. And the maidservant as well. She's repugnant, and I don't want her left around blackmailing us."

Considering the matter settled, Serafina glanced toward the depths of the labyrinth. "Is all well down there?" she asked diffidently. "I depend upon you to take care of things, you know."

His gaze narrowed and he gestured toward the pit of hell made for him by his mother. Where she'd intended to take Alexa. "Why don't I show you around? You can get to know some of our guests."

She shivered. "No, I'm afraid it's a little too unsavory down there for me to visit more often than I must. And we should find Alexa and calm her."

Her nervousness pleased him. He stepped closer, intimidating her. "Yes, you prefer to pretend that none of that exists. Yet you banish me to these dungeons every night to maintain order. To live among your victims."

"It's the way things have been done in our families for centuries, dear. The women upstairs, the men down. Why object at this late date?" She pushed past him in the direction of the house and he let her leave him behind.

"Why?" he whispered when she'd gone. "Because I hate this. Hate you for making me live like this." He stood there, thinking of Eva as he often did now, as a way of escaping reality. She represented a fresh start. If he could have her, he had a feeling he could find his way out of this hell. Thoughts of her made his prick stir. He put a hand over it and squeezed, relishing the small sexual pain. Yes, if anyone could, Eva would save him.

17

It was twilight by the time Mimi and Lena returned home, looking disheveled and exhausted.

"Where have you two been?" asked Eva, ushering them inside. "We've been so worried! I've been roaming the neighborhood searching. Poor Pinot is out looking for you still."

Mimi shot a mutinous look at Odette. "We—"

Lena spoke over her, drowning out the rest of her words. "We wanted to see the ruins, so we walked there on our own." She sent Mimi a warning glance, thoroughly confounding Eva.

"Don't you understand how dangerous that was? You must never ever do such a thing again," said Eva, hugging them to her. Mimi cuddled close and Lena shivered. "You're chilled, and dusty. Odette, help me get them into a hot bath."

But when Odette came near, Mimi drew back and Lena stepped in front of her in a protective maneuver. "We can undress ourselves."

"What's going on?" Eva demanded, looking from them to Odette.

"Girls are growing up," Odette supplied, her lips forming a

creaky smile. "Wanting to do things for themselves. That's good, *si?* Independent."

"I suppose." The girls were obviously angry with Odette about something, but they weren't in a mood to say what. "Go on, then," Eva told them. "You both look exhausted."

"Can we sleep here tonight?" Mimi asked.

"With me?" The girls only asked to sleep with her when they had the occasional bad dream. "Well, of course," said Eva. "If you'd like. But not when you look like little chimney sweeps. Get to your baths."

The girls were unusually quiet and made quick work of bathing. Once they were in their nightgowns, Odette gave them some chocolate, their customary bedtime drink. Then Eva tucked them in her bed, gave them each a kiss, and at Mimi's urging also bestowed a kiss on her doll, and they both fell into exhausted slumber.

"What happened between you and the girls?" Eva asked quietly when Odette returned from dropping their filthy clothes in the laundry.

"Truth is, I took them to the market," Odette murmured, handing her a mug of hot chocolate. "They ran off to the ruins when my back was turned."

Eva took a sip. "Why didn't you say anything earlier when Pinot and I were looking for them?"

"Thought it best they learn a lesson for their waywardness, having to make their own way home."

Just then they heard the creak of the gate and Eva went to the window. It was Pinot. "The girls have come home," she called softly down to him. "They were wandering the ruins on their own, can you believe it?"

He shook his head over their foolishness, then said, "They're all right?"

She nodded.

"I'm off then, to Capitoline, unless you need me."

"What's on Capitoline?" asked Odette, coming to the window.

"That's my business, old lady." He winked at Eva and walked off, whistling.

"Got a new love, that one, and I can never find him when I need him," Odette groused.

Eva smiled. "It's good that Pinot is making friends. The girls should be encouraged to do the same. Maybe it would stop them from wandering off in search of entertainment."

Going back to sit at her dressing table, Eva set down her mug and began taking the pins from her hair in preparation for bed.

Odette came behind her and took over the job. "Don't forget, those girls are comfortable roaming the streets. It's where you found them. Nothing's going to happen to them out there."

Eva's brows rose. "This from the woman who's always giving me such dire warnings about safety, and how I'm going to be found floating in the Tiber? No, that part of their lives is over. They're our family now and we must look after them, do you understand?"

Odette nodded grudgingly.

"I'll arrange to find some children their ages in the neighborhood."

"Think that's wise?" Once Eva's hair was unbound, Odette began brushing it. "If anyone finds out they're fey, it's trouble for us. Little girls have big mouths."

Eva caught her eye in the mirror. "I want them to have friends. I didn't as a girl and I sorely missed them."

"It was for your own good that you were kept from the other young ones in ElseWorld. Might've guessed what you were."

"I know." Eva sighed. Growing up, Fantine and Odette had always kept a close eye on her, waiting for signs of her blood to will out. On her eighteenth birthday, the signs they'd awaited had finally shown themselves. Her menses had finally begun— far later than it had in the few other girls of her acquaintance— shocking her body with cravings she didn't understand or know how to cope with. Her nights had turned restless and she'd begun to awaken from sleep, her thighs clenched tight, trying to hold on to the pulses of pleasure that spontaneously visited her body high between her legs.

She had withdrawn from the company of other young ladies then, finally understanding what her mother and Odette had tried to explain all those years. That she was different. That something about her was shameful. That it was dangerous to get too close to those who might expose her for what she was.

"Umm that feels nice," said Eva, enjoying the feel of her mother's silver brush running through her hair. "Just like when I was a little girl."

"You still my little girl. Always will be," said Odette. "Your *maman*, she had an angel's hair, but you got the hair of a witch. Just like your father's."

Eva frowned, laying a hand over the brush to still its stroke. "What?"

"Oh, my mistake," said Odette, smoothing a hand over her hair. "Just thinking too hard about the wedding."

"What wedding?"

"Yours with Patrizzi, *bambina*, what else?" She began braiding Eva's hair for sleep, something she hadn't done since Eva was in her teens.

Eva's frown deepened. "Didn't you hear what I said last night? I was caught out, in Dane's arms. Gaetano Patrizzi saw us. The very last thing he must want now is a wedding with me."

"It's gonna be all right with your Gaetano, you'll see." Odette patted her arm.

Eva pulled away, an unsettling feeling filling her. "You have blinders on if you think Signor Patrizzi would take me to wife. I've as good as cuckolded him before all of society. I'm only glad he didn't announce our engagement before it happened."

"Don't worry about all that. I fixed things with Signora Patrizzi," Odette announced proudly. "All gonna be well."

"You spoke to his mother?" Eva rose slowly to face her. She put a hand to the dressing table to steady herself, suddenly feeling a bit dizzy. "When? How?"

"Never you mind that. You gonna have what you want. Gonna wed your human. Have your own *bebes*. Won't need to go picking them off the streets." Odette smiled and smoothed Eva's hair over her shoulders. Then her hands went lower, covering Eva's breasts.

Eva knocked her touch away and slid from her and the table. Something strange was going on here. "Odette, that's inappropriate."

Odette just shrugged and turned the silver brush in her hands, pulling long raven strands from it. Eva backed away from her, stumbling, her thoughts becoming confused. "What you said before, about my father's hair. How do you know his was dark?"

A faraway look entered Odette's eyes. "He was a handsome one, your father. Might as well tell you his name since Signora Patrizzi has it now. Angelo Sontine. Fantine thought I didn't see she was falling in love with him. I did, but I was too late in getting rid of him. Still, he had to be punished for putting you inside her. And I made sure he was." A smile creased her lined face. "Used my gift on him. Had to do what's right for us. You understand, don't you?" Wrapping the long strands of Eva's hair around two fingers, she tucked them inside the little pouch she carried in her pocket.

"And now you think to use your gift—your powers—on me?" asked Eva, assuming Odette planned to make some sort of magic with the use of the strands.

"Already started on that, *bebe*. You stay quiet here in your bedchamber for a week or so. Give me time for to carry out some plans I've made for Lord Satyr."

Eva raised a shaking hand to her forehead, trying to think. "The chocolate you gave the girls and me. You laced it with one of your roots or spices, didn't you?"

Odette hooked an arm around her back. In spite of herself, Eva leaned heavily on her, feeling too drowsy to resist. "You just rest. Get this Satyr out of your head." Gently, she led Eva to the bed, where she pulled back the covers for her and pushed her to lie next to Mimi and Lena, then tucked her in as if she were a child as well. "The three of you won't get up to any mischief in here. Won't even know I'm gone. Odette will take care of everything."

Eva sighed into her pillow, only vaguely aware of the sound of the door being locked from outside. By the time Odette's ungainly step was moving away down the hall, she was asleep.

Much later—though it seemed only minutes had passed— Lena and Mimi were tugging her awake and the late afternoon sun was already beginning to drop toward a pinkened horizon.

"Goodness! How long did we sleep?" Eva said, sitting up.

"All night and most of today," said Lena. "When Odette left the garden just now, the gate squeaked and woke us."

Odette. A chill slid over Eva. She could hardly believe what the woman had told her yesterday, but she did believe it, and it terrified her. She had to get herself and the girls to safety before Odette returned.

"I need my toilet, but the door's locked," said Mimi, hopping from one foot to the other.

Eva pointed toward the bathroom. "Use mine. And don't forget to wash your hands in the basin." Sliding from the bed, she fought off her grogginess and went to brush her teeth at the basin in her room, then tried the door.

"It's locked, I told you," Mimi called from the bathroom, sounding grumpy.

Eva found a hairpin and got on her knees, trying to pick the lock. "What happened yesterday?" she asked Lena over her shoulder. "You didn't really wander off on your own, did you?"

"Odette said demons will get us if we tell," Lena hedged.

"She can't conjure demons," Eva assured her.

"I knew it!" Lena said in satisfaction. "She's just a mean old woman. Yesterday, she left us in the park and drove away with a fine lady in her carriage. We got cold, so we walked home."

Eva gave her thin arm a quick squeeze, then went back to jiggling the lock. "I'm sorry that happened and glad you're safe. Odette's unwell. I want you both to stay away from her from now on." She tried not to think about her father and the fact that he'd met his end by Odette's hand. Of how Fantine had waited all those years not knowing the true reason he hadn't come for her as he'd promised. What misery Odette had caused! How dare she think she'd done it for their own good. She'd been hurt by men herself, but no one had realized how it had twisted her. How could they have missed it all these years?

When the lock proved impossible, Eva began throwing on her clothes, her mind racing to formulate an escape plan. This room that had jailed her during Moonful had now become a far more terrifying prison.

"I'm hungry," Mimi complained, wandering out of the bathroom.

"I know. We need to find a way to get out of here," said Eva. Going to the window, she opened it and leaned over its wrought-iron railing. They'd break their ankles or worse if they tried jumping.

"If you were Rapunzel, you could let down your hair," said Mimi, reading her mind.

Eva turned from the railing and kissed the top of her head. "Brilliant, Mimi!"

Lena brightened, immediately grasping the plan. "We can tie the bedsheets together."

"And perhaps extend them with a dress or two," added Eva. She ripped the sheets and coverlet off the bed and began knotting them into a makeshift rope by which they might descend. A half hour later, she tied one end of the rope to the railing and dropped the rest of it down until its far end dusted the asters in the garden.

Going quickly to her dressing table, Eva located her mother's journal and her silver hairbrush, and stuffed both in her pockets. Then she took a deep breath, gathering her courage. "I'm going to go down first. And then you'll follow me one at a time."

"Like little monkeys," said Mimi.

"Only quieter," cautioned Lena. "In case *she* comes back."

"Yes, we must all be very, very quiet," Eva agreed.

"Like little monkey mice!" Mimi improvised in a squeaky, mouselike whisper.

"Exactly," said Eva. "Be careful and remember to hold on tight. I'll wait for you below." With that, she swung her leg over the railing and began a precarious, unskilled descent.

Sometime later, she breathed a sigh of relief as the three of them found themselves in the garden without mishap. But when they reached the iron gate, Lena hung back. "We can't go out in our nighties. And barefoot!"

"We have to," said Mimi, sounding quite adult for once. "If we stay, Odette might come back and get us."

"*Vite!*" Eva whispered. The gate gave a harsh squeal as they passed through it. Then they ran, the three of them scurrying toward the sunset.

"Where are we going?" Mimi whispered, sounding excited. To her, this seemed an adventure.

"To Dane's," Eva decided, trying to sound confident. "Lord Satyr's."

"Will he want us?" asked Lena, and it broke Eva's heart to hear the uncertainty in her voice.

"Yes," Eva assured, praying it was true. But how they would get there was a mystery. When they passed a wagon already hitched to a horse and only awaiting its driver and passengers, Eva hesitated only briefly before motioning the girls to get in.

"We're stealing!" said Mimi, looking both scandalized and delighted.

"Only because we're in danger. We'll return it tomorrow, with an apology and payment for the use of it," said Eva. "But hurry now, get in. Monkey mice, remember?"

Miraculously, the owner of the wagon didn't hear them drive away, for no one pursued them. Several blocks later, they passed Pinot on foot, heading toward the townhouse.

"What's all this?" he said, leaping onto the wagon's tongue.

Eva eyed him, a little wary. Her foundations had been rocked by Odette's betrayal, and she wondered for a moment if she could trust him.

"Odette locked us up," Mimi announced. "She's bad."

"That's not news. That old lady is as rotten as spoiled fruit." Pinot hopped onto the seat and took the reins from Eva. "Where are we going?"

As they made their way to the grove, Eva told him what had happened. His face turned grim and he gave a long, low whistle. It was dusk when they reached Aventine Hill and the grove.

Dane met them on the porch of his home, a questioning frown on his face. "What's happened?" he demanded. He looked masculine and capable, and the sight of him made Eva want to fall into his arms.

"Odette locked us in the bedchamber, but we escaped on the bedsheets and stole a wagon!" Mimi cackled gleefully.

Dane made a suitably impressed sound, but his frown deepened. "Well, I'm glad you had the good sense to come here afterward," he told her, as he lifted each girl down.

"We don't have to go back?" Lena asked him.

"No, you don't have to go back," said Dane. "Not ever."

Reaching for Eva, he lifted her easily from the wagon, his hands at her waist. An arrested expression came over his face and he paused, leaving her dangling in midair, her toes a few inches shy of the ground. Holding her weight seemed to cost him no effort as he searched her eyes with a ferocious concentration.

She cocked her head. "Is it all right that we've come?"

"I'll see to the horses," Pinot interrupted, after the strange silence stretched too long.

Dane lowered her against him and she slid to the ground. "Just so it's clear, I tried to see Alexa, but she has gone from Rome," he informed her. "My letter breaking off our betrothal follows her now to Venice. She and I have no futher obligation between us. Do you understand?"

She nodded at the vehemence in his tone. Seeming satisfied at that, he turned away as if forgetting her. "There's lodging here for you as well," he told Pinot. "For as long as you like." The two men's gazes met, and Pinot relaxed under the welcome he read in Dane's.

"That goes for all of you," Dane announced, herding them inside. "Come. Consider my home yours."

Eva ushered the girls ahead of her, wishing he hadn't made promises in front of them that he might not be able to keep. They'd been let down often enough by the adults in their lives. Once inside, Lena took Mimi's hand and they both studied the magnificent house uncertainly as they walked through. The front room was enormous, with a sweeping staircase and a chandelier that tinkled eerily as they moved past, disturbing the air. Gaslight hissed in lamps here and there, providing little in the way of illumination. All here was gloomy, appearing to have been untouched in a decade or more, with dust on every surface and grime on the windows. The furniture was covered with white dropcloths that made chairs, sofas, and tables appear to be ghostly figures.

"Is it haunted?" she heard Mimi whisper.

"No, just dirty," Lena informed her practically and with little regard for Dane's feelings.

"Lord Satyr hasn't resided here very long," Eva told them, hoping the girls hadn't embarrassed him, but curious about the house's condition herself. It had obviously once been beautiful and could be again with enough care.

"Can we sleep with you?" Mimi asked Eva, sounding a little nervous.

"Not tonight," Dane replied in an unshakable tone. Eva looked at him, but he'd glanced back at the girls. He had seemed preoccupied ever since he'd lifted her down from the wagon, and it worried her. By showing up uninvited at this hour with her entourage, she hadn't given him much choice in whether to provide lodging. Did he wish they hadn't come? "I'll have the dryads ready rooms for everyone," he said, and she was only slightly reassured.

"Dryads?" asked Mimi, immediately intrigued. "Like the tree spirits in the fairy books?"

Dane nodded. "They've been working to bring my house to order, for as you and your sister noted with such candor, it has been neglected for years. Lucky for us, they began their labors in the sleeping quarters, so you'll have clean beds."

Fortunately, the girls took to their ethereal nursemaids on sight, who in turn fussed over both of them in the maternal fashion common to such nymphs. Eva didn't question their presence in his home, for it had also been traditional in Else-World that landowners take in such creatures when the trees they inhabited reached the ends of their lives.

And so it was that less than thirty minutes after their arrival, Eva found herself alone with Dane in the shadowy corridor outside the girls' new bedchamber.

"What the hell happened?" he demanded, folding her against him.

Earlier she had tried to be strong for the girls' sake, but now worries burst out of her. "I've learned something terrible. That Odette, my maidservant, killed my father, before I was born."

His hand moved over her back in soothing circles and she felt his lips on her hair. "I'm sorry, Eva."

She nodded her cheek against his shirtfront. "There's more I'm afraid, just as bad. Odette plans to do you harm. She went out this morning and locked us in the house."

He curled a hand at her nape and drew back, bumping his forehead to hers. "You're safe here. With me." She went on tiptoe and touched grateful lips to his. "Thank you, but your safety is more at issue." Something shifted in his face and he turned her, ushering her down the hall.

"Where are we going?"

"To my chamber, at the other side of the house where I can have you to myself."

Sudden excitement bubbled in her, but she still worried for him. "You must take this conspiracy against you seriously, Dane."

"I do. But I seriously believe I can defend myself against one elderly maidservant." They turned another corner, moving past a fireplace so large she could have stood inside its hearth. And then past a wall of mirrors, then another of windows.

"You didn't hear her. You—"

"Shh. There's nothing we can do about her tonight. I need to have you now. To know you're here and real and mine. Tomorrow is time enough for serious matters."

Moments later, they went through a door. She stopped inside the room he'd shown her to, standing in the middle of a fine Persian carpet, and surveyed the massive olivewood bed hung with dark burgundy. She heard the door click shut behind her and turned to see him lean back against it. The halo around him gleamed pure silver but was strangely turbulent. Her eyes dropped to his, found them ruthless on her.

"What is it telling you?" He pushed off from the door and moved toward her. "My aura. You were studying it for clues to my mood. Does it inform you I'm glad your serving woman revealed herself a lunatic so that you wound up here in my bedchamber tonight?"

"Dane." Her lips firmed, the schoolmarm again.

Dane chuckled to himself, low and dark. "It's true." He circled her slowly, prowling, drawing blunt fingertips over her, a light touch at her waist, hip, back. "But what else does it tell you, I wonder?" A pause. Then gently, "That I know your secret?"

Her green eyes went wary. "What secret?"

"That you are satyr. Like me." The words were soft, accusing.

But she stepped back from them, as if hit by a physical blow. "Don't be ridiculous."

He ignored her denial, stalking her toward his bed. Lifting her and tossing her back upon it, and looming over her with hands planted on either side of her. "I scented you tonight before you had even arrived at my door. And it brought to mind your scent that first time we met in the grove last Moonful, something Dante had made sure I'd forget. Since then, you've been doing something to disguise it. What?"

She managed a brittle laugh. "Honestly! First Odette reveals her insanity, and now you."

He dragged her higher on his bed, raining hot kisses on her throat, her mouth. Holding her with those big hands that always before had made her feel safe. Only she didn't feel safe now. She felt exposed, scraped raw by his discovery.

"What are you afraid of?" he asked. Her lips trembled and she folded them inward as if to hold in her confessions. "Eva." His voice was a low growl.

"That you'll tell!" She pushed against his chest in emphasis.

"That I'll be caged in some laboratory and studied like a bug on a pin. That Mimi and Lena will be put out on the streets when I'm not here to protect them. I've kept this secret for twenty-two years. And you wonder that I'm afraid to reveal it?"

"I'm not going to tell anyone."

"What *are* you going to do?" she demanded in a ravaged voice.

"Do?" His mouth touched hers, butterfly soft. "I'm going to undress you. Here on my big bed, and kiss you, and hold you, and come inside you. All." A kiss. "Night." Another kiss. "Long." His hands came between them, unfastening her bodice, putting his plan into action.

"But shouldn't we . . . don't you . . . care what I am?"

"Oh, I care," he said, stringing more kisses along the pale flesh he was uncovering—her breasts, her ribs. "I care deeply. And I'm about to show you just how very, *very* deeply."

Her terrible secret was out to him at last, but strangely Eva could only feel relief and a fierce need to have him do just as he suggested. To feel connected to him. She rolled from him and both came to their knees on the mattress. In a hurried rustle of wool, silk, and linen, they undressed themselves and each other in the dim golden light. They spoke in hushed, excited voices.

"Leave the stockings," he said when her hands went to her garters. She nodded, devouring him with her eyes. He was so handsome. Sculpted like a statue of some powerful Roman god come to life, its phallus angling tall and ardent from a dark nest.

Needing to touch him, she put her palms on his chest and kissed his throat, and felt the shudder that ran through him when their bodies pressed close. "What about Dante? Will he come?" she asked.

His hands had cupped her buttocks and now were squeezing and massaging them in a voluptuous fashion. "I imagine we'll *all* come," he said, sounding distracted. She glanced over her shoulder and saw he was looking to their reflection in the window glass, watching his dark hands shape and reshape her twin ivory globes. "But I will be in control."

Catching her eye with his roguishly wicked gaze, he bodily turned her to face their reflection as well, her silk-encased calves sliding between his on the mattress. Save for her stockings, they were naked there together on their knees, his chest and cock and thighs warming her backside.

His fingers traced over one of her garters and the expanse of silk it held high on her thigh, as if he enjoyed the fact that the clasp restrained the stocking and forced it to conform to her shape. She watched his hands play over her body then, exploring. Eventually, he cupped her breasts, rolling her flesh between the heels of his hands and the flats of his fingers with such relish that she sensed he'd saved this for last. Sensation fluttered high between her legs and her inner tissues moistened, as if in anticipation of where all this must ultimately lead. A breath soughed from her and her head lolled back on his chest. Her hand lifted to curve at the side of his throat.

"Your hands always seem to wind up here," she noted breathlessly. Beneath lowered lashes, her eyes were riveted on the mesmerizing pinch and twist of the long, blunt fingers drawing out her nipples.

In his reflection, she saw his slow smile, the predatory glitter of his eyes. "Your breasts beg a man to touch. So firm, and high, and white." He drew her hands to hold their lush weight and showed her the motion he liked, and then watched her fondle herself in his stead with a look of intense satisfaction on his face. "Gods, that's so beautiful, Eva," he said reverently. And with his eyes on her in such hot approval, she did feel beautiful.

Behind her, he shifted slightly, found his cock, and with his fingers, guided it between her legs. Pressing it lengthwise along her slippery folds, he sawed along them, making her tremble.

"I'm wet," she said softly, and heard the apology in her tone.

Their eyes met in the glass and the desire in his lightened her heart. "I love that you go wet for me," he said in a voice gone hot and dark.

The hand at her hip went lower over her abdomen until his second and fourth fingers pressed at her pubic bone, one on either side of her clit. Gently, they forked upward, spreading her, exposing her sensitive nub to the cool air. She gasped, shocked at his daring.

"But how naughty you are, little Eva," he murmured in feigned censure, his gaze riveted to their reflection. "So naughty, showing me your sweet pink clit." Her eyes widened, uncertain.

In the glass, they looked so decadent together, him a burnished, broad-shouldered, masculine god towering protectively over her more feminine frame. Her hands still on her breasts. His hand splaying her private flesh in this almost obscene manner. Yet the very sight of them like this sent a tumultuous burst of excitement fizzing and sparking through her veins.

"How shall I punish you, I wonder?" he continued in a gentle scold.

"I don't know," she whispered, tentatively entering the game. "I can't help such things." She arched, tilting her hips back, the movement parting her slit so she flowered naturally for him, beckoning him inside.

He sighed as if he were a tutor sorely disappointed in his pupil. "How shall we endeavor to check such hedonistic impulses?" At odds with his words, he nestled himself there at her quivering center; and then he was rising in her, his mushroom knob stretching her labia wide. Something brushed her clit. The callused tip of his middle finger.

She moaned. His breath came, warm at her ear. "I'm appalled, dear Eva. I begin to think you might have done this before." The tantalizing touch came again at her clit.

"No, no, I haven't . . . monsieur."

He made a soft, disbelieving sound. "You won't get out of your punishment so easily, mademoiselle. Not with lies." His length pushed higher in her then without hurry, in a measured glide that made her writhe against him, wanting more. But a band of steel wrapped itself around her waist and held her firmly now, refusing to accommodate her impulse toward a headlong rush. Instead, he took his sweet time, restraining her with his body at her back, and his thighs crowding on either side of hers so closely that it was as if her knees had been bound together. Her slit and channel were compressed more tightly than she'd ever been for a man's invasion. And still he pushed on with maddening slowness, opening her snug haven with sure, steady power.

"Gods, I can feel my cock fucking every inch of you," he groaned. His features were drawn and tense, his restraint obviously coming at a cost.

"I need you deeper," she begged, knowing suddenly that this was to be her amatory punishment in his game—this withholding.

"No, not yet," he whispered. And still, he didn't fill her completely, but only began to thrust in short, shallow pulses that stroked his bulbous knob in such a way and on such a particularly sensitive spot within her that her inner tissues began to shiver and sob for him. His fingers toyed with her clit in the softest of torturous, titillating strokes. She was a void now, nothing more, nothing less. An emptiness that wept to be filled and fulfilled. She felt confined, dominated, controlled. She wanted it to go on forever, yet at the same time she wanted to scream for relief.

She lifted her lashes and gazed at their reflection. Saw his dark head bent to her shoulder, his mouth on her throat. Saw the desire etched on her face, the raw tension in his. Saw his hands, big and strong on her pale flesh. "Deeper, please, Dane."

"I'm sorry, Eva." He kissed her nape with gentle regret.

She wanted to wriggle lower on him, to widen her legs and move her body so as to force him to give her what she craved. Yet at the same time, she was thrilled by the fact that she could not. By the fact that he was in complete control. Only he would determine the strength and pace of their mating. Only he decided how she could move on him. Only he decided how deeply he would fill her.

Here was the sort of man she'd dreamed of in her solitary bedroom. A man who would take charge in these matters. A man who knew what to do with a woman. Who knew what she needed, and had the confidence and strength of character to give it to her. Or to withhold it for their mutual pleasure.

Something shifted in her heart then, some terrible, wonderful, wrenching emotion that she knew with a certainty would forever connect her to him from this moment on. In the glass, she saw her mouth move, watched her lips silently forming three powerful, binding words. *I love you.*

Though she made no sound and he couldn't have seen, something seemed to give way in him. His hands captured the bones of her hips and he took her with a single, mighty thrust. She cried out as she felt his thick phallus tunnel through her compressed channel like some slick erotic fist.

"Your so tight like this," he rasped, his gaze sweeping over her reflection as if to possess all of her. "So fucking tight."

"Yes."

"So fucking mine."

"Yes, I'm yours. Yours, Dane," she vowed.

With a masculine growl of satisfaction, he ebbed from her and then plunged again, mating her with a series of vigorous slams that shuddered her breasts. In this, he owned her, taking what he wanted of her, yet offering her rapture in the taking. A raw, curt groan tore from his throat as he drove so deep and high that she was lifted from the bed, and her body held aloft only by the thick, quivering cock in her cunt and his broad hands on her flesh. Held so tightly, she felt his balls lift tight at her bottom, felt the warm burst of seed that pulsed through his shaft. It shot from him and fountained inside her in a rapid series of hot, hard gushes.

She cried out, overwhelmed by sensation. But impaled so thoroughly, she could only ride him and thrill to his body's domination of her own.

His fingertip pressed at her thrumming clit and rubbed gently. "Come for me," his velvet voice urged. And with a soft gasp of feminine surprise, she did, melting over him, breaking on the crest of her own orgasm, her tissues fisting him and gulping greedily at the semen he pumped like some pagan volcanic god licking tongues of fire at her womb.

"Oh, thank Gods, thank Gods," she whispered, glorying in his gift to her, in his allowing her to reach her pleasure and experience his.

"Eva." Her name on his lips was a rough benediction, and he wrapped his arms around her and held her tight. They clung there on their knees forever it seemed, caught in a carnal spell, arching under each clench, each spill; undulating together as one body, one moan.

Long, delicious moments later, their breathing slowed and they lay together on his big bed, her on her back and him alongside. Head propped on his fist, he gazed down at her. "You never said how it is that you disguise your scent." As if unable to stop himself from touching her, his fingers wandered to play gently in her moist nest of curls. She sighed with pleasure and shifted her legs, luxuriating in the wonderful slip and slide of the semen he'd deposited in the void between them.

"I drink a powder made from crushed olive pits," she murmured. "The only suitable olives in all of Rome grow somewhere here on your land."

"Which is what brought you to me that first night," he surmised, now tracing feminine folds still slippery with his leavings, and finding more of himself on the insides of her thighs.

She nodded, flushing under the effort of pretending to ignore the fact that he had begun painting moisture in soft swirls over her still-trembling clit. "Where did you find the ones you sent me that day with your payment?"

"Near the temple at the northern corner of my property. Why?"

"I'll have to gather some and try my hand at making the powder myself, for I will need to resume taking it tomorrow." She encircled his wrist as his touch on her turned more carnal. "Dane!"

He leaned close and his beak of a nose nuzzled the hollow of her throat where an Else's scent was most intense. "I prefer you like this. Your taste and scent as natural as the Gods intended. It makes me wild to have you again." And then his body was covering hers and he proceeded to show her just how wild she in fact made him.

Eva woke sometime close to dawn to see him standing at the window. Something about his melancholy stance made her sit up and call to him, "Dane?"

He shook his head and turned, meeting her eyes. "No."

She tugged the covers higher over her breast. Not Dane. But this wasn't Dante either. It was the other one who had come in the study that afternoon just before his leave-taking. The one with the moody gray aura. She hadn't known what he was then, but now . . . "Daniel?"

He nodded, his expression intense, urgent. "Tell him. Bona Dea. You must tell him."

And then his demeanor and aura altered, and he was Dane again. He ran a hand over his overnight beard, looking surprised to find himself at the window. "Damn it's chilly." He slipped into the bed, his arms sliding around her.

She wrapped her own around him. "Something happened just now," she told him. He looked at her, alert with tension.

As she went on to explain what he'd said, panic filled his face, a raw terror come and gone in a flash. "Bona Dea. The goddess?" he asked. "What sort of warning is that?"

"I don't know. But there's something else. When you left me that first morning in my study, you—Daniel—mentioned her then as well. I'm sorry I didn't tell you before. I didn't realize it was important."

He fell on his back among the covers. "Maybe this has something to do with Luc, or maybe it's simply madness."

"You are not mad!" She followed him down and kissed him then, passionless, caring kisses meant to heal. They heated somewhere along the way, and soon he was pulling her over him and filling her again with the delicious warmth of his seed.

His arms around her, Dane lay awake until dawn, afraid that if he slept again he might lose himself, his brothers, or her in his nightmares.

18

The next morning, Eva froze on the front stairs listening to Dane and his brother lock horns in the salon below. They'd obviously been at it for some time, for Bastian seemed to know everything.

"Aligning yourself with her is too damned dangerous!" Bastian argued with a chilling certainty. "What if the Council discovers that she's of satyr blood and that you've harbored her?"

"That won't happen!" Dane argued.

"Oh? Yet you discovered her secret in a matter of days! What if she falls ill at some point? Or becomes full with your child and spends her mornings retching as some women do? Fat lot of good her powders will be to her if she can't keep them down. You won't be able to hide what she is! She could ruin your chances of finding Luc. Get you locked up again."

"I won't let them shove her into a laboratory to be studied like some fucking animal!" Dane exploded. "I've had enough of their doctors myself to last a lifetime."

"You don't intend to keep her here?"

"I do. She won't need the powders forever. An Else female eventually takes on the scent of her mate. Mine will soon mask what she is."

"You hope. How do you know that will work with her? She's an unprecedented phenomenon. None of the usual rules will necessarily apply." Bastian's tone lowered, grew more persuasive. "The Council wants you back, Dane. Desperately. You're their prized Tracker. You said yourself the only way they'll let you stay here when they find you is if you've followed their rules. Wed a human bride and breed her."

Eva pressed a hand to her lips in dismay. Dane had come through the gate without permission? She hadn't known. It made his position here all the more untenable.

"I'm going to wed Eva and damn the consequences."

"Ninety thousand fucking hells, Dane! Don't be stupid about this. I don't want to lose you again. No woman is worth that." The sound of a fist striking a hard surface put the period on Bastian's ringing statement.

Behind her, Eva heard Mimi and Lena come skipping down the stairs. Turning, she put a finger to her lips calling for silence, then waved them ahead of her toward the kitchen. Both wore their own dresses now. Just after dawn, Pinot had rousted Dane's brothers out of bed with news of all that had happened, and the three men had gone to Eva's townhouse in search of Odette. They hadn't found her, but Bastian had come here afterward, bearing a trunk of Eva's and the girls' clothing, while Sevin and Pinot continued searching for Odette.

Bathed and clothed, Eva had come downstairs just now eagerly seeking Dane, with warm memories of their night together dancing in her head. But the brothers' argument had doused those with a bucket of frigid reality.

She took Mimi and Lena's hands and the three of them finished the stairs, found a basket of muffins and tea on the kitchen sideboard, and then scampered out the back door. Bastian was right. Her presence here was a danger to Dane and his family. She would have to go, but she couldn't bear to think on it yet. First, she would take the girls to explore a bit in the fresh air. She would find her olives and leave it till later to formulate a plan for the future.

In the front salon, Dane grew tired of Bastian's coercion and sliced a hand in the air. "Enough! There is something else I need your expertise on. Maybe you can prove yourself more helpful with it than you have been thus far with your asinine orders." Unfazed by Bastian's glower, he went on, "Last night I spoke to Eva in the voice of Daniel, the third personality we all met in Sevin's salon."

Bastian's eyes sharpened. "And?"

"And I—Daniel, that is—said: 'Bona Dea. Tell him.' Bona Dea was a goddess. I know that much. But what is the message I'm to take from this?"

With a concerned frown, Bastian ran through what facts he knew. "The cult of Bona Dea was vitally important in ancient Rome, but the rites associated with her worship were as much a mystery then as they are now. Her worshippers were solely female. The presence of males at her ceremonies was strictly forbidden. The women even cloaked male statuary before they began."

"That urn in your tent in the Forum," Dane prompted. "The man beating the girl."

"Bona Dea was the daughter of Faunus," said Bastian. "A man infamous for pursuing an incestuous relationship with her. Mythology has it that he beat her with sticks of myrtle and got her drunk on wine, hoping to have his way."

"That's it?" asked Dane.

"Not much more is known. Does any of it mean anything to you? Evoke any memories?"

Dane rubbed the back of his neck in frustration. "Not a damn one."

"There are more detailed references to the cult in the texts in my office. I'll go and return with any news. You'll be here?"

"I'll be here. With Eva."

Muttering something dire about obstinance and asses, Bastian headed for the door.

Meanwhile, Eva and her girls were exploring the temple that stood in the grove. With the help of Fantine's journal, which she'd brought in her pocket, it had been a simple matter for Eva to locate it. For it was the one landmark her mother had managed to clearly map.

"It's cleaner than the house," Lena pronounced.

"And smaller, like a little castle or a playhouse!" agreed Mimi. Both girls were right. The temple was, in fact, a charming, gleaming white circular structure with a portico around a partially enclosed central area. But it was the trees surrounding it that Eva had come for. They had an otherworldly look—their bark like silvered satin, their branches gnarled, their olives plump and perfect.

Emptying the crumbs left from the muffins, she began filling the basket she'd brought with olives. If they must leave Rome soon, she would need to take as many of the pits as she could with her, in order to make her powders.

The brilliant mosaic on one wall of the temple had fascinated Mimi and Lena, but Lena eventually came to sit among the roots at the base of a tree near Eva, drawing in a sketchbook Pinot had included in their trunk. Mimi hardly noticed and was concocting a fantastical adventure in which the temple featured prominently. "This can be the palace," she was saying. "And this is the playroom where I play because I'm the princess and . . . Look! There's the queen."

"Well, aren't you a pretty little thing? What's your name?" asked a refined feminine voice.

"Princess Mimi."

Eva whipped around, shocked to see Serafina and Gaetano.

Dane had bespelled his land against intruders, yet here they stood in the temple on either side of Mimi! A tall, rectangular portion of the wall mosaic had been turned and now stood at an angle, revealing itself to be a door. And beyond it a dark tunnel yawned into a seemingly infinite darkness. Fear flared in her, for there was something sinister about mother and son now.

Her first impulse was to run to Mimi, but then she remembered Lena, who was obscured from their view by the tree trunk. "Don't move. Stay quiet," she whispered between clenched teeth, hoping Lena wouldn't choose this moment to turn disobedient.

"Are you really a queen?" she heard Mimi ask in her clear, innocent voice.

"Yes, how did you guess?" said Serafina.

"Come here, Mimi," said Eva as she warily neared the trio in the temple. Pushing past Serafina, she snatched at the girl, hoping to steal her away, gather Lena, and make for the house, but Gaetano grabbed her arm in one hurtful hand and Mimi's in his other.

"Let go!" Mimi shrieked, abruptly sensing danger.

"Get away from her!" Eva yelled, dropping the basket she hadn't realized she'd still been holding. Several olives tumbled from it onto the marble floor.

Serafina picked it up. "Good of you to do our work for us," she said, peering at the olives Eva had collected. Nodding at her son, she tipped her chin toward the entrance to the tunnel, and though they both fought him, he dragged Eva and Mimi through the mosaic door. Once inside the cool, dim tunnel, he released Eva but blocked her escape. As if she would have left Mimi alone to face whatever fate they had in store for her! Hefting Mimi high in his arms and away from Eva, he pulled something from his pocket and held it to her nose. Mimi's struggles stilled.

"What is that?" Eva demanded, punching at him. "Give her to me. What do you want with us?"

Hoisting the now limp Mimi over one shoulder, Gaetano shook his head. "She's too heavy for you. I just gave her something to calm her. We're not going to hurt you." But Eva knew he lied. His gaze, which had once seemed so innocuous, now made her want to bathe it away.

She cast a quick glance beyond him through the door, which Serafina was quickly closing. No sign of Lena. Good girl. She'd stayed hidden. Gaetano followed her gaze, suspicious. With his free hand, he lifted one of the gaslight lanterns that he and his mother must have left just inside.

"Don't take Mimi," she pleaded, pulling his attention back to her. "Let her go and take only me. I'll do whatever you want. Please."

His aura leapt toward her and his eyes glinted. He still wanted her. Maybe she could use that to her advantage. If she lived long enough.

"Don't try your tricks with him. He's loyal to his family." Having secured the door from inside, Serafina lifted the remaining lantern. "Let's go."

"Where?"

Serafina smirked. "Why, to the playroom your girl so clearly wished for." With that, she turned and led the way, her lamp held high. Behind her, Eva felt the weight of Gaetano's covetous stare.

And she felt the bump of something in her pocket as well. Fantine's journal.

After what seemed like miles of walking, they emerged from the tunnel into a spacious circular room with a small raised platform at its center. Serafina set her lantern in a sconce near several others that already burned and set the basket of olives on a small table. Quickly, Eva pulled the drooping Mimi from her captor and sat on the platform, holding her tight on her lap and gently rocking her. Until the girl woke from her stupor, they could not attempt an escape, for Eva couldn't move quickly if she held her.

As her eyes grew accustomed to the brighter light here, she saw that numerous rooms branched off from the main space. Through an open door, she spied a young woman who looked about sixteen seated in a chair. Her face was placid, the vacant stare of the drugged. An elderly blind man knelt at her side. The girl moaned as some sort of cuplike device was roughly detached from her breast, leaving a thin red circlet of chafing around her breast's circumference. The cup was then summarily reattached to her other breast, eliciting another moan.

"Stop! What is he doing to her?" Eva started toward the scene, but then drew up short, fearing that Gaetano and Serafina might snatch Mimi away when she passed.

"That's our newest. Nella, a fey," Serafina said blithely. Dane had been right, then. This woman did know about their world! "Poor dear," Serafina went on. "Her breasts swollen with milk and no child to feed. Sergio is only pumping it from her. We use it as an ingredient in our rejuvenating face cream, which sells for fifty lire a gram. Alexa gave you some recently, did she not?"

"But that's wicked! Criminal!" said Eva, scarcely able to credit what she was hearing. It made her violently glad she'd never opened the jar she'd been given.

"That disapproving look on your face will result in wrinkles," Serafina advised her.

Wrinkles? Was the woman insane? "Does Alexa know about this?" Eva demanded.

"Alexa?" said Gaetano, shooting his mother a hate-filled look. "No, my dear sister developed a sudden and urgent distaste for Rome yesterday, packed her things, and left for a visit to our relatives in Venice."

"I'll write to them this afternoon," Serafina said sharply, and Eva sensed the tension between them and wondered if she could employ it as a wedge. "They'll send her home."

"It's you who should be locked up, not that girl!" said Eva, unable to hide her abhorrence.

Annoyed, Serafina came closer, bending to look her in the face. "How old do I look to you?" Beyond her, Gaetano rolled his eyes.

Eva gaped. "What is that to anything?"

"I'm forty-eight," she said fatuously.

Though she looked far younger, Eva refused to be impressed.

"That girl in there does a great service. As do the others," Serafina insisted, making a sweeping gesture that encompassed the other doors. "Their donations of breast milk, semen, tears— even their blood and urine have uses in limited quantities— offer the promise of youth to thousands of our aging clients."

There were others like that poor girl behind each of these doors? It was too horrible to imagine! At all costs, she must avoid being shut into one of those rooms herself. She must keep them talking until she could think of some sort of plan that would allow her to escape with Mimi. "How do you know about us—about my world?"

"An ancient ancestor of mine, Faunus, had a liaison with an ElseWorld female. She died giving birth to their daughter. And through that daughter, my family discovered your kind's uses." Serafina smiled. "Back in those days, the wealthy ladies of Rome had to make do with charcoal, saffron, chalk, and lead in their cosmetics. Can you believe it?" she tsked. "But with the use of fluids Faunus's daughter provided, my matriarchal ancestors concocted new cosmetic recipes. The women of ancient Rome leapt at our superior offerings that made their skin smooth, replenished thinning hair, and kept them young. It made us rich, but we didn't forget our humble beginnings. We named our products after Faunus's daughter, who'd helped us so much in our discoveries. Bona Dea. Grateful women worshipped her as a goddess and flocked to her temples to receive treatments, so desperate for them that they turned a blind eye to the inner workings of our business. It is much the same today."

"Bona Dea." The words Daniel had spoken! Eva's eyes widened as everything suddenly fell into place. "You abducted Dane and his brother all those years ago, didn't you? And brought them here."

Gaetano broke his moody silence to make an irritated sound.

"Don't be jealous, Tano," chided Serafina. "You have her now." Unmollified, he snatched up some keys and opened another door, revealing the young man inside. His features were handsome, his hair dark and overlong, hanging down his back. He rose unsteadily to his feet and she saw he wore only a linen loincloth. His face turned slowly toward them, his eyes blinking open. They were silver! Like Dane's. Oh, Gods, was it—it had to be . . .

"Lucien?" Eva called in a tremulous voice. His head cocked and his eyes fastened on her in a slightly more lucid way as if he'd recognized his name. "It's you, isn't it? Dane and your brothers, they're still looking for you. They haven't given up. They love you."

His eyes bored into her, intent and fascinated. And hopeful?

"He doesn't understand you." Gaetano gave a loud clap and Lucien's fascinated gaze flew to him instead. "See? Anything draws his attention. He's drugged."

"As long as you've woken him, you might as well give him the onions," Serafina ordered, and like an obedient dog, Gaetano went back into the tunnel to fetch. When he came back, he carried an oddly shaped funnel and a round white onion and a knife, and he headed into Luc's cell.

"What are you doing to him?" Eva demanded. She half stood to go to them, but Mimi's weight sent her down again. If she caused too much trouble, they might lock them up as well. If only Dane could know his brother lived. She longed to tell him somehow. Her gaze went to the exit.

"Don't try anything stupid," said Serafina. "He's not going to hurt him. The onion is only to bring on the boy's tears so my son can siphon them off." She seemed entirely incapable of comprehending that what they did here was wrong!

Serafina moved over to the cabinet, took a knife and bowl from within, and then began slicing the olives Eva had picked and collecting their pits in the bowl. "Forgive me for being such a poor hostess, but we are quite desperate to have these olives. The calming agent we use on your kind is made from the pits. In small doses, it dulls your scents, but in large quantities, it lulls your minds as well. Since we lost the grove, our guests have gone without enough, and that makes them restless."

Eva watched the knife blade cut precisely and another pit flew into the bowl. "Is that what we are to become?" she asked faintly. "Your guests?"

Instead of replying, Serafina offered, "You look like your father, did you know?"

Bile rose in Eva's throat. "Did you trap him down here as well?"

"Don't be silly. Angelo knew nothing of this. He was visiting Rome from Florence when we met at a social function. Lord, he was so handsome, a dark angel. Women flocked to him. But he wanted me. Until your whore of a mother came. I hated her for taking him." The cut of the knife grew louder with her anger. Then she glanced at Eva and said cruelly, "Your maidservant poisoned him."

"So I learned yesterday."

Serafina gestured with her knife toward the doors that ringed the room. "But you didn't know that she's here, did you, in one of the rooms? Came wandering around this morning at my home, hysterical. Accusing us of hiding you. Threatening to go to the *polizia*. I couldn't have that."

Although Eva would never forgive Odette for all she'd done, the woman had been like a second mother to her and she didn't want to see her tortured! "Can I see her?"

Serafina shook her head. "She's drugged for now, but is far too old to be of use to us. She'll be flushed into the Tiber as soon as Gaetano can manage it."

Poor Odette! To have fallen into the hands of those responsible for the drownings and doomed herself to the very fate she'd long feared. Terror threatened to immobilize her and Eva fought it down.

Serafina straightened, dusting her hands. She'd finished her work—the pits were piled in a small mound. "Tano, come out and watch her! I'm going to the scullery." She hefted her lantern and went back into the tunnel.

When Gaetano emerged from Luc's room, Eva felt his eyes on her and ducked her head. Mimi stirred and her chest tightened with worry for her. Poor Lucien. Poor Odette. And the others here. She felt battered, almost numb from all the terrible revelations thrown her way one after another.

With all her heart she wished that she could protect Mimi from whatever was to come. The fact that her captors were so free with damning information surely meant they had no plans to release them. She would do anything to save Mimi. Anything.

Gaetano's thigh came into her peripheral vision as he came closer. A hand feathered on her hair. She wanted to slap it away. But instead she did what she knew she must. Calmly, she raised her gaze to his and forced a gentle smile. "I still care for you, you know," she said in a soft appeal. It was a ridiculous statement, but the only gambit she could contrive at the moment.

Unfortunately, he wasn't so easily fooled. "Is that why you

humiliated me with Satyr?" he scoffed. "Because you care for me?"

"I—"

"I only wish you could have seen your lover when we brought him here. He wasn't much use then. The young ones never are. Still, we gave him the onions. He hated that. Cursed us and fought worse than anyone we've had down here. Didn't help him, though. We got what we wanted. Every day for a year." His eyes found hers. "Has he had you?"

When he read the truth in her face, his lips took on a cruel curve. "Well, I had *him* once. Not with my prick, but with the handle of a flogger."

Oh, Gods! It killed her to think of Dane as a boy, here with this demented man. "You're a decade older than he. A man to his child then. How could you!"

Distantly, Eva heard Serafina return. Gaetano sighed and said softly, "Lord, I'd give a kingdom to be able to tell that bastard how he and his brother passed their time here."

"Don't," she begged quickly. "He's been hurt enough. Please, promise me you won't ever tell him."

His eyes slowly swept her, lingering on her bosom. "What'll you do for me in return?"

19

Eva. No. Gods, no!

Terror stabbed Dane's chest as he stared into the dark tunnel beyond the mosaic door. It had been sealed, but he had just wrenched it open with his bare hands. This was how he and Luc had been taken! He remembered now. Through this door and into this gaping abyss. How could he have forgotten it all this time? A year after his abduction, he'd been found wandering in the Forum. So he'd concentrated his efforts to find Luc there these past weeks. Fucking waste of time! Instead, the secret of his brother's whereabouts had been right here under his nose.

"You have to find them!" Lena's tear-soaked cry jerked him back to the present. His heart had very nearly stopped when she had appeared at the house just now, telling him that Eva and Mimi had been abducted from the temple.

He took her thin shoulders and gave her a little shake. "You've done well in bringing me here, Lena. Now stop crying and tell me what happened."

Looking frightened of his stern tone, she obediently launched into speech. "We came here so Eva could gather the olive pits so no one will guess that she's satyr." She covered her mouth, her eyes wide. "I wasn't supposed to tell that. It's a secret."

"It's all right," Dane told her impatiently. "What else?"

Lena pointed to the tunnel. "A lady and a man took Eva and Mimi away through there." She made as if to step inside and search for them, but he snatched her back.

"No! Listen to me, Lena. Go back to the house. Wait there for Pinot or my brothers and tell them what has happened. Tell them I've gone into this tunnel to find Eva and Mimi."

"But—"

"Promise me."

"I promise," Lena said bravely, though her thin body was trembling so hard that her teeth rattled.

"Good girl. I'm proud of you." The words slipped from him with surprising ease, an echo of his own father's approvals to him and his brothers long ago when his family had owned this land. He turned her body toward the house and gave her a little push. "Go."

As she went, he grabbed a lamp from the temple and lit it. Dante and Daniel were both awake inside him—an unprecedented occurrence. Dante never came for anything other than physical gratification. And Daniel—he'd never come at all when Dane was aware. But now both were making frenzied pleas to stop him from entering the tunnel. Begging him to let his brothers go instead.

I'm not waiting for them to help! Dane replied in a soundless shout. *The trail will grow cold and Eva could be . . .*

No. No, she would be fine. Arrogantly, he refused to let it be otherwise and steeled himself against any possibility of losing her as he'd lost Luc.

Heart slamming in his throat, he stepped across the threshold into the jaws of hell. Even with the lantern, it was nearly pitch-black in the tunnel. As he loped through the darkness, the walls seemed to undulate, choking at him, trying to close in on him from every side. His head swam with his own fears and those of his alternate personalities as they fought with him and themselves.

Let's go back. I'm frightened. I hate this place! This from Daniel.

And then Dante joined in the chorus. *You see what you're doing? Panicking him. No good can come of this. Do you want to wind up in another asylum?*

Go back go back go baaaack!

No! I have to find them. Have to. Have. To. Left. Right. Eva. Mimi. Luc. Eva. Mimi. Luc. Keep. Moving.

The trail wound crazily, then fifty yards on, it forked. If he chose wrongly, he could waste precious minutes. Which direction? He held the lantern higher.

There was something just ahead, in the direction of the right fork. A rectangle of white lying on the ground. Running to it, he snatched it up. A sheet of paper, limp from dampness seeping through the walls and collecting in puddles on the floor. The word *Evangeline* caught his eye, written in a spidery feminine hand. It was a page from Eva's mother's journal!

He lifted the lantern again and moved farther in that direction down the tunnel. Nothing but black. But then he saw another rectangle of white on the floor. His boots slipped and slid as he rushed toward it. Another page. And farther ahead, another. Eva must have dropped them one by one, leaving a trail her captors had missed! He dropped the two pages to the ground there to mark the path for his return trip. When he would have his rescued loved ones in tow.

Or when your brothers follow to find your bodies! That from Dante, ever the optimist.

Almost paralyzed by claustrophobia and fear for Eva, Luc, and Mimi, Dane followed the trail of pages, one after another. Dante railed and Daniel begged as he zigzagged through honeycombed catacombs and areas of subterranean ruins, a fallen pillar here, a cracked marble slab there.

We remember this, don't we? he murmured silently to the two companions in his mind. *The dank, close atmosphere of stillness where time means nothing. The frustration. The anguish.*

Flashes of memories came, horrible ones tearing at him.

It had been Moonful, thirteen years ago. He'd been sneaking through the night, curious to observe the mysterious event that occurred under the full moon, when all the adults disappeared into the wilderness and did not return home until dawn. Unknown to him, Luc had followed. They'd begun arguing. And then that mosaic door in the temple had opened. Cloaked figures had ushered them inside the tunnel. He and Luc had fought, but they'd been boys, helpless. The next thing he knew he had been shown to his new quarters, an airless, windowless cell. And then the drugs. He'd become an object, one with no rights. Not even to his own body or mind. And now, his abductors had stolen fresh prey.

These are secrets you don't need to discover.
Go back.
Pain lies ahead.
Nooo!
Let it rest.
Pleeease.

"How much farther? Is Luc down here?" he asked, mumbling to himself in the darkness like a crazy man. "When I find Eva, will I find him as well?"

When he would have answers, now the voices fell silent. Grimly, Dane pushed on, cautiously now, for he never knew when he might turn a corner and come upon someone.

Then suddenly, he drew up short, his eyes keening. Eva's little book lay at his feet. She must have dropped it here as some sort of final clue. He was getting close.

At the sound of a door opening, he froze. Murmured voices. He moved stealthily, peering around the corner to see who awaited him. Eva! Looking tired and vulnerable, but unharmed. And Mimi on her lap, and Gaetano standing beside them in the center of the room. And Serafina on the far side. With a knife.

Bonadeabonadeabonadea! Daniel shrieked in his brain.

"Promise me you won't ever tell him," Eva was saying to Gaetano in what appeared to be a private conversation.

"What'll you do for me in return?"

"Anything," she vowed recklessly. "And let Mimi go. If you do that, I'll stay here in these rooms with you without argument. I'll do whatever you want."

The hell she would.

"Share my bed? Be Persephone to my Hades?" Gaetano's hand smoothed Eva's cheek, and a primitive urge to kill sent Dane surging forward a step. But his Special Ops training kicked in, halting him. The crime scene in progress wasn't volatile at the moment. The best way to protect her was to survey matters for now. Others could be hidden behind those doors, foiling any headlong attempt he made at rescue. It wouldn't help Eva or Mimi if he got himself killed.

"I hear you scheming and making bargains over there, mademoiselle," Serafina threw over her shoulder. Setting the knife aside, she dumped olive pits in a mortar. "But has my son told you of his 'little difficulty'?"

Gaetano's face mottled. "Don't, Mother."

Crushing the pits with a pestle, she smirked at him. "Your little French *puta* should know what she's getting in her bargain." She glanced at Eva. "He's impotent. Can't get hard enough to put himself inside a woman."

"You just had to tell her, didn't you!" Gaetano exploded. "But we both know what caused my 'difficulty,' don't we? Do you think I'd forgotten what you did to me, Mama? You and your 'ladies'?"

Brows raised, Serafina said, "Are you speaking of your occasional attendance at our business meetings as a boy? Innocent afternoons of family and friends with tea and cakes? That was years ago. You loved those little cakes with the lemon frosting back then, remember?"

Gaetano's jaw twisted and a wildness lit his eyes as venom came pouring out. "I'm speaking of mothers. With sons. Fathers with daughters. Perversions. And you know it."

She looked at him then with vague surprise. "The Daughters of Bona Dea must carry on the family traditions. I make no apology. It's why you need your own wife and children. To do the same one day."

Crossing the room, Gaetano loomed over her. "Shut up!"

Foolishly, she didn't. "You are not so innocent in all this yourself," she went on. "While the Daughters are upstairs at our worship each month, don't forget who leads the Sons of Faunus down here to make use of these creatures."

"Shut up, Mother!" Gaetano grabbed her, his eyes bulging with rage. The pestle clattered to the floor. His hands squeezed her throat. "Shut. Up."

Good, thought Dane. Let him kill her. Save him some trouble. His eyes went to Eva. Come on. Come on.

As if she'd heard him, Eva suddenly jumped up and set Mimi on her feet. Tugging her along, she ran toward him. Serafina saw and raised a hand in their direction, pointing. But Gaetano was oblivious.

Eva burst into the tunnel, and Dane caught her wonderful weight in his arms and hugged her near. Pressing her face into his shirt, he whispered at her ear, "I left the pages you dropped as a trail. Can you find your way out?"

She nodded up at him. "But—"

"Take my lantern. Get Mimi out." She might not go to save

herself, but she would go for Mimi, who was strangely docile for once.

Eva put a hand on his arm, her face full of tenderness. "Your brother Luc," she whispered. "He's here, alive. In the room with the door there that's ajar. There are others, held captive in the other rooms."

Gladness and pain and longing twisted inside him, but he only nodded. "Go." He pushed her off as he had Lena earlier. Her eyes were full of emotion and words she wanted to speak, but he wanted her out of here. Now. "Wait at the house with Lena. Wait for my brothers." *Wait for me.*

"Please be safe and come to me soon. I love you," she whispered. And then she was gone, taking Mimi with her.

Across the room, Gaetano was still choking his mother, murmuring, his voice full of grief and hate. Dane picked up the small knife on the cabinet as he passed it and then was at Gaetano's side, the blade at his throat. "Open the doors. All of them. And I might let you live."

Gaetano jerked, a comically startled look on his face. Serafina dropped at his feet, dead or close to it. "Sergio!" Gaetano shouted.

A blind guard ran out of one of the rooms and into the tunnel in the direction opposite the one Eva had taken, and was heard cursing in the distance as he banged into walls he couldn't see.

Dane gave Gaetano a hard shake.

"Do it yourself," Gaetano railed at him.

A door creaked open. Luc. Taller now, but still Luc. "I'll do it."

At the sight of him, Dane's heart threatened to crack. It was his brother's voice, yet older, and so tired. So many years lost to this godsforsaken place. "Luc." He swallowed pain. "Lucien, I'm sorry."

Luc only smiled in return, an eerie, angelic curve of his lips. "It's all right, Dane. I knew you'd come back for me."

"You're cutting!" Gaetano screamed, craning back from the knife at his throat.

As they watched, Luc took the keys from a hook and began unlocking each door. Pulling out victims, one by one. The last door opened to reveal Odette lying ominously still on a narrow cot, a vial of poison in one hand. "She's dead," Luc said with an unnatural calm. Gods, was it just the drugs or was something else wrong with him?

Volcanic anger surged through Dane, ready to blow, and he bodily threw Gaetano into one of the now empty cells. The asshole stumbled back and hit a beam support full force, knocking it a few inches back. Dust drifted down on them.

"Why did you let me go all those years ago? Why not Luc as well?" Dane gritted, stalking him. "Answer me!" He slammed his hands on Gaetano's chest.

"I didn't let you go! We have to exercise them." Gaetano waved toward the seven wraiths gathered now out in the main room with Luc. "That's how you escaped. We'd tethered you too loosely and you were at the end of the line. You wandered off and somehow found your way to the surface." His eyes went cruel. "Then only your brother was left to entertain us."

With a mighty roar, Dane rammed him against the tunnel support again, so hard that he fell. Bits of tuff showered them.

"Are you insane?" Gaetano asked.

Dane's hands fisted with a rage to kill. "I'm what this place made me."

"No, Dane. It's dangerous." It was Luc's voice, a voice without inflection. Luc standing beside him, calmly. Too calmly. Luc staring at Gaetano, and then higher above him, gazing fixedly at the beam overhead. The silver of his eyes seemed to glow brighter for a moment. Then came a great groaning sound, that of rock and wood cracking and splintering. Luc put a hand on Dane's arm. "It's going to cave in."

"Fuck!" Dane barreled into his brother, pushing him ahead

and out of the cell. Gaetano scrambled to stand, but then screamed in horror as loose chunks of tuff began to crumble and rain on him, becoming a torrent. The ceiling crashed in and the cell door burst off its hinges as a ball of debris and dust whooshed out into the main room.

"Let's get the hell out of here!" Dane yelled. He and Luc herded the other witless creatures ahead of them out into the tunnel, following Eva's path. Behind them volcanic rock caved in, crushing everything below in a great fall of tuff, mosaic, and marble. In seconds, Gaetano, Serafina, Odette, and their insidious evils were buried forever.

A blast wall of dust spewed into the tunnel, chasing Dane, Luc, and the others through the labyrinth, threatening to suffocate them. Fifty yards in, it eased up, and a few yards on, they met Bastian.

"What the hell?" Bastian said when he saw the dust-covered group.

"A cave-in." Dane coughed. "Luc's with me. Eva?"

Bastian's gaze darted to Luc and emotion distorted his face. But all he said was, "Sevin has Eva. We met her halfway, and he took her and the child out. Let's go."

Together, they led their precious cargo through the tunnel and out into sunshine, fresh air, and freedom.

Sevin was waiting for them in the temple.

"Eva?" Dane demanded again.

"At the house with her girls. Said to bring you up there the minute you came." Then he did a double take. "Lucien? Gods, are you—"

"Home." Luc smiled a beatific smile that encompassed all three brothers. "I'm home."

It was nightfall by the time all seven of the Patrizzi victims' names and situations had been determined. They and Luc slept now under the care of the night servants, and their futures would be sorted out over the following days. Dane hadn't had the time he wanted with Eva yet and was itching to get his hands on her. To assure himself she was whole and well and his. But still he must wait while she insisted on putting her girls to bed.

Bastian and Sevin had joined him in his office, one of the few clean rooms in the house, and he sensed their intention to speak of things he didn't want to discuss.

To forestall them, Dane said, "Down there in that chamber of horrors today, Luc moved an overhead beam somehow, causing the cave-in that killed Patrizzi." He had his brothers' immediate attention. "Not with his hands, but with his mind, or his eyes. I don't know. I've never seen anything like it."

"Damn. A talent?" Sevin ventured.

"Possibly," Bastian said thoughtfully. "Though I don't remember it from before we lost him. However, he was only five, and—"

"Why don't we just get it out in the open once and for all. What happened to him, the way he is now—it's my fault," Dane said with quiet certainty. "All of it."

At that, both brothers sat forward. "The hell it is!" said Bastian.

"I knew it!" said Sevin. "You've been blaming yourself all these years. But what of the night servants who were supposed to be watching over us? And Bastian and I were older than you. Why isn't it their faults or ours as well?"

But it was hard to relinquish a long-held guilt. "Luc wouldn't have gone out that night if I—Gods, if only I hadn't been so damned nosy."

"It was a boyish prank," Bastian insisted.

"Hell, if I'd thought of the idea of playing at voyeur during the ritual, I'd have done the same thing you did," said Sevin. "We were all curious."

"Just think of what our brother has been through." Dane

scrubbed a hand over his face. "The memory of that hellhole was what Dante and Daniel kept from me all this time. Dante took over my mind when I was sexually assaulted down there. And Daniel put himself in charge of the memories of who my abusers were and the location of the subterranean dungeon. Both only wanted to save me from pain and terror back then but didn't know how to stop doing so afterward when the danger had passed for me."

"They aren't your enemies at all," said Sevin. "They're your protectors."

"Only a strong mind could have come up with such coping mechanisms," said Bastian. "Others might have gone insane instead."

Dane shot him a sardonic glance. "So you don't think I belong in an asylum?"

"No, though I sometimes have my doubts about Sevin."

"I love you, too, brother," Sevin replied with a sardonic grin.

Dane chuckled, as they'd intended. Then his head swiveled to the door and he slowly rose to his feet. Eva was coming.

Seconds later, his heart leapt. She was in the room with him. Lena held her hand on one side and Mimi on the other, both in their long girlish nightgowns. Eva's eyes locked on him, full of an emotion he didn't yet understand. "The girls wanted to say good night before they—"

Suddenly, Lena broke away from her, her face wild, almost panicked. She looked from Dane to Bastian to Sevin and to Dane again.

"What is it?" Dane asked, thinking something new must be wrong.

Shocking them all, she barreled toward him then and wrapped her small arms around his middle, hugging him with her face buried in his shirt. "Thank you for saving us."

Dane's arms rose in surprise at her unexpected embrace; but then he slowly lowered them to her back and his expression filled with a new warmth Eva hadn't seen in him before. That of a parent reassuring his child. Their eyes caught over Lena's head and Eva melted inside, hoping. Never one to be left out, Mimi raced over to join in the hug and was immediately included. And then Dane opened an arm to Eva, and she went to join in with a laughter that was a mix of relief and joy. And something more precious.

"We'll bid you good night," said Bastian. Dane glanced up to see him and Sevin leaving the room and nodded to them in farewell. Satyr blood linked them, and they'd sensed the depth of his feelings for this woman and were glad for him. Though Bastian still worried, he was reconciled.

"You and your nieces are welcome here," Dane told her once they'd gone. "Forever. You're part of my family now."

Eva pulled slightly away and looked up at him, her adoring expression making him feel heroic.

"We're not nieces. We're orphans," Mimi informed him.

Dane caught Eva's eye. "It's true," she confessed.

"But we can't be orphans anymore," Lena corrected. "Orphans don't have homes or families."

"What, then?" asked Mimi.

"Would you like to be my daughters instead? Our daughters?" Dane asked, his eyes never leaving Eva's. Tears filled her vision. As the girls enthusiastically embraced this proposal, he quirked a brow at her over their heads. "Is there anything else I should know about you?"

Dashing her tears away, she pretended to contemplate. "Hmm. Let's see. I'm the only female satyr in existence, my girls are not nieces, I wasn't afflicted with the Sickness. I believe that's the entirety of it."

Dane stilled. "What was that last one?"

She smiled at him, fully aware that that last bit was news to him.

He shook his head in amazement "Damn, woman. A fertile female satyr?"

"So you see what a prize I would be to the Council," she said.

His eyes softened. "But an even greater prize to me. Marry me, my love?"

The Tracker Dane had worried would come arrived three weeks later. He came only hours before the full moon was to make its appearance and brought with him an administrator laden with books and papers. Both were sitting unannounced in Dane's study, lying in wait when he walked in.

Bastian and Sevin were absent from the city, having escorted Luc to Tuscany and through the interworld gate. A kineticist in ElseWorld professing some experience with Luc's sort of preternatural abilities had offered to work with him. But the brothers would take no chances of losing him to ElseWorld's asylums as they had Dane, and had insisted on traveling there with him while Dane oversaw matters here until their return.

"Are you here to arrest me?" Dane asked the Tracker, going to sit at the massive desk Eva had purchased for him. The entire house gleamed now under her care, and the smell of lemon polish and beeswax and fresh air and joy mingled here as it had in his boyhood.

The administrator looked taken aback at his nonchalance. But the Tracker swiftly got down to business. "Military prison or rejoining your operative unit. Those are your two options."

"I choose a third one," said Dane, his eyes going to the window and Eva beyond it. She was in the yard playing a rowdy game of croquet with Mimi and Lena. Having come to see to the household accounts as he did weekly now as part of his new accounting business, Pinot was enjoying the game as well.

The Tracker's gaze followed his to Eva, and Dane scented

his immediate appreciation for her many attractions. "Who's that?"

"My wife."

The administrator went on alert. "You wed without permission?"

"The Council wanted a wedding," said Dane. "Go back through the gate and tell them they got one."

"Her name?" asked the administrator.

"Evangeline Delacorte."

"Human?" asked the Tracker.

"A fey-human mix," Dane lied smoothly.

The persnickety administrator began fussing. "I know her. She's a Marital Broker. Prepared her visa myself to send her through the gate." He frowned. "She's had the Sickness."

"Not so, as it turns out," Dane informed them, truthfully this time.

"But she was tested," the administrator insisted.

Dane leaned forward, interrupting. "Tests are fallible. She's not infertile, I tell you. Tonight is to be Moonful. I'll make sure my seed takes in her. In another month I'll have the children you require of me."

"But what sort of children? Not human as we requested," tutted the administrator.

Dane's eyes narrowed. "No."

The Tracker eyed him, weighing the truth of his words. "Children at least. That's something." A shared camaraderie flashed between them, that of men bound by service and training. A moment later, the Tracker stood and waved his companion toward the door.

"But—" the administrator protested, sputtering.

"We're done here," the Tracker stated unequivocally. "Lord Satyr is to be congratulated for securing this ancient grove again for our world. And he has wed. It's plain to see he's besotted with his new wife. If they don't conceive, we can find him again easily enough to reopen the matter with him."

He ushered the administrator out the door. As he followed, he turned back to Dane with a sardonic half smile. "These children you're planning to make with her. If they cannot be human, make them satyr, will you?"

Dane grinned slowly. "I'll do my best."

With Eva as his mate, the man had no idea how easy that request would likely prove.

20

Mere hours later, Eva flew through the olive grove on Aventine Hill, her gown fluttering in the breeze. Her slippers were wet from the dewy grass, betony, and rosemary that grew low on the forest floor. Dane followed in her wake, not attempting to catch her but still enjoying the chase. It was Moonful, and his hunting instincts were keen, his blood running high.

A gentle misty rain was falling, the sky overhead a pendulous gray. Although the moon was in hiding, its pull on them was strong. It wouldn't be long now.

Dane slowed when he saw where his delectable quarry was headed. The temple. The mosaic was gone from it now, replaced with one removed from another ancient site and brought here. This one depicted harvest scenes showing grape and olive pickers with their baskets and nets, the vats and the urns, and the wild celebrations in which consumption of wine and olives featured prominently. The tunnel beyond the mosaic had been blasted to rubble, twenty yards deep so no door would ever open here again to steal their joy. Still, back at the house tonight, he'd posted ten night servants to watch over Mimi and Lena, all with strict orders to keep them safe. Some fears died harder than others.

His beloved Eva awaited him on the temple steps now, her dress damp and clinging, her long hair in rivulets on her shoulders and crowned by a wreath of olive, like a beautiful pagan goddess.

"Nice gown," he told her, drawing near.

She held the skirt of the long, simple linen shift wide on each side of her, and his eyes dropped to the way its sodden fabric molded her thighs and the shadowy vee where they joined. "Do you like it? It's from a design I found in one of Bastian's books. The traditional dress of a virgin on her wedding night in ancient Rome. Note the embroidery." Her fingertips skimmed the decorative stitching over her breasts. Her nipples were dark circles, poking at the rain-soaked linen that covered them. They would be cool in his palms, his mouth.

His brows lowered. She'd drawn his gaze there on purpose, offering enticements in hopes of luring him into ignoring the fact that she'd brought him to this vile place. He moved closer and she kicked off her slippers, excitement lighting her eyes.

"We've been married over a week now," he informed her. "It's not our wedding night. I distinctly remember our wedding night." He reached overhead for a gnarled branch, plucking an olive from it, juicy and plump.

She glanced at the small green oval he rolled between his forefinger and thumb and blushed, remembering exactly what he'd done with a very similar olive on their wedding night. Rouging it over her slippery folds, separating her petals, and tucking it delicately inside her core and . . . She sighed with remembered bliss. Although he didn't know it, she had saved that small olive, carefully placing it in a velvet box within a treasure trove that also contained the portrait of him Lena had made that day in her study and the neatly folded wrapping paper from the box of olives he'd sent her afterward.

"But this will be our first Moonful here on your land," she coaxed softly. "I made this gown to celebrate it."

"Eva." Her name was a primitive growl in Dane's throat. He took the steps to stand just below her.

"Dane." A stairstep above him, she put her hands on his shoulders, her reply light and teasing. Then more earnestly, she said, "Let it happen here. Our first Moonful together. Let it happen where your ancestors mated, where they made love and babies under the full moon long before we were born. Let us heal here together, join our bodies in the ancient way for the first time."

Tension crackled between them, electric and waiting, and then Dane peeled off his shirt, trousers, and boots in a flurry, leaving them lying on the stairs. He came to her and tossed something on the raised altar beyond them. Something he'd been carrying. A coil of rope. She shivered, anticipation coloring her eyes darker. His hands went to her waist. "This will be a first for us both, for I've never had a Moonful of my own, one without Dante."

"And I have had far too many on my own." She inhaled his warm scent and moaned softly. The longer she was in his company, the more easily she could discern it as distinct and precious among others. "I brought something as well, earlier today."

"Another surprise." He sounded wary.

She turned away, going to the altar. "The wedding ritual entails wine, but I thought for tonight"—she held up a bottle and tilted it, filling her palm with viscous amber—"olive oil." Setting the bottle aside, she returned to him and cupped her palms around him, massaging his cock and balls until they glistened. And all the while he watched her with stormy silver eyes, enjoying the sight of her doing this service for him. The backs of her fingers stroked his abdomen, making it quiver and ripple. His skin was smooth there. But the muscles beneath were extraordinarily taut. With the coming of the moon, his second prick would emerge. "It excites me to know how you'll Change here," she whispered.

He grabbed her wrists, his voice tight with emotion. "I want to be in you when it happens. I want you to feel it."

She drew a harsh breath and sunk her teeth into her lower lip, nodding. "Yes. Yes."

She took his arm and they hurried to the altar. It was slick and puddled with rain, but she readily knelt on the marble ledges that jutted from the base of it.

He picked up the rope he'd brought, and her eyes watched him uncoil it. With experienced fingers, he looped and knotted it securely around her wrists, binding them together. He nodded toward the altar that stretched before her. "Will you be cold?"

She shook her head, smiling slightly. "Not for long." Still on her knees, she half-lay facedown on its surface so breast and cheek met cool, rainslicked stone. Her breasts settled into the slight depressions where the slab had been worn smooth by the breasts of other women who'd prostrated themselves here in earlier centuries. He drew her arms up and tethered her to the mooring that protruded at the head of the altar, then came to stand in the hollow of the jutting ledge, between her splayed thighs. And she awaited his pleasure then as generations of females before her had awaited the pleasure of his male ancestors.

Her damp, ceremonial gown clung, delineating the cleft of her buttocks. He lifted the back of the linen length high, unveiling her. "Gods, I wish you could see how beautiful you look, bound here, half naked, and so open for me," he said.

He tilted her hips up, noting the telltale signs of the moon's effect on her—the deep crimson flushing of her folds, their unusually plump petaling around her feminine core. Pouring oil in his palm, he cupped it to her there and she moaned, rubbing against his hand, massaging herself until she was dripping with it. Another symptom—hypersensitivity. Then he dribbled more viscous amber along the crevice of her bottom, anointing her with oil from olives planted here by the ancients from his world. He spread her cheeks, massaging it into her pruney ring, hearing her whimper as he slipped a finger inside. The signs were here as well, a general puffiness, a responsiveness to the merest touch. "I can't wait to come inside you here," he said, his voice low and dark.

"Dane." It was a moan, a plea. "Why is it so . . . intense?"

"The Calling," he told her. "Without your powders to inhibit it, the moon has affected you physically in this way, made you incredibly sensitive and responsive. And so fucking beautiful."

"Oh, Gods, I'm not sure I can wait much longer. I need to . . . the moon, where is it?"

He rinsed his hands and then poised his crown at her slick center. She cried out when he pushed inside. This first joining would be quick and raw and pagan, but they had the rest of the night. He commenced fucking and she met him thrust for thrust, her tissues already milking at him. "Damn, Eva. You're so tight. So hot. Close to coming already."

Overhead the clouds shifted and gently rumbled, and the moon's first light found them. Together, they shouted their joy as his second cock erupted from him, nudging along her rear crease and spearing high. Pulling back slightly from her quim, he grasped this new shaft with fingers that shook. Then in a smooth motion, he positioned it at her rear opening and pushed inside in long, oil-slickened, dual glides until she held him more deeply and fully than he recalled any woman having done.

She screamed and arched up, her arms pulling at the ropes, pushing against him, trying to make their joining harder, rougher, more primal. And he was right there with her, bucking into her in hard slams. The sound of their moans and gasps and the wet slaps of heated flesh echoed in the temple and more gently through the grove to disappear among the trees and mist.

Dane's chin lifted, his throat tight as he gazed at the heavens, seeking the moon's beneficence. "With my seed, let us bring life this night," he murmured. Through the gnarled branches grown heavy with olives overhead, he saw the clouds shift and part for the luminous light he and his mate craved. With the strengthening of this drenching glow, he came in her with a great roar, both his cocks pumping hot spurts of syrupy semen into her simultaneously. She came almost immediately, her thighs shaking and her tissues fisting him as her cry rode the cool, rain-soaked air.

Eva fainted briefly, and when she came to, a haze of ecstatic sparks danced in her vision. His pelvic cock had already receded into his flesh, not to return until another Moonful. Yet still she felt so full of him, so full of his seed that it dribbled from her.

The sparks in her vision had dwindled to an iridescent glow. She lifted her head slightly. An iridescent hand worked at the ropes tethering her, untying them. She gasped. Shimmerskins! Two. Both male. Muscled male. Her gaze went lower. *Very* muscled.

Her ropes released and she pushed up with one cock still inside her. "Dane?"

"Think of them as a belated wedding gift," he said from behind her, his prick beginning to rock in her again.

"But—"

"It excites me to share you, when and how we both want it. I'll direct them and sometimes direct you to please them for my enjoyment. Will you like that?"

Luminescent hands swept over her breasts and downward as the first Shimmerskin knelt before her. A hot mouth covered her clit. A tongue pressed, stroked.

Passionate tears filled her eyes, blending with the soft, pattering mist. Resting back against him, she nodded and twisted slightly to draw his lips down to hers. "I love you." Her words fell on him like rain on parched, cracked earth and he soaked them in.

"And I you," he said solemnly in return, his gaze full of emotion as he wrapped strong arms around her.

Dane mated her there until dawn, on the altar where his ancestors had mated their women for centuries. Against the wall, on the steps. They made love in the cleansing rain and among furs and pillows in the central room, reconsecrating this temple with their passion. Making this land pure and whole again. And whispering sweet words of love.

EPILOGUE

Lying in bed the next morning, Eva turned her head to smile at Dane, feeling love well up in her. He was asleep, and so beautiful. So strong and good, and so wonderfully hers. Carefully, so as not to wake him, she rolled toward the bedside table and pulled a small leather-bound book from it. Yet another gift from Dane, to help heal her loss of her mother's book, which lay buried in the labyrinth. This new journal was filled with crisp, blank pages only waiting for her to record the joys of her future days. She took up a pen, the urge filling her to start. For this felt like a new beginning—the morning after her first Moonful with Dane. Her husband. What a delicious word it was when applied to him.

I shall begin with how things are.

I am married now to Lord Dane Satyr, and we have legally adopted Mimi and Lena as our own. Mimi dogs Dane's footsteps and is turning into a farmer before our eyes, fascinated with his olives and grapevines. Lena dotes on Lucien like a little mother and misses him now that he has gone to ElseWorld.

Pinot and his lover exist in bliss in their small house on Viminal Hill, but we see him often as he does our household accounts and investments as part of the financial business he has begun. As for Odette, she is dead, and I can't bring myself to speak of her yet, so I shall move on to happier matters.

Bastian has recently made some new discovery in the Forum, a House of Vestals. He has an uncanny knack for locating such amazing things, almost as if he already knows where to look and only has to dig there to find them. I still hope to secure a wife for him, but I fear I may have to look to the museums, for marble statues seem to be the only females that hold his interest.

Sevin works overlong at his Salone di Passione, *and I think he may be too successful at it, for he seems always to be there. I hope to see him wed as well, but first I shall work on his brother.*

My dearest friend Alexa had been found innocent of wrongdoing in the Patrizzi affair. But she is devastated by her family's betrayal and is filled with guilt at the cruel devastation they caused. In a strange way, all that has happened has brought us closer. For I now know her secrets and she knows mine.

Dane and his brothers learned the identities of the others involved in Serafina's ring of evil and have bespelled each into forgetting the cult entirely. It wasn't possible to reveal the whole matter to the Roman courts, of course, so their punishments must come in time as surreptitious means are found to diminish their fortunes and positions in society and government. And surely, the continuing rise in fame and fortune of the Satyr lords here is a punishment of sorts to them already.

The Council continues to warn that any day now Else-World may be exposed. But we exist in a cocoon of happiness here in Rome, and the threat of that larger danger seems distant.

Daniel no longer comes, and Dante visits only when Dane occasionally calls upon him to join us in carnal engagements. This seems to feed some need in Dane, and I confess I enjoy the unexpectedness of it.

I am happy. Truly happy, for my beloved occupies my heart and mind and body in a way that is entirely fulfilling. I am no longer in danger of discovery, for it is assumed by all the ElseWorld creatures who visit us or who pass me on the streets that the scent clinging to me is due to the touch of my husband's flesh upon mine. And he does touch me often, as if to assure himself I am real and his.

I hope Fantine would be pleased to know that I have wed such a man as this. She would like that he is wealthy, and that he and his brothers are welcome in the highest circles of Roman society.

But I care only that he loves me. That I am safe. That I am—

Eva gasped and dropped her pen, feeling a strange sensation come over her. A fluttering. Her eyes widened and her hand went to her abdomen. There it was again under her palm! A flutter. Oh! Glory!

She felt the coverlet being tugged away. A hand smoothed down her back. She glanced over her shoulder.

"Yes, I'm awake, my beloved," Dane growled, smiling in that sexy way of his. "And wanting attention from my wife." He turned her, pulling her across his body. The linen sheet was tented, his prick a pole beneath it, but he wasn't demanding anything of her and only kissed her in a slow, sweet mating of lips.

The fluttering came again, and he felt it where her belly met his and drew her back. Slow realization darkened his eyes. "Eva?" It was a question. A blaze of hope.

She moved his big hand to cover her abdomen and smiled into his eyes. "Yes, my love. It seems your seed was potent last night. I am *enceinte*. In a month we will see what sort of wonderful child we made together last night."

Joy lit his face. "Yes, my sweet satyr wife, we shall indeed."